The Rise of Yellowhenry

By

Stevens McClellan

Table of Contents

Chapter One

The drop wasn't all that much. Twelve feet or so, but he could see scattered, jagged volcanic rock under the carpet of pine needles below. Going back up was out of the question—thirty feet without the assistance of gravity. Not a chance. He figured he could probably drop his rifle into the pad of pine needles below without causing a great deal of damage. Unless it bounced and slid into the rocks farther down the slope, it would survive. He was willing to chance a seven- or eight-foot drop for himself, even though he couldn't see all the rocks. He knew from experience that the rocks were set in a lava base. They wouldn't budge. A broken leg would be a hell of a price to pay for getting unlucky.

So, he gently dropped the rifle. It struck the springy pine needle pad, tumbled, and fetched up against a scraggly, mostly dead, and stunted mahogany tree. Lucky. Without the rifle restricting his movements, he felt more confident about making another move to ease down another four feet. The rock knob he set his left boot against didn't hold, however, and his backpack strap got hung up. He dropped down the rock face unceremoniously and uncontrollably.

He survived with only one injury. When he inventoried his parts, all was well except for one leg. The left one bent off to the side at the knee. It didn't hurt too much, but his try at straightening it with his hands didn't help. So, he wedged his boot into a crack between a rock and a small tree. Then, he threw himself downslope and shoved off against another rock with his right leg. He passed out from an explosion of pain he hadn't imagined.

Two hours later, and in the dark, he came to. He sat up and felt his leg. It was almost straight, so he shifted around and unwedged his foot. He couldn't, however, stand on that leg. The pain nearly dropped him again. Since building a fire was out, he crawled down to his rifle and burrowed into the pine needles. He heaped more over himself and the rifle. He shivered violently for most of the night.

At daylight, he scuffed a clear spot in the pine needles with his hands. Then, he butt-scooted his way to the mahogany tree and attacked with his hand ax. He always carried his hunting knife on the right side of his belt and his hand ax on the left. The exertion warmed him up, so he was able to set a fire pile. From his small backpack, he pulled out two plastic pill bottles. One held cotton balls infused with Vaseline. The other was stuffed with kitchen matches, the heads of which had been dipped in light oil.

He used a cotton ball to ignite his fuel. Soon, he had a warming fire and took his first look at his leg in daylight. A splint was the only option. He carried a packet of nylon cord in his backpack, so after chopping a pair of branches to size, he wrapped and tied the pieces above and below the swollen knee joint. He tested the leg. The pain was intense but dull. He could move as long as he kept the splinted leg downhill. When he came to a game trail that angled downhill, it led him north toward the head of the drainage he was in, so that was where he trudged.

Joe Yellowhenry was deep in the wilds of his tribe's reservation. Worse, no one knew he was there, and no one cared. Even better, neither did he. Joe was a half-breed by birth. His mother was Norwegian, and his father was Cree. The twenty-five-year-old stood six feet two inches tall. He was broad-shouldered and lean at 186 pounds.

He looked Indian, with dark brown hair and skin, but his blue eyes and hints of Scandinavian features revealed his mother's side. He was raised by his father's people after his mother died when he was four. Soon after, his father fell into a deep funk and ended his life. Joe and his sister were raised as a community project by their father's people. When she was seventeen, his sister, Pheonia, married a white man and left the reservation. Joe had no interest in following her into a lifestyle he didn't understand. He preferred the subsistence lifestyle the reservation provided. Getting lost for a month or two in the wild was his favorite way of connecting with the land.

By the time Yellowhenry was into his second hour, hobbling along with a branch crutch padded with moss and lichen, he was two more miles in and by the creek. He also had food. A rabbit and a grouse hung from his belt thanks to his ability to throw rocks. Always on the lookout for a good rock, he had found three as he hobbled along.

The bird and the rabbit were proof of his ability to hunt simply by throwing rocks. A smooth, pullet-egg-sized rock was his favorite, but size was more important than smoothness. Give him a three-inch opening, and whatever blocked it would take a good smack. From fifty feet, he was very unlikely to miss.

Now, he was looking around at things. He had food and water handled. What he had to make—or find—was fire and shelter. In his shape, finding shelter would be better than building it. The vigorous stream at its headwaters sprang from broken underground rock structures. Yellowhenry focused his gaze on the sides of the watercourse. He looked across at a band of black rock that rose close to fifty vertical feet. Two hundred yards of climbing through grass, brush, trees, and rock to get to it soured the idea for the moment. He could see openings to caves, some with faint trails leading away. He liked that side of the stream, though—it had southern exposure. Then he looked at the north side, the one he was on. More caves. It was closer to the stream, and the climb to it was shorter and less impeded by downed branches and logs of pine and fir trees in the bowl below a cave he had his eye on.

Using a foldable drinking cup, he drank as much water as he could, knowing hydration was key. Pissing a couple of times during the night wouldn't bother him. When he felt bloated, he tucked the cup back into his pack, hitched up his pants to adjust the weight of the grouse and rabbit, and began his painful climb to a rock band seventy-five yards above him. A half-hour later, he was peering from a rock ledge into the confines of the pit he had chosen in the rock. He used his crutch to stab some loose rock at the top. It dropped away, leaving the opening about four feet high. He liked it. "Bear and I will tussle for this," he thought.

Inside, the cavity was spacious—seven feet high, ten feet wide, and who knew how deep. Before the cave dropped off at the back end where the bear went into its depths, the floor was nearly flat for thirty feet. In the gloom, Yellowhenry took stock. A few old deer bones were scattered around. It smelled of must and old bear and cat piss.

He kicked at the dust on the floor and watched it settle. The lighter-than-air particles drifted upward and toward the mouth. "Fire toward the mouth will work," he said loudly, checking his voice. It worked but sounded strained from the screeching he'd done with his dislocated knee. But there was more screeching to come, he knew.

Shelter secured, Yellowhenry turned his attention to the fire. A pine tree that had spent its eighty-year life shallowly rooted in the thin soil at the upper edge of the fifty-foot-high band of basalt had lost its battle to a small avalanche that hit it head-on the previous winter. Now it lay ready to serve as firewood. After two hours of labor, a pile of branches and a couple of pieces of fractured trunk decorated his commandeered shelter. Another hour of work yielded enough brush to block the cave entrance at night.

A small, nearly smokeless fire crackled merrily, toasting the plucked grouse Yellowhenry had skewered on a green branch spit he'd cut from the brush. The skinned rabbit carcass lay on its hide beside him. When he judged the grouse done, he sprinkled it with salt from the supply he always carried on bush trips. Yellowhenry loved the salt and would come out of the outback just to replenish his stash if he ran out.

Half an hour later, with the cracked grouse bones tossed over the ledge, Yellowhenry turned his attention to the rabbit. Using a pair of short lengths of wire he had freed from a small coil in his backpack, he secured the rabbit to another spit. Patiently, he waved the headless body back and forth at the top of the flames. After about thirty minutes, he sampled a bite, decided it needed a little more time, and gave it another ten minutes.

Satisfied with the rabbit, he set it aside on a pair of branches to cool and turned his focus to the snowshoe rabbit skin. Using a debarked piece of pine branch as a solid surface, he carefully worked his knife to scrape away the blood, fat, and tissue. Once the skin was clean, he spent another half hour kneading and rolling it back and forth over the pine branch.

Chapter Two

Darkness had descended on the shallow canyon where Yellowhenry was holed up. When he got in his firewood, he'd also scooped up armloads of pine needles and carried them into the cave. Before banking his fire with two large chunks of tree trunk and stretching out on the bed of needles he'd made, he packed the cave mouth with brush. Using his backpack as a pillow and keeping his rifle close, it wasn't long before he slipped into a dreamless sleep.

Sometime after midnight, a rustling sound of an animal stirred him awake. Something was trying to push past the brush plug at the cave's entrance. Slowly and quietly, Yellowhenry brought his rifle into position, sitting up with his legs stretched toward the cave mouth. He waited, silent as a snake, his entire focus locked on the rifle's peep sight.

A faint glow from the banked coals of his fire made the animal hesitate as it tugged at the tightly packed brush. It growled quietly. The odor of the raw rabbit skin and the cooked carcass overpowered its caution, and the animal resumed pulling the wad free of the cave's entrance.

When Yellowhenry saw the big head poking through a gap in the branches, he dropped his front sight under its chin and pulled the trigger. The roar of the Winchester .30-06 was immense inside the cave. For nearly ten minutes, Yellowhenry could hear nothing. Not even the sound of his own voice as he shouted came through the ringing in his head.

With the splint off his knee, he had to crawl awkwardly. His left knee had swollen and stiffened, still partially out of the socket. He stirred the fire and crawled over to see if what he had shot was on the ledge before the cave. It wasn't, so he crawled back to his bed and tried to sleep. It took nearly an hour before he finally fell into a restless slumber.

Daylight seeped slowly through the cave mouth. Yellowhenry was awake and waiting for it. The last of his wood had gone into the fire sometime between the shot and first light. The fire had nearly burned out. As he waited, he gnawed on a haunch of rabbit. He was warm enough, but he had a big day ahead. He finished the meat, re-splinted his leg, and hobbled out to see what his shot had brought down. Just as he thought, a black bear was sprawled halfway to the creek. But first things first. He had planned something while gathering wood the day before.

He'd discovered a tree with a sturdy branch about eight feet off the ground, which gave him an idea. He carried his nylon line with him to the tree where he cleared out the ground next to it and tossed the line over the branch. He tied one end to his left boot and heaved his leg up by pulling on the free end. When he had it high enough to dangle by kicking his right leg off the ground, he began jerking as hard as he could. He bit down on a thumb-sized piece of branch and screamed intentionally, hoping to keep himself from passing out. It didn't work.

When he regained consciousness, it was midmorning. He lay flat on his back with the nylon line piled on his legs, so he sat up and looked at his left knee. It was back in the socket. He removed the splint and tried testing the knee. It wouldn't bend, but it didn't deliver the blinding shot of pain he expected. Using his crutch, he climbed to his feet and put some weight on the leg. It hurt, but he could stand it.

Yellowhenry then hobbled down to the creek where he removed his boots, waded out, and sat on a rock at the edge of a small waterfall in midstream. His naked left leg was being splashed by the icy water. It ached like hell, but he was finally able to flex his knee. He kept it immersed for half an hour before moving to the bank. The rabbit skin, which he'd thoroughly scrubbed with sand and water, was laid out on a rock. He wrapped the skin, hair side in, around his knee joint and tied it tightly with the lengths of line from his splint. Then he made his way to the bear.

He laboriously dragged the 225-pound carcass down to a flat spot beside the creek and began his work.

Eight hours later, a happy man had stashed a fresh bear hide, head attached, hair side down, in his cave. On it, he piled the boned-out bear meat. His leg had healed well enough that he was crutching it less often. He was already keeping an eye on the first of the meat drying on a rack. His only concern was the gut pile, bones, and the blood-soaked ground where he had processed the bear. That's why he had a double pile of firewood stacked against the cave wall.

His plan was to dry the meat night and day until the task was complete. He ate heartily. While working the drying racks, he also worked on his bear hide. He scraped the hide for two days, moving the meat stash aside as he scraped. Over the next two nights, he listened to scavengers below. Twice, he blasted the mouth of the cave when animals crept near while he was sleeping. He'd used small strips of rabbit skin for earplugs, so he could tolerate the rifle blasts. His labors now included a wolf and a bobcat.

Yellowhenry's cup runneth over. He skinned out his latest two animals after hauling them half a mile down the game trail beside the stream. His leg was improving even more. While still sore, it allowed him to function as a lame man rather than a cripple. He kept the skins and heads. He split open all three animal skulls for their brains. More scraping, followed by stretching the skins on green-branch hoops, set the wolf and bobcat skins up for a final treatment of washing and softening with a paste of brain and bear fat. Yellowhenry worked his bear hide in the stream, washing the skin side with water and sand to cleanse it of the residual fat, blood, and tissue from scraping. He brought it back to the cave to dry and, as it dried, he worked his brain paste into it. When finished, the hide was cured and pliable.

By notching and fitting tree branches, he built a crib that was about six inches high, three feet wide, and seven feet long. He filled it with pine needles. At night, he folded himself inside the bearskin, stretching out on top of it during the day. After curing the hides, he fashioned a vest from the wolf and bobcat skins, using strips of rabbit skin to tie the pieces together. He spent his days gathering wood. He wasn't sure how much he needed because he wasn't sure how long he planned to stay. Cave fever was a real phenomenon he'd known a time or two, and he knew he wouldn't winter there. He figured he'd pull out as soon as the snows that were already burying the highest peaks came down to the ridges above him. He was into his twentieth day on this particular walkabout. A week more, and he'd head back out. Eating nothing but meat, even though he had a good supply of salt, was getting tiring. His leg was also a pain in the ass whenever he had to sidehill.

To avoid boredom, Yellowhenry hunted the brush along the stream for grouse and rabbits. The snowshoes were turning white and were easy to spot. He could've bagged a half dozen in a morning if he wanted, but the fur wasn't ready yet, and he didn't believe in waste. He limited himself to two animals—two grouse, two rabbits, or one of each. He mixed the bounty with the bear meat. While he liked the taste of all three, five days into his final week, he pulled the pin. He hated leaving his stash of meat. There were still around sixty pounds of good dried bear meat left, plus some rabbit. He thought about what to do. His bear hide weighed close to ten pounds. His rifle added six or seven more. His backpack and its contents amounted to another ten pounds. He figured he could carry seventy-five pounds on good legs. But with only one good leg, he piled everything on the bear skin. By gathering the hide into a pouch, he tried walking with it. The best he could handle was around sixty pounds. He pulled half of the bear meat out and piled it up at the back of the cave. While it wouldn't go to waste, he regretted not having it to share with people when he got out. He took two rabbits and left four.

He used pieces of his nylon cord to close up the bundle, rigging it with a forehead strap and armholes. He had to cut the bearskin to make it work. He could sew the bearskin back together when he got home. The fifteen-mile trek began early the next morning. Yellowhenry wasn't in a hurry. Rest stops were frequent, and by sundown, he still had ten miles to go, even though he'd already climbed nearly that many miles of up-and-down trail. He burrowed into a thicket of thornbush next to the creek to spend the night. He used his hatchet to clear out a space large enough to spread out the bearskin. He moved rocks around as much as he could to hollow out a sleeping spot, and after a supper of cold bear meat washed down with creek water, he settled in for a night without fire.

Chapter Three

It was early afternoon the next day when he found the horse in the country that was flattening out into a grassy valley. Or, perhaps, the horse found him. As soon as he noticed the horse approaching, he quickly dumped the pack and walked away from it. Then he stopped, and the horse nickered and walked up to him. He chuckled.

"Hi, boy. I know what you are, and I know that, somehow, you got lucky. Let me take a look at you."

After walking around the horse, a sorrel gelding, he knew it was considered used up.

"Now, how did you avoid your fate?" Yellowhenry asked.

Old horses like the sorrel were often taken out into the mountains and staked as bait for guided bear hunts. They were usually shot. This one had somehow failed to cooperate with the hunters. Yellowhenry sized the horse up. From its teeth, he figured it to be around ten, which was really not old for horses. This one needed to have its teeth floated, however. An uneven bite had led to the horse's thin and generally rundown appearance.

"Let's you and me team up," Yellowhenry said. "I just hope you don't run off when you get a stronger whiff from my bear pack than what you're getting off me."

The horse followed as the man walked the fifty yards back to his pack. It stopped short, snorted, and shook its head, but it didn't run. Yellowhenry opened the pack and pulled out the remaining length of his nylon cord. He walked to the horse and quickly built a hackamore, placing it on the animal's head. Then he swung up onto its back, reined it back around, and rode away from the pack. The sorrel was well-trained and responded obediently to everything its rider asked of it.

Yellowhenry spoke quietly as he rode in a circle that ended at the bearskin mound. The horse shied at first, but after riding away and coming back several times, it came to accept the pack as harmless. Getting the pack loaded on the horse's back took another period of time, familiarizing the horse. Finally, Yellowhenry was able to crawl onto the horse's back with the bearskin pack resting between his legs and in his lap.

By sundown, Yellowhenry could see the lights of the Indian village, so he decided to ride on in. His house, or shack, was a three-room affair dominated by the main room, a fifteen-by-twenty-foot combination kitchen, dining, and living room. Two bedrooms, both ten-by-twelves, completed the layout. The place was snug, didn't leak, and was set on a good foundation. It had a good well, and its water was accessible by a standard pump stand. A small porch fronted the living room door. Yellowhenry slept in the bedroom to the right of the living room. He had converted the second bedroom into a sort of mudroom. He had cut a door into its back wall, and a pair of steps led to his backyard. Thirty yards or so across the yard was his corral and horse shelter. Four bales of hay were racked up above the shelter where a horse couldn't reach them.

He hadn't had a horse for several months. He'd sold the last one he had when he took a month to go hiking in the southern Rockies. Now, he had another one.

Yellowhenry dumped his pack to the ground and slid off the sorrel. He opened the gate to the corral and led the horse inside. Beneath and against the back wall of the shelter, he had built a feed bunk that butted against a metal horse trough. Stepping up a four-rung ladder nailed to the right side of the shelter and opposite the horse trough, he broke open one of the hay bales and pulled off a couple of flakes of hay, tossing them into the feeder. The horse walked under the shelter and nosed the hay before starting to feed.

"You'll do fine with hay like this," Yellowhenry promised, laughing. "Even with teeth like yours. We'll do a little dentistry tomorrow, then you'll get a treat. Oats. I'll get you some water in a minute."

When he didn't have to prime the pump after one of his excursions, he counted himself lucky. This was one of those times. He'd only had to jack the long handle a dozen times or so before water started splashing into the open-topped discharge chute. He filled a plastic five-gallon bucket and dumped it into the trough. The well pump was located halfway between the house and the corral. He lugged four bucketfuls across the yard.

"There you go, horse," he said as he climbed into the corral. The horse finished a mouthful of hay and swung his head over and down to the water, where he drank deeply. Yellowhenry pulled a curry comb off an overhead nail that had been hammered into the back wall of the shelter and began curry-combing the sorrel. As he worked, he talked to the animal.

"Let's get you all handsomed up, boy. Combed tonight, tomorrow your teeth, mane, and tail. I'll pull out that mane and tail and trim that broomtail of yours. Trim those toenails. You need a name. I'm gonna call you Hi Boy. Not because you're tall—fourteen and a half hands is good, but not tall. The first thing I ever said to you was, 'Hi, boy.' Get it?"

The horse chose that moment to nicker in contentment. Yellowhenry laughed.

"You got it." He patted the horse's rump. "There you go. That'll hold you for tonight."

He lugged the pack into the mudroom and left it there as it was while he flipped on the lights. Then, he went back outside and unhooked a galvanized metal tub from its nail on the back wall. For the next twenty minutes, he pumped and lugged water into the house, filling the tub halfway. Then, he started a fire in his wood-burning kitchen range. He had left the woodbox full when he'd gone on his walkabout, and now he was thankful that he'd thought ahead. He filled his teapot with water to heat. While he waited, he used a hand mirror to look at himself. He decided to trim his bangs and leave the rest of his hair alone. Even though he lived on the reservation, he preferred to keep his hair collar-length in the white man's style. His beard wasn't much, but it made him look scruffy when it grew out. He shaved a couple of times a month. Tonight would be one of those.

With the water heated to his liking, Yellowhenry stripped and set his Levi's, shirt, and socks to the side. He eased butt-first into the tub and held the sides opposite each other. He had to keep his left leg mostly straightened out. He lathered up quickly and used warm water to rinse off the soap. He kneeled on his right knee on a towel and used shampoo on his hair. Before dumping the tub, he used a washboard to scrub his laundry. Then he dumped the tub and added clean water to rinse his clothes.

After cleanup, Yellowhenry checked the freezer of his refrigerator. He found a package of frozen corn and carrots. He pulled it out and placed it in a pan of warm water. Clad in his home nightwear—pajamas over cotton briefs, house slippers, and a bathrobe—he pulled the bearskin bundle into the kitchen and spread it out. He pulled the bear meat out and stored it in six one-gallon glass jars. The rest of the stuff he put away. He used a sponge to clean dirt and grease off the hide.

He used a piece of a curry comb to clean the hair side. Meat was something he wanted no part of at the moment. His meal was the entire package of vegetables, washed down with well water. It was delicious.

Voices woke him the next morning. He pushed the curtain at his bedroom window aside and looked toward the corral. Two men were leaning against the rails and were talking about the horse.

One of the men was a tribal policeman. Yellowhenry swung out of bed, stepped into his slippers, tugged on his bathrobe, and walked out to talk to the men. He knew both and greeted them by name.

"Mornin', Nate, Horace," he said amiably.

The men shook hands. Nate Baldwin was the policeman. Horace Greene was a big-game hunter and guide who conducted business both on and off the reservation.

"Haven't seen you for a while, Joe," Baldwin said. "Where have you been?"

"Headwaters of Lost Horse Basin. Lookin' around."

"Find anything?"

"Bear. Got a piece for ya. You, too, Horace."

"No thanks," Greene said. "Got plenty."

The men visited for nearly fifteen minutes before Baldwin said, "Nice horse."

"Found him on the way back."

"Found him?"

"Wild horse," Yellowhenry said.

"No. Loose horse," Greene said. "My horse."

"Then he was a bait horse," Yellowhenry said.

"He got away before I could shoot him," Greene said. "Thanks for bringing him back."

Baldwin looked at Greene. "By tribal custom, you cut your ownership."

"Only by the view of informal law. I could have gone and got him myself, but I was busy."

"You didn't. So, he's my horse," Yellowhenry insisted.

"I have money invested," Greene said.

"How much?" Baldwin asked.

"Fifty dollars."

"No, no," Yellowhenry said. "No one pays

fifty for a bait horse. Especially you. I'll give you ten dollars."

The men dickered for ten minutes while Baldwin listened. They finally settled on twenty dollars, which was five more than Greene had paid for Hi Boy. Yellowhenry led the men back to the house where they sat at the kitchen table. He went into his bedroom, pulled a twenty-dollar bill from a stash he kept in a hideaway spot, and rejoined the two at his table. Before he handed over the twenty, he placed a tablet on the table and wrote out a bill of sale.

"What's that for?" Greene asked.

"Protection."

"Protection from what?"

"It's for the horse. Anyone who takes him without my permission would be guilty of horse stealing. There are serious penalties for that," Yellowhenry said.

"Like what?"

"Ask Nate."

"Hanging, for one," Baldwin said. "Doesn't happen very often. Usually comes with a fine of $500 or the value of the horse, whichever is greater."

"You think I would steal your horse?" Greene asked Yellowhenry.

"No. But there are others."

"What if I don't sign?" Greene asked Baldwin.

"Then you'd have abandoned the horse. Ownership goes to Yellowhenry by right of possession."

Greene stared silently at both men for a moment. "All right, I'll sign."

Baldwin witnessed the sale, and Joe handed Greene the money. Then he pulled down one of the gallon jars of bear meat and handed it to Baldwin. It went without saying that the container would be returned. The men visited for another twenty minutes before Baldwin and Greene left. Joe put the bill of sale into the bundle of legal papers he kept with his cash.

Chapter Four

With his purchase of the horse completed, Yellowhenry dressed in fresh clothes and pulled out his farrier's bag. He added his float file and speculum and walked back out to his horse. He used a nail to pull the tangles out of Hi Boy's mane and tail, thinning them out. He cut the tail to hock level, then trimmed the hooves until they were neat and unsplit. The most worrisome part of the care was floating the horse's teeth. He placed a halter on the horse and tied him to a post of the corral. Then he manipulated the animal's jaw as though placing a bit in its mouth. He placed the hand rasp in Hi Boy's mouth and began sawing it back and forth on the right side. At first, Hi-Boy jerked his head, but Yellowhenry kept a firm hand on his nose. He quieted him down and continued the treatment. Then he looked into the mouth and was satisfied with that side. He moved to the other side. The horse stood quietly and let Yellowhenry do his work.

When he finished with the left, he touched up the right side. "You are a good patient. Didn't have to use the speculum," he said, smiling as he patted the horse's neck. He curry-combed his horse just to touch him up. Then he walked to his mudroom and came back with a flat metal pan containing a scoop of oats. Yellowhenry set it down and climbed up to get another flake of hay. Hi Boy tucked into the oats and ignored the hay. Yellowhenry laughed, "You candy lover, you." Water came next, and then he used a scoop shovel to remove Hi Boy's overnight horse apple deposit. "You're on your own for a few hours now," he said. But he chained and locked his corral gate.

Yellowhenry went in through the back door of his house and came out the front carrying one of the gallon jars of bear meat. He walked to his next-door neighbor and knocked on the door. Presently, the door opened, and a white-haired woman stood before him. "There you are, Sand in His Shoes," she said happily, using his Indian name. "Come in, Joe. Let's talk."

"Hello, Minnie," Yellowhenry smiled. He handed her the jar. "Bear meat."

"Oh, thank you. I will love it. Next time you go off, come get me. I'll go with you. Keep you warm at night," she giggled.

"Minnie, you know I can't handle as much woman as you," he laughed with her. He thought to himself, however, 'Forty years ago, Minnie Graves. Forty years ago.'

"Oh, Mama would be gentle with you," she grinned. "But you have clean thoughts for Minnie and something for her to do."

"Yes. I have a horse."

"I know. I saw. Very nice horse. Others like him, too. That's why you locked the gate."

"I paid Horace Greene for the sorrel. He wanted him back."

"Horace Greene is a bastard. He only needs horses for bear bait. That horse is too nice a horse for such a bastard."

"I'm glad you think so. Would Minnie be able to watch my horse?"

"Does your horse have a name?"

"Yes. He is known as Hi Boy. Why do you ask?"

"I like to know the names of horses I ride."

"You don't need to ride him over here," Yellowhenry said. "He is locked in the corral."

"I will ride him there, where he is, so he gets to know me. Does he come to a whistle?"

"I don't think so."

"Then I will teach him," she said firmly.

"I just hoped you could let me know if someone comes by and checks on him."

"If you want me to watch your horse, I can watch him much better if I am with him."

"Yes. You are right. If you wish to watch him that way, I will be grateful."

"It's little enough to do for some good bear meat," she said.

Yellowhenry limped a half mile to the Indian center. There, he checked the bulletin board for notices of anyone needing him for horseshoeing or other types of horse care. There were three: two for shoeing and one for worming. He pulled the notices for horses needing to be shod. The one for worming he left a note. 'Have to call a vet. I do not offer that service.' He knew the request for deworming came from when he used to do that work. The problem was that the over-the-counter medications he tried usually caused him to have to go back and repeat—and repeat again. The veterinarians had access to better stuff.

From the community center, he walked to the tribal police station. "Sand in His Shoes," the woman officer at the counter smiled. "What do you need?"

"Game report," Yellowhenry answered.

She turned around to a set of open-faced cabinets behind her. "What kind of report?"

"Predator."

She handed him a form, and he checked off bear, wolf, and bobcat. Then he marked on a map where he had shot the animals and added a brief description of the circumstances. He also noted that he had taken and tanned the skins as well as processed the bear meat.

She read the report and asked coyly, "Would a girl have to come to sleep with you to get a piece of bear meat?"

He chuckled, "Amy, you just come on over. I have a jar with your name on it. Other services are not required."

"Darn it," she said. "I was just hoping to get lucky. The bear meat was my excuse."

"You'd do better to just take the meat," he laughed. "I wouldn't want to disappoint you."

"You are too modest, Joe," she said.

"Yeah, maybe," he said. "Is Kaden in?"

"Let me see if he's busy. I'll be right back."

Yellowhenry watched her as she swung down from the stool she was sitting on. Amy Doans was twenty-six, tall, and willowy. She was well-proportioned and toned. Her black hair combed straight back fell to the center of her back, and she walked with a straight foot plant that bespoke athletic ability. Facially, she was attractive, with dark eyes, a straight nose, full, sensuous lips, and high, distinctive cheekbones. She was a widow with two children, four and six years old. Her husband, Marvin Fletcher, had been a tribal policeman killed during a traffic stop a year earlier. His killer had yet to be discovered. After his death, she reverted to her maiden name.

While he waited, Yellowhenry flipped through the wanted posters pinned to a bulletin board on the wall across from Amy's desk. He wasn't paying too much attention—they were mostly for fugitives from out of the area. Then he came across one that surprised him. It was for Talon Greene, son of Horace. He had been arrested as an accessory to murder, posted bail, and then disappeared without making his court date. There was a thousand-dollar reward for his apprehension.

Amy's voice interrupted his reading, "I see you found the flyer on Talon Greene. You going after him?"

"Says here he's armed and dangerous. Last seen on this reservation."

"Yep. He's somewhere on the way back. Laying low," she said.

"I'm not a bounty hunter," he said. "Somebody else's job."

"Somebody else's money, too. I'd go after him if I didn't have kids."

He looked at her to see if she was serious. "You mean that don't you?" he asked.

"Damn right, I mean it. A thousand dollars would mean a lot to me."

"Amy, that country back there is huge. No roads, to boot. I've been out in it a month at a time in different directions, and I haven't seen all of it. A man could get lost back there and never find his way out. He might not ever be found even if he were being looked for. It's as close to the old ways as you can get."

"I don't care. I'm keepin' my ear to the ground. If I get the right information, I just might have my mother watch my kids, take a leave of absence from here, and go after him."

"I don't advise you to do that. Come see me before you go off half-cocked."

She grinned at him and rolled her tongue over her upper lip. "If I do that, I'll get off full-cocked, Joe. When can I come see you for my bear meat?"

"Well, anytime, I guess," he said, turning red.

"Okay, I will. Kaden's waiting for you."

Chapter Five

Kaden Bull was the tribal chief of police. He had been for thirty years. At sixty-five, he was starting to slow down and think about retirement. His full head of hair was streaked with silver, and he parted it on the left side and combed it back. At six feet three inches tall, the strength of his barrel chest was impressive despite its overhang above his belt. He weighed 235 pounds and had a deep, booming voice that commanded attention when necessary. Otherwise, he was soft-spoken and intelligent. "Sand in His Shoes," he greeted when Yellowhenry walked into his office. "I see you've been out to the Lost Horse country."

"Hello, Kaden," Yellowhenry said. "Yes, I would still be up there, but I wrecked a knee. Had to come out."

"You all right?"

"I'm going down to the clinic to see if I can get it scoped out. I'm sure I've got some loose cartilage floating around in it."

"Sorry to hear that. You didn't happen to notice anyone else up that way, did you?"

"I didn't. No campfire smoke either. You must be interested in the whereabouts of Horace's kid."

"They've added another thousand to his capture. Seems like he was more than just an accessory. He's wanted for murder," Bull added.

"Damn. That's harsh."

"I feel for the people. Horace is a shithead, so I do not care for him. But I'd like to see this boy brought to justice by one of our own. It'd help with the way we're viewed to turn him in ourselves."

"Yeah, I agree," Yellowhenry said.

"So, what did you want to see me about?" Bull asked.

"I'm back for the winter. Gotta rustle up a job."

"You just missed a chance. I put Enos Clay on last week. I can put you on the auxiliary board. That's the best I can do right now."

The men sat silently as Yellowhenry thought. "If I went after Talon Greene while on the auxiliary board, would that mean that as an officer of the law, I'd be disqualified from receiving the reward money?" he finally asked.

"No. Not as a temporary officer, which is what being on the board is."

"I could carry a badge?"

"Sure."

"I'm okay for a while. Got to have this knee looked into. If Talon is still missing, in a couple of weeks maybe I'll look into that."

"You'd be risking snow," Bull observed.

"I wouldn't go back so far that I'd get snowed in. I have a horse. Wouldn't want to lose him that way. I'm figuring that with heavy snow, Talon will move closer to the low country. Horace is likely supplying him. Track Horace and find Talon."

"Yeah, well, if you get there first," Bull said. "Others will be hungry for that money too. It isn't on the flyer, but they've added that the reward is good, dead or alive. Here's a badge. Good luck."

Yellowhenry limped into the tribal clinic, checked in at the desk, and sat down to wait. He was called in and placed in an examination room, where he waited for an hour. The doctor came in and said without preamble, "I'm Dr. Kirby. You have a bum knee. While I glove up, take off your pants."

The exam was brief and painful. "Good news and bad news," Kirby advised as he stripped off his gloves. "You aren't bone on bone. That's the good news. You have broken pieces of cartilage that need to be trimmed and some loose pieces that need to be removed. We can't do that here. I'll refer you to a specialist in Billings. Give it two days, then call to see when they can schedule you for surgery. In the meantime, use ice to get the swelling down, and stay off it as much as you can. Check out some crutches when you leave."

"What about wrapping it?" Yellowhenry asked.

"That'll help. Ace bandage. I'll wrap it for you so you can see how to do it."

With his knee wrapped, Yellowhenry found he could walk significantly better. He had checked out both crutches and a cane. He used the cane to walk to the grocery store, where he bought a bag of party ice. Then he walked back to his place, where he found Minnie riding Hi Boy in a circle in the corral. He smiled and waved before entering his house. He put the ice in his freezer and leaned the crutches in a corner.

With his cane in hand, he walked out to the corral. Minnie was riding the horse in the opposite direction. When Yellowhenry leaned against the corral rails, lifting his left knee to the bottom rail for relief, she kneed the horse, and he walked across the corral to his boss. "This is a fine horse," Minnie declared. "When you sell him, I want the right of first refusal."

"That's good to hear, Minnie," he smiled, "but you don't have a place to keep a horse."

"I'll keep him here. You won't be using it."

"Yeah, you're right. I hadn't thought of that. Okay, you have the right of first refusal."

"This horse doesn't need a bridle. He'll go where you want with hand and knee pressure. He's a very smart horse. Watch this."

She slid off the right side and began walking across the corral. Hi Boy turned to go with her but stopped and stood quietly when she held up her hand and said, "Stay." When she reached the far side of the corral, she crawled between the rails, walked twenty yards beyond the corral, and sharply whistled. The horse trotted toward her and stopped by the corral with his head thrust out toward her. She walked to him and murmured something as she stroked his muzzle lovingly. Then she crawled through the rails, grabbed his mane, and swung aboard. Hi Boy delivered her to Yellowhenry's side of the corral. She hopped off and grinned. "He learns quickly."

"How did you get him to come to your whistle?"

"Bribery. Like all horses, he loves carrots."

"Well, it's amazing how you've done all this so quickly. Did anyone come by?"

"Yes, that bastard. He shook your lock and chain. Said that wouldn't stop him if he decides to reclaim the horse."

"He knows you'll see him."

"He'll come disguised and at night. You should have a big dog that sleeps with your horse."

"Are you a big dog, Minnie?" Yellowhenry laughed.

"Don't laugh. I would sleep here with this horse. I would shoot that bastard when he shows up."

"That would be a good shooting," Yellowhenry agreed. "I'll talk to him."

"Why are you pushing that cane?"

"I ruined my knee joint. Have to get it scoped out."

"That cane is an old man's tool. You need a walking staff. I have one for you. I have herbs for a poultice that will help that knee, too. The horse will be fine for now. Come with me."

The pair walked to Minnie's house. Its layout was the same as his. "You'll need to skin out of those pants," she ordered. "Let me get a towel so you can cover yourself."

"Well, shoot," he grinned. "And here I was, all hopeful."

She cackled. "It warms my heart to hear that, but not anything else. You need to find a woman, Sand in His Shoes, before you waste away, too."

"I agree, but the women I run into have no sand in their shoes. My woman will have to have a little wanderlust in her soul, or she'll be left behind."

"Men," Minnie pretended disgust. "All a bunch of love-'em-and-leave-'em types. Women don't have sandy feet because they bear all the children. It takes a lot of stayin' home to raise a passel of kids. Here's a towel."

When he was seated bare-legged in front of her with a towel over his lap, she began her ministrations. She seemed to have a magical way of manipulating his knee so that it didn't hurt. "What are you doing?" he asked.

"Just settling stuff into better positions. That doctor is right. Get it scoped. This poultice will take away pain, but you'll need to wrap over it. Keep it in place. He referred you to Billings?"

"He did."

"It'll be at least six weeks before they fit you in."

"Six weeks? Why so long?"

"Think about it," she said. "You're a back-of-the-bus sitter, like it or not."

"Well, I don't."

"Good. Maybe someday you can change that situation. For now, we've got to get you along as best we can. There, now you can put your pants on. I won't look. Much."

"I might just flash you, Minnie. Keep my hopes alive," he laughed.

"Go ahead. I won't tell."

With his pants back on, Yellowhenry hefted a six-foot walking staff. "What's this made of?" he asked. "It really has a tight grain."

"My husband said it was black walnut, but I don't know for sure."

"It's really a nice staff. Are you sure you want me to use it?"

"I'm pleased to give it to you. Now you need to get back to your house. You have company comin'."

"I do? How would you know that?"

"Amy called me to take her kids tonight. Her mother is her regular sitter. Something special is comin' to you."

"I didn't ask her to spend the night. I told her I had some bear meat for her. I was just gonna give her that. Doesn't take all night."

"Don't be stupid, Joe. Take all night. She needs it and, believe it or not, so do you. Now git."

Chapter Six

An exhausted Yellowhenry and Amy Doans were both asleep when the shot rang out. He instantly scrambled over her naked form and, naked himself, darted to the window of his bedroom. It was just after daylight, and shadows were still deep. He could see that a rail was down on the far side of his corral. A man was disappearing into a low fold in the ground about fifty yards beyond the enclosure. Hi Boy was nervously running back and forth as another rifle shot boomed through the morning stillness.

"Stop your goddamned shootin'!" the running figure bellowed. "I'm leavin', I'm leavin'."

Hi Boy bolted across the corral, leaped the fence where the rail was down, and galloped after the running man. A keening whistle came from the corner of Minnie's house. The horse checked his run but seemed to want to keep going. Another whistle stopped him. He turned and began trotting, with his head up, back toward the corral. He stopped at the corral, but she whistled a third time, and he trotted around the corral and past where Yellowhenry was watching, disappearing toward the white-haired figure with a lever-action .30-30 in one hand and a carrot in the other.

With everybody dressed, Hi Boy back in the corral, and the rail back in place, Minnie was wielding a spatula, turning pancakes in one pan and eggs in another. Amy and her kids were sitting on a bench at the back of the kitchen table, leaning against the wall. Yellowhenry was seated at the end of the table, sipping black coffee. "Are you sure that was Horace Greene?" he asked again. "I mean, it was dark enough that his face was hard to see. He could have had someone else come for the horse."

"What's the difference?" Minnie asked. "If you want to find out who it was, go to the clinic and see who's bein' treated for a wounded ass. Did you see him flinch at my second shot? I got some meat on the end of that one."

"I'll call the clinic from the office and ask about a gunshot wound," Amy said. "That will make it official."

"That's a good idea. Let me know how good my aim was," Minnie said as she plopped pancakes in front of Amy's kids. "You two are next," she added.

"I'm good," Yellowhenry said.

"Yeah, so am I," Amy said.

Minnie turned and looked at them as she poured more pancake batter into her frying pan. "I'll be the judge of that," she grinned. "You should see yourselves. All pale and sunken-cheeked. I'd be ashamed of myself, turning such survivors as you two loose on the world."

Amy's son looked up from eating his pancake. "How come your cheeks sank, Mom?" he asked.

"James," Amy said, "do my cheeks look any different now than they did yesterday?"

"No."

"See? Mom's just fine. Don't worry about it."

Minnie giggled and kept her back to the table. Yellowhenry covered his face and looked sidelong at Amy.

She ducked her face and didn't look at him, but her shoulders shook with laughter.

After Amy and her kids left, Minnie examined Yellowhenry's knee."Did you experience a stiff leg last night?" she asked.

"No. In fact, now that you mention it, I didn't even think about it," he answered.

"That's good. In two ways," she smiled. "I'll replace this poultice for you. But be more careful than you were last night."

With his pants back on, he left to take care of Hi Boy. From there, he took his new walking staff and walked uptown to the police station. Amy greeted him professionally before winking at him.He smiled, pleased. "Any news from the clinic?"

"Not yet," she answered. "Did you look down there where that guy disappeared to see if there was any blood?"

"No. I will now, though, before I go see Horace."

"I didn't hear that, did I?" she asked. "You planning to take the law into your own hands?"

"I'll come back and see if someone can go with me," he answered.

"Good. I am a witness, you know?"

"You saw? I thought you were still in bed."

"I wanted to see just like you did. I was right behind you. I saw the guy runnin' and hollerin'."

"Can you identify the guy?"

"You're gonna find Horace Greene with a sore ass. He might not go to the clinic today. If he infects, he will. Three days if you want to wait."

"I don't. Minnie saw him and heard him say the padlock and chain wouldn't stop him if he wanted the horse. All three of us saw someone trying to steal my horse. The sooner we face this, the better."

Yellowhenry was combing the ground beyond his corral. He wasn't coming up with anything, so he looked at the corral where the rail had been taken down. Then, he looked at his bedroom window and realized he was offline. When he found the tracks of the runner, he also found spatters of blood. He followed the trail down to a road a half-mile down the hill. The blood stopped at the edge of the road where a small puddle had formed. The footprints tracked in and around the puddle and then away, bloodstained, for thirty-five feet where they disappeared. 'You closed the door on your trailer walked to the door of your truck and drove off, he thought to himself. 'Quite a distinctive tread on your truck, too', he surmised. Then he walked back up to his house. He was quite pleased with the assistance of the walking staff. Minnie was busy working with Hi Boy. "Hit that bastard in the ass, didn't I?" she asked smugly.

"You hit something. He bled all the way down to the road. Didn't go to the clinic, though."

"He'll infect."

"That's what Amy said, but I'm not waitin' for that."

"He'll be layin' for ya. Today, he is a wounded, angry man. Wait till he is a sick and wounded man. Have Kaden investigate. Have him or Nate or one of the other deputies look into this. Playing vigilante is going off half-cocked. It's a bad way to go."

"Why do I have to have a lawyer for a neighbor?"

"Be thankful. Forty years ago, I would have tracked that bastard down and shot him like a mad dog. Things are different now. Now, everybody has a lawyer whether they know it or not. Now, those old behaviors are lawsuits."

"Didn't stop you from shooting this morning."

"I'm different, and I caught him in the act of trying to steal a horse. I'm not going over to his house, though, to finish the job like you are."

"I just want to talk to him."

"Don't. Set up your case for attempted horse theft. Have the police go talk to him. Don't you see the difference?"

"Yeah, I guess I do."

"Wow. A man who can think. Tell Amy. She needs someone like you."

Chapter Seven

Nate Baldwin took copious notes as he investigated the shooting of Horace Greene. He examined the rail that had been removed and measured the distance from where the blood spatter started back to where Minnie had fired the shots. Her interview included his examination of her .30-30 rifle. He made plaster casts of the tread marks at the road and noted measurements from the blood puddle to where the bloody footprints disappeared. Interviews with Yellowhenry and Amy Doans were conducted. When all was said and done, Yellowhenry decided not to press trespassing charges. Together with Nate Baldwin, he went to Horace Greene's home to further investigate the attempted horse theft.

Baldwin looked at the tread pattern on Greene's truck. It matched his plaster of Paris casts. He photographed the pair side by side and measured the length of the truck from the driver's door to the end of the horse trailer. The measurements matched those taken on the road.

He was just finishing his work when he heard Greene shouting from his front door. "What the hell do you think you're doing?"

Baldwin motioned to Yellowhenry, who was sitting in the patrol truck. Yellowhenry climbed out, and the two approached the edge of the porch. Greene was leaning heavily against the door frame. "Horace," Baldwin said mildly, "Your attempt to steal that horse you sold to Joe is what I'm nailing down."

"That wasn't me," Greene asserted.

"Horace," Baldwin said, "It was you. Your ass is running blood down your leg right now, in case you haven't noticed. You left a blood trail down the hill behind Joe's place. You need to go to the clinic and get some help. Right now. But, you're luckier than you deserve. Yellowhenry isn't pressing trespassing charges today. He's going to wait to see if you try it again. He can press charges until the statute of limitations runs out."

"How long is that?"

"Three years."

"To hell with it. He can keep the damned horse."

Baldwin turned to Yellowhenry. "Anything you want to say?"

"When I file, I'll also add criminal trespassing."

"Aww, to hell with you, half-breed. You'll have to live to press charges," Greene spat angrily. Yellowhenry stiffened, and his jaw hardened.

"Joe," Baldwin asked, "Are you sure you want to wait?"

"No, I don't. I've had a sudden change of mind. I want to charge Horace with attempted horse theft and criminal trespassing right now."

"Horace, you are under arrest," Baldwin said. "Step down here and put your hands behind your back."

"Oh no, you don't. You aren't takin' me anywhere," Greene shouted, as he spun in the doorway pulling a shotgun from behind him. The gun was a double-barreled, side-by-side shotgun. He fired the first barrel at a diving Baldwin, catching him in the back of his right thigh. The second barrel was aimed at Yellowhenry, who had jumped behind the still-open door of the patrol truck. The blast of birdshot shattered the police insignia but failed to hit Yellowhenry. He dove through the door and immediately grabbed the sawed-off shotgun Baldwin had placed in a vertical dashboard rack. Sliding across the seat, he exited from the driver's side. He came up by the front tire of the truck and fired a round, which took the door of Greene's house off its upper hinge. After firing his rounds, Greene retreated. The sudden screams of terrified women echoed through the destroyed door.

Baldwin was dragging himself toward his vehicle when Greene reappeared, leveling the shotgun at him. "Nate!" Yellowhenry yelled. "Roll!" Whether it was Baldwin's roll or the blast from Greene's shotgun that turned him over, Yellowhenry couldn't tell. His immediate reaction to Greene's shot was to fire his own. The double-aught buckshot split the edge of the door frame and struck the left side of Greene's sternum. Wooden splinters tore through the wound channel and exited out of the man's back. Greene was blown off his feet, and by the time his drumming legs stilled, he was dead.

Yellowhenry rushed to Baldwin and assessed the damage caused by Greene's last shot. The pattern of number six birdshot had spread enough that, while the pellets were embedded in Baldwin's back, his heavy jacket had slowed them, leaving them less than an inch deep. "Nate, let's get you to the clinic. They'll be able to patch you up there."

"What about Greene?" Baldwin asked.

"Gone."

"Good. Let's get outta here. You drive."

42

Chapter Eight

Amy was entertaining Yellowhenry at her place a week later.

Her kids were spending the night at Minnie's, having the time of their lives as she led Hi Boy around the corral in circles with the kids on his back. James kept kicking the horse's sides to get him to go faster, but Hi Boy ignored the effort.

Following dinner and a TV movie, Amy and Joe were conversing in bed. "With Horace dead, you can't follow him to Talon," Amy said. She was lying on her side, nude, as she spoke.

Yellowhenry was on his back, looking up at nothing in particular. "I thought you were hot to go get him. What happened to that idea?"

"I have our kids to watch out for," she said, nudging her hip into him.

"Our kids? What the hell are you talking about?" he asked in alarm. "You aren't, are you?"

"If I am, what are you gonna do about it?"

"What do you think I should do about it?"

"Marry me, of course," she said, suddenly solemn. "You aren't the kind to go around planting bastards, are you?"

"Well, no. I was assuming you were on the pill. I guess."

"Joe, I haven't known another man since my husband died, so I haven't needed the pill. You are the first. And my plumbing seems to be working just fine. You are my only plumber. You're the only one I want, too. Isn't that how you feel?"

"I haven't thought that far ahead. This is only our second date. I'm just…"

"Taking free milk because you don't want to buy the cow?" she finished for him, sitting up and looking straight into his eyes.

"How did we get to this point? We were talking about going after Talon Greene," he said, trying to deflect her challenge.

"We got here because you laid claim to me. And I accepted. When you get me, you get my kids—and the one you planted in me."

"How do you know that? It's only been twice."

"With my husband, it was the first time. After James, I went on the pill for fifteen months. When I stopped using the pill, I was pregnant so quickly, we figured it had to be the next first time. Get used to it, Joe. I'm a first-timer."

He sat up and faced her. They were both sitting cross-legged. "If you are, Amy, we'll get married."

"Okay," she said. "That takes care of the business end of it."

"What other end is there?" he asked.

"Love and family," she said. "I'll wait for love. I'm not sixteen, expecting you're bangin' me because we're in love. There are other issues, too."

"Issues?" he asked.

"Where we live. I like your place, but we'll need to add on to the house. I'd say a pair of bedrooms off the side of your living room—to the right side there."

"How do we pay for that?"

"Go get Talon Greene. We can have the bedrooms added, unfinished, for fifteen hundred. We can finish the inside ourselves with the five hundred left over."

"Okay, assuming I bring him in, we get the reward, add on the bedrooms, and you have our baby, how do we make a living? Did you ever think of that?"

"Yes. No more Sand in His Shoes, I have. I checked into our future before I came over to your place and staked my claim."

"Really," he said, looking at her in growing amazement. "How do I fit into that?"

"Kaden is quittin'," she said. "You will take his place."

"Aren't you rolling the dice pretty hard here, Amy?"

"Tell me your plan," she said.

"I don't have a plan. I didn't have a family when I came over here tonight. How could I have a plan already?"

"Good point," she said. "So in the absence of your plan, let's move ahead with mine. If you come up with a better one, we'll switch to yours."

"Amy, if I may ask," he said, "What makes you think I'd be the one selected to take Kaden's place?"

"Well, Nate Baldwin was first up. But he is transferring to the state patrol. Enos Clay is too green. You have served several times on a temporary basis. Kaden likes you, and when I told him you and I are getting married and you'll need a steady job, he said he'd support your candidacy to the tribal elders. That should do it."

"How did you figure all that out?" he asked.

"My dear," she said patiently, "I have an A-type personality. Get used to it. I can't help it any more than you can help being a C-type."

"What type am I?"

"You are a C. That's why you take off for long stretches of time. It's the anti-social part of you. You're into detail. Those are two parts of you that I know, so far."

"What happens when I take off again, Amy, if it's something I can't help?"

"Do it on manhunts and lost people searches. Hell, you have one right in front of you now. Go have fun. You can call it a one-spouse honeymoon."

"We're getting married tomorrow, aren't we?"

"How long do you want to wait?"

"Well, hell, if we're gonna do this thing," he said, leaning toward her, "let me lay claim to my bounty."

She smiled, kissed him, and slipped beneath him, gripping him firmly between her thighs.

The next day, Amy took an hour off her work. She and Yellowhenry stood before the tribal holy man who wed them according to the tribe's customs. When they had completed their vows and been declared husband and wife, the holy man told them to go to the county seat as soon as they could and legalize their nuptials in the eyes of the county and state.

Chapter Nine

After their wedding, Yellowhenry met Amy's mother. Anna Doans' husband had died of tuberculosis when Amy was ten. She was their only child. Anna was fifty and, like her daughter, athletic, direct, and attractive. She had never remarried. "Well," she said when Amy brought Yellowhenry home, "I see what she likes. I've heard of you, Sand in his Shoes. You are a good match for her. You will be a good father. I can tell these things."

"Thank you," he said. "I hope you will help with our children. A good, strong grandmother is a blessing."

Anna looked at Amy. "He says the right things. Does he do the right things?"

Amy smiled. "That's why I grabbed him, Mom. I didn't want him sampling other wares."

"Uh, I'm right over here," Yellowhenry said.

The women looked at him and laughed. "You'll have to get used to us," Amy said. "We haven't had a man around here for a long time. We're used to talking about them, not to them."

"I hear you are building a nursery at your place," Anna said.

"A nursery?" he questioned. "A couple of bedrooms is what we've talked about."

"With Amy, as quick as she is, you better think about one of those bedrooms as a nursery."

"Well, it's just a plan right now. First, I have some work to do to get the money."

"Your 'first' is too late because of weather time. You need to get the framing, roof, floor, and siding up before snow flies. I'll loan you the money to get that started while you're after that killer," Anna said.

"If that doesn't pan out, it will take a long time to pay you back," he said. "I can't do that. No offense. But the add-on comes after I bring Talon in."

"Amy, you need to talk to Joe," Anna said.

Amy looked at her husband and then at her mother. "No, Mom," she said. "This decision is Joe's. We'll be just fine as we are, even if we have to wait till spring to add on."

Yellowhenry didn't go man-hunting right away. So, he had a break-in period for himself and Amy, which involved Yellowhenry sleeping at Amy's place for two nights and his own place for two nights. They had taken a day to go and legalize their marriage at the county courthouse. He was doing his best to be a father to James and Susan, but his need for privacy was not something he was able to give up completely. He used Hi Boy as his excuse. In addition to improving the horse's overall condition, Yellowhenry wanted to get him hardened up for going after Talon Greene. He shoed him and then saddled him every other day, riding him an increasing number of miles over ten days. While he was doing that, he also shoed other horses. He gave it up when his knee started getting sore again.

He was back at Amy's house and was walking her to work when she announced quietly, "Honey, guess what?"

"I don't know," he said. "What?"

"I'm late."

"Late? I don't think Kaden cares if you come in a little late."

"Not that kind of late, Joe."

"Oh," he said. "Like in baby-makin' late."

"Yes. I told you I'm a first-timer. I hope you don't hold it against me."

"Well then, guess what? So am I. Let's do this thing together," he said, pulling her into his arms and kissing her passionately.

"Hey, you two," a man in a passing car yelled, "Get a room." Then he waved and grinned good-naturedly at them.

They waved back, and Amy hollered, "We already have, Sam." The man honked his horn for them.

"Ames, I'm taking off today," Yellowhenry said, using his term of endearment for her.

She stopped walking and threw her arms around him, holding him as he embraced her. "Are you sure we need to have you go?"

"Need? Maybe not, but if I'm going to step into Kaden's shoes next month, I want to have this done and out of the way. As police chief, I'd be ineligible for any reward. And to tell the truth, we could use the money."

"It can't wait?"

"If I'm going, it's time. There's snow up high that will force him into the low country. I have a pretty good idea where he is. If I'm right, I'll spot smoke. That'll be where he is. I shouldn't be more than a week or so."

They had arrived at the police headquarters. She reached for him and kissed him fiercely. "Don't make me a two-time widow, Joe. Whatever you have to do, don't risk that."

"I'll be careful," he said. Then he kissed her goodbye.

Chapter Ten

In an ironic twist of fate, Yellowhenry had acquired a pack saddle and the use of a pair of mules that had belonged to Horace Greene. The mules were kept in a pasture owned by Enos Clay who had bought them from Greene's widow. Clay had approached Yellowhenry with the idea that the mules could be useful assets to the tribal police force. They had pitched the idea to Police Chief Kaden Bull who had modified the concept to a fee-use on an as-needed basis. Clay would retain ownership of the animals but would make them available when the police needed them. Yellowhenry's effort to apprehend Talon Greene was the first use of the animals by the police force. The pack saddle was Yellowhenry's. He had bought it outright as he had plans for pack trips with his new family.

He took both mules. They were big animals, black over light tan. Neither had names, so Yellowhenry named them. The bigger of the two was a jake. Yellowhenry called him Bray and the other, a jenny, he named Jay. Bray carried the pack saddle and Jay carried an open-top double pannier with a bale of hay on either side. She would also carry Talon Greene on the return trip.

It was a clear sunlit day and Yellowhenry was in an ebullient mood. He had left at mid-morning. His unhurried departure had allowed him time to double-check his supplies and equipment. Having a horse and two mules was a luxury he knew of but had seldom bothered with in his walkabouts. Having animals to care for added a serious burden to his days. As he rode, Yellowhenry kept his left leg free of the stirrup and his butt shifted to accommodate the angle of the stiffened knee joint. Minnie had insisted that he pack the ingredients of her special poultice. He had enough stuff for three applications. It pissed him off every time he thought of the stupid antic that had caused his injury. He had enjoyed scaling rock walls, free climbing and never falling. Now, he was wiser but wounded. It reminded him of the old saying about bull riders. 'There are many bull riders, but no old bull riders.'

Nevertheless, he was a happy man to be out on another solo excursion and getting paid. 'It couldn't get better than this,' he thought. His direction was northeast into what was called the Moose's Ass Canyon. The Moose Creek drainage was one of the best places on the reservation to hunt that regal animal. The creek poured, however from a deep, steep walled trackless canyon. It was really more a gorge than a canyon. The canyon was a serpentine affair that zig-zagged for miles from its headwaters before spilling out into a series of willow-draped meanders, oxbows, side pools, and stretches of swamp. Perfect moose habitat.

Moose's Ass Canyon was named by an old timer, Chief Bold Hawk, who had hunted the outflow of Moose Creek. He scoffed at youngsters who wanted to explore the headwaters. He could have called them a bunch of horse's asses for their folly, but he didn't. He asked, instead, "Why would you want to climb into the moose's ass?" The amusing analogy had stuck to a piece of the country that had, up to then, been unnamed. Yellowhenry suspected that Talon Greene had crawled into the rocky reaches of the canyon until he could figure out how to plot an escape.

Talon Greene had always been a pudgy, sullen youngster who was contemptuous of his father, Horace. He didn't hate the man, he just didn't believe in catering to white men who paid bloated fees to hunt deer, elk, moose, sheep, goat, bear, and lion on reservations. That it had been a successful way of making a living for his father didn't matter. Neither did Talon have an alternative in mind that his father could pursue to make a living. He was just one of those teenagers who rode along in contempt on their parents' coattails until the parents shook them off. Horace had had enough when the youngster had insulted a client and refused to help cater to the moose hunt they were on. That had happened three years prior. Upon the return from the hunt, Horace had turned the eighteen-year-old out. "You go find your own way if you're so damned smart. Then come back and tell me what I should do," he had said.

Talon had gone to Billings where he fell in with a group of dissolute young men who formed a loosely constructed gang. They were a mixed-race lot who got by, peddling soft drugs, shoplifting, and committing petty crimes. As a result, they all carried stolen handguns. Talon's was a short-barreled Smith and Wesson semi-automatic forty caliber which he carried in his boot. Word had come in that a wealthy homeowner had snowbirded to the Southwest, leaving his luxury home loaded and vacant. The gang's leaders decided to move on the fat score.

Five of them crept under the cover of darkness to a window leading into a storage room on the ground floor. Using a glass cutter, they had managed to successfully enter the main body of the house without setting off alarms. There they spread out looking for loot that they stuffed into burlap bags they carried tucked under their belts. None of them noticed the security cameras that recorded their activity. What they did notice was a pair of Rottweilers that exploded from a basement doorway where a house sitter had turned them loose. The man was yelling at the top of his voice, "Attack, attack, attack!"

The gang members began firing wildly at the dogs. It was a crossfire without discriminate targets. The dogs tore out the throats of two of the thieves, the gang shot and wounded another pair of their own, before downing the dogs, and Talon became the unluckiest of all when he saw the house sitter waving his arms and yelling wildly. Without thinking about it, Talon unloaded his forty-Cal semi-auto of his four remaining shots at the gesticulating shadowy figure fifteen feet from where Talon had forted up behind a recliner. Two of the shots found their mark. The man was struck once in the neck and once in the forehead just above the bridge of his nose. He had died instantly.

With two of their members killed by the dogs and the dogs and house sitter killed by the gang, the remaining three grabbed all the loot bags and left through the back door as security alarms were blaring all around them. Police were soon upon the scene and discovered the massacre which had been dutifully recorded by two security cameras on the ground floor and by one near the back door where the three gang members had fled.

Of the two wounded gang members, one needed surgery to repair the wound he had from a round that had entered his trunk under his right armpit. The bullet had hit a rib and deflected into the lung. The twenty-two-year-old was coughing up blood. The other wounded gangster had suffered a minor leg wound that didn't need professional attention. When the three reached their car, Talon was instructed by the slightly wounded leader to drive to the hospital and into the emergency entrance. There the badly wounded comrade was jerked from the backseat to the sidewalk beside the hospital where he fell to his side. Talon and the leader tore out, leaving their gangmate to the emergency room staff.

The hospital workers arrived quickly and began treatment of the wounded gang member. They also immediately notified the police that a gunshot victim had just been processed into the hospital for emergency surgery. Two hours later the police had interviewed the gunshot victim. He refused to talk for the first two days. A BOLO had, nevertheless, been issued for the other two, Talon and a young black man named Alexander Johnson. Both were known by the police. Flyers with their pictures were also printed and circulated. It was one of those that Yellowhenry had seen. Five days after the incident, with the assistance of the wounded gang member who had acquired a public defender attorney, the police had identified Talon as the shooter who took out the house sitter. They had cut a deal for the gang member's testimony. He had identified Talon as the shooter shielded from the cameras behind the recliner, and the reward for Talon was doubled.

In the meantime, Johnson had dropped Talon off at the boundary of the reservation a mile's distance from the village. The young man had sneaked onto his father's property and hidden out in the stable. His father had found him the next morning, and after listening to his son's truth-altered tale, had loaded up a pack train and escorted him into the Moose's Ass. Horace had ridden out and resupplied his son once since then. Johnson had been captured two hundred miles to the west and returned to Billings.

Now, Talon was watching a three-animal packtrain, thinking his father was coming to resupply him again. The packtrain was moving slowly as it wended back and forth along the watercourse of Moose Creek. "He will be here in the morning," Talon said to himself as he turned and retreated to his camp a half mile into the rocky and rugged reaches of the Moose's Ass.

Yellowhenry had been relaxed for the first two days of his ride, but now as he neared the Moose's Ass, he kept a weather eye out for a possible ambush. When he was a little less than half a mile from the mouth of the canyon, he dismounted and pulled the saddle gun he had stashed under his right leg. Leading Hi Boy, he walked until he was a quarter mile closer, then he stopped and set up camp. "Come on mules," he said. "Ol' Talon will know you. You get to be out there in the meadow where he can see you." He led them to water before hobbling both animals and giving each a flake of hay. With no need to graze, he knew they would be close to where he left them come morning.

He repeated the process for Hi Boy but hid him in the thick cover of willows near the stream. "Talon won't know you," he said to the horse, "so you have to stay out of sight." Then, he pitched his own camp, built a small fire, and heated a can of beans. He had a couple of slices of cooked bacon he'd saved from breakfast. With a pot of coffee and a slice of bread, he ate the bacon and beans. It was fully dark when he finished cleaning up his cooking and eating utensils. He slept under a two-man A-frame tent, set up inside the screen of willows. Afterward, he walked out to check on the mules and relieve himself. It was a clear night, and as he checked the mules' hobbles, he looked toward the mouth of Moose's Ass. To his satisfaction, a tendril of smoke curled against the black rock of the canyon wall.

Yellowhenry returned to his tent and crawled into his sleeping bag which he kept unzipped. He slept soundly without fear of being surprised. Bray had a habit of sounding off just before sunrise. He did the same thing with the approach of predators. Yellowhenry kept his rifle loaded and at his side. The previous night, Bray had opened up in the middle of the night and Yellowhenry had popped up and fired a shot off into the air. A snarl and the sound of a bounding animal rewarded him. He had gone to check on the animals of his packstring to find them spooked but otherwise fine. So, he was confident that, come morning, he would be up and around by the time Talon worked his way out of the canyon. Trying to do so in the dark would be dangerous, and Yellowhenry was also confident that his quarry would be expecting his father. His guard would be down, so coming out before daylight would be unnecessary.

Bray broke the frost-bitten morning air as he had every morning on the trip by hee-hawing just before dawn. Yellowhenry rolled out and scouted around the immediate area of the camp. He carried a flake of hay that he broke apart for the two mules. He left them hobbled. Hi Boy nickered when Yellowhenry gave him a small flake of hay. The horse had been able to access water so Yellowhenry left him hobbled where he was. Satisfied that the animals were settled, he stepped into the willows and leaned against a tree to wait.

Yellowhenry watched Hi Boy as he waited. An hour after sunrise, the horse started looking intently at something that seemed to be approaching from upstream. A few minutes later he saw a figure approaching cautiously. Yellowhenry moved to shield himself behind the tree and watched a young Indian walk up out of the creek and into the campsite. He looked around and called, "Dad? You around here?"

Yellowhenry stepped out from behind the tree. "No, Talon," he said. "Your dad isn't here."

"Who are you? How did you find me?" Talon said, turning to run.

Yellowhenry triggered a round from his Colt .45 that whistled just past Talon's head. "The next one won't miss," he shouted. "Stay right there. Talon Greene, you are under arrest for the murder of Simon Gallagher." Yellowhenry then read him his Miranda rights. "I also have some sad news for you. Your father is dead."

"What?" Greene said sinking into a squat. "What happened?"

"He tried to steal a horse. That one down there in the willows. He trespassed to do it. When he was arrested, he started shooting. He wounded the arresting officer and was killed by the man who was pressing charges."

"Whose horse?"

"Mine. Your father sold him to me. I have a bill of sale witnessed. Then your father was wounded by my neighbor who caught him attempting to steal the horse back early one morning."

"So, you killed my father?"

"Yes. I'm sorry. He gave me no choice. He shot first."

"And now you're going to take me in?" Greene asked angrily.

"The law is Talon. I represent the law," Yellowhenry said, holding up his badge.

"What if I won't go?" Talon pressed.

"Let me lay all the cards on the table, here," Yellowhenry said severely. "You are wanted for murder. There is a bounty posted for you, dead or alive. I want to take you back alive, but the choice is yours."

Greene began shifting in his stance and looking off thoughtfully. Then he rolled and came up with his pistol blazing. Yellowhenry had not been fooled. His shot took Greene through the right forearm, knocking the pistol from his hand after two of Greene's shots went zinging off through the willows. Nevertheless, he scrambled for the loose pistol. Yellowhenry's second shot hit the handgun sending it skittering out of Greene's reach. "Stop!" he yelled. "I don't want to shoot you."

Greene froze and sat up. "Okay," he said. "I quit for now."

"Let's make this clear," Yellowhenry said. "I'm through shooting to keep you alive. You can go back dead if that suits you."

"One of us goin' back dead suits me," Greene said, grinning. Then he looked at his arm. Blood was flowing down his wrist and into his hand and fingers. Still grinning he began licking and sucking the blood from his fingers. "What're you gonna do about this?" he asked.

"It's not much more than a scratch. You take care of it. I'll watch."

"You're a real bastard, ain't ya?"

"Enough of one to put a hole in you that you can't lick. Now pull that knife out of your belt scabbard and toss it over there by that pistol."

"I can't," Greene replied, "I'm bleedin' here."

"Okay. I'll shoot it off for you."

"No. Don't do that. I'll get it, I'll get it." He slowly reached down, unsnapped the retainer strap, and pulled the knife slowly from the scabbard. As he readied to toss the knife, he gripped it by the tip of the blade. Yellowhenry's shot broke the blade and knocked the knife out of Greene's hand.

When the echo of the shot settled down, he said, "Thanks for your help, Talon. We're making real progress here. Another four or five shots and all I'll have to do is throw you over the back of that jenny over there. How'll that be?"

"Don't hold your breath. I ain't done yet."

"Neither am I," Yellowhenry smiled evilly. "And I got the guns. Now get down on your belly with your hands behind your back."

"Make me."

Without warning, Yellowhenry's right arm flashed like the strike of a snake. The rock, one of his favorites, struck Greene in the side of his head just above the left temple. The young man folded and flopped, completely unconscious. Yellowhenry walked over and pushed Greene's hip with his boot. Satisfied that he was out cold, he picked up his rock and put it back into his jacket pocket. Then he retrieved the broken pieces of the knife and threw them into the willows. The pistol was still functional, so he stuck that in his waistband behind his back.

With Greene down and his weapons removed, Yellowhenry pulled a length of nylon cord from his pack saddle and tied Greene's hands behind his back. The forearm wound was still bleeding but would soon clot, so he didn't worry about that. Then he tied his ankles together. All Greene would be able to do was roll when he came to.

With the prisoner in hand and stable, Yellowhenry set about breaking camp. He took his time, making sure the animals were watered and fed. He gave them a bait of oats before loading them up with saddle, pack saddle, and panniers. With everything loaded and ready to go, he pulled a rope from the pack saddle and placed the loop around Greene's neck. He untied his feet and jerked on the rope. Greene, who had been faking unconsciousness, groaned. "I can't get up."

"Okay," Yellowhenry said, swinging aboard Hi Boy. "I'll drag you." He looped the rope around the horn of his saddle and began riding away at a walk. At first, Greene tried resisting but the noose around his neck began strangling him, so then he ran at Hi Boy. Yellowhenry calmly kicked his horse into gear and jerked Greene to the ground where he floundered, running on his knees for a short way before flopping to his belly.

Yellowhenry kept the rope under control. He let Greene get to his feet. "What the hell do you want me to do," he wailed.

"Walk," was the response.

"I thought I was gonna ride the mule."

"She's busy haulin' hay. You can ride her though when you're dead."

"I can't walk all that way."

"You behave yourself and after a few hours, we'll see if we can figure out how to give you a ride."

Chapter Eleven

Yellowhenry took it slow and easy, stopping occasionally to give Greene a chance to rest and for the mules to close up. Instead of stringing them, he let them follow on their own. He had shifted the rope to Greene's waist. The hours passed slowly. Once when Greene complained that he was diein' of thirst, his captor obediently stopped, dismounted, and held his canteen while Greene drank. Then he spit the last mouthful into Yellowhenry's face. "How do you like that? That's what I think of you."

"Makes my job easier, Talon. I'm thankin' ya," Yellowhenry said calmly. He swung back into the saddle and picked up their pace. A half-hour later, Greene was stumbling. He began yelling obscenities. Then he fell. Yellowhenry dragged him a short distance before stopping to look back. "Are you gonna get up and walk, or would you just as soon be dragged?" he asked.

"You can't keep doin' this to me," he yelled. "It's inhumane treatment of a prisoner."

"When you start actin' human, I'll treat you like one."

"I wanna ride."

"Behave yourself, and we'll see what we can do."

"All right, I'm behavin'."

"We'll see how you do next stop."

An hour later, Yellowhenry looked back. Greene was beginning to stumble, so he stopped and swung down from his saddle. He coiled the rope as he walked back to Greene.

The water canteen was slung over his shoulder. Greene was standing, head down, and breathing heavily. "Let's get some water into you," Yellowhenry said. Greene tipped his head back and drank.

"Joe," he said, "I don't think I can make it."

"We only have an hour, maybe two, till camp."

Greene sank to his knees. "I'm done, Joe. Drag me if you have to."

"Are you really gonna behave yourself, or is this just a cover for another one of your stupid pranks?"

"No more of those, I promise, Joe. Let me ride, please."

"All right," Yellowhenry said. "Walk back to the jenny."

It took Yellowhenry's help to get Greene up onto Jay's back. His feet were thrust down into the hay to the bottoms of the two panniers. Yellowhenry retied his prisoner's hands in front of his waist. Then he strung the mules and Hi Boy, nose to tail. For the next hour, they made good time. Yellowhenry looked back from time to time. After a half hour, Greene was riding slumped forward, asleep.

It was near sundown when Yellowhenry decided to pitch camp. He had selected a grassy slope leading down to Moose Creek. Greene had awakened and was sitting, waiting to be helped down. "You can get down, Talon. You don't need my help to do that," Yellowhenry said.

"Get down and do what?"

"Sit on your ass and keep your mouth shut. Behave your goddamned self."

"What is it with you adults? My old man was a pain in the ass, too," Greene groused as he slid off the mule's back.

"Well Talon, when you get to be an adult, maybe you'll figure it out. Oh, wait. Dang it, I forgot. You have a date with death's needle. You'll never make it to adulthood. You'll just die with that as one of the great mysteries you never figured out. Damn, that's sad," Yellowhenry shook his head sadly. "Yeah, that'll be a real shame."

"Fuck you," Greene spat.

"You're not asking a question, are you, Talon?" Yellowhenry grinned. "If you are, I'll pass. You just aren't my type."

The back-and-forth insulting continued as Yellowhenry cared for the stock. Greene sat in one place and watched. With the animals watered, hobbled, and fed, Yellowhenry set up his camp for the night. "No fire, tonight, Talon," he said. "No wood. Cold camp. Here's your chuck for supper." He tossed him a piece of smoked bear meat.

Greene caught the offering in midair. "What the hell is this?" he demanded.

"Bear."

"I don't like bear meat."

"Then give it back and go hungry. That's all we got."

"No. I'll eat it. Why didn't you shoot one of those muleys we saw today? We could be havin' a feast right now."

"I'm saving you for your real last feast. You'll enjoy it a lot more if you haven't had one before."

"You're havin' a real good time with my fate, aren't you?" Greene asked bitterly.

"Naw. I'm just japin' ya a little. It's called gallows humor. Enjoy it. You know, make the best of the things you have left. Look at the snow on the mountains over there. It's beautiful. This may be your last time to see something like that."

"I never liked snow."

"Well, where you're goin', that won't be a concern," Yellowhenry grinned.

"Ha, ha. Real damned funny. You haven't got me in, yet."

"Thanks for the warning," Yellowhenry said, tossing the canteen to Greene. "Drink up. We have to get settled in for the night. You'll need your rest for the walk tomorrow."

"Walk? I thought I was ridin'," Greene said.

"You walk when you behave. Threatening me with some unspoken plan of escape is not behavin'. So, you walk."

After Greene drank his fill, Yellowhenry asked, "You gotta piss?"

"Why? You wanna watch?" Greene asked.

"I'll take that as a 'no'," Yellowhenry said, rising and walking to where Greene sat. "On your belly."

"Go to hell," Greene spat.

Yellowhenry's boot caught Greene squarely under the chin, knocking him to his back. "You can't win. Get used to it. By God, if I have to drag your stupid ass to death and take you in dead, I'll do it. Do you understand? The state would rather have me do that than take you back alive. It would save them a hell of a lot of money. You're wearing my patience damned thin, Talon. Quit acting like a punk kid. We're still a day or two out. Think about how much more of your bullshit I'll take. Now, belly down, hands out front."

Greene rolled over slowly and pushed his arms out in front of himself. Yellowhenry untied his hands and retied them behind his back. Then he tied his ankles and strapped his hands and ankles together. When he was finished, Yellowhenry tossed his saddle blanket over him. "Sleep tight," he said.

"I could freeze," Greene said grimly.

"Stay under that blanket. You might make it."

The next morning Yellowhenry rolled out in twenty-degree weather. Greene was stretched out partially under the saddle blanket, shivering uncontrollably. "Mornin', Talon," Yellowhenry said. "Time to rise and shine. I need this saddle blanket. You just stay right there, okay? I'll be back as soon as I get the animals saddled up." Twenty minutes later he was back. "Woo, Talon. It's brisk this mornin'. Makes a man want to get movin'. Know what I mean?"

Yellowhenry untied Greene and set him up to walk with his hands tied in front. "My feet are frozen stiff," Greene complained.

"We'll go slow. Give your blood a chance to get to circulatin'. That's the best medicine for the chills. You'll be sweatin' in no time."

Half an hour later, Greene was walking along briskly. Yellowhenry had kept track of Greene's pace and kept Hi Boy to match. "Hey," Greene hollered. "I need to take a piss."

"Okay," Yellowhenry said. "Go ahead." He backed Hi Boy up a couple of steps to put slack in the rope.

"I don't want you lookin'," Greene sniffed.

"Turn your back, then. You have fifteen seconds. Fifteen, fourteen, thirteen, twelve,..."

"All right," Greene said. "I'm doin' it."

It took a minute, or so, and Yellowhenry waited patiently. When Greene turned around, he asked, "All better now?"

Greene heaved a sigh, "Sure, Joe. Let's go."

Chapter Twelve

The second day passed much like the first, except that Greene stopped complaining. The weather remained clear and cool, with a high of thirty-six degrees. By early afternoon, Yellowhenry loaded Greene onto the jenny, and they made much better time. When it came time to pitch camp, Yellowhenry expected the wrangle he'd experienced the night before, but it didn't happen.

Greene slid off the jenny and stood passively while Yellowhenry cared for the animals and set up camp. They were in a wooded area, and the clearing Yellowhenry chose for their camp was surrounded by abundant dead wood for a fire. He kicked away leaves, needles, and duff from a small area to clear space for the cooking fire, then started gathering branches and piling them up nearby. He kept an eye on Greene as he worked. After dumping an armful of branches, he turned to get more when he heard scuffling behind him. Expecting to see a charging Greene, he instead saw Greene kicking away detritus from around the fire pit."We'll need a bigger fire, Joe," Greene said. "I'll help. We can't have another night like last night."

Yellowhenry studied him, searching for any sign of deceit in his voice or manner. There was none."All right, Talon," he said. "You can help, but I'm not gonna untie your hands."

"I didn't expect you to," Greene replied. "I just wanna help, so I don't freeze to death."

With the two of them working together, they gathered enough wood for a fire to last through the night. Yellowhenry broke out his last can of stew, adding some diced bear meat. When it was ready, he served it up evenly between them, adding a lump of the last of his bread—the heel. "Eat up," Yellowhenry said. "This is the last of our grub. If you don't cause me any trouble tomorrow, we'll be at the village by nightfall. We can eat good there."

"I'm through with trouble, Joe," Greene said. "I just want to get this over with."

"I'm glad to hear that, Talon," Yellowhenry replied. "But I'll have to see it to believe it. No offense. Here, have some water."

Greene took the canteen, drank deeply, and handed it back. "So, Joe," he began, "they'll find me guilty of shooting that guy. But what happens after that?"

"Could be a couple of things. You could get the death sentence, but I doubt it. The shooting wasn't premeditated. Life in prison is possible. So is thirty years. You'll definitely get jail time. No way around that."

"What happens if I get the death sentence?"

"They'll send you to death row at the penitentiary at Deer Lodge. You'll wait there until all your appeals are exhausted."

"How long does that take?"

"I'd like to say six weeks, but that won't happen."

"Why do you say that?"

"Because, Talon, when the system delays execution for fifteen years as they do now, the murderer becomes another victim. The people he killed are lost to time. Forgotten. There's no justice in that. And no deterrence either."

"I didn't plan to kill that guy, Joe. I thought he was gonna shoot me. Everyone was shooting at anything that moved."

"Talon, you need to explain that to your defense attorney. That alone will probably keep you off death row."

"If I get prison time, is there a chance of parole?"

"Well, hell yes, there is. The average time spent in prison for murder—just plain, simple, old murder, not premeditated—is seven years. That's if you behave yourself and are a model prisoner. Not like the dipshit you've been with me."

"Hey, that's over, Joe. I'm serious," Greene said. "I apologize. I won't be any more trouble. Not for you. Not for the prison."

"Well, good. If you can keep that attitude, Talon, you'll be out before you're thirty."

When they finished their stew, Yellowhenry swabbed out the pot and the tin plates as best he could with a dish rag. Then he set up their sleeping arrangements. "Talon," he said, "I hope to hell for your sake that everything you said tonight is the God's honest truth. But I can't take chances. I have to tie you up. I hope you understand. I'll keep the fire going tonight so you don't get so damned cold."

"That's more than I deserve, Joe. I understand, and I won't be trouble," Talon said.

Yellowhenry broke out the blankets he'd brought for Talon in the first place. Talon was honestly grateful and didn't ask why they hadn't been given to him the night before. "Damn, Joe," Talon said. "This is nice. Thanks. Thanks a lot."

"You aren't pissed because I didn't give them to you last night?"

"Nope. I got what I deserved."

"All right, then. Hands in front. I'll move some wood over here with you. If you wake up and the fire's down, you can stir it and add wood. I'll have a pistol in one hand and my rifle in the other. If you try to take me, you better do it right. Because if you fail, I'll kill you."

"You have nothin' to worry about, Joe," Talon said. "I ain't gonna do nothin'."

With Talon wrapped in his blankets, the firewood nearby, and the fire banked, Yellowhenry spread his ground cover on the opposite side of the fire and laid out his sleeping bag. He stacked firewood between himself and Talon so that if the latter tried to approach him with a branch, he'd have to go through the barrier first.

Talon watched and said, "You don't need to do that, Joe. I give you my word, I ain't gonna bother you."

"Well, that's all well and good, Talon, but any man willing to break into another man's house, steal his stuff, and shoot his housekeeper would probably find telling a lie pretty easy to do. And any lawman willing to believe that lie is taking a chance with his own life. I'm cutting you some slack, but I'm not givin' you the rope to hang me. Now, good night. We have a long day ahead of us tomorrow."

It was a long night for Yellowhenry. Whenever he found himself nodding off, he jerked awake and looked across the fire at the form of his prisoner. He got up twice to step off, make water, and check on the stock. He stoked the fire both times. Talon slept the sleep of the dead. Not once did he awaken to tend the fire.

Finally, Yellowhenry slept. When he awoke, he sat up instantly and looked toward Talon Greene. He was sitting, hugging his knees, and gazing into the fire. He noticed Yellowhenry sitting up, looking at him. "Good morning, Joe. I know you didn't sleep too well. If you want to grab another hour, I'm good tending the fire."

Yellowhenry looked at the lightening sky and saw a low, slaty gray buildup of cloud cover. "Gonna snow, Talon," he said. "The earlier we get out of here, the better. You tend the fire; I'll break camp."

The first serious snowstorm of the season commenced within the hour. Yellowhenry took stock of landmarks, hoping that the storm would open up at times, allowing him to see the horizon and make course corrections to their line of travel. With snow piling up at an inch an hour over the following six hours and the horizon obliterated, Yellowhenry hoped that they weren't traveling in a wide circle. At first, he was hunkered under a blanket he had thrown over his shoulders. Later, he tented under it. He had given a blanket to Greene as well. Whenever he looked back to check on him, it amused him to think of Greene as something out of a Charlie Russell painting. He was a hunched figure with his hands clutching a snow-clad blanket. His gaze was down to the neck of his snow-covered mule. He looked, for all the world, the epitome of the condemned.

The intensity of the storm lessened in the early afternoon. It was then that Yellowhenry noticed Hi Boy resisting the direction of travel his boss was trying to get him to take.

"All right," he said to the horse, "If you think we should go that way, we'll try it." So, he gave the horse his head and re-tented under his blanket in the same way Greene had. He only looked up from time to time to make sure Hi Boy wasn't leading them off a cliff.

It was nearing dark, and the horse and mules were walking through nine inches of fluffy snow. It had nearly stopped snowing, but the wind on the backside of the passing front had picked up, drifting the snow and piling it up in drifts against anything that stuck up above the surface of the ground. Yellowhenry became worried and was processing how to spend another night out in much worse conditions when he noticed Hi Boy walking more quickly. The horse shook his head and shuddered, spilling snow off his neck and rump.

Presently, they topped a low rise, and Yellowhenry let out with a happy hoop that caused Greene to look up. The lights of the village shone faintly through the driving snowcloud they were traveling through. He grinned when

Yellowhenry hollered, "Hey, Talon. Look at that. Another twenty minutes to hot chocolate."

Chapter Thirteen

Yellowhenry rode directly to police headquarters. He caught Kaden Bull just leaving after spending a shift and a half on duty. "Well, I'll be damned," Bull exclaimed. "Look at what the cat dragged in. Who do you have under that blanket on the mule?"

"It's me. Talon Greene, Sheriff," Greene spoke before Yellowhenry could answer.

"No shit?" Bull said, squinting into the darkness. "Well get down here and let me take a look at ya, Talon."

Yellowhenry slid off Hi Boy and walked back to Jay. He reached up, "Let me give you a hand, Talon," he said. Greene piled off, mostly in Yellowhenry's arms. They staggered into the light spilling from the open door of the police quarters.

"See? It's me," Greene said, apparently happy to be in custody.

"I do see that it's you, Talon," Bull said. "Now. I'm going to do you a favor." He reiterated the same Miranda Rights that Yellowhenry had voiced when he arrested Greene.

"We already went through that, Mr. Bull," Greene said.

"Good. Now we've made double sure. It's very good advice, son. Especially when you leave here. I'll notify the authorities in Billings in the morning. They'll send someone over to pick you up in a day or two. Roads will have to be plowed out first. Now let's get you inside. You look like you're half frozen. You, too, Joe."

"I'm All right, Kaden," Yellowhenry replied. "I've got to take care of this stock. Then I'll be back to file a report."

"All right, then," Bull said. "We'll be here."

Yellowhenry rode back to his own place. He was surprised to see it lit up. He opened the corral gate without dismounting and rode into the corral. On the ground, he unsaddled Hi Boy first. He led the horse in under the shelter. Flakes of hay were already spread out in the feeder and there was water in the horse trough. When he turned around, someone was pulling the panniers off Jay. "Hi, honey," Amy called. "You're back. I was worried about you," She dropped the panniers and walked into her husband's arms.

"My god," Yellowhenry said. "You feel wonderful." He kissed her long and hard. "How did you know I'd be back tonight?" he asked when they broke apart.

"I didn't. I've been staying here for the last two nights. I put hay down and packed water for the stock. Supper's on inside."

"You are unbelievable. Do you know that?" he asked as he turned to pull the pack saddle off the big jake. "As soon as I finish with the stock, I'll be right in."

"I'll help," she said, pulling the curry comb down from its nail. She led Jay into the shelter next to Hi Boy and began to quickly groom the mule as it dropped its head into the trough to begin sucking up water. Yellowhenry pulled the packsaddle free of Bray and set it aside next to his saddle and the panniers. Then he led him into the shelter, as well.

"I'll wipe the jake and Hi Boy down with a blanket. I'll curry comb them in the morning. With all three in under the shelter, they'll be warm and happy tonight," he said.

"Did you find Greene?"

"He's over at the jail. Kaden's with him. I've got to go back and file a report."

"You're going into the house and warm up first Joe," she said.

"I'll have to hurry."

"That's fine, but you need to get into some clean dry clothes and have a bite to eat. And before you sleep with me, you're taking a bath. I'll set up the tub."

"Where are the kids?" he asked, startled. "I'm not getting into the tub with them watching."

She laughed, "I'll do that, honey. The kids are at my place with Mom."

When Yellowhenry had his equipment stashed in the mud room, he walked into the kitchen to find Amy setting out a plate with mashed potatoes, gravy, green beans, and a slab of meatloaf. Slices of bread and a block of butter were on the side with a steaming cup of coffee. "What the hell," he exclaimed. "Did you cheat on me and this is your way of making up?"

"Yep," she said. "I was a whore with a fresh monger every night. Aren't you proud of me?"

"If you feed me like this when I get back, I'll leave more often. Who's your monger tonight?"

"My favorite one," she said sitting next to him. "Can't tell you much about him. He's been gone so long, it'll be like the first time." She leaned over and blew into his ear.

"Stop that," he said. "I'll look like a three-legged stool when I walk into the sheriff's office if you keep that up."

"Okay," she said. "I'll save it. Did you have any trouble with Talon?"

"At first, he was a shit, to put it mildly. Lasted for two days, but last night and today, he was a model prisoner."

"What made him change?"

"Punishment and kindness."

"Punishment. You'll have to tell me all about it when you get back from filing your report."

He had been eating rapidly as they spoke. He swabbed up the last of the gravy on his plate with a slice of bread, stuffed it into his maw, and wiped his mouth with the cloth napkin she had set out for him. "I will," he said. "As soon as I get back. I'll change clothes then." He kissed her then stepped out the back door and headed for the police station.

"You're back sooner than I expected," Bull said when Yellowhenry walked through the door into the tribal police headquarters. "Talon's back in the cell block. I fed him. Wasn't much, but I promised him a good breakfast in the morning. He was thankful and truly grateful. Told him he could shower down and clean up in the morning, too. He said that I needn't go to so much trouble. Can you believe that?"

"I can. Started yesterday when he figured out he wasn't gonna escape. We had a conversation about his sentence and parole, and if he was given jail time instead of the death penalty. I told him parole comes to model prisoners a lot quicker than to shitheads. Seemed to straighten him right out. He's practicin' is my guess."

"Do you think he could get the death penalty?"

"He could, but if he has a decent attorney, I'd bet not. The shooting wasn't premeditated. It was a bunch of stupid people bent on thievery. Then they ran into an unexpected shitstorm. Hell, I'd bet that if the surveillance video is closely looked at, the house sitter was shooting, too."

"Well, that's out of our hands. The report form is there on the deputy's desk. The claim check for his capture is with it. You can fill them out in the morning. I want to close up shop tonight, and you have the best wife on the reservation waiting for you. How the hell did you punch her dance ticket anyway?"

"You'll have to ask her, Kaden," Yellowhenry replied. "That was all her idea. She was the one doing the sweeping off the feet thing. All I know is she said something about free milk, and the next thing I knew, I was buying the cow."

Bull laughed heartily, "That's my girl, by god," he enthused. "Everything kept tied up nice and tight with a pretty red bow. Nothing salacious intended, Joe, but I love your woman. Forty years ago, I would have been giving you a run for your money on that one. But I'm just happy for her, now. And don't you give her a reason to get unhappy? You hear me?"

"I won't, Kaden," he said. "I just keep discovering more and more reasons to be happy with her. Hell, she's one of those women no man deserves."

Chapter Fourteen

A month later, Amy stood inside the add-on to Yellowhenry's house, surveying its progress. After the season's first snowstorm, the weather had moderated for two weeks, allowing a contractor to complete the framing, roofing, flooring, and siding without interference. The interior work had followed—insulation, wiring, and drywall. Yellowhenry sat on an overturned joint compound can, watching his wife pace thoughtfully between rooms. "Penny for your thoughts?" he asked after she crossed the space for the third time.

"I'm wondering if we should wallpaper the nursery after we paint the walls."

"How much money do we have left?"

"It's not about how much we have left. It's about how much we have. I thought we'd still have five hundred after paying the contractor," she admitted. "I was wrong. But don't worry—we do have five hundred."

"Amy, how much did you have to kick in?"

"It was my fault. It's all right," she said dismissively.

"Amy," Yellowhenry pressed, "how much?"

She turned to face him. His expression was steady and unyielding. "Two hundred and ninety dollars," she admitted at last.

"All right. Now we're getting somewhere," he said. "Sweetheart, your five hundred dollars isn't going to cover floor coverings, insulation, furniture, paint, doors, and wallpaper. Do what you really want to be done first, and we'll see where we are. I'll pitch in whatever we need to make it happen," he added, rising to his feet. "I'll do all the labor. I'll seal the drywall joints now. Can't paint until the compound dries. I am at your command."

Amy kissed him quickly. "What do you think of this idea? We move into this bedroom and make the other one the nursery. Susan can use it until the baby comes, and James can take your old room. That way, when the baby wakes up screaming, we'll be right next door."

"Well, that makes sense to me," he said. "Let me get to spacklin'."

Over the next two weeks, Amy directed Yellowhenry until he felt nearly overwhelmed. His love for her, however, outweighed his tendency to retreat. For the first time, his self-perceived craving for isolation took a backseat.

When the project was finally complete, the two lay in bed in their new bedroom.

"Honey," Amy said, "it's beautiful. And now it's done before you take over for Kaden."

"Thank God," he replied, heaving a sigh of relief. "You know, you're the one who has to tell Susan she has to give up her bedroom when the baby comes."

"I've already talked to her. I think she'll be all right."

"Uh, huh. And she'll be good with moving into her brother's bedroom too?"

"Well... maybe not."

"You've got your eye on my mudroom, don't you?" he asked suspiciously.

"Honey, honey, honey," she said sweetly. "Only if I can sweet-talk you into finding another way to store your stuff."

"Like what?" he asked warily.

"Like better. Like a full-on stable with a tack room."

"Are you serious? I'd love that, but even with the new job, we won't have the money for it."

"I'm selling my mother's house. It's not on reservation land, and a white man wants to buy it to build a general store. We can have a stable built before the baby comes, and then we'll just convert the mudroom back into a bedroom."

"You're serious, huh? How come you get to sell your mom's place?"

"It was actually my husband's. I couldn't stand living there after he died, so Mom and I swapped."

"Where will your mother live?"

"She'll move back into her leased house."

"I wish I qualified for a bigger allotment," he said wistfully.

"Are you sure you don't?"

"I've always been told that half-breeds don't. I've never bothered to inquire. I'm just amazed the elders let me become head of the tribal police force."

"Our people believe in inclusion, as long as you're at least half. Your father was full."

"Well, I see that. I've got a 99-year lease on this place," he said.

"That's because this reservation is held in trust by the U.S. government for our tribe. The tribe can lease to tribal members. You still have to pay on the lease, don't you?"

"Well, yeah," he muttered. "I'm not a full tribal member, though. Now I'm wonderin' if my lease is legal. All the more reason a bigger allotment would be nice."

She reached over and ruffled his hair. "I'll do some research. Who knows? We might get rich."

He turned to her, studying her shadowed face. "I already am rich," he said. "You're worth more than money. But if you can find us some cash, go ahead."

They laughed together, holding each other until they drifted off to sleep.

Chapter Fifteen

With their immediate needs settled and Yellowhenry able to work his desk job as tribal police chief, he had gone to Billings and had his knee scoped. While the long-term news was bleak, the immediate benefit was amazing. After the initial discomfort from swelling subsided, he forgot about his knee altogether. It was only after long days when he was on his feet for extended periods that the joint ached. He treated it by taking aspirin. He would have used Minnie's poultice but she had run out of ingredients. "You will have to take me to the mountains, Joe," she beamed. "We'll look for herbs and be friendly."

"Minnie," he laughed. "Maybe we'll find an old buck up there."

"Ha," she giggled, "There are many ways I could use an old buck. He just wouldn't last long."

"That's what I'm hoping for, Minnie. I wouldn't either."

"Aren't you sweet," she said. "Maybe we better take Amy, too."

"Remember what you said about sand in a woman's shoes? That it takes a lot of stayin' at home to raise kids. Well, it might just be you and me after all. Amy is close. A month, maybe."

"No hurry. The herbs have to go dormant. The middle fall is the time. Indian Summer. I'm just teasing you, but think about it. We could take your whole family. It would be a lot of fun."

"I think that's a great idea, Minnie," he said. "I'll talk to Amy. We'll make it a date."

It was late May when Yellowhenry was subpoenaed to testify in the Talon Greene murder trial. The other two survivors of the shootout that killed Simon Gallagher had turned state's evidence to testify against Greene. They had received reduced sentences, seven to ten years, for their testimony.

The state was seeking the death penalty. Yellowhenry was called as a character witness for the defense. His testimony was a positive for Talon. Only upon cross-examination did he testify to the antics he had to deal with before Greene became manageable without severe suppression tactics. He had to admit that Greene had attempted to shoot him at the time of the arrest. The prosecuting attorney asked Yellowhenry if he believed in capital punishment. He was surprised when the answer was, 'No.'

"This man is accused of first-degree murder, and he shot at you, yet you do not believe he deserves the death penalty?"

"The way the death penalty is managed in this country, it's pointless. Appeals run for fifteen to twenty years. The victim is forgotten, and the perpetrator becomes the victim who is remembered. If you're going to jail someone for twenty years and then kill him, you might as well jail him for life. Neither justice nor deterrence is served when executions are carried out twenty years later."

His statement saved Talon's life. The jury came back and asked if they could consider a different sentence. The judge advised that they could. The jury found him guilty of second-degree murder. He was sentenced to fifteen years to life with the possibility of parole after ten years.

Yellowhenry hung around for an extra day. He wanted to talk to Talon. A visitation was granted and the two faced each other on opposite sides of a plexiglass divider. They spoke to each other through telephone receivers. "Well, how do you feel, Talon?" Yellowhenry asked.

"A lot better now that I know. My attorney said your testimony saved me. I want to thank you for that."

"I don't know about that," Yellowhenry said. "I hope you do the right thing now, though. The way things are with prison overcrowding   and minority rights, I'd be surprised if you don't qualify for parole in seven years, maybe less."

"You think so?"

"Yes. Doesn't make prison a cakewalk. You'll have to ally yourself with a group that gives you protection. The most dangerous thing about prison is the prisoners that surround you. Hate to say that, but it's the simple truth."

"How do you know who to trust?"

"See if you can befriend the prison librarian. You might get some decent advice from him. If that doesn't work, think about how your gang figured things out. The rules are about the same. Some you can trust and some you can't."

"I'll do that, Joe. Thanks for the advice. Is there any way you can go back into the Moose's Ass? I left my mother's .243 up there, leanin' against a rock. I'd kinda like to make sure she gets it back."

"I'm afraid not. I'm the sheriff now, so most of my time's spent in the office. We don't patrol that far back, either. Spring runoff probably swept your whole camp into the willows. That rifle—unless some moose hunter stumbled on it—is gone for good."

"Damn. I wish I'd thought about it while we were up there."

"Well, there's some good news, Talon."

"What's that?"

"You're finally thinkin' about someone besides yourself."

Amy went into labor in early July. After two births, she was hoping for an easier time of it, but when she still hadn't delivered after twelve hours, she looked at Yellowhenry and asked somewhat bitterly, "What did you do to me? Plant an elephant?"

"I'm sorry, Ames," he said. "If I could do anything different, I would."

"Ohhhh, damn!" she squealed, "Hold my hand, here comes another one."

"Attagirl," the attending nurse exclaimed, "now we're gettin' somewhere." She turned to a second attendant, "Go get Dr. Laurence."

Dr. Sandra Laurence came into the delivery room of the tribal clinic a couple of minutes later just as Amy was pushing through another contraction. The doctor was there just in time to catch a large baby boy that accented the final push. Yellowhenry stayed while his baby was cleaned up. The nurse handed the baby to Amy who smiled wondrously as she gazed at her son.

"Sand in his Shoes, Jr.," she said, "looks like he could go hiking with his papa right now."

Yellowhenry looked at his wife and son with tears flowing unabashedly, "In time, Ames," he choked, "In time. The baby and Joe were sent their temporary separate ways, while Amy stayed to pass the   placenta and get cleaned and stitched up. Then she was taken to her hospital room where she slept for fifteen hours.

Yellowhenry was standing at the window of the hospital nursery comparing his son to three other babies. He felt pretty good. The ticket in the bassinet identified the mother and father and gave the baby's sex, weight, and length. A voice behind and over his shoulder rumbled, "Pretty good job, Joe. A boy, twenty-three inches long, and eleven pounds nine ounces."

Yellowhenry turned, "Hey, Kaden. I didn't see you come up. Too busy lookin' at my boy," he said. "I guess he's pretty big, huh?"

"Oh, yeah," Kaden laughed. "You just made the playground a whole lot bigger, though."

Joe looked quizzically at his old boss, "I did?"

"Hey, forget it. It's an old joke. How is Amy doin'?"

"Asleep the last time I looked. They said she should be wakin' up pretty soon, though. They want the baby to feed."

"Well," Kaden said, "A nurse just picked up the baby, so we better wait for a while."

"I don't think Amy will mind," Yellowhenry said.

"Then you go, Joe. You should be there for your son's first feeding. I'll be in the waiting room. Come get me when you're done."

"Oh, yeah, I see what you mean," Yellowhenry said sheepishly. "Amy might feel uncomfortable nursing with both of us watchin'."

"Definitely. Come get me when the baby goes back to the nursery."

Yellowhenry was stopped at the door by one of the nurses. "Give us just a few minutes," she said. "The baby needs a little coaching."

Five minutes later, Yellowhenry was pacing nervously when the nurse stepped out of the room with a smile. "Okay, Mr. Yellowhenry, you can come in."

Amy looked up and smiled when her husband walked hesitantly into the room to see their baby held in the cradle of her left arm. She raised her right hand to him and pulled him down to sit on the edge of the bed. "Joe," she said dreamily, "He's so beautiful."

He kissed her as tears sprang to his eyes. "Damn it," he said. "I can't quit cryin', for God's sake."

She laughed, "Good. A little pain in this deal for you makes me feel better."

"It isn't pain. I don't know what it is," he said. "I just wish I could stop."

"I hope you can't," she laughed again. "It's time to name your son, honey. I want you to do it."

"You're sure?"

"Yes."

"Okay, then. I'm going to name him Kaden Joseph Yellowhenry."

Amy gasped and a flood of sudden tears streamed from her eyes. "That's perfect," she

said as she cried.

Chapter Sixteen

In the final two months of her pregnancy, Amy had supervised the construction of the new stable, and the addition of oil heat to the house. She had stopped working for the tribal police, so she was responsible for the stable becoming more of a barn with four stables than a one-horse stable. Nevertheless, the added storage space, made Yellowhenry happy to give up his mudroom. He connected the corral to the stable so that by leaving the door at the corral end open, Hi Boy had access to the new stable. He padlocked the opposite door of the breezeway. He was still guarding against horse thieves.

When Amy and Kaden came home from the hospital, Yellowhenry found the home scene markedly changed. The baby was the center of attention; both when he was sleeping and everyone had to be quiet, and when he was screaming his head off and he wouldn't be quiet. It set his father's teeth on edge. As a result, he found more and more ways to be involved in police work. When it got to the point that he left at six in the morning and didn't come home until dinner or even later, including weekends, Amy called him on it. As he was getting ready to leave for work, she said. "I need a paternity test."

"A paternity test? What do you mean?" he asked.

"I want to be able to prove you are Kaden's father?"

"You said I was the only one, so you ought to know," he said. "So, why do you need a test?"

"So when Kaden gets old enough to ask if he has a father, I can prove who he was."

"I guess I'm not doing too well, am I?"

"In my experience, you are an abject failure. Your behavior as a father creates the kind of individual you chase around and put in jail all the time."

"I just haven't had any experience raising kids. You're doing such a great job; I just sort of went to the sidelines."

"Okay, good enough," she said. "I'll pack your things and your uniforms and set them out on the porch for you so when you come home tonight; you won't have to run into the game from the sidelines."

"Ames," he said in a panic. "Let's discuss this. I don't want to leave the house."

"To me, that isn't it at all," she said. "You went to the sidelines on being a father, and I'm going to the sidelines on being a wife. It seems like an even trade to me."

He sank into a chair at the kitchen table. His negligence hit him like a brick in the face. For several minutes, he sat staring at his shoes. She busied herself preparing the household to begin its day. Finally, she turned to her husband, "You better get going. Your sidelines await."

Just then, Kaden started crying from the nursery. Amy started to get him, but Yellowhenry caught her arm. "I've got it," he said. He changed the baby's diaper. Even used baby powder. When Kaden kept fussing, he put him on his shoulder and walked him around the nursery and then into the kitchen. Amy grinned, "Can't nurse him?"

Yellowhenry blushed, "Ames," he said, "That one's above my pay grade."

"Honey," she said, sitting down and exposing her right breast, "give him to me. There's nothin' to it."

He sat down nervously glancing away. James came from his room and leaned against his mother. "Morning, baby," she said, pulling him close with her left arm and kissing him on the cheek.

"Morning, Kaden," James said. "Mom, I'm hungry."

"What do you want today, sweetie, cereal or a real breakfast?"

"Cereal."

"I'll get it," Yellowhenry said, rising from the table. "What flavor, James?"

"I dunno," the little boy said.

"Okay, come on over and pick your pony," Yellowhenry said, pulling three different cereal boxes down from an overhead cabinet and lining them up on the counter. "This is the Black Stallion," he continued, pointing to bran flakes with blueberries. "And this is the Stud Muffin," he said flicking the frosted mini-wheats box. "And this is Black Beauty, the queen of sugared cornflakes."

"I can't choose, Dad," he said. "You choose."

"All right then," Yellowhenry said, "Let's have a race." He began shoving the cereal boxes back and forth on the counter. "And they're off! It's the Black Stallion in the lead by a head over Black Beauty with Stud Muffin a half a length behind, but now with a hundred yards to go the Black

Stallion and Black Beauty are neck and neck, you can't put a sheet of newspaper between them, but here comes the Stud Muffin. Oh, My God, the humanity! Stud Muffin wins by an eyelash."

James giggled, "Dad, I want Black Beauty."

"Black Beauty? But, she didn't win, James. What are people gonna say about this house, when a loser can come back and be a winner?" he cried.

"I don't know," James said.

"I don't either. I guess we're just cockamamie around here, huh?" Yellowhenry said as he poured cereal into a bowl for his stepson.

"Yep."

"What's that mean?" a tousled-headed Susan said as she came from her bedroom.

Yellowhenry set James on a high stool at the counter, set out a spoon, and poured milk from the refrigerator over his cereal. Then he picked up Susan, "Ask James. He knows."

"What's cocks and Amy's mean?"

"Losers are winners," James answered.

"Oh," she said.

"Would you like cereal this morning?"

"Yeah, I guess so."

"Let me guess," Yellowhenry said, "You don't know which one?"

"I don't know."

"Okay," he said, "let's play a game. Which one don't you want?"

"That one," she said, pointing to the bran flakes.

Yellowhenry set her down on the floor. "Close your eyes," he said as he put the other cereal boxes behind his back. "Okay, open your eyes. I have the boxes behind me. One in each hand. Pick one of the hands."

She started to lean around to get a look. "No, no. You can't peek. Pick a hand."

"That one," she said pointing to his left.

He made a great show by presenting mini-wheats. "And the winner is, for the second time in two races, Stud Muffin. 'Oh, you can't keep a good horse down'," he sang.

"Dad. Dad," Susan said.

"What? Do you have something you'd like to say, little girl?" he asked.

"I want Black Beauty," she giggled.

"Well, folks, there you have it," he exclaimed. "This is the house of cockamamie."

He set her on her special stool, the one with the booster cushion, and poured her cereal and milk.

He looked at Amy and wiped his brow. "I love you," she mouthed. "There's orange juice in the refrigerator for the kids, honey," she said. He poured a glassful for each one. Then he sat down next to his wife.

His son was looking solemnly at his father with his mother's left nipple in his mouth. He wasn't sucking, so Yellowhenry reached over and pushed Amy's breast, popping the nipple from the baby's mouth. The baby immediately sucked it back into his mouth. He nursed for a moment, then stopped. Yellowhenry popped the nipple free again. Kaden grinned and grabbed the nipple again.

They played for a little while, until Yellowhenry said, "I better get going. Do I have a bed here tonight?"

"Kiss me, Joe," Amy said. When they parted, she said through tears. "You do."

Chapter Seventeen

Even though it was a labor, Yellowhenry gradually learned how to be a father to all his kids. With Amy's patience, now that she had his attention, he learned that being consistent and steady both in reward and punishment made fatherhood a little easier. Amy was very proud of his efforts. The complete turnaround was such a relief that she became more affectionate. On the camping date with Minnie during a beautiful Indian Summer, she snuggled in especially close one night and asked, "Guess what?"

He laughed. "Every time you ask me that, we're pregnant."

"Are you okay with it?" she asked.

"Well, of course," he said, nudging her. "Let's think about it later."

"You have to be quiet, honey," she said, yielding herself to him.

With oil heat and a snug stable, the family weathered a mild winter. Except for collaring a few drunks, dealing with traffic accidents and issuing traffic citations, and jailing an occasional abusive husband, Sheriff Yellowhenry and Deputy Enos Clay found a comfortable routine at the sheriff's office. Enos took over the morning duty, arriving at seven to start a big pot of coffee on an electric range. Yellowhenry had become so spoiled with oil heat that he convinced the tribal elders on the council to drop wood heat for oil in the police headquarters. Enos found being at work so appealing that he nearly fell into the same trap

Yellowhenry had. Enos' wife, Shirley, was a plump and happy woman most of the time. But when she was pissed off, she wasn't subtle.

Enos discovered his error when his wife, pregnant with their third child, showed up at the office with a diaper bag, their two-year-old son, and eight-month-old daughter. She sat down on the love seat that was a part of the furniture, popped a naked breast from her blouse, and began nursing her daughter. Enos was in the cell block, sweeping out a jail cell. Yellowhenry was in his office when he heard the noise of people in the outer office. He walked through the door of his office and stopped. "Hey, Shirley," he said, "can I help you with something?" The sight of her breastfeeding, he took in stride. He had watched Amy and Kaden so often that it had become natural. In fact, he realized that the native women considered it a duty to motherhood and an entirely normal behavior. Nursing mothers in public places was commonplace.

"No," Shirley said. "I just decided to make this place home. My husband is always here; I want him to know his children. To do that, we have to come here."

Enos heard the conversation and came out of the cell block to stand in shock and embarrassment. "Shirley, what the hell are you doing here?" he demanded.

"Oh, hi," she said. "Don't I know you from someplace? You look so familiar, like one of my old boyfriends. Oh, I know. You are the one I find in my bed every once in a while, aren't you? Ha! I've got it. You're my husband, soon-to-be wannabe husband."

"Sheriff, I'm sorry about this," Enos said, hustling to sit beside his wife, where he began whispering fiercely.

"Enos," Yellowhenry said, "Come into my office."

Enos rose and bent his face down into his wife's, "See what you've done, now?" he growled.

"Have a seat," Yellowhenry said as he sat behind his desk and rummaged around in a drawer. "Ah, here we go." He pulled out a pair of cellophane-wrapped cigars, tossed one to Clay, and unwrapped his own. Then he pulled a couple of kitchen matches from the center drawer.

"Sheriff, I don't smoke no more," Clay said.

"I don't either. Never have, except on very special occasions like this one. You'll need to wet that down. It's pretty dry," Yellowhenry said as he wallered his own cigar around in his mouth. "I don't have to give you an order here, do I?"

"No, I just don't understand what this is all about," Clay said as he began wetting down his smoke.

"I'll explain in a minute," Yellowhenry said as he struck a match on his pant leg and touched the flame to his cigar. He reached across the desk and held the match for Clay until his cigar was drawing smoothly. Then he shook the match out and tossed it into his waste basket.

Clay puffed a couple of times, "Damn, Joe," he said. "This is a fine smoke. Almost enough to make me take up the habit again."

Yellowhenry grinned, "That's an expensive cigar. It really deserved to spend its days in a humidor," he said.

They smoked for a few minutes before Clay's nervousness overcame him, and he asked, "I'm not getting fired, am I, Joe?"

"Oh, no. You aren't failing in your work, Enos. You are failing in your marriage. In your job as a father. I know because I was doing the same thing. Amy taught me the same lesson Shirley laid out before you. Start being a husband and a father, or take a hike."

"Really?" Clay asked.

"Think about how your waking time is balanced between your work and your time interacting with Shirley and the kids."

"Waking time. You mean sleeping, working, and family time?"

"That's right, Enos. Subtract sleeping time, say six hours; of the remaining eighteen hours, how much time is work? The balance is your family time."

Clay sat smoking his cigar thoughtfully. "Well, I've been putting in twelve-hour days. Sometimes more than that, depending on what's happening here. So, I'd guess, around six hours."

"Okay. From that six, take off the time your kids sleep beyond your six hours."

"Well, two or three hours, I'd guess."

"Okay," Yellowhenry continued, "You're down three or four hours. Do you devote any of that to holding your baby or playing with your kids?"

"Well, no. I guess not."

"Same thing I was doing. How much time does Shirley get for herself away from the kids?"

"I've never thought about it. She doesn't. But isn't that her duty? Her responsibility?"

"It is, and she is doing a great job. She is also a good wife for you while taking care of that responsibility. She is telling you that if you aren't going to be a husband and father, she would be just as well off without you in her life."

"Well, she sure likes my paycheck," Clay said.

"She'll still get a big chunk of it. You know how the council is about men who leave their wives and children. She'll get most of your paycheck and most of your allotment. All of your children's allotments when they qualify. You can't hide behind a paycheck, Enos. Take the rest of today off. Take your family home and start working as a husband and father."

"This sounds like I should go home and kiss her ass," Clay said resentfully.

"You should, Enos. Shirley is a marvelous woman. She and Amy have become close friends. I know how she is. Thank your lucky stars you have such a partner. If you don't, this smoke will commemorate the beginning of your life as a family deserter. So smoke to the finish of your married life or to a new beginning of it. I hope it's the latter because that's the one I chose, and it's been wonderful. Wonderful in ways I didn't imagine, Enos."

When Clay returned to his desk in the outer office, his family was gone. He walked out to the reception desk and asked the woman who had taken Amy's place, Barbara

Premminger if Shirley had left a message. "She said to tell you she was going to Amy Yellowhenry's for a while before she went home."

"Thank you," he said and walked out. When Shirley came home that afternoon, he was playing with a Labrador puppy. Pulling it around with an old sock clamped in its mouth.

"What's that, dinner?" Shirley grinned at him.

"Ho, ho," he said. "No. This is my apology. I want to be a good husband and father. This little guy is Chaco. He is a chocolate Lab. The kids and I will care for him and train him to be housebroken."

"I didn't even expect you to be here. Did you get fired?" Shirley asked.

"No. Joe told me to go home and take care of my family. If you'll have me, that's what I will do."

Shirley carried their baby to her bassinet in their bedroom and laid her down. The child was asleep. Then she walked back and sat beside her husband, who had their son on his lap as he continued playing with the growling puppy. She leaned against her husband and whispered, "Welcome home."

Chapter Eighteen

In the late spring, two significant events occurred. Enos told Yellowhenry he wanted to sell his mules. "I'm not getting enough use money to pay for their keep, Sheriff."

"Let me see if the council will buy them," Yellowhenry said. The fact that a lost boy had gone fishing in the backcountry and required the use of the pack string to rescue him helped the argument. The council agreed to purchase the mules. Yellowhenry agreed to stabilize them and take care of them. He submitted feed bills, boarding, and vet bills to the council but provided his farrier care free of charge. As a result, Bray and Jay became bosom pals of Hi Boy.

Then they disappeared. Yellowhenry had gone to do the morning chores—cleaning up overnight waste in the stables, carrying water, and putting down feed—when he found the padlock shank to the outer door cut in two. The animals were gone. He tracked them down to the bottom road where Horace Greene had parked when he tried to steal Hi Boy.

Since that attempt, and because of his hunch that Liam Greene, Horace's younger brother, had vowed some retribution for his brother's death, Yellowhenry had freeze-branded Hi Boy with his own brand, the Lazy Y Bar. The brand was applied to the right front shoulder. He had also branded the mules with the tribe's brand, the Circle C, on the left hip.

When he had confirmed that the pack string had been stolen, he put out a stolen stock alert. Two days later, an anonymous tip came in that two mules and a horse had shown up at a ranch a hundred miles to the south of the reservation. The rancher, Wes Edom, had bought them from an Indian with bills of sale on Cree Reservation stationery. When Yellowhenry contacted the rancher, the man declared the sale bona fide. "I have bills of sale on tribal paper," Edom declared. "That's good enough for me."

"Who was the man who sold the animals?"

"Let me look. The signature is Yellowhammer, something like that."

"Could it be Yellowhenry?"

"Yeah, it could be that. It's sloppy. Kinda hard to read."

"What did the guy look like?"

"Like an Indian. Hell, they all look alike to me."

"Okay," Yellowhenry said patiently. "I am Yellowhenry. Tribal police sheriff. I did not sell those animals. The horse is mine. The mules are the property of the tribe. All three are branded. They were stolen. A stolen stock alert was issued, and all law enforcement was notified. I need a description of the seller because he was the thief. If I can find him, I might be able to get your money back. If he is a member of the tribe, I can guarantee it. I can also guarantee that you do not have the right to retain stolen stock. You know that, being a rancher."

"Well, Mr. Indian Sheriff, our further conversation will be through my attorney."

Yellowhenry turned the matter over to the tribal attorneys, who outsourced the case to a legal firm in Lewistown. By the time the attorneys finished their haggling, Edom had agreed he had bought stolen stock and given a rough description of Liam Greene. Yellowhenry and Enos Clay had arrested Greene and brought him in for questioning. He denied everything, but Yellowhenry had sent his mugshot to the attorneys, who had put Greene in the picture lineup for Edom. He had identified Greene immediately. Greene, however, was out on his own recognizance and had disappeared.

Edom agreed to return the stock but declared the animals had been turned loose on a remote corner of his ranch. The road to it had, supposedly, been washed out, so the only way to reach the horses and mules was by horseback, a four-day endeavor. He declared he would bring them out during his fall roundup, or an Indian contingent would be given a five-day pass to retrieve the animals. At the end of five days, the Indians would be declared trespassers.

After some discussion that included dissension, the council had agreed to fund a retrieval expedition. A pair of horses had been hired for Yellowhenry and Clay. They had rented a horse trailer and pickup and set out for the Flying Eagle ranch near Christina, Montana. While they traveled, they discussed what they were likely to get into. "Those animals are not where Edom said," Yellowhenry declared. "He has them stashed in a pasture out of sight, but not where he said they are."

"How are we gonna find 'em?" Clay asked.

"You noticed that portable bull horn, didn't you? I'll show you when we start on horseback."

The pair of Indians pulled into the Flying Eagle ranch headquarters near sundown. The place was a collection of ranch houses, bunk houses, barns, stables, and corrals leading to barbed wire fenced pastures. Yellowhenry knocked on the ranch house door and waited while voices hollered inside the house. It was a woman who answered the door. "Yes?" she asked.

"I'm Sheriff Yellowhenry, and this is Deputy Clay. We're here to retrieve stock stolen from the Cree Indian Reservation."

"Oh, that," she said. "Hold on. Wes," she hollered, "Those Indians are here."

"Tell 'em they get five days startin' tomorrow," he yelled. "And they don't stay on this ranch tonight."

"You can start tomorrow," the woman said.

"I heard," Yellowhenry said. "We'll be back at daylight tomorrow."

"Where are we spending the night?" Clay asked as they drove out of the ranch yard.

"Well, thanks to your wife and mine, we have a survival basket in the backseat. We have a couple of bales of hay, so we need to find water for the horses. Let's go back to that bridge we crossed a mile or so back. Maybe there's water in that stream."

Clay was driving, so he swung their rig around, and they drove to the bridge. The road leading to the bridge was wide enough that they could pull off the road. They drove down to a side road and turned around. They pulled off the road near the bridge and unloaded the horses. The men led them down to the stream, where the horses drank their fills. Then, they were tied up to the trailer and fed hay. The men plundered their food basket, being careful to leave enough to last for five days in case they needed it.

"That rancher isn't going to feed us. We'll be lucky to fill our canteens," Yellowhenry said.

They slept in the truck, with Yellowhenry taking the front. The next morning, just after sunrise, they pulled into the ranch headquarters. They pulled off to the side of the yard and were met by a ranch hand.

"Is this a good place to park?" Yellowhenry asked.

"Yeah, that'll do," the hand said. "I'm Zane Hammond. I'll be riding along with you, fellers."

"Fine," Yellowhenry said. "Will we be permitted access to water for ourselves and horses?"

"Oh, yeah. There's water as we go. First, you can fill canteens at the pump over there by the stable."

Fifteen minutes later, the trio were saddled up and riding through scattered juniper and sagebrush leading up toward a long ridge that ranged for miles from the northwest to the southeast. Both Yellowhenry and Clay had saddlebags strapped behind their saddles. The country was sectioned off by fences that were accessed through gates. After the first gate, Yellowhenry rode off by himself to a rise where he pulled the bull horn that dangled by a strap looped over his saddle horn.

"What the hell is he doin'?" Hammond asked Clay.

"Sounds like he's whistlin' into that bullhorn. Loud, ain't it?"

"Carries like a damned coyote howlin'. You Indian boys got some strange behaviors workin' if you don't mind my sayin'. No offense intended."

"Oh, none taken," Clay assured him.

"What's he up to now?"

"He's lookin' around with binoculars," Clay answered as he pulled his field glasses from his left saddlebag. "See up there toward the top of that low ridge? There's a band of what looks like horses walking along through the junipers. From the looks of 'em, they're likely wild. Do you have wild horses in this country?"

"Yeah, there's a few. We try to keep 'em thinned out. Why'd you ask that?"

"One of those mules we're after is a jenny. The horse and the jake are gelded and show no interest in her, but a stallion will. If he steals her, though, he'll chase the other two off. They will follow at a distance that doesn't threaten the stallion. So we'll want to check as we go."

"That horse and those mules are ten miles as the crow flies and four fences from here. It's a day and a half up there. You boys did come intendin' to stay overnight, didn't ya?"

"We're good for two nights. How about you?"

"Two nights? I was told to pack for one. Why would we be out more than that?"

"Because we're gonna check to see that the stock we're lookin' for hasn't come down off that big ridge into this lower country."

"I told you there are fences. Those critters can't cross four fences," Hammond argued.

"You mean fences like these?" Clay asked.

"Well, yeah."

"With my field glasses, I can see two places where the fence we just went through is down. Wild horses will know exactly where to cross your fences, so there is every reason to prospect the country as we go."

"Well, hell. Suit yourselves, I guess. But I ain't stayin' more than one night."

"We wouldn't expect you to. We'll be all right if you want to go back early," Clay said.

"Just make damned sure you don't try to overstay your five-day permit."

"We wouldn't dream of it."

The three zigzagged their way for the rest of the day without finding Hi Boy and the mules. Yellowhenry caused a lot of coyotes to howl, but that was the extent of his efforts to whistle his horse out of the gullies and low ridges they had ridden by. With the sun taking a low slant and shadows lengthening, Hammond led the way to a hidden stream that rose from a low rocky head, flowed for a quarter mile, and then sank underground. It created a green grassy strip in which willows and thornbushs grew. Three mule deer bounded away as the riders rode off the dry hillside down to the stream. Quail flew up and away only to settle back down fifty yards from where they started. Cottontail rabbits hopped quickly into the thick cover of willow and thorn.

Hammond rode to where the stream pooled before it sank into the ground. "This is where we'll camp tonight," he announced. "Mr. Edom is right fond of this little place. Keeps the stock out of it. You can drink the water right there before it goes underground. It runs over a rock bed for about a quarter of a mile. Purifies the water. It's the damnedest thing. I've drunk that water a hundred times and never had a problem. I do recommend you strain it through a cloth when you drink from your canteens, though."

"Thanks," Yellowhenry said. "Maybe we oughta drink and fill our canteens before we water our horses. I'll hold your horse for you, Zane, while you drink."

"Appreciate it," the cowboy said, swinging down and pulling the bridle reins over his horse's head. He handed them to Yellowhenry, walked to the edge of the pool, unsnapped the cuff of his shirt sleeve, and pulled the sleeve over his fist. Then he bellied down and sucked up his fill of water, using his shirt sleeve as an impromptu filter. "Damn, that's good," he smiled happily. "Best water in the place. I never get over just how good that water tastes. I'll hold you fellers horses while you fill up."

"Well," Yellowhenry said to Clay, "in for a penny, in for a pound."

When the two Indians had finished slaking their thirst, they filled their canteens. They had to agree that the water from the seep was everything Hammond said it was. Then the three men watered their horses. When they had a spot picked out to spend the night, it was getting dusky but full dark was a half hour away. "Zane, are the rabbits and quail here harvestable?" Yellowhenry asked.

"Well, yeah, but shootin' 'em just blows 'em apart. It's a waste of time and effort."

"So, if I knock off two or three, we could spit 'em on a fire, then?"

"Well, yeah. Sure enough. How're you gonna do that?"

"If you and Enos can gather up some of the dead willow around here, I'll see what I can do. I'll be back in fifteen minutes. Enos, my camp hatchet is in my right saddlebag."

Yellowhenry rose and melted away along the willow and thorn line so swiftly and silently that it made the hair on Hammond's neck stand up. The first throw knocked a flying quail from the air. It bounced and fluttered wildly before Yellowhenry rapped it in the head with a piece of willow branch he'd picked up. He also retrieved his throwing stone. With the bird dangling from his belt, he moved slowly and with quiet stealth until he saw a rabbit sitting quietly, hoping not to be noticed. Its head was all that Yellowhenry saw in a small opening twenty feet away. It was an easy target in the thornbush, so he exchanged his favorite stone for a pickup he'd found and didn't mind losing. The stone was a ninety-mile-an-hour blur that killed the rabbit instantly.

Yellowhenry couldn't find the stone that he'd used to bag the rabbit, but he would look to replace it as they rode the next day. With a bird and a rabbit in hand, he turned and walked back to the campsite. He tossed the rabbit to Clay, who quickly had it dressed and skinned. Yellowhenry breasted out the bird. "Damn," Hammond said in admiration, "you fellers don't mess around, do ya? I'll get the fire goin'. Just how in hell did you do that, Joe?"

"I rock 'em," Yellowhenry said.

"With rocks. I'll be damned if that ain't the neatest trick I ever heard of. You must have a hell of an arm on you."

Clay was busily attaching the rabbit to a green willow branch with lengths of wire from Yellowhenry's saddlebag. "He does, for sure," he said. "You don't want him against you in a rock fight."

With their horses hobbled and grazing on the green grass of the seep and the men sitting in a comfortable circle around a small fire, sharing the lightly salted meat of Yellowhenry's bounty, Hammond commented. "If you fellers eat like this, all the time, a man would be proud to become a tribal policeman." Neither Yellowhenry nor Clay commented, so he framed it in the form of a question. "Any chance a that happenin'?"

Clay looked at Yellowhenry and grinned slightly, obviously indicating that the ball was in his court. "Well, there are qualifications," Yellowhenry said carefully as he cracked a rabbit leg bone and sucked out the marrow.

"Like what?" Hammond persisted.

"You'd have to have a fair amount of Cree Indian blood for the tribal council to even consider you to start with. Some experience in law enforcement always helps, and a clean legal record is essential."

"Would a quarter blood be enough?"

"These days, my guess is it would. Something positive in a resume would help."

"What does that mean?" Hammond asked hopefully.

"That the applicant had done things to help the tribe or its members in some positive way."

"A guy just doesn't have an opportunity like that when he lives so far from the reservation," Hammond said wistfully. Clay glanced at Yellowhenry with a broad grin stealing across his face before he looked away, hiding his face and keeping from laughing out loud.

"Yeah, it is a really rare opportunity," Yellowhenry agreed, forcing a sad face. "Tribal members have a tendency to stick pretty close to home. Getting out like this, for example," he added, waving his hand to encompass the ranch, "doesn't happen very often."

Hammond stiffened but said nothing more. The men spent another hour staring at the fire and indulging in idle chitchat before turning in for the night. The men slept in their clothes on the dry ground. They used Yellowhenry's hatchet to gouge out hip holes, and they covered them up as best they could with their saddle blankets. The following morning, having broken camp early, the three rode up into the rising sun at the top of the ridge. Yellowhenry turned to head up into the long ridge they had been directed to the day before. "Hold on there, Joe," Hammond called. He wore a smirk on his face. "Let's go this way."

"Let's go that way," Enos said, raising his arm like a cavalry officer and mugging Yellowhenry. "Follow me."

Yellowhenry looked at the two, "Is this why we suffer fools?" he muttered to himself.

Hammond's lead took an hour to sidehill to the bottom of a steep drainage with a dry stream. He turned toward the headwaters and said, "This way."

Enos, grinning broadly, turned to Yellowhenry, who scowled and shook his head. A half-hour later, the watercourse disappeared into the mouth of a box canyon. A hundred yards further on beyond the mouth, the canyon opened up into an area roughly a quarter mile long by half that wide. It was closed off by a gated fence. A seep at the far end provided water for a band of seven horses that appeared to be grazing on the grass growing around the seep. Yellowhenry waited until Hammond opened the gate, and then he whistled. One of the horses jerked its head up and looked at the source. Another whistle spurred the horse into a trot toward the gate. "I'll be damned," Hammond said. "So, that was the horse you was whistlin' at yesterday. Who'd a thunk it."

"Do you think there is a chance that those two mules up there are branded with a Circle C on the left hip," Yellowhenry asked.

"I don't know, but it would definitely be worth a look," Hammond grinned.

"I'll go get 'em. I mean, look at 'em," Clay laughed as he loped toward the animals in the spring.

Yellowhenry identified Hi Boy to Hammond with the brand on his right front shoulder. "Well, that has to be the horse in question," Hammond shrugged. "You'll have no problem from me if you can get him off the ranch."

"That's an 'if' you need to explain," Yellowhenry said as he fitted a hackamore over Hi Boy's head.

"You were never to find your horse. Even with your bullhorn, you never would have found him. Edom isn't stupid, though. As soon as you guys came up dry and left the country, those brands were to be altered, and after they healed, your string would be incorporated into the ranch's stock."

"But if we found the stock?"

"You were to have an unfortunate accident."

"I see. Are you going to be involved in our disappearance?"

"Not now. We need to figure out how to get you and your stock off Edom property," Hammond said.

"Then what?"

"I don't know. It's something we'll have to figure out, " Hammond said.

"Well, here comes Enos with the mules. He needs to hear this," Yellowhenry said.

"How do we want to trail 'em?" Clay asked.

"Nose to tail unless Zane thinks we should do something else," Yellowhenry replied. "Something else has come up. We need to do some brainstorming. Let's picket the stock to the fence so we can sit down and talk."

After explaining the situation to Clay, he asked, "So, what changed your mind, Zane?"

"Last night. Got me to thinkin' about my grandmother. She was Cree. I didn't know her all that well, but everything she did was honorable. My granddad was the happiest man I knew. It was because of her. He didn't last six months after she passed. And then you guys. Decent, good men. I just can't go along with Edom's scheme. I won't," Hammond answered. "I'm leavin' this ranch when you guys do."

"Then let's figure out how to do this," Yellowhenry said.

With their plan underway, Hammond rode back to the ranch headquarters, timing his arrival to occur after dark. He carried the keys to the Indians' rental truck. He took care of his horse, carried his saddle and bridle to the rental truck, placed them in the trailer, and walked to the ranch house where he reported. "What are you doin' back here?" Edom demanded. "You were told to stay with those Indians."

"Ran out of grub, Wes. It took a day and a half to get 'em lined out on the trail up to the high pasture. But, by tomorrow night, they'll be up there. Yellowhenry is carryin' a bullhorn he whistles into. That horse will come to that whistle. Hell, he rode to every ridge and break in the country whistlin' into that damned thing. That's why getting 'em lined out to the upper pasture took so long. I'll tell you one thing. We've got more damned coyotes than you shake a stick at."

Edom laughed, "Damned coyotes. Can't live with 'em, can't live without 'em. So, they'll have burned up three days of their permit by tomorrow night. They'll be lucky not to get shot as trespassers before they get back here. I take it they didn't find the box canyon."

"No, they didn't find it," Hammond said.

"All right, go on to the bunkhouse. You'll stay here tomorrow, and I'll take the other boys with me. We're goin' skunk huntin'. Hell, we might shoot a few coyotes, too," he laughed.

Hammond slaked his thirst at the ranch yard pump. Then, he quietly entered the bunkhouse and went to bed. Yellowhenry and Clay stayed the night at the Box Canyon.

Chapter Nineteen

Yellowhenry and Clay were at the second gate Hammond had given them instructions to when Clay asked, "Joe, why are we doing all this backtracking to gates? There isn't a fenceline on this ranch that isn't down in several places. What if we just cut our way out of here? We have your fence pliers in your saddle bag."

"Cutting fences is a real taboo in ranching country, Enos."

"Yeah, well, the last time I checked, so was hiding stolen stock and shootin' Indians."

"Good point. If we just cut fences, we can also stay off the ridgelines. It makes me nervous every time we reach the top of a ridge. All right, let's drop back into the bottom and stay there."

Edom instructed the three ranch hands who would be riding out with him to intercept the Indian lawmen. "Don't shoot until I give the order," he said, handing out rifles and ammunition. "Don't shoot the horses, whatever you do. Burying men is one thing; horses are something else." Then he mounted his horse and commanded, "Follow me."

When the four horsemen of the Flying Eagle disappeared over the first ridge, Hammond, who had been watching and waiting, gathered his personal belongings. He loaded them into the back seat of the pickup, then hustled to the corral where his horse was chomping hay. Hammond had stashed the animal there the night before. He led the horse to the trailer, loaded and tied him securely. Afterward, he started the pickup to let it warm up. While he waited, Wes Edom's wife emerged from the house and approached the driver's side door. "What are you doing, Zane?" she asked.

"Wes wants this rig moved out of the yard."

"Why?"

"He didn't say, and I didn't ask."

"Okay, but why are your personal stuff and horse loaded up?" she asked.

"I'm giving notice, Sal. I'm leavin' with those Indians if they get back here alive."

"But, Zane, you have pay coming. And why wouldn't you wait here for the Indians?"

"Wes rode out with the other hands. All of 'em carryin' rifles. He has no interest in returning the stock. No interest in letting the Indians come back out, either. Keep the pay; it's only a week's worth anyway."

"Wes wouldn't do that, Zane. Where did you get that idea?"

"Maybe you didn't notice or hear, but Wes told the men to ensure not to shoot those Indians' horses. I don't plan to be anywhere near this place if murder becomes the order of the day. Even if it is Indians."

"Before you leave, can I get you to saddle a horse for me? I'm going to stop Wes before he does something stupid," she said in alarm as she turned hurriedly back to the house. "Just tie the horse to the corral. I'm going to change clothes."

Hammond rushed to the stable and pulled her saddle and saddle blanket out of the tack room, piling them into the breezeway as he hurried to the corral. There, he roped the boss's wife's favorite horse and led her to the stable. He bridled the mare and threw the saddle blanket and saddle to her back. He was tightening the cinch when Sal Edom came striding across the ranch yard to the stable. "Here's your pay, Zane," she said, handing him an envelope. "Don't argue with me about it. You've earned it. You've been a good hand. There's a little extra, too. If you need a reference, have them call me, not Wes." She stepped up to him as he finished cinching the saddle and kissed him on the cheek.

"Thanks, Sal," he said, "I appreciate it." Then he strode to the pickup, jumped in, and pulled out in a circle to the exit road. He waved as he passed the rancher's wife. She waved back as she swung into her saddle and took off at a trot in pursuit of her husband. Hammond drove down to the main road and turned to the right toward the bridge across the creek drainage, where he expected to meet the Indians. He drove to the side road Yellowhenry had used to turn around and repeated the process. Then he pulled down to the wide spot near the bridge and waited.

Yellowhenry and Clay were making good progress as they trailed down the dry watercourse toward the road, where they expected to find Hammond and their pickup and trailer. With one fence cut and just the gate at the main road to go, Yellowhenry felt like they were going to get out Scot-Free. What he didn't know was that Edom's wife's attempt to head off the assassination only served the opposite. While she had the best of intentions at heart, her intercession gave her husband pause to reconsider what had happened overnight. "Sal," he had yelled at her. "You're telling me you paid that turncoat bastard, and now you're trying to tell me to stand down. Go back to the house. I'll deal with you later. Come on, boys, we've got to pull leather. That sonofabitch has led those Indians to the box canyon. They're gettin' away."

The first bullet was a whine that Yellowhenry, Clay, and Hammond heard as the missile went sailing by overhead. A moment later the booming blast of the rifle reached their ears. Hammond yelled, "It's Edom. He's coming down the draw. Two hundred yards out."

Yellowhenry spun to see a dust cloud being raised by a group of horsemen. "You two get the stock behind the trailer. I'll get a rifle from the pickup and hold 'em off." Seconds later, Yellowhenry was braced against a fence post and was pumping lead from a .30-30 rifle. The horsemen were a hundred yards away in the wide open when Yellowhenry's lead hit them. He was firing to wound, not to kill either men or horses. He fired four rounds and clipped Edom in the right shoulder and one of his cowboys in the right thigh. All the riders jerked their horses down and spun them to race back the way they had come. "Start loading the stock," Yellowhenry shouted.

Clay and Hammond sprang to action. They had to cram the animals into the trailer. They weren't able to tether them. The animals, being unfamiliar with one another, began to rear, bite, and kick. The men had barely closed the gate when a bullet spanged off the side of the trailer. Yellowhenry turned to see what was happening behind him. "Go," he yelled. "Take the rig and get out of their line of fire. I'll catch up." Then, he returned to exchanging fire with the enemy. Edom's crew had taken refuge in a line of scrub juniper. That allowed them to focus their fire. Edom was out of action, but Yellowhenry could hear him bellowing commands. Yellowhenry's .30-30 was close to the end of its effective range, so despite his misgivings, he fired two quick shots at larger targets. His first was a headshot of Edom's horse. The horse dumped on its haunches and side and began running its death throes. The second was a body shot to a horse that squealed and ran bucking up the sidehill before turning back down and blowing through the line of men in the junipers. Its squealing and fountaining blood unnerved the men as they leaped to avoid being overrun.

Yellowhenry took advantage of the disruption by turning and running down the road after the pickup and trailer. He very nearly made it unscathed when a wildly flung shot of desperation caught him in the left calf, knocking him down. He struggled to his feet and, limping badly, continued to hurry as best he could. More shots began tracking him, and he took another shot that burned a crease in his left shoulder. Then, he was around the corner of a cut slope just above the road and out of the line of fire. The pickup and trailer were fifty yards ahead of him. Both Hammond and Clay were working desperately to tie off as many of the horses and mules as possible. Neither noticed Yellowhenry limping toward them. With the mules braying and the horses squealing and kicking the trailer sides and tailgate, they couldn't hear him shouting either.

Finally, Hammond caught Yellowhenry out of the corner of his eye. He was standing on his right leg twenty yards away with his rifle barrel jammed down into the road supporting his left side. "Holy shit," he exclaimed, "Joe's been shot."

Clay finished tying off another horse and turned to see what Hammond was yelling about. The two rushed to aid their wounded comrade. "I need a tourniquet on my leg," Yellowhenry said urgently. "Then we need to haul ass before they get down to the road and start shootin' again."

"Jesus," Hammond said, "If I'da known quittin' was gonna be like this, I woulda waited."

The two men dumped Yellowhenry into the passenger seat of the crew cab. Clay grabbed a length of rope and handed it to Yellowhenry. "Here you go, Joe. I'm drivin'." While he applied the tourniquet himself, the men loaded and took off. Later, they would find where three rifle bullets had hit low on the back of the trailer in an obvious attempt to flatten the tires. "How bad are you hit, Joe?" Clay asked when he had driven them clear of the immediate danger.

"Leg is pretty bad. Gonna need a doctor for it. The shoulder isn't too bad. A few stitches. We need to drive down to Lewistown to the hospital. Give us a chance to see how much damage the stock has done to themselves. We'll need to report to the sheriff's office, too."

Wes Edom and his cowboys were encouraged enough by the obviously wounded Indian that Edom told the two healthy ones to run down to the road and finish him off. By the time they got there, their only target was the horse trailer's rear end. When they climbed back up to where Edom and their wounded counterpart sat, they had to endure a tirade from Edom. When the two took exception to his shouting and declared that if he didn't shut up, they were taking the two remaining horses and quitting, he finally settled down and gave them a half-assed apology. It took their help to get him on one of the two remaining horses so he could ride double down to the road and up to the ranch house. They did the same for the wounded cowboy.

When they rode into the ranch yard, Sal, who had seen the blood on the shoulder of her husband, was waiting for them. "I heard a lot of shooting. Are you hit bad?"

"I'll live, but those goddamned redskins got away. Killed my horse and ol' Henry, too."

"We put some lead in that Indian sheriff, though, Mrs. Edom," one of the cowboys, Josh Harris, said.

"Let's talk about that later," she said. "Help me get these two into the house where we can see how bad shot up they are. And don't you say one damned word to me, Wes, about dealing with me later. You're lucky that sheriff was shooting to miss your fat ass. Anyone else would have plugged you dead center."

Yellowhenry ordered Clay to drop him off at the emergency entrance to the Lewistown General Hospital. "You boys go down to the stockyards and settle the stock," he ordered. "When you have that done, unhook, gas up, and come pick me up. Here's a fifty, Enos, for gas. Get a receipt. I'll call the sheriff's office and file a report as soon as I can after I get stitched up."

An hour later, the Fergas County Sheriff, Larry Barnes, listened aghast as Yellowhenry told him what had happened. "Well, Sheriff Yellowhenry, I'll have to call Wes and get his end of it. You know that, don't you?"

"I figured."

"I'll need you to stay in town until we get this thing sorted out."

"I figured," Yellowhenry returned.

With his leg sutured and bandaged and seven stitches in his shoulder, Yellowhenry used the hospital's crutches to work his way to the front entry. Clay and Hammond had parked in the main lot before the hospital. "Let's get out of here," he said, laying the crutches aside in the entryway. "The sheriff wants us to stay here while he gets a statement from Edom. Yeah, like, we want to hang around for that. Let's git." He began hopping to the rig. "How's the stock?"

"They ain't happy, but they're loaded. Except for a few bites and a lame leg or two, they seem to be all right," Clay answered.

"Good. We're going back up Highway 19 through Grass Range. If they come after us, and they will, if we can get onto the Belknap Reservation, it's a short jump from their northern boundary to ours. Staters and county won't chase us on a reservation. We need to move fast."

Larry Barnes placed his call to the Flying Eagle Ranch. "Wes, Sheriff Barnes, here. I just heard the goddamndest tale. Got a call from that Yellahenry. Indian sheriff from up north. Claims he got into a shootout with you and your hands while he was retrieving that stolen stock. You know, from that lawsuit, n' all. That right?"

Edom launched into a long explanation. When he finished, Barnes commented, "That ain't nothin' like what Yellahenry said." He listened to some vitriol from Edom.

"Wes, I'll look into it, but it ain't a matter of whether I believe you or him. Hell, I wasn't there. I know he doesn't vote in this county, Wes. Yeah, I know where he is. Yeah, I can have him picked up. Sure. You can pick the stock up. We'll unload it at the stockyards. That's All right, Wes. I know you didn't mean that about the election. Okay, All right. I'll get right on it."

The deputy Barnes sent to the hospital swung into the emergency room on the heels of an ambulance delivering automobile accident victims. No emergency room personnel were available to talk to him for nearly half an hour. Then, they sent him to the business office, where he was held up for fifteen minutes while paperwork was tracked down. "Sheriff Yellowhenry checked out an hour and a half or so ago. Account paid in full."

"Hey, Sheriff. Willie, here," the deputy reported. "Say, that Indian sheriff? He's gone. Checked outta the hospital an hour and a half ago. Nobody here knows which way he went. Well, there was no reason they knew to pay any attention. He just paid his bill and left, hoppin' on one foot."

"Hour and a half ago. Is that right? What took so damned long, Willie?" Barnes demanded. "Wes ain't gonna like this."

"Hey, don't shout at me," Willie hollered. "The hospital was backed up. Had an emergency. And since when do I need to tap dance to Wes Edom's fiddle music? I thought you were the sheriff."

"Okay, okay, Willie. Don't need to shout. I get it."

Barnes's next call was to the state patrol, where he asked for an immediate BOLO on a Native American driving a black Ford three-quarter ton pickup, pulling a horse trailer possibly full of stolen stock. Yellowhenry was not identified as a sheriff. Then Barnes called Wes Edom. "Hey, Wes, that Yellahenry got outta town before we could detain him. We got a BOLO workin'. Staters will get him."

"Damn it, Larry," Edom shouted. "We needed that sonofabitch here, in our own bailiwick. This makes a damned serious shooting very complicated, Larry."

"Well, it might get hairier, too. That sheriff. That Yellahenry? He said he called and alerted that law firm. You know, the one that handled the lawsuit about the stolen stock? Yeah, that one."

"Oh, for Christ's sake. I don't want this in a courtroom. Damn it, Larry, this is all your fault."

Barnes, suddenly angered, stiffened in his seat, "What did you just say to me, Mr. Edom?" he shouted. "This is my fault? Is that what you said to me? Be advised, you fat sonofabitch. I have a statement here from a fellow police officer, which, at this very minute, I'm taking as gospel. You got that, you liein' asshole? And don't you ever try to threaten my job again? You got that?"

"Hey, Larry, I am sorry," Edom said in a panic. "I've been shot, man. Indian shot, to boot. I'm under stress here. I do apologize. I just wasn't thinkin' straight."

"Your story is a lie, Wes," Barnes continued to shout, "I'm holdin' on to it. I could turn it over to the attornies and let you try to defend it, but I'm not. I'm cuttin' you one damned big favor. You call back in the morning and refile your report when you're not so stressed. It better be damned close to what Yellahenry had to say, or I'm gonna file your first account of what happened, and you can sweat about thirty pounds off your fat ass tryin' to defend it. You got that, Wes?"

"Jesus, Larry," Edom pleaded, "I'm sorry. Yeah, let me call you back in the morning after you and I have had some time to settle this down."

Sal, who had been leaning over her husband's shoulder unnoticed, had heard the entire conversation. "Well," she said, "he hung up on you. You silver-tongued sonofabitch, you."

Edom jerked around but hunkered down as pain flashed through his shoulder. "Damn it, Sal. Don't sneak up on me like that."

"Sorry, lover. Now that you've finally decided to come clean, you can go to town tomorrow and irrigate that wound properly before your big fat ego isn't the only thing that gets infected."

Chapter Twenty

It was dark, and Yellowhenry and his two accomplices were sailing along, thinking they were just about home free, when a Montana State Patrolman passed them going in the opposite direction just as they turned off Highway 191 onto #66. "That was a stater," Hammond announced.

"Looks like he's turnin' around," Clay said.

"We're only about half a dozen miles from the Belknap boundary," Yellowhenry said. "Enos, play dumb and drive the middle of the road. Stop just before we cross onto the reservation. I'll see if I can bluff our way out of this."

By the time the patrolman had turned around and retraced his route, adding the distance that Enos had driven, the pursued and the pursuer were two miles from the reservation boundary. The patrolman turned on his lights, expecting the driver of the pickup to pull over and stop. When that didn't happen, he pulled out to make sure he was seen. Then, an oncoming car forced him back into his lane. When the car passed, he pulled out again, only to have the rear of the trailer shift into the center of the narrow two-lane highway. At that point, he turned on his siren. Three-quarters of a mile later, the pickup and trailer stopped in the center of the road. The patrolman got on his loudspeaker. "Pull forward to that sign up ahead. It's wide enough there for you to pull over."

Enos drove past the sign announcing the boundary to the Belknap Indian Reservation. The patrolman pulled up behind the trailer, stopped, and walked forward. "Tell him,"

Yellowhenry instructed, "That you didn't pull over because there was no safe place to move the trailer off the road."

The patrolman rapped on the window with his flashlight. Enos rolled the window down. "Why didn't you stop back there when I turned my lights on?" the cop asked.

"With that trailer, there was no place to pull over. I finally stopped in the middle of the road. This was the first wide spot. Sorry."

"All right. I'll let it go this time. I need your driver's license."

Yellowhenry took over. "Actually, officer, you don't. He is a Native American on a Native American Indian Reservation. I am a Native American Tribal Police Chief. Here are my credentials."

"There is a BOLO out for this rig issued by the Fergas County Sheriff."

"Do you have FBI approval to enforce that BOLO on a reservation?" Yellowhenry asked.

"I was in continuous pursuit, so I don't need FBI approval."

"No, you were not in continuous pursuit. We stopped, and you directed us to the reservation. That was when you lost jurisdiction. But that BOLO from a county sheriff carries very little weight on a reservation. In this case, it is also without merit."

The patrolman had not noticed Hammond in the backseat. He decided to bull his way through using the race card. "I don't have to take this kind of crap from a pair of thievin' redskins," he said. "No white man would take your word over mine, anyway."

"This one would, Officer Tibbetts," Hammond said loudly, reading the officer's nametag and leaning into view from the backseat.

"Who are you?" the patrolman asked in surprised belligerence.

"Zane Hammond, a white man. Citizen of the United States of America willing to stand and testify in a court of law that you used racial slurs in an attempt to intimidate and deprive these two Native Americans of their rights, and, furthermore, on an Indian Reservation, no less. How do you think that report will be received by the FBI office in Helena tomorrow morning, Officer Tibbetts?"

"What do you know about any of this?"

"Everything. I've been involved in it from the time it started until now. You would be well advised to stand down, sir. You're risking your badge on an unenforceable BOLO issued by a county sheriff in a jurisdiction where you have no authority and where that county sheriff sure as hell has none."

"He is correct, Officer Tibbetts," Yellowhenry said. "You have seen my credentials. Whether they mean anything to you or not, they mean something to the FBI. In this situation, your captain will likely find them also meaningful."

Tibbetts stood uncertainly before saying. "Give me a minute." Then he strode back to his car. He fiddled around for a couple of minutes before returning to the pickup. "All right, you can go. Just be sure you stop at the roadblock when you drive off the reservation. Then you will be in our jurisdiction."

Yellowhenry responded quickly before the other two could speak. "Thank you, Officer Tibbetts. We appreciate your concern and how you've handled this situation professionally. Let's go, Enos," he added with extra force in his voice.

Enos quickly shifted into gear and rolled up his window. "I wanted to give that snooty bastard a piece of my mind," he said.

"I know, and I don't blame you," Yellowhenry said. "Just be satisfied that we won. Before we leave this reservation, I'll have to call our law firm in Lewistown. The headquarters of the Belknap Reservation are at the northern entry. They have corrals there. That's where we'll stop, water the stock, and get some shuteye. I'll call as soon as the lawyers hang out their open sign. Probably nine o'clock. I know the sheriff up there at the headquarters, too. We might get a bale or two of hay for the stock and some vittles for ourselves."

Enos pulled into the headquarters and shut everything down. The men slept as best they could. The stock did, as well. At seven o'clock the following day, a tribal police officer approached and tapped politely on the driver's side window. It woke Enos from the first spell of solid sleep he had had all night. Nevertheless, he was also polite as he rolled down the window. "Do you boys need some help?" the officer said.

"We'd appreciate a little assistance, but you must talk to our leader here. This is Tribal Police Chief Joe Yellowhenry. You might have heard of him."

"Of course. Our chief is inside. If you'll follow me, I'll take you to him."

Yellowhenry opened his door and stepped with his right foot on the running board. When he swung his left leg to the ground, it collapsed, and so did he. "What happened to him?" the tribal officer asked, alarmed.

"Damn it," Yellowhenry ground out between tightly pursed lips. "I'll need some help here, I guess."

Hammond was the first to reach him. "Give me a hand, Joe," he said. "I'll pull you up." With Yellowhenry stabilized, he could hop on his right foot with Hammond's help. The four made their way slowly to the headquarters. Enos explained what they had gone through.

"You mean he took one to the shoulder, too?" the officer asked.

"Yeah. A few stitches are all. His leg is what it will take a while to heal."

"Damn, that's harsh. Let me go get Chief Piersoll. Just take a seat here in the lobby. I'll be back shortly."

"What's up, Ian?" Piersoll asked as the young officer burst into his office.

"We got Joe Yellowhenry out in the lobby, all shot to hell," he exclaimed.

"Is his life in danger?" Piersoll asked as he bolted from his chair.

"No. Shoulder and leg. He can't walk on his own."

"Well, that's bad enough. We got a BOLO on him yesterday. This has to be tied to that."

Yellowhenry tried to rise when Piersoll entered the lobby. "Hey, Michael," he said. "Sorry for the intrusion."

"Good lord, Joe," Piersoll waved him back to his seat. "I thought you were at least a half-blood. You're as pale as your companion here. Damned near white. What the hell happened to you?"

"All in a day's work, Michael. Meet my deputy, Enos Clay. This cowboy is Zane Hammond. Damned good hand."

The men shook hands. "I see you've met Deputy Ian St. James," Piersoll said. "I've got to hear the tale behind the BOLO. That had to come from something pretty damned wild."

Piersoll and St. James listened spellbound as Yellowhenry told the story, starting with the original theft. "My God," Piersoll said, "Edom, I know a little about, but that Greene bunch. Wow! It sounds like the best of that lot is the young one who went to jail."

"I can tell you I'm gettin' damned sick and tired of havin' shootouts with 'em," Yellowhenry said.

"So, how can we help?" Piersoll asked.

"I need to call our tribal attornies in Lewistown and see the BOLO status. We have a load of stock in our trailer. They need water, feed, and maybe a place to clean out the trailer. Maybe a bite to eat, if that's not too much trouble. If it comes

to it, we could use a police escort over to our place,"
Yellowhenry said.

"Would you like to use a wheelchair in here?"

"No. I'll hop," Yellowhenry answered.

"Okay," Piersoll said. "Right this way."

Yellowhenry's call to Lowe, Jones, and Dunn was
answered by Grayson Lowe. "Mr. Yellowhenry, what has
that idiot Edom done now?"

Lowe listened quietly as Yellowhenry told him what
had happened on the Flying Eagle Ranch. "So, all you want
from this is the BOLO quashed?" he asked.

"Is that possible?" Yellowhenry asked.

"Yes, but let's see what else," Lowe said. "For starters,
the charges would be the illegal secretion of stolen stock in
violation of a court order, assault with a deadly weapon on a
peace officer, and attempted murder. Those are for Edom's
behavior towards you and Deputy Clay. They also apply to
the behavior of the men who aided Mr. Edom. Most of those
also apply to the favor of your accomplice, Zane Hammond.
When you and your deputy press charges, all those men
should go to jail. Hammond also has grounds for a civil suit.
All of this must be turned over to the sheriff's office and the
district attorney. In fact, it is your responsibility as an officer
of the law to do so."

"I don't have jurisdiction down there," Yellowhenry
said.

"Of course, you don't have jurisdiction off the
reservation. This has nothing to do with your policing

authority. That will be taken care of by the sheriff's office and or the Montana Highway Patrol."

"The sheriff's office put out that BOLO. He wanted me arrested."

"Sounds like Barnes," Lowe said. "We can file these charges for you as your attorney of record."

"Okay, do that. I'd like to have that BOLO pulled first, so I can get back to my office without the highway patrol on my ass."

"That will be done within the hour. Check back in with my office as soon as possible after you reach yours."

Yellowhenry handed the phone receiver back to Piersoll. "I could hear parts of your call, Joe. Sounds like your attorney knows his business."

"I'm glad I don't pay his bills. He represents our tribe."

"We are unloading your stock, by the way. We thank you for the manure. It does go nicely on our gardens," Piersoll smiled.

The two lawmen visited for the next half hour. All of the men then went to a small on-site cafeteria where breakfast was prepared. While eating, Piersoll's receptionist came in with a report that the BOLO had been withdrawn. "I'm glad to see this," Yellowhenry said. "Is it possible to get a copy?"

"Certainly," Piersoll said.

"Then we'll be shoving off as soon as we're finished here," Yellowhenry said.

"We can give you an escort if you'd like," Piersoll offered. The offer was declined.

Chapter Twenty-One

Yellowhenry and his team were unmolested by the highway patrol as they drove to their own reservation. A roadblock had been set up to interdict the men as they left the Belknap Reservation. It was still there when Enos pulled into line behind a pair of vehicles. The people in those cars were curious about what was going on. They were given general and vague information about a miscreant the patrol was interested in apprehending. When Enos pulled up to the patrolman manning the stop, Enos had a copy of the BOLO cancellation in hand. "There you are," the patrolman said pleasantly. "Oh, you have a copy of the BOLO withdrawal. We set up this traffic stop to inform you not to worry about it. Have a nice day." The traffic stop was immediately withdrawn.

Enos drove to Yellowhenry's home first. There, he and Hammond assisted the injured sheriff into his house. Amy met the rig as it pulled up near the stable, and the corral cleared the way of toys so that Yellowhenry could be deposited into his personal easy chair. While the other two men left to tend to the stock, Amy kissed her husband silly and demanded all the details of his excursion.

He had barely finished telling the tale when Minnie Graves knocked on the door. So, he told her an abbreviated version. She immediately attacked his injuries. When she peeled the wrapping off his left calf, she took a moment to carefully sniff both the entry and exit points of the wound channel. "This one needs the help of the clinic," she said. Then she looked at his shoulder wound. "Not much more than a scratch. After the stitches come out, if they infect you, let me know. I have the stuff to take care of that. I see you got that horse back. I need a ride on him."

"Take a look at him, Minnie. He's been in a bitin', kickin'" feud for two days. He might need one of your poultices," Yellowhenry said.

"I see an extra horse, too."

"He belongs to a cowboy who helped us. He's hoping to get on with the reservation police force."

"Does he speak the people's tongue?"

"Some. His grandmother was Cree."

"That helps. He can learn more."

"I will speak to the council," Yellowhenry said.

Later that day, with the rental rigs and horses returned, Yellowhenry had Enos bring the tribe's one squad car around to drive him to the tribal medical clinic. There, Dr. Sandra Laurence examined the wounds. "The shoulder will be fine," she said. "You can clip and pull the stitches yourself in another two weeks if it doesn't get infected. Just keep a clean bandage on it. Change it daily. The leg needs some work. I will numb it up so I can trim the tissue a bit. You'll need to come by twice a week so I can see how you're doing. With some antibiotics, it should heal in a couple of months. You'll be able to pack your newborn by then. That's about when Amy is due. I'm restricting you to no more than a ten-pound lift until we're sure this leg isn't going to throw clots. I'm putting you on blood thinners, as well. I'd suggest you restrict your police work to your desk as much as possible for a month or so."

"I'll need this on paper, Doc.," Yellowhenry said. "For the sake of my department."

The regular monthly meeting of the tribal council occurred four days later on a Thursday night. The chairman of the board, Cecil Crow, and fifteen of the seventeen council members were in attendance, so the quorum for making financial decisions was satisfied. After approving routine expenditures, the exceptional expense requests were considered one at a time. When they came to Yellowhenry's requests, the expense sheet for recovering the stolen stock was approved without dissension. Three members of the council questioned the medical expenses arising from the gunshot wounds Yellowhenry experienced. Their concerns were notwithstanding. His last item required his personal justification, so Clay had driven him to the meeting.

"All of you have a copy of Doctor Laurence's instructions regarding my recovery," Yellowhenry stated. "My request to add a deputy is partially because of my recovery protocol and partially because, with 1,814 members living on the reservation, we need a deputy to cover our office and the jail during overnight hours. Deputy Clay comes on duty at seven in the morning. He works until five, goes home to dinner, and comes back at six for three more hours. If prisoners have an hour off for lunch, that's a nine-hour day. When we have prisoners, it's twelve hours.

"I work from seven to six. An hour off for lunch. That's a ten-hour day unless a case takes us out of the office. When that happens, there is no one in the office except for our receptionist. She works from eight until five. She eats her lunch at her desk. In the field, we work around the clock. We do all we can to provide decent service. We usually take vacation days one at a time. On a per capita basis, our people deserve better. Our police department is dead last of all tribes of comparable size in terms of budget and personnel. I am hopeful that we can do better. Thank you."

"Thank you Sheriff Yellowhenry," Chairman Crow said. "Now, if you would be so kind as to allow us to go into executive session, we will advise you in writing within forty-eight hours of our decision."

When Yellowhenry had been delivered back to his home, Amy asked, "So, did you get the approval?"

"Don't know."

"Why?"

"They have to discuss and debate in a closed-door hearing," he said.

"Why can't they do that in an open-door hearing?"

"It's so that honest opinion can be exchanged without concern for the feelings of the petitioner. In this case, me.   They'll advise me in writing in a couple of days."

"Well, at least Zane will be okay. Minnie has grabbed him. I don't think she's charging him rent. He just buys the groceries. With you being laid up, maybe they'll fire you and put Zane on full-time. With no sheriff and just a couple of deputies, they can save money. Each deputy works twelve hours. Voila! If they need extra help, they can bring you in off the auxiliary board. You can make your rounds on horseback. No extra charge."

"That's pretty strong language, my dear," he said. "What brought that on?"

"Don't forget, I used to work in the tribal police office. I know how cheap the council thinks. You get one uniform top per year that you wear over your own Wranglers or Levis, Joe. I know you're grateful for the job. However, they think they did you a forever favor by putting a half-blood on as sheriff. That favor allows them to justify in their own minds that you don't need a raise this year. They won't even provide their own police chief with his own squad car. But I see their point. He offers his own horse. I think you should put a hitching post right outside your office and ride Hi Boy over there and tie him up. You know, let everyone know this is a real one-horse town."

"Before I do that, I'll have to have another job lined up. That's for sure."

"The Montana Highway Patrol would probably put you on within a month. And, guess what?"

"I'd have my own patrol car."

"Bingo!" she said. "You'd make at least half again as much as you do now, have a retirement plan, and be able to work eight hours a day."

"I'd get kicked off the reservation," Yellowhenry said.

"No. Now that we're married, your 99-year lease attaches to me. A full-blooded woman. So, you'd be another half-Native American who lives on but works off the reservation. Some of them might grouse about it, but other than refusing to talk to you, they can't do a damned thing. And when they fire you, you can take their mules over and tie them up where you were tying up. Hi Boy. Then they could brag that they have a two-jackass town."

"You know, honey," he said, "as outlandish as all that sounds, if they turn me down, I'm gonna make it happen."

"I'll support you every step of the way," she said fiercely as she leaned over her belly and kissed him.

Chapter Twenty-Two

Three days later, Yellowhenry was on the phone with the Lewistown attorney, Grayson Lowe." Sheriff Barnes and a pair of deputies arrested that bunch at the Flying Eagle Ranch. They were arraigned and charged with the crimes you and I spoke of. They've been released on bail."

"Well, I'm surprised the sheriff didn't tip 'em off before he went out there. I have to apologize for not calling you when I got back."

"That's okay. The BOLO was quashed. That was my only concern at that time. You and those other two who were with you will have to testify or give sworn statements about what happened. That's why I called."

"With our work schedules up here, the statements would work better for us," Yellowhenry said.

"Very well," Lowe said. "Your tribal attorney can assist you with that."

The men ended the call with mutual good wishes.

When Yellowhenry hung up, Barbara Premminger, the woman who had taken Amy's old job, stepped into his office, "Chairman Crow is here to see you."

"Good, send him in."

The two shook hands and sat down. Crow was dressed in a business suit with a string tie. He was sixty years old and had a full mane of white hair above a hawk-like face. He stood five feet nine inches tall and weighed two hundred thirty pounds. He liked to think his sober countenance was dominant in all his relationships. Without a preamble, he spoke. "Joe, I wanted to deliver this to you personally. I'm sorry to say that the council did not approve your request. This is the written advisory." Crow handed over a sealed envelope.

"Before I open this," Yellowhenry asked, "is there more I should know other than the request being denied?"

"Nothing in the written statement, but an oral declaration of reprimand was approved on a split vote. I am to tell you that your presentation, which ranked our police department as last in commensurate tribes, was not appreciated. Some members even doubt it's true. Your annual performance review will be appended to the effect that no raise in pay is warranted. I'm sorry to have to deliver this declaration to you. I, personally, did not support it, but I am not a voting member of the council."

"Well, Cecil," Yellowhenry said, "this doesn't surprise me. Thank you for letting me know."

"Is there anything you want to say in response to this action by the council?"

"No."

"Joe, this would be a good time to clear the air. I will deliver your message verbatim."

"Thank you. I appreciate the council's consideration."

"Well," Crow said, smiling as he rose to his feet, "I will let them know that you took the reprimand like a true gentlemen. Personally, I appreciate your professionalism, Joe. I truly do."

Yellowhenry smiled, "Thank you. I appreciate the professionalism of the council, too."

Crow looked slightly startled, "Does that mean more than what's on the surface?"

"Don't let it bother you, Cecil," Yellowhenry responded as he limped painfully to escort the man out of his office. "It's just mutual business as usual." Crow left, frowning uncertainly.

"Well, well, well," Amy said. "Another move downward and onward. What are you gonna do about it?"

I'm going to check in with the world and see what my prospects are. I don't want to do anything precipitous. I want to talk to Enos and Zane to see if they'd be interested in running the tribal police department. County elections are coming up. I might run for sheriff.

"We would have to move off the reservation."

"I hate moving. Maybe you and the kids could stay here. I could visit on weekends."

"Ho, ho, ha, ha," she responded. "A man's dream come true. Visit the rez on weekends and have your own private chicken ranch. Well, your chicken is out there eatin' hay."

"On second thought, maybe I'll just check in with the highway patrol."

"That's what I like about you, honey," she said, "you're so thoughtful."

"I am going to implement your idea, though. I'm gonna ride Hi Boy down to the office and let him shit on the pavement in my parking spot."

Amy laughed in delight, "I can't wait to see how Cecil will spin that. Professionally speaking."

"I'm goning to tell him Hi Boy is my personal squad car."

"You know what they'll say about that. They'll call for your badge."

"When they do that, they get two jackasses. It'll be a twofer," he said.

Yellowhenry did call the highway patrol. He was referred to human resources in Helena. Cicely Roper took his call. "You say you are recovering from a gunshot wound and won't be available for a couple of months. Is that right?"

"Yes. I was retrieving stolen stock from a ranch down Christina way and got into a shooting scrape."

"We heard about that. Indian sheriff took down a fat cat named Edom. You're that guy?"

"I am."

You're quite a celebrity, Mr. Yellowhenry. But why are you interested in leaving your reservation? You should be a hero up there."

"Well, life moves differently on a reservation. Let's put it that way," Yellowhenry commented.

"So, let me send you an employment application. We have three retirements coming up in the next ninety days. As a man of Indian blood and law enforcement experience, you will be a prime candidate for one of those positions. Actually, there is one opening coming up in your sector," she advised.

Yellowhenry had to make adjustments to saddle his horse and get mounted the next morning. He also conceded to the use of crutches, which he had scored at the tribal clinic. By stepping up onto his overturned galvanized bathtub, he was able to grab the saddle horn and spring off his right leg to the saddle's seat. When he reached down to pick up his crutches, Minnie and Zane were standing by the corral watching.

"Whatcha doin', Joe?" Minnie asked.

"Goin' to work."

"Well, Sheriff," Zane said. "Just let me know whenever you need your horse tended to. I'd be glad to saddle him up and unsaddle him for you."

"I just might take you up on that, Zane," Yelllowhenry said.

"What're you gonna do with Hi Boy while you're workin', Joe?" Minnie asked.

"I'm savin' the tribal council money. This horse is my transportation. He'll be tied up in front of the office during the day."

Minnie looked at him in disbelief. "Do you know what that will look like?"

"A town with a horse tied up in front of city hall," he said, deadpan.

Minnie began giggling, "The council really pissed you off, didn't they?"

"Oh, not at all, Minnie. They just declared the standards they like. I checked the codebook for the conduct of the tribe. I'm just meeting the standards of the code."

"I take it they turned down my application," Zane said.

"Only temporarily. Don't give up hope. If you can hang in for a couple of months on the auxiliary board, they'll have a change of heart."

"If Minnie can put up with me, I can do that."

"Piece of cake," Minnie said. "If you start gettin' rank, I'll crawl into bed with you. Take you down a peg or two."

"Looks like you got it made, Zane, you lucky sonofabitch, you," Yellowhenry laughed.

"Is anybody sleepin' in the loft of your stable, Joe," Zane chuckled.

"I might need a place of refuge in a couple of weeks."

"All right, you two," Minnie added. "Come on, Zane. Every lamb needs a good breakfast before he's taken to slaughter."

"Woo! I'm goin' to work where it's safe," Yellowhenry laughed, turning Hi Boy toward town.

There was a lamp post off to the side of the entrance of the tribal hall headquarters. It was set in the center of the parking spot reserved for the tribal police office. Yellowhenry rode up to it, leaned over, and dropped his crutches on the sidewalk out of the way. Deputy Clay had been tipped off not to park there. The sheriff lay down over the horn of his saddle and swung his right leg over Hi Boy's rump so he could position himself belly down. Then he slid down to his right leg, loosened the saddle cinch, and hopped to tie up the horse. With his crutches set, he went swinging along to his office.

When he had settled in behind his desk, Clay came in grinning, "You did it, huh?"

"Did what?" Yellowhenry asked innocently.

"Rode your horse and tied him up in our parkin' spot."

"You don't have a problem with that, do you, Enos?"

"Oh, no. It's just what I was expectin' all along. The police chief has dibs on the department's parkin' spot," he said as he returned to his own desk. He rubbed his hands together briskly as he laughed and added, "This is gonna get good, Sheriff."

The first one to notice the horse and say anything was Barbara Preminger. "Joe," she said, "Someone tied a horse up in the parking spot. He looks like that sorrel of yours."

"That's because he is."

"But we park the car there."

"We used to. I've added Hi Boy to supplement our rolling stock. It's an improvement to the department," Yellowhenry said seriously. "It's in the city code book."

"Okay, whatever," she said uncertainly, turning to look at a broadly grinning Deputy Clay.

For the next hour, various people dropped into the sheriff's office to see what was happening. Many people passing by Hi Boy stopped to pet him. He endured their attention patiently. When he relieved himself, urinating in a broad splashing stream and dropping his defecation to the asphalt, the curious became concerned. "Hey," one of the women workers from the tribal chairman's office said, "someone needs to clean up behind that horse and get him out of there."

"Oh, that's the sheriff's horse. He'll be parking him here on a regular basis," Barbara said.

"A horse? What's this town come to, for God's sake," the lady exclaimed.

"Well, it's a town with a horse," Barbara said mildly. "It's all according to town code. The code book is right here. You can look it up. It's right there. See? The sheriff shall provide his own horse."

"Oh, my word," the woman said, suddenly understanding the image. "Wait till Cecil sees this."

When Cecil Crow finally came walking down from the Rocking Horse Café located four blocks to the east of tribal headquarters, it was almost ten o'clock in the morning. He had been hosting a breakfast meeting with the owners of the Langston General Store, who were planning to stage a grand opening in ten days. Two blocks from the headquarters, a man driving by in the opposite direction slowed down and yelled at Crow. "Hey, Cec! Congratulations on your one-horse shit hole."

Crow had started to smile and wave, but he stopped and dropped his arm. At that moment, a woman walking his way spotted him. She marched to him, grim-faced, and began shaking a finger at him. "You listen here, Cecil. That mess down there will not be tolerated. It's an obvious insult to the tribal council because we didn't give Sheriff Yellowhenry his way. That man needs to be fired. Today!"

"Emmy, hold on," Crow said. "I've been in a meeting. I don't even know what you're talking about?"

"Well, go to work, and you'll find out," she said angrily. "This cannot stand."

By the time Crow made it to headquarters, Hi Boy had added to his pile. Flies had also made their busy appearance. The horse stood hipshot, sleeping quietly and swishing his tail. Crow finally saw what people were laughing or shouting about when he was half a block away. "What the hell?" he blurted. He began hustling. Without stopping at the reception desk, he stomped into Yellowhenry's private office. "I want that horse removed immediately and the horseshit with it!" he shouted.

"Have a seat, Cecil," Yellowhenry said mildly, "before you have a stroke."

"What's the meaning of this," Crow demanded as he sat on the edge of one of the two straight-backed wooden chairs fronting the sheriff's desk.

"Well, I'm only trying to improve my office, so I checked the codebook. It requires the sheriff to provide a horse. Now, instead of having just one squad car, we have a squad car and a horse. Right up to code."

"I don't care what the codebook says about your office of a hundred years ago. It doesn't apply now,' Crow said, using his right hand to smack his left for emphasis. "I could fire you right now for this obvious attempt to dishonor the tribal council."

"If you try that, I'll sue for wrongful dismissal," Yellowhenry said calmly. "The codebook is an agreement with the federal government on the operation and administration of this tribe. To amend or change the codebook, a tribal vote is required with 65% approval. Then, the Bureau of Indian Affairs has to sign off on the proposal. I am simply following the code, Cecil. Don't try to go to the tribal council and come back with their declaration to terminate me for cause, either. I don't think your declaration would be worth toilet paper in a federal court."

"Joe, work with me here," Crow said as his face blanched. "What do you really want?"

"I want you to appreciate that my horse is adding to the police department," Yellowhenry said seriously. "A car and a horse are better than just a car. In my current condition, the horse will help me. It will free up the squad car for patrol duties rather than splitting time to transport me around."

"Don't you see that with that horse standing out there shitting and pissing on the street in the space reserved for the police department, people are calling this a one-horse shit hole?" Crow exclaimed, screwing his face into a mask of concern.

"I can't control what people think, Cecil," Yellowhenry said just as seriously. "I do see your point about the pissing and shitting, though. Why don't you have a sanitation swing by every three or four hours to clean up the mess?"

"I'll tell you who I will go talk to, by God," Cecil said. "Right now, too. I'm gonna go see our attorney. There has to be something we can do about this."

"Be sure to let me know what you come up with."

157

Chapter Twenty-Three

After the lunch break at noon, Tribal Chairman Crow came back from his meeting with the tribal attorney. He had been advised that, technically, the sheriff was operating according to code. The attorney suggested that Crow offer Yellowhenry a raise to expedite the removal of the horse or maybe provide a rental car until a vote could be taken to change the code. Hi Boy was again tied up in the police chief's parking spot. Yellowhenry had ridden him home for lunch, giving him hay, oats, and plenty of water.

When Crow came back, Hi Boy had done a good job of adding to the mess—juice, flies, and horse apples. The odor was pungent and penetrating. The chairman hurried into the police department's inner sanctum, where he found Yellowhenry on the phone. "Have a seat, Cec. I'll be right with you." He returned to the phone call. "Sure, I'm willing to negotiate. Cecil just came in, as a matter of fact. I'll let you know what we come up with."

"Sheriff, I'm not negotiating until that mess and that horse is removed," Crow said severely.

"Well, good enough," Yellowhenry replied. "I'll remove the horse this afternoon at five o'clock. You can have sanitation remove the waste this evening. We'll talk tomorrow, but that horse come back in the morning, Cecil. That was the tribal attorney on the phone when you came in. He advised that you were briefed on code."

"Damn it, Joe," Crow began pleading. "Work with me on this thing. We cannot have a horse tied out front like this. It's giving us a black eye."

"Maybe it's a blessing you're overlooking, Cecil. I can see a billboard in my mind's eye. 'This is the Real One-Horse Shit Hole. Welcome to the original. We live up to our creed!' It's rude, it's crude, but think of the T-shirt and sweatshirt sales. Caps, banners, and boots. It would put us on the map, Cecil. Hell, open your mind, man. This is a one-time opportunity. Who could drive by a sign like that without checkin' us out?"

"Oh, for Christ's sake, Joe. Listen to yourself," Crow said. "Do you want to be the police chief of a place that advertises itself like that?"

"Well, Cec, when that place is trying to throw me out on my ass, I'd say that place gets whatever happens in the meantime."

"What if we gave you a raise?"

"You can't do that until the council meets next month. No offense, but I don't trust that the council has my interests at heart," Yellowhenry said.

"How about a rental car to replace the horse?"

"In writing?"

"Yes, in writing, Joe."

"Three conditions. One: the new car is to be retained until a replacement squad car, no less than two years old, is secured for the exclusive use of the police chief. Two: a second full-time deputy of my choosing is hired. Three: the

Sheriff reserves the right to employ his horse as directed by the codebook," Yellowhenry concluded.

"I can have a rental car here in a couple of days. You can take the horse home in the meantime, and I'll have the attorney draft a temporary agreement," Cecil said, getting to his feet and putting on his businessman's air.

"Car first," Yellowhenry said. "You'd best get the sanitation department on it. Anyone could sue, claiming a health issue."

"Damn it, Joe. You're being unreasonable here. Work with me, will ya?"

"Work with me... Let's see, I don't get a raise, I don't get a part-time deputy, and I'm told to shut up and be a good boy. All this while I was recovering from gunshot wounds received in the line of duty while conducting tribal business. And I'm supposed to work with you?" Yellowhenry said slowly.

"All right, I get it. I get it," Crow said. "I'll have sanitation clean behind the horse."

"See," Yellowhenry said, "we're making progress already. We were a one-horse shithole. Now we're just a one-horse town."

Yellowhenry continued to ride Hi Boy to work for nearly a week. A new car rental had to come out of Great Falls. Crow delegated the task to accounting, but no rush was put on it. The holdup was that the driver needed to be bused back to Great Falls or have a return car. A rental return would be available in seven days, so that was the arrangement. In the meantime, Chairman Crow had to walk past the horse in front of headquarters. Tribal council members came by to express disapproval. Barbara greeted all of them with the codebook. Only two of them insisted on bracing Yellowhenry.

Billy Braddock was the first. "Sheriff, you can stick that codebook up your ass. Get that goddamned horse off the street, or I will."

"Don't sweat it, Billy," Yellowhenry said. "Your wish is my command."

"Good. I'll be checkin'," the disgruntled man growled as he left.

With his leg wound getting better by the day, Yellowhenry was using a cane. He walked out to Barbara's desk. "I've got to get Hi Boy off the street. Billy demanded it. I need your help."

"What do you want me to do?" she asked.

"Hold the door open for me," he said. He limped over to his horse, untied him, and led him into the lobby of the tribal headquarters, tying him to the back of a heavy lattice-backed chair. By bumping Hi Boy over, Yellowhenry had him standing parallel to the doorway and against the back wall. The horse looked for all the world like a sculpture placed there intentionally.

Billy Braddock came striding by to see if his threat had been honored. He felt even more emboldened when the horse was gone from the street. He walked in the sheriff's office without noticing Hi Boy in the lobby. It was one of those moments when a person is so focused on intent that prominent objects go unseen. "Hello, Billy," Yellowhenry said when Braddock came striding into his office unannounced.

Barbara followed closely on the heels of Braddock. "Sorry, Sheriff," she said. "He just walked by without saying a word."

"That's okay, Barbara. I've got it. Have a seat, Billy."

"I'd rather stand. Now that I've caught your attention about that horse, let me clue you in on how this office is going to operate."

Yellowhenry leaned back in his chair. "I'll tell you what, Billy. Put your clues on paper, and I'll see what we can do."

"You can take notes."

"Can't do that, I'm afraid."

"Why not?"

"Because the tribal attorney can't interpret hearsay. If you really are so damned sure of yourself, be brave enough to put it in writing, sign it, and turn it in."

"Like I did with that horse? I didn't have to put that in writing, did I?"

"That was the one exception I'm giving you. Put the rest if it in writing, or you'll just be wasting your time and mine."

Braddock put his hands on Yellowhenry's desk and leaned forward. He didn't notice Enos Clay walk into the outer office. "If this attitude doesn't change, I'll be putting my thoughts in writing all right. All over your face."

Clay stepped into the doorway of the sheriff's office with a big grin plastered on his face. "That your horse in the lobby, Joe?" he asked.

"What horse?" Braddock said, turning toward Clay.

"The one standing in there against the back wall."

Braddock went striding out to see what he had missed.

"Enos, follow him," Yellowhenry ordered. "Don't let him bother my horse."

When Clay reached where the enraged Braddock, standing with bulging eyes, gawking at Hi Boy, he quietly slipped his nightstick from his service belt. Braddock reached for the reins. "Don't," Clay said loudly.

Braddock spun. "I'll do any damned thing I want, Deputy."

"Not quite, Billy. One thing you will not do is mess with the sheriff's horse."

"Oh, yeah? Try and stop me," he said angrily as he turned back toward Hi Boy. He grabbed the reins, but the alarmed horse jerked his head and took a step backward. Braddock tried to follow, but he didn't see Clay step with him and deliver a blow to the right side of his head that knocked him out.

Yellowhenry was standing in the doorway to the sheriff's office and watched what had happened. "Leave him there for right now," he said. "When he comes to, we'll jail him and book him for assault against me. He threatened to beat me up just before you came in. I'll move Hi Boy back out to the street now."

With the horse settled down and Clay handling the door, Yellowhenry limped and led his horse back to the lamppost in his parking space. Hi Boy immediately anointed the spot generously, relieving both bowels and bladder. Yellowhenry laughed, stroked his horse's nose, and patted him on the neck and shoulder. "You're a true gentleman, Hi Boy. That would have been more than even I could have tolerated in the lobby."

Braddock was still stretched out when the sheriff returned. Clay was standing near the prone figure. "Let's splash water on his face. See if that'll bring him around," Yellowhenry said.

Clay borrowed a 16-ounce drinking mug from Barbara and filled it half full with cold water. He rolled Braddock to his back and splashed his face. The man drew a sharp breath and struggled into a sitting position. He reached up and touched the lump on the side of his head. Then he looked up at Clay. "What the hell did you hit me for? I was just going to get that goddamned horse out of the lobby for chrissakes."

"You are under arrest for assault," Clay responded.

"Assault? Assault on who? I didn't hit anybody."

"Striking, even touching, is battery. Assault is the threat to commit battery. You threatened the sheriff. Get up, you're going to jail."

"I am a tribal councilman. Let me go talk to Yellowhenry. I can't be thrown in jail."

"Bring him back to my office, Enos. I'll talk to him. You and Barbara will bear witness."

While holding his head with his right elbow on his knee, Braddock sat in a chair in the sheriff's office. "Sheriff, I'll lose my seat on the council if you throw me in jail. I apologize for my actions. I will have nothing more to say about you or your department."

"All right, Billy. I won't file charges against you right now. I can do that later if you change your mind and try to take the law into your own hands again."

"You have my word, sheriff. I'm done with this," Braddock said.

"Barbara, do we have some aspirin out front?" Yellowhenry asked.

"We do."

"Go get some aspirin, Billy. Thank you for changing your mind."

Chapter Twenty-Four

The second council member who insisted on confronting the sheriff was Emogene Chandler, known as Emmy. As a mother of six children, she was used to giving orders that were obeyed. So, she ordered Yellowhenry to remove his horse. "Emmy, I need the horse to improve our police department," he said.

"That's horse crap, and you know it. This is just a gambit to embarrass the tribal council because you didn't get your way. It's as clear as the nose on your face. Take that horse home now," she demanded.

"I am following the code book, Emmy," Yellowhenry said.

"Oh, to hell with the code book. It was written for a different time."

"I'll tell you what, Emmy. If you can get a directive from the United States District Attorney instructing me not to bring my horse to work, I'll take him home and leave him there."

"To hell with him, too. This is just common sense. It doesn't require an attorney to litigate."

"Emmy, this is one time we are following the code book instead of your common sense."

"Cecil will hear from me. You can count on it."

"Please feel free to talk to him. I already have," Yellowhenry said, "but I'm sure you can comfort him."

"Damn you, Yellowhenry. I knew we should never have hired a half-breed. I've been against you all along. I'm gonna see you're kicked out of office if it's the last thing I do. To hell with you and that goddamned horse you rode in on," she said as she slammed out of the office.

Barbara came back and looked in on Yellowhenry. "She isn't very happy, Joe."

"She never liked me to start with; now she hates my guts. It comes with the territory."

When Amy saw her husband limping toward the house from the stable, she met him at the door. He saw her and grinned tiredly, "You are a sight for sore eyes," he said.

"How goes the horse war?" she asked.

"Another round in the books," he said. "So far, they haven't fired me."

"Well, that deserves a kiss," she said, stepping into his arms. He embraced her gratefully. "How are you doing?" he asked, patting her swollen belly where their next baby rested.

"She has been a little bitch," Amy said. "She loves to kick. She's wearing me out."

"Between her and the horse war, we're both gettin' the crap beat out of us," he said.

"Isn't the attorney supposed to draft something for you to keep you from riding Hi Boy to work?"

"Should get it in the morning. But the rental car is still two days away."

"Honey, I'm worried that somebody is gonna do something bad to Hi Boy," she said, looking out her kitchen window. "Here comes Minnie. She looks worried, too."

Yellowhenry met her at the door, "Come on in, Minnie," he said. "What's up?"

"Joe, quit takin' our horse down to city hall," she said.

"I haven't reached the point where some needed changes are being made, Minnie," Yellowhenry advised, smiling at the thought that she was considering Hi Boy as 'our' horse.

"You don't hear what I hear. At first, the people were on your side. You were stickin' it to the council, and the picture of the town as a one-horse shit hole was kinda funny. But it's gone on too long. Now, the people think you're stickin' it to them and their town. There are whispers about gettin' rid of that 'damned' horse. Not rustlin' him either. You're puttin' him in the crosshairs, Joe."

"That serious, eh?" he said.

"Yes. You are in that position where you win a battle and lose the war. Making our horse a casualty so you can win your battle is bad medicine. You are past the point where the people would have sympathy for you if somebody shot our horse. They would say, too bad about the horse, but the sheriff is the one who kept puttin' him there with his shittin' and pissin'. They're sayin' enough is enough."

"Okay, Minnie," Yellowhenry grinned. "I'm at the point where I can walk to work if I take my time. Do me a favor, though."

"What do you need?"

"Keep an eye on our horse. Make sure no one tries to take him from the corral."

"That's a guarantee, Sheriff," she said. "I've done it before."

"One thing, though. This time, shoot to warn 'em off. I don't want to deal with any dead or wounded rustlers right now."

"I'll do my best to miss, but if they get too damned grabby, asses are good targets."

"That's fair enough. Where's Zane?"

"He's sparkin' that oldest Chandler girl."

"Emmy's daughter?" he asked, surprised.

"She's the one. Lily. Just turned nineteen. How a pretty girl like her came outta that witch is beyond me," she said disgustedly.

"Well, tell Zane I want him to report to work tomorrow. The attorney is supposed to deliver the approval to hire a deputy."

"What time are you leavin' for work in the mornin'? I'll have him walk with you."

"Six thirty, or so," Yellowhenry said.

"I'll have him ready to go," she said.

The following morning, Yellowhenry briefed Hammond as the two men slowly made their way to the sheriff's department. "There is some bad blood against me on the tribal council because I am only half-blood. That will spread to you. Don't take the bait. Detach from it and take note of who it comes from. I'll be right up front with you. The mother of that girl you've been seeing is mainly against anyone less than full-blooded. She hates me with a purple passion. Have you noticed anything along those lines?"

"So, that's what it is," Hammond exclaimed. "Lily's mother leaves the room when I show up. Lily says her mom is furious about our seeing each other. Lily says she's moving out as soon as possible, and her mother can go to hell."

"Sounds like Lily is as strong as her mother. Or is she just rebelling against one issue coming from her mother?"

"Well, I don't really know. I guess I'd have to observe them when I'm not around to see how they get along," Hammond said.

"Yeah, I'd say so, especially if you were to get really serious. But that's your business," Yellowhenry said. "Today, I want you to ride with Enos on patrol. We'll do the same tomorrow. We're getting a temporary unit and a rental the day after tomorrow. You and I will share it. It won't be lighted, so I'm getting a temporary dashboard light that plugs into the cigarette lighter."

"So, I'm for sure on with the department?"

"Let's put it this way. If the tribal attorney tries to welsh on me and Chairman Crow, or Crow on me, the horse is coming back. You will be assigned to tend and guard him. The people are getting antsy about this one-horse war, and I don't want my horse getting shot. Keep your fingers crossed that the deal I made with Crow goes down this morning."

With Clay and Hammond off on patrol, Yellowhenry waited impatiently for the written order from the tribal attorney. Finally, he called the attorney's office. After some obvious secretarial delay, he was connected with Tribal Attorney Albert Silverhorn. "You are calling about the draft from Chairman Crow."

"I am," Yellowhenry said.

"There seemed to be a problem when Cecil left the other day. He called me later and said he wanted to hold up on that. He wanted to check with a couple of other tribal council members. Seems like Emmy Chandler, in particular, was against it."

"Well, that's disappointing. Please advise the chairman that the horse will be back at work this morning. Also, the two mules belonging to the tribe will accompany the horse. I am no longer in the business of boarding the tribe's stock."

"I don't advise you to do that," Silverhorn said quickly.

"Why is that?"

"Credible threats about the shooting of your horse have been heard."

"That's why an armed guard will be stationed with the animals. Any armed threat will be met in kind," Yellowhenry said as he banged the receiver down.

Then, he walked into the outer office, reached the two-way radio receiver, and called the squad car. "Enos, come back to headquarters as soon as you can."

Fifteen minutes later, Enos and Zane came walking into Yellowhenry's office. "Boys, we need to tighten the screws. I need you to go to my place, bring the tribe's mules up, and tie them to the front doors. I am not going to board their stock starting now. Be sure that the mules are well watered. Bring Hi Boy in and put him in the third cell. I have been told that credible threats are being made against his life. I want him placed in protective custody. Don't water him. Be sure you check with Minnie so you don't have to dodge her lead while you're gathering up the stock."

When the deputies left, Yellowhenry asked Barbara to get in touch with Cecil Crow. He told her to transfer the call to him when he called. An hour later, all the stock was in place.

"Sheriff, Chairman Crow on line one," Barbara said, buzzing over the connection.

"Thanks for checking in, Cecil," Yellowhenry said pleasantly.

"Before you get all twisted up, Sheriff, all I wanted to do was get some support from the council."

"I understand, Cecil, and I want you to know that I'm not tying the horse up on the street. There have been, according to Albert, credible death threats against the horse. So, he is in jail in protective custody. There are, however, two mules owned by the tribe tied up to the doors of city hall.

If someone wants to come by and shoot them, it's okay by me. I am not boarding them starting immediately."

"How much farther are you gonna take this, sheriff? Do you really expect to hang onto your job through all this?"

"Maybe, maybe not. We'll probably find out after the press conference this afternoon."

"What did you just say?"

"It'll be great, Cec," Yellowhenry said. "I keep giving you all these chances to put the town on the map. Just think of the exposure. Indian sheriff puts horse in jail in protective custody. One horse town upgrades to two jackasses. I'm having pictures made that can be disseminated to any newspaper looking for an unusual feature story. I'm notifying the local radio stations, too."

"You can't do that!" Crow shouted in anger, exasperation, and desperation.

"Oh, but I can," Yellowhenry said. "I've been told by the tribe's attorney that people are threatening to kill a legal asset of the police department. Until those threats have been investigated or until I decide the asset can be safely housed elsewhere, the investigation is warranted, including calling a press conference to alert the public to be on the lookout for suspicious activity and to call in with credible information about those who may be planning to attack the department's asset. I was sure you would want to be present to make a statement."

"Aw, shit," Crow said. "Don't do anything until I talk to Silverhorn."

"I'll give you half an hour, and then I have to announce this press conference to give the news media time to get here so they can file their stories for the evening news. We're right up against the blades here, Cec."

"Make it an hour," Crow said.

"So you can call Emmy Chandler and get her approval? Now that I think about it, you have fifteen minutes," Yellowhenry said and slammed down the phone's receiver.

All members of the police department had been listening to Yellowhenry's side of the conversation. "Are you really gonna call a press conference?" Clay asked.

"Ask me again in fifteen minutes," Yellowhenry said. Barbara, while we wait, could you send me the contact numbers for the local newspaper and the radio stations?"

"I can do that," she said.

Eight minutes later, Barbara buzzed Yellowhenry, "Albert Silverhorn on line one."

"Yes, Albert?"

"Give us a couple of hours, and we'll bring down a proforma draft of the temporary agreement for you to look at," Silverhorn said.

"Albert, you are a liar, and Cecil Crow is too. You've had over a week; all you've done is prevaricate. No proforma. The goddamned contract, as stated and signed by Cecil Crow. You have one half hour, period. If that is not done, I'm calling radio and print media to advise them that a press conference will be held in front of city hall right where those jackasses are shitting on the steps. You got that, Albert? Good!" He slammed down the receiver before Silverhorn could say more.

"Are they gonna do it?" Hammond asked.

"I think so, but just to make sure the mules are there where we need 'em, you and Enos go out and guard 'em. Enos, get Zane an auxiliary deputy's jacket and service belt from the storage room. Make sure the sidearm is loaded. I'll guard Hi Boy while you guys do that."

Yellowhenry pulled a rifle from the rack behind his desk and pushed one of the straight-backed chairs out into the main office area. He set up in front of the door to the cell block, sat down, and waited. Twenty-seven minutes later, Barbara came back and said, "Attorney Silverhorn and Chairman Crow are here to see you."

"Okay, show them in, and then stand beside me." He propped the rifle upright on his knee and faced the door to the reception room.

"Now, what the hell are you doin'?" Crow said, stopping to look at the sheriff with a rifle in a position from which it could be quickly employed.

"I'm guarding a prisoner in protective custody. You can see him in the far back cell behind me."

"You are insane," Crow blustered, "That's your horse. I didn't believe you'd go this far, but you have."

"Ask Silverhorn there. If he doesn't lie, he'll admit that he told me death threats have been made against my horse."

"I did say that, Cecil."

"Who cares?"

"I do, Cecil," Yellowhenry said, looking at his watch. "Now, you have one minute to produce the agreement in question."

Silverhorn stepped forward to hand a folder to Yellowhenry. "Give it to Barbara," he said. "Now, Barbara read the agreement out loud. All three conditions."

"Why don't you just read it yourself, sheriff?" Crow asked.

"Because I don't want to until I've heard it. Go ahead, Barbara."

She read it carefully, adding punctuation marks as she went. "That's what I was told, Sheriff," Silverhorn said when she had finished.

"Let me look at it, Barbara," Yellowhenry said, reaching out with his right hand. He read the document and then asked, "Barbara, do you have a pen?"

She handed him a pen, and he signed and dated the document. Then he drew a line and printed 'Witness' beneath it. He had her sign as the witness. "Albert, you have a copy for your files?" he asked.

"I do."

"The extra copy here is for Cecil?"

"Actually, that's your copy; the signed original is for Cecil," Silverhorn said, glancing at Crow.

"Now, it's mine. Cecil can have the copy after all of us have signed it. Barbara will witness that copy as well."

"You're going to hassle us right down to the paperwork? I can't believe it," Crow said.

"Believe it, Cecil," Yellowhenry said. "You lie, and I hassle. If you don't want to do it, have it your way. I'll give you ten seconds to decide."

"Albert, what should I do here?"

"My advice is to sign it and quit trying to subvert the terms of the agreement," Silverhorn said.

"All right, but I can tell you, the tribal council is going to not like this."

Chapter Twenty-Five

With the document signed, and Zane Hammond an official deputy, the men took up the question of the tribe's mules."Now, what are you going to jam up our ass?" Crow said irritably.

"I have an area that is too small for four animals. They churn my corral into a knee-deep mud bog after a rain or a snowmelt. It's unhealthy and adds too much work to care for the animals."

"Where were they before we bought 'em?"

"Enos sold 'em to the tribe."

"Then we'll put the mules back there."

"Barbara, will you go ask Enos to come in here, please?" Yellowhenry asked.

A few moments later, Clay stood in front of the gathering. "You wanted to see me, Sheriff?"

"I do," Crow said. "You need to take those mules to your place."

"All due respect, sir, but I'll have to decline. With my family growing and my work here at the police department, I just don't have time to care for horses or mules."

Crow looked sourly at Yellowhenry. "I suppose you have an answer for this, too."

"Just an option, Cec," he said. "My lease is for the usual hundred sixty acres. It's unfenced except for my corral.

If the tribe would agree to fencing in two twenty-acre parcels, I could properly take care of the mules."

"And your horse, too, I'll bet," Crow said bitterly.

"I will point out that the tribe, according to the code book, has the right to utilize the sheriff's horse in the execution of the sheriff's duties."

"So, you can bring the horse to town, tie him up, and have him shit and piss all over the street whenever you want. Is that your plan, Sheriff?" Crow retorted.

"No, Cecil," Yellowhenry, suddenly angry, shouted. "It isn't. But whenever we have to go into the backcountry for lost people or hunters or to go after criminals, we have to go on horseback. That's the utilization I have in mind for the horse. And you can't go back there for any time without a pack string, so the tribe would benefit from healthy mules, too. I'm not trying to do anything but improve my department. Maybe you should start thinking about that instead of running scared of Emmy Chandler."

"I resent that remark," Crow yelled.

"Resent all you want, Cecil, but also stop and think at some point. Your job isn't easy. There are times when you have to think of the greater good, not the best compromise you can make with your detractors."

"Albert, you're the expert," Crow demanded. "How much have I just been slandered?"

"You haven't been, Cecil," Silverhorn answered calmly. "If you bothered to listen, you've just been given expert advice on how to be the leader of this tribe."

"I'll be the one to decide that," Crow said hotly. "Sheriff, I'm ordering you to take these animals back to your place until the council can determine their final destination."

"I'll take my horse back to my place. The mules can go to yours."

"Did you hear what I said?" Crow responded. "I gave you a direct order?"

"And if I don't follow it, you'll do what?"

"I'll fire your ass, by God!" Crow shouted.

"Cecil, you need to settle down," Silverhorn warned sternly. "You do not have the authority to act like a dictator. You've put the tribe and yourself in a position to suffer a severe lawsuit for wrongful dismissal."

"Wrongful or not, at least he'll be gone," Crow continued.

"Cecil, he'll win the lawsuit, prevail in a substantial award for damages, and get his job back. That's the simple truth, whether you like it or not," Silverhorn advised.

"Goddamnit to hell," Crow roared, "what am I suppsosed to do with animals and nowhere to put 'em? What the hell is wrong with you working with me just one fuckin' time?"

"Stop yelling," Yellowhenry demanded. "Approve a voucher for fencing material. I'll put up the goddamned fence without charging the tribe a dime."

"I only have the authority to approve purchases up to a thousand dollars," Crow said, finally dropping his voice.

"So, do that," Yellowhenry said. "I'll fence as far as that much material will permit."

"I'll agree if you take these smelly animals out of here."

"Not until I have a purchase voucher."

"Here," Crow said in exasperation. "Take this credit card and get what you need. If you go over a thousand, the difference will come out of your pay." With that, the chairman stomped out of the sheriff's office without parting words for anyone.

"That went well," Barbara smiled as she walked out to the reception room, where she checked voicemail. She came back a moment later. "Sheriff, the rental car is here. The driver came in early."

"Well, Zane, let's go see what we have."

The delivery driver was in the front lobby. "Here are your keys. I'll need a ride into town so I can pick up the return car."

"No problem," Yellowhenry smiled. "What kind of vehicle do we have?"

"Well," the driver said, "it doesn't really look like a cop car."

Yellowhenry stood, looking at a humpbacked, short-coupled looking SUV. "This is an SUV?" he asked.

"Yes sir," the driver answered.

"How does it drive?"

"Very nicely, Sheriff. It's quick, responsive, and comfortable. I see you have mules. Put the back seat down, and you have plenty of space for hay."

"What do you think, Zane?" Yellowhenry asked.

"I think I'm gonna cry when we have to return it," he grinned. "Lily will love it."

Yellowhenry laughed. "So will Amy. This thing is a real hog hauler. She can get all the kids in there."

Chapter Twenty-Six

The fence building became a community project. With daylight until after nine PM, most of the work was done by men who volunteered to help in the evenings. The infamous episodes of the horse war were widely known. A weekly off-reservation paper had picked up the story and published the tale. The horse being jailed for protective custody and the concept of a one-horse town resonated either in laughter or in embarrassment. Both reactions caused people to want to see the stock taken care of.

Yellowhenry opted for metal fence posts for a three-strand fence; two smooth-wire lower strands and a barbed wire top strand. A thousand dollars worth of fencing wasn't enough for two twenty-acre pastures. Yellowhenry and Amy added five hundred of their own money to finish the project. The two deputies alternated evenings. Zane Hammond came over with Lily who helped, using a fencing plier to attach wire to posts. She was a good worker and her bright outgoing personality endeared her to Amy and Minnie who supplied lemonade and cookies to the people working on the project.

The second evening that Hammond and Lily volunteered, her mother, Emmy, made an appearance. "Sheriff," she said, "that deputy of yours is trying to manipulate my daughter illicitly."

"Really?" Yellowhenry asked incredulously. "Do you want him jailed?"

"If she was your daughter, what would you do?"

"I'd congratulate her, Emmy?"

"She's barely of age, Sheriff. She doesn't know about men. Especially those of mixed blood."

"Emmy, you just don't want mixed-blood grandchildren. Lily is smart and well-balanced. The more you try to tell her what to do, the more she is likely to do something else. Why don't you pick some battles instead of trying to fight them all?"

"Well, Mr. Sheriff Know it All, I have picked battles. You and that whitebread deputy of yours. I'm gonna stay with it until I get both of you. Preserving the purity of our blood is a noble cause, even if you don't believe it," she said defiantly.

Lily, who had been working on the lower-end run of the two pastures, had seen her mother walk past the stable toward where Yellowhenry was seated in a portable lawn chair with his left leg elevated on a second chair. "Oh shit," she said to Hammond, "what's Mama doing here? Hey, babe, I've got to get up there." She hung her fencing pliers on the strand of wire she was working on and strode up the slope to where her mother was speaking with Sheriff Yellowhenry.

"Is this about me?" Lily demanded of her mother.

"As long as you are living under my roof, being concerned about who you hang out with is my business," Emmy declared.

"I figured. What if I was down at Hill's Pool Hall hangin' with those guys? Would you care about that?"

"You could take up with one of those and improve over who you're hangin' out with now," Emmy said.

"Your same old bullshit racist claptrap, Mama," Lily said. "I doubt it will ever happen, but I'll pray that someday you actually grow up." Then she walked back down to where she had been working, threw her arms around Hammond's neck, and kissed him passionately.

Yellowhenry looked up at Emmy, "What can you say, Emmy? The kids these days. You just never know."

"Well, I know one thing, Sheriff," she snarled, "You can kiss my ass."

With the fencing job completed, Yellowhenry added resting shelters in each pasture. The material had been donated and a number of men volunteered the labor. Then Yellowhenry started billing the tribe for boarding and maintenance. Cecil objected until he had to walk past the mules tied up in the sheriff's parking spot. "Damn you, Yellowhenry," he had said, "if you ever leave the police department, I'm going to celebrate for a week."

"I can see it now," Yellowhenry said. "You and Emmy Chandler dancing cheek to cheek."

"Don't laugh," Crow growled, "It'd be worth it."

The birth of Yellowhenry's and Amy's daughter was nearly coincidental with the birth of Shirley and Enos Clay's daughter. The kids were born two days apart in late August. Amy named her daughter Bella Lou, and Shirley named her daughter Millie Joice. Both fathers were relieved that the births were without complications. The families were able to get together for a celebration a month, or so, after the births, thanks to Zane Hammond's employment as a second deputy.

The women chatted happily while the men sat out and smoked a fine cigar. What made the occasion special was that Minnie smoked a cigar with them. "You managed to do a fine thing for our horse," she said. "For all those other animals, too. I don't know, however, how long that tribal council will keep you. There are vipers on that council who do not want white blood in positions of influence over tribal affairs. It makes them feel inferior. You would be well advised, Yellowhenry, to move on. Find other work off the reservation. There are others who live here but work outside. They do not pose a threat to the vipers on the council who are planning to bite you. You should become one of those who do not threaten the council."

"Is there something specific you know about, Minnie?" Yellowhenry asked.

"When I hear the people whisper and then shut up when I walk by, I know there is something foul being hatched up. I heard one say 'Sheriff Clay' before she closed her big yap."

"Was that Emmy Chandler, by chance?" he asked.

"It was. She and that bastard, Crow, make no bones about their hatred for you. She has the red ass because you hired a man whiter than you are who is sparking her daughter. Crow has the red ass because he lost the horse war. They are up to no good, Yellowhenry," she said severely, pointing her cigar at him. "Your days are numbered, I'm afraid. But, there is good news. I have a brother who is a Montana State Highway patrolman. Works out of Bozeman. He tells me that there is talk of half an Indian who is being scoped out for the patrol. Up this way."

"Well, I won't lie. I am that half an Indian. The job won't be available until after the state fiscal year ends at the end of this month. I'll decide what I'm going to do then."

Chapter Twenty-Seven

When Liam Greene had jumped his recognizance bond, wanted posters had been distributed for his capture and return. He had had so many narrow escapes that he could scarcely count them. His initial strategy was to assimilate into neighboring tribes only to find that every single person was accounted for. Extras were unwanted. His reservation idea quashed, he tried to hide in plain sight within the general population only to find that police officers, local, county, and state, from the smallest burg to the cities, kept at least a casual eye out for the wanted.

With his nerves nearly shot, Greene decided to return to the geography he knew. His appearance was clandestine under the cover of darkness. He rapped quietly but insistently upon his mother's door. When she cracked the door enough to peer out, he whispered, "Mom, it's me, Liam."

"Come in quickly," she breathed. "What are you doing here, Liam?"

With the door closed, she pulled all the curtains before she turned on a small reading lamp. "I'm tired, Mom. I can't get any rest. I'm constantly lookin' over my shoulder, runnin' from one shithole job to another. I can't take it anymore."

"Then, go to Yellowhenry in the morning and turn yourself in," she advised.

"Never," he said fiercely. "The only thing I want to do with that sonofabitch is kill him. I need your rifle."

"I don't have it anymore. After your father died, it went to Horace. Talon had it with him. When Yellowhenry caught him, he didn't have it. It was left in the Moose's Ass."

"What about Dad's guns?"

"With him gone, I didn't need them and I needed the money, so I sold them. There are no guns in my house," she said.

"All right," he said, "I know guys with guns."

"Don't tell me that, Liam. I can't get involved. Do what you have to do, but don't pull me in. You can stay here tonight and I'll feed you breakfast in the morning, but then you have to go."

"Okay, Mom," he said. "At least that's a start."

The reward for the capture of Liam Greene wasn't much, $500, but when it was simply tied into a tip line that, if it led to his arrest, was enough to claim the prize, those willing to put his head on a plate were rife. That was what put the entire tribal police force on red alert. An anonymous tipster had called the tip line reporting that Greene had been seen the previous evening in the vicinity of his mother's home.

"Let's set you two at the back door before I knock on Maddie's door," Yellowhenry instructed as he deployed his men. "No shooting first, so be sure you have good cover. We'll all be on walkie-talkies. As soon as you are in place, call and say, 'All set.'"

When he received the 'All set,' Yellowhenry stepped off to the side of the door and rapped on the frame. After the second set of raps, the door was opened. Through the screen door, Maddie Greene stared at Yellowhenry who was looking at her from the angle created by his standing off to the side. "Why are you here?" she demanded.

"To search for Liam, Maddie."

"He ain't here."

"Has he been here?"

"No."

"Well, Maddie, I still need to search the house."

"Why?"

"He was seen approaching your house last night."

"What if I don't give you permission."

"Then you will be arrested for giving aid to a felon."

"Come in under protest."

"Noted," he said. Yellowhenry drew his service weapon and checked each room with the gun at the ready. When he was finished he found Maddie sitting in the living room. He holstered the sidearm and sat down beside her. "I'll ask you again, Maddie. Was Liam here?"

"No one's been here but me," she insisted.

"You keep a neat house, Maddie."

"Always have, since I was a girl."

"You had breakfast this morning, I see. The dishes are draining on the rack. Are any of those from last night?"

"I don't let dishes stack up, Sheriff. Those are my morning dishes."

"So, why are there two of everything in the rack?"

She looked at Yellowhenry, stunned. "Am I under arrest?"

He patted her hand. "No, Maddie. But, please, if you hear from Liam or see him, please notify us immediately."

She nodded without looking at him. He showed himself out.

Yellowhenry called his deputies out to the front of the house. "He was here. Had breakfast and vamoosed."

"Is Maddie going to stand muster for assistance?" Clay asked.

"No. Call it a mother's get out of jail free pass."

"Where do we go from here?" Hammond asked.

"Back to the office. See if anyone else has called the tip line."

As soon as the men walked into police headquarters, Barbara said, "Liam Greene is trying to score a gun. A tip came in that one of his acquaintances was asked for a rifle."

"Any idea who that tipster was or the location the call came from."

"I called back. It was Naomi Tarlie. She said her son told Liam Greene that he wouldn't loan him a rifle to shoot the sheriff."

"The Greene's, for chrissakes," Yellowhenry said, wearily. "I hope this one isn't strike three for me."

"I think you better go guard those horses," Barbara said. "Every time a Greene, excepting Talon, tangles with you, it begins with that horse and those mules."

"All right, it's between me and him," Yellowhenry said. "You guys cruise the streets. You have pictures of Greene. If you see him, assume he is armed. Look for someone carrying a rifle. Be damned careful when you arrest him. I'm going to stake out the stock and see if he makes an appearance."

"All of you should go vested up," Barbara said.

"She's right," Hammond said. "A guy with a grudge and a death wish against the sheriff. We shouldn't take him lightly."

"All right, let's do it and get going," Yellowhenry said. "Maybe we can get the jump on him before he knows we're aware that he's here."

Liam Greene was not having the response he expected from his old friends. None of the first three were willing to loan him a gun of any kind. All of them said he ought to turn himself in. The last one Allen Tarlie said he had a reward out on him for $500. Tarlie told him there was a hotline that tipsters could call anonymously. "Are you gonna rat me out," Greene had asked, glaring at his old friend.

"Naw. Ain't into that, but I ain't into aiding and abetting your shootin' no sheriff, neither."

"Look, all I want to do right now is get a rifle so I can get into the backcountry for a few months. I shouldn't have said anything about shootin' Yellowhenry, but you have to understand he killed my brother."

"Your brother sold him a horse and tried to steal it back, Liam. And he shot at the sheriff first. Then you rustled that horse and the tribe's mules. Yellowhenry got shot to shit gettin' 'em back. Think about all that. You ought to turn yourself in. Your runnin' is just gonna make it a lot worse for yourself."

"I won't give Yellowhenry that satisfaction. I may lose the feud, but it won't be because I quit."

When he reached home, Yellowhenry parked the rental car out front. It was ten thirty in the morning, an unusual time for him to come to the house. Amy met him at the door. "What's up? You're wearing a bulletproof vest, and you look worried and tense," she said.

"Liam Greene is in town. He's trying to get a gun. A tipster said he's going to come gunnin' for me. I want you to take the kids and go over to Shirley's. Stay there until you hear from me. Take the rental car. The keys are in it."

"Okay, can you help me load up?"

"Sure, the quicker you get over there, the better."

Ten minutes later, Amy pulled away from the house and Yellowhenry headed for the loft of the stable. He had armed himself with his .30-30 and a box of ammunition. He had no sooner settled into a corner from which he could scan the corral and pastures than he heard Minnie calling from down in the breezeway. "Joe, where do you want me?" she asked.

He scuttled over to the edge and looked down. She had her own .30-30 in her hands and was looking up at him. "Minnie, this is different. Liam Greene is in town and is trying to arm himself so he can come huntin' me."

"That doesn't change my question, Joe. Where do you want me? You know I'm not gonna back down."

"Minnie, it could be hours before he shows up, or he might not show up at all. I'm workin' on a hunch that he'll go for the livestock if he can't get a shot at me."

"I agree with you. Where do you want me?"

"Crawl up in the overhang of the old shelter in the corral and wriggle in behind those hay bales. That'll give you protection and a decent field of view. I've got the pasture covered from here. If he comes up here, we'll have him in a crossfire. Make sure he shoots first, Minnie. I'll try to arrest him, but I doubt he'll throw down whatever weapons he has, so if he shoots first or if I have to shoot first, then you can unload on him. You are hereby authorized to be an auxiliary tribal deputy sheriff."

"All right, I won't let you down Sheriff Yellowhenry. You can count on that. Is the stock okay in the pasture?"

"Yes. Down there they are more likely to draw him out. Up here, they'd be in the line of fire for someone. Us or him."

"Got it," she said and hustled into the corral and across to the shelter. She slipped over a hay bale, settled her gun across it, and waved to Yellowhenry that she was ready.

Chapter Twenty-Eight

Greene finally scored a rifle. A stolen .308 with a full box of ammunition was given to him by a seventeen-year-old whose mother hated Yellowhenry. Brian Chandler did not personally care too much about his mother's passionate distemper towards the sheriff. He had found the horse war amusing but mostly wanted to please his mother. Greene, who had dated Brian's sister, Lily, called her on the phone for assistance. She told him to get lost. "I am seriously involved with a deputy sheriff," she said. "If you think I'm going to help you, you are out of your mind. I'd arrest you right now if I could."

"You're a red apple bitch," he hissed as he hung up the pay phone he'd called from.

She called the tip line first, then the sheriff's office.   She advised Barbara about the call. There were only two pay phones in town, so Barbara called the squad car and gave the information to Enos Clay. The phone booths were on opposite ends of town, and the deputy drove in the wrong direction. Brian Chandler secreted the rifle and ammunition into his car and drove in the right direction. He spotted Greene on the street, tapped his horn to gain the fugitive's attention, and swung to the curb next to him.

"Get in, Liam," he called. "I've got what you need."

"Brian? Brian Chandler, is that you?" Greene asked as he leaned down to look at the youngster.

"Yes. Get in. We need to get off the street. The sheriff's department is looking for you."

Greene quickly slid into the car and ducked down in the seat. Within minutes, Chandler had them on the road to the bottom below Yellowhenry's property. A small stream bordered the road, and a band of willows bordered the stream. Greene grabbed the rifle and ammunition, and as soon as Chandler stopped, he stepped out of the car and into the willows. His parting, "Thanks a lot," was barely heard as Brian hit the gas and departed.

Yellowhenry and Minnie waited all day. The only breaks to their vigil were piss breaks. Minnie hollered each time she climbed down into the corral, "Don't look, Joe." He gratefully averted his eyes. Finally, as darkness was settling in, he called it off.

"He's waiting for it to get dark. Let's call Hi Boy up from the pasture. If you want to do that, I'll get some oats, and we'll stall the entire bunch tonight."

She whistled a couple of times, and a minute or two later, the sorrel nuzzled her shoulder as she led him into a stall. "No carrot, this time," she said, stroking his muzzle, "but look. Here comes Papa with some candy." She closed the stall door and walked down the breezeway to where Yellowhenry was rattling his oat bucket. It had the desired effect. The mules and Hammond's big bay gelding horse came trotting up to the stable. The bay's name was Hammer, short for hammerhead, which he was until Hammond had broken and trained him.

"Let's put the mules together in one stall, Minnie, and Hammer in one of his own."

With the animals grained, they put flakes of hay in the mangers to hold them overnight.

"As sticky-fingered as that Greene bunch is, we better set up watches on this stock all through the night," Minnie said.

"I agree, but I'll put Zane and Enos into the rotation. Three-hour shifts will be more manageable with four of us than six-hour shifts with you and me."

"Those Greenes have a love affair with the Moose's Ass," she said. "I'll bet a dollar Liam wants an outfit so he can disappear up there."

"The Moose's Ass," Yellowhenry chuckled. "What a name that is."

"I knew Bold Hawk," Minnie grinned. "He was the one who named it. He laughed at how stupid people are. Stupid name, stupid people, he was always sayin'. He was proud of the older man's wisdom. He said at his age, everything was trying to screw him but women. I proved him wrong on that one. He died happier because of it."

"I'll bet," Yellowhenry said. "Well, I'm locking this end of the stable tonight. The other end is locked all the time."

"It's the shits, Joe. Life is going to hell when everything has to be locked up constantly. We never used to even have locks on our doors. Do you know why I don't wear panties?"

"Uh, I really don't, Minnie, but I think you're gonna tell me anyway."

"As a cop, you need all kinds of information, Joe. Take advantage. I don't wear 'em, so I don't have to lock 'em up."

"That's wise, Minnie. Yes sir. A lot of logic, there."

Amy and the kids came back just after dark. Yellowhenry wasn't happy, but she prevailed. "Joe," she said, "Enos and Shirley don't have enough beds for all of us. Has Greene been here yet?"

"No."

"Good, then you'll be here to guard us. Otherwise, you'd be out there chasing him around."

"Okay, honey," he said. "Just put the kids down early."

The three lawmen rotated their shifts at the stable to cover the jail as well. They dug in to wait out the fugitive.

Liam Greene walked up to the lower fence lines of Yellowhenry's new pastures and knelt. He scanned for the horses and mules in the dark, hoping to skyline them. When he saw none, he figured they were inside the stable. It was close to midnight when he pressed his body along the backside of the stable to discover a lock. He crept back around, keeping to the dark side. He peered at the front side doors from the corner. He knew where to look for a lock. He spotted it easily, turned into the shadow of the stable, and walked away into the dark. Two hours later, he led a saddled stolen pinto mare away from the sheriff's from a rundown stable on the opposite side of town. He also had a set of saddlebags strapped down behind the saddle.

Greene's next stop was at the new general store. His break-in was smooth and practiced. He found a wrecking bar from the stable where he stole the horse. He used it to force the back door. He loaded all he could find and that he and the horse could pack. He had a backpack loaded with stuff he couldn't attach to the mare, stuff in the saddlebags, or hang from the saddle. By daylight, he had managed to clear the outskirts of the village. He was well on his way past the end of the road into the Moose's Ass drainage.

With nothing to show for the stakeout, the sheriff's department crew assembled at headquarters the following morning. Coffee and doughnuts were provided by Yellowhenry. All three were gathered in his private office as they fleshed out what hadn't happened the night before. Then Barbara came in with two theft reports. Ben Thomas reported a stolen horse, saddle, and saddlebags. The Langston General Store reported a back door break-in. They included a laundry list of missing items.

"Well," Yellowhenry said. "He beat us boys. Any bets on where he's headed?"

The deputies stated the obvious simultaneously, "Moose's Ass."

"So, are we going after him?" Hammond asked.

"I'd like to know how he's armed," Yellowhenry said. "From this list from Langston, there was no rifle stolen. He had to get a rifle from somewhere. You don't go into that country back there without one."

"Why wouldn't you just assume he does and go from there?" Enos asked.

"I may have to, but the difference between a .30-30 and a .3006 is a factor I'd like to know for obvious reasons. That ought six can pick you off at four hundred yards. A .30-30 is lobbing at that range."

"That makes it pretty clear. You'll have to go in with a bigger bore than our saddle guns," Hammond stated.

Barbara buzzed in at that moment. "Phone for you, Zane," Yellowhenry said, handing the deputy the receiver.

He listened quietly before saying, "Thank you, honey. Don't let your mom get to you. If we have to, I'll come get you and your stuff. With Minnie's help, we'll figure out something."

"What was that all about?" Yellowhenry asked.

"They're missing a .308. Emmy is pissed at Lily for reporting it gone. Her younger brother is involved. He handed it off to Greene, along with a full box of ammo. Emmy is threatening to boot Lilly out of the house. She doesn't want Brian charged as an accessory."

"Another reason for Emmy to hate my guts," Yellowhenry said. "The kid is a juvenile, so if Greene doesn't shoot anyone, he'll get a slap on the wrist. If someone does get shot with that rifle, then it's a whole other ball game. Now, Zane, here's a thought for you. Go get your girl, meet with the tribal holy man, and get married according to tribal custom. Then, Lily and you can live legally with Minnie. The only thing you might have to add is a little bigger bed. Langston General is going to have a hell of a bed sale when they launch. It's just a thought, and I apologize if I've overstepped my bounds."

"I'm not sure Lily is at that point, Sheriff, is the only thing."

"From that comment, I presume you are," Yellowhenry said.

"I'm crazy about her, Joe. She's all I think of," Hammond said earnestly.

"Well, get a ring and give her a chance to tell you to go to hell," Yellowhenry grinned. "I just don't envy you, your mother-in-law."

It was while Yellowhenry was getting outfitted to go after Greene that Hammond dropped by on patrol and walked into the sheriff's stable. "Hey, Sheriff," he said, "I've taken your advice. I spoke to Minnie about Lily, and she is as excited as she can be to have her move in with me. So, I got a ring from Langston. While I was there, they added a couple more items to the stolen list. Two boxes of .308 ammunition."

"Well, Greene is loaded for bear. Sixty rounds of high-powered stuff. It won't help me to count his shots. He has plenty. So, you're gonna pop the question, then?"

"Tonight."

"I wish you and Lily the best. She's a great girl, Zane. You couldn't do better. I'll have a cigar with you when I get back."

"What if she says 'no'?"

"The odds she'll do that are a hundred to one. But if that one comes up, we'll smoke to unrequited love."

Chapter Twenty-Nine

Yellowhenry's departure was a day later than Greene's. He rode Hi Boy and trailed Bray. The pack saddle on the mule was stocked for a five-day trip. Even though it was somewhat more awkward, he had eschewed his saddle gun for a bolt action, scope mounted .3006. It required him to hold the neck of the rifle with the barrel poked into the scabbard. He carried his customary coil of nylon cord. As he rode, he fiddled with different loops connecting his rifle to his saddle horn. Despite his aversion to them, he had yielded to Amy's tearful assertion that he wear a bulletproof vest. "You are responsible for four children right now, Joe," she had sobbed. "Why is it that you are the one who always goes out and risks his life?"

"I'm the sheriff," he'd said.

"Yeah, for a tribal chairman and some ungrateful council members who don't appreciate it and would rather that you die, get fired, shot, or quit," she had spat.

"Well, honey," he had said, "this is likely to be the last one I'm the leader of."

"I just hope this isn't your last one, period," she had added, turning away from his attempt to kiss her goodbye.

"Jeez, Ames," he had said. "You're taking this whole thing harder than you should. It comes with law enforcement at any level."

"Oh, sure it does. So you go out and get shot at by Horace Greene. Then, Talon Greene tries to shoot you. Then that bunch down in Christina gets their turn to shoot at you. Now, Liam Greene gets his turn. Do you know how much sleep I get when you go on your goddamned manhunts?"

"I know it's tougher on you…"

"None!" she shouted, turning away as Bella, who was on her mother's shoulder, began crying. "Not one fucking wink, Joe," she continued as she ran into the house.

He had ridden away with a more sober perspective on his sense of duty. Amy's pricking his conscience about the lack of appreciation on the part of tribal members weighed on his mind. It gave him a pressing concern for caution, especially when he hit the wooly covert of willows that blanketed the Moose Creek drainage. He was fortunate in one way. The weather was fine. Warm and sunny.

Liam Greene was toward the upper reaches of Moose Creek near sundown of the second day. He was planning to set up camp where the creek came splashing from the mouth of the gorge. He had reworked the way he loaded the pinto mare so that she carried more, and he carried less. The backpack was tied down like a rider to the saddle. He carried the rifle and led the horse. The added weight was meaningless to the mare, but its absence was a great relief to him. Together, the pair had covered enough ground that if trouble hadn't found them, he would have carried his supplies far enough up the gorge that he could have turned the horse loose. There was no way for the horse to navigate the narrow up-and-down pitches of tortured black rock inside the orifice of the canyon.

It wasn't so much the jerk on the halter rope that surprised Greene as the sudden splashing rush of a large animal coming at him through a screen of stunted willow adjacent to the pond he was passing. His cry of alarm and attempt to run so he could turn and shoot were in vain. He hadn't chambered a round as he traveled. If he had, just triggering a wild shot would probably have turned the cow moose back to her calf. As it was, his working the bolt was a fraction too slow. The cow lunged, her front feet like pistons hammering the back of his neck, head, and upper back. He was driven forward to land face first. The cow pressed her attack as he scrabbled, yelling at the top of his voice. That only spurred her to stop his movement and noise making. To her, it was like trampling a snake. Any small motion he made caused her to attack his core. A blow to his head finally knocked him unconscious. The cow left twice and came back to pound the inert form some more. Finally, she disappeared with her five-month-old calf in tow as she splashed and swam across the pond and into the willows beyond.

The pinto mare galloped back downstream in virtually the same tracks she had made coming up. She occasionally bucked, losing bits and pieces of stuff Greene had packed her with. At one point, she stepped on the halter rope, dropping her to her knees. When she pulled herself back to her feet, the loosely fitted contraption had been deposited on the trail. Then, she settled down into a mile-eating trot as she headed home.

Yellowhenry was alerted that an animal was approaching when Hi Boy stopped, his ears pricked forward and nickered. The Sheriff quickly dismounted, pulling his rifle with him. The pinto came through the willows and stopped fifteen feet from Hi Boy. She returned his greeting and walked forward to touch noses. The saddle had turned under her belly, so Yellowhenry stepped to her, stroking her neck and speaking softly. She stood quietly as he dropped the saddle. He was going to let the mare go on her way, but instead of slapping her on the butt, he changed his mind. He made a hackamore using some of his nylon cord and tied her off to Bray's tail. He strapped the saddle back onto her, mounted Hi Boy, and continued, using the easily discernible trail left by the passing to and fro of the mare.

Greene heard himself groaning, so he figured he wasn't dead even though he couldn't move his legs. He tried moving his hands and arms. That he could do so despite lightning-like spikes of pain that shot from his spine and down his arms to his fingertips gave him hope that he could somehow survive. He began manipulating his upper limbs until he could heft himself enough to get his right hand to his mouth. Then he began an earsplitting whistle that echoed into the maw of the Moose's Ass and repeated itself. At first, he whistled over and over. As darkness fell, he found himself growing hopeless and morose. He whistled out of anger every fifteen minutes or so, like an animal caught in a trap and full of desperation.

Yellowhenry had planned to pitch camp well short of the canyon so he could move in just before daylight. His hope was to surprise Greene with enough gathering light that he could have the best of both darkness and light to make his arrest. Then, Hi Boy began moving nervously and tossing his head. His ears were shot straight ahead. Fifteen minutes later, just as Yellowhenry had found a spot to camp, he heard a weird echoing sound that repeated and then went silent. He feared that a mountain lion was on the hunt. After waiting for ten minutes, he began unsaddling the mare. Then the whistle emanated again, except that this time it was repeated so that the echoes overlapped. It was clearly manmade. He unsaddled the mare and pulled the packsaddle from Bray. He tethered both animals to willow trees. Then he swung up onto Hi Boy, and with his rifle loaded and at the ready, he moved into the gathering gloom toward where he figured the sound was coming.

One more time, as he rode, the whistle and its echoes burst from the canyon's mouth. It was near enough that Yellowhenry heard the whistle before the echo. He stopped and quietly dismounted, ground-tying Hi Boy. Moving slowly and stealthily, he eased with his rifle foremost, parting willows as he went. Fifty yards farther on, he spotted the figure of Liam Greene just as he was placing his fingers into his mouth. "You don't have to whistle, Liam. I've got you. You're under arrest."

Despite the situation, Greene began laughing. "No shit, Sheriff. What gave you your first clue?"

Yellowhenry chuckled, "You have the right to an attorney."

Greene laughed even harder. "I want the bastard present before I admit anything."

"You got it. From the looks of the ground here, you must have pissed off a cow moose, eh?"

Greene's laughter stopped abruptly, "I think she broke my back. I can't feel anything below my waist."

"Why didn't you fire off a round? That would probably have turned her."

"I was gonna do that, but she hit me before I could jack the bolt."

"Well, I guess it's too late to tell you that in moose country…"

"Travel with a round in the chamber and the gun on safe," Greene said ruefully. "So, what do we do now?"

"We have to camp right here. We'll figure out how to get you back to town in the morning. Where's your rifle?"

"I think I tossed it out ahead of me. Why?"

"We need to get it back. I've got to go back for the stock. Half an hour or so. You'll probably feel better if you have it. Who knows, the cow might come back," Yellowhenry warned.

"Aren't you afraid I'll shoot you?"

"Not really, Liam. You do that, and you'll never get out of here." After a few minutes of casting back and forth in the total dark, Yellowhenry stepped on the rifle where Greene had chucked it when the cow first hit him. He picked it up and jacked the bolt, seating a fresh round into the chamber. "Here you go," he said, "I can't guarantee that the barrel isn't plugged. It was dug into the ground pretty good. But, if you have to shoot at something, having the gun blow up and kill you might be better than the alternative."

An hour later, Yellowhenry had a fire going, the stock tethered and hobbled, and a pot of canned stew beginning to bubble. After taking the rifle from him, he sat Greene up into a sitting position with his back propped against the pack saddle. "Nothing hurts below my lower back," Greene said.

"I figure my spine is gone down low. My arms are sore but getting better all the time. Ribs are screamin' a riot, but I'm so damned grateful that cow didn't finish me off, I don't care."

"Can you feed yourself?" Yellowhenry asked.

"I think so. I was able to use hands and arms pretty good when I was whistlin'."

That proved to be the case, much to Yellowhenry's relief. What became an embarrassment, however, was Greene's need to relieve himself. There was nothing for it but the Sheriff's having to become a health care worker. He had to roll Greene to the side and hold him while he evacuated his bladder. When he had him buttoned back up, Greene asked, "What do we do when I have to shit?"

Yellowhenry looked at him, "I don't want to think about that. Just try not to."

It took a half hour to pitch the tent and get the bedding laid out. Greene had stuffed a wool blanket into the left saddle bag that had been attached to the saddle on the pinto. It was still there, so Yellowhenry spread it out over Greene. He could string a line from a willow tree to a stob on a stump. He used it as support for his A-frame tent. He cut a pair of forked willow branches and used them as support at either end of the tent. This helped him get the two through the night.

Chapter Thirty

In the morning, Yellowhenry started his day helping Greene make water. Then he made a pot of coffee and fried up some bacon, the fat of which he sopped up with frying pan toast. Putting the two together made a breakfast sandwich apiece. "I appreciate this, Joe," Greene said.

"I hope you say that when we get back to town," Yellowhenry said.

"Why wouldn't I?"

"Have you ever spent two days on a travois behind a horse?"

"Never been on a travois, period. Why?"

"You're not likely to think too much of it."

"Is there some other way?"

"Belly down over a saddle," Yellowhenry said.

"I'll try the travois."

"Thought so. I'll be back in an hour, or so. Here's your rifle, in case something comes lookin' for horsemeat. I'm going up top to get a couple of poles and some cross members for the travois. Shouldn't be more than a couple of hours."

Yellowhenry rode Hi Boy and trailed the mule, saddled with the pack saddle, up into the timber above the creek. After locating a stand of lodge pole pine, he used his camp hatchet to drop a pair of eighteen-footers. Then he added a pair of shorter more slender specimens and strapped them, two to a side of the mule. When he returned to the campsite, he found Greene had rolled over, wet his pants, and couldn't roll back. "Joe, I'm sorry," Greene said. "I tried to hold on, but it ain't like it used to be. I shit my pants, too."

"Goddamnit, Liam. I'm beginnin' to wish that cow had just finished the job."

"How do you think I feel?"

"You're right. Sorry. I should have thought about that. It's a good thing we are about the same size. I've got an extra pair of pants in my saddle bags." 'How the hell am I gonna clean you up?' crossed his mind. 'Things are about to get shitty.'

"Joe, would it be possible to heat some water? You know, in that pot you heated the stew in last night."

"I'll never eat anything out of it again."

"Probably a good idea. I didn't even know I'd shit, Joe. I was just tryin' to take a piss."

For the next hour, Yellowhenry heated water and after pulling Greene's pants off him, cleaned him up, and redressed him in his spare pair of jeans. Then he sloshed Greene's pants in a shallow pool at the side of the creek until they were as clean as he could get them. Following that, he built up the fire and draped the wet pants over Greene's stolen saddle. "What's gonna happen to me when we get back, Joe?"

"Well, you stole my stock, Liam. That's what you were runnin' from. I'll pull those charges. You're payin' a heavier price with your back like it is than any prison would give you. We'll return the horse and saddle you stole. We'll ask those folks not to press charges. The General Store, maybe we can set it up so you can work off what you stole from them."

"How am I gonna do that, Joe? I can't even walk."

"Therapy Liam. You'll operate from a wheelchair. Hell, in a year or two, you could be racing in a speedchair. Count yourself lucky. Soldiers coming back from the non-wars do it all the time if they can. Some of them have it a hell of a lot worse than you do."

"That doesn't make me feel a hell of a lot better," Greene said. "I should have finished the job that moose started."

Yellowhenry walked over to where the rifle Greene had gotten from Brian Chandler lay on the ground. "Who did you get this rifle from, Liam?" he asked.

"Brian Chandler. His mom is on the council. She doesn't like you, so she turned a blind eye."

"Really," Yellowhenry grinned. "Well, well, well. I can't have this rifle around you after what you just said. Too much temptation for a murder-suicide. You understand don't you Liam?"

"Yeah, I guess so. But I wouldn't shoot you, Joe. I wouldn't."

"Well, my wife wouldn't forgive me if I didn't remove obvious opportunity since you have a motive. In a fit of depression, you could forget yourself and take the opportunity to trim my wick."

"I ain't motivated, Joe."

"You and I both know that if that cow hadn't attacked you, Liam, we could have been in a shootout because you wanted to avenge your brother. You can put that idea on hold, but as a lawman, I can't." He jacked the magazine of the rifle empty, the rounds flying out over his right shoulder in bright bronze flashes of light. Then he walked to the creek bank and like a stationary discus thrower, twisted his torso a couple of times before heaving the rifle out over the creek and into a pond on the opposite side where it splashed loudly and sank to the bottom.

"Jesus, Joe, that's harsh. That's no way to treat a rifle."

"I know," he grinned happily. "Maybe when you get settled, you can come back and retrieve it for Emmy. Just so you know, tossing that particular rifle was a rare pleasure."

It was nearly noon when Yellowhenry had the travois rigged and strapped to the saddle of the pinto mare. He used a blanket over the drag poles and attached it with some of the same nylon cord that he used to secure the cross members. Greene was lying on his back on the contraption, hanging onto the poles on either side. "You ready, Liam?" he called from upfront of the three animal trains that were tethered nose to tail with the mare trailing the mule.

"I'm ready," Greene hollered. "Let's give it a try."

Yellowhenry eased out along the main game trail beside the creek. With the willow thicket pressing in on both sides, he had slung the two drag poles barely wider than Greene's body. He hadn't gone a hundred yards before the man dumped off the side. "What do we need to do to help you stay aboard?" Yellowhenry asked.

"My legs just pulled me off, Joe. I don't know what to do."

"Are you able to keep your upper body in place?"

"Yes."

"All right, I'm gonna rope your legs to the travois."

With his legs stabilized Greene was able to hang on. Two hours later, Yellowhenry stopped to water the horses in a shallow crossing of the creek. It was then that the mare squatted and relieved herself in a yellow spray that showered Greene from head to foot. "Goddamn that horse," he spluttered. "If I had that rifle, I'd shoot her if it meant I had to crawl to town. What are we gonna do now, Joe?"

"Just fuck me," Yellowhenry said, disgustedly. "Hang on, Liam. I'll douse you off. As warm as it is, you'll dry by the time we make camp." For the next ten minutes, he used the cooking pot to pour water over Greene, sluicing off the mare's piss.

"Don't tell nobody about this, Joe," he pleaded. "It's gonna be bad enough with my back broken."

"Liam, as long as you behave yourself, and I don't have to throw your ass in jail, nobody will hear of this unless you tell 'em."

For the first time in his ordeal, Greene sobbed. "Thank you, Joe. You're a good man."

"That's All right, Liam," he said as he patted him on the shoulder. "Let's get out of here. With any luck, we'll be back in town by dark tomorrow. We'll get you into the clinic, and I'll see what I can do about your charges."

Chapter Thirty-One

Yellowhenry rode into the emergency room entrance just after dark the following day. His shouts brought the crew out to see the horse train standing in the bright light. At first, the travois went unnoticed. "Is that you, Sheriff Yellowhenry," the emergency room doctor asked in complete surprise. "Are you all right?"

"Yeah, but that's Liam Greene on the travois back behind the pinto. He got moose stomped up near the Moose's Ass. Broke his back and probably cracked some ribs. He's paralyzed below the waist. He's all yours now. I'll be back to check on him tomorrow."

The crew quickly went to work to transfer Greene onto a gurney, and they hustled into the clinic. Yellowhenry dismounted and coiled up the rope he'd used to tie his prisoner down. Then he remounted and rode to his place. Minnie and Zane had heard Yellowhenry's horses nickering to Zane's bay, and they came walking down to see what was going on. Amy came out of the house, too, hurrying, "Joe," she cried, clutching his leg, even before he could swing down off Hi Boy. "I'm so sorry about what I said. Forgive me. I didn't mean it."

"Ames," he said, leaning down to kiss her, "there's nothing to forgive. I love you too much to hold anything like that against you. If you can get the yard light, I'll take care of this stock."

Presently, a light mounted on the front of the stable turned on, and Zane and Minnie were there looking at the travois. Trailing them by a few yards was Lily Chandler. Yellowhenry swung down to the ground and faced a barrage of questions as he worked with Zane's, Minnie's, and Lily's help to strip the animals and put them on feed and water. "If he has a broken back, will he go to jail?" Zane asked.

"I'm dropping my charges for horse theft. That poor bastard is gonna suffer more from his broken back than if I sent him to prison. He was even suicidal a time or two comin' out. I had to keep him away from guns the last couple of days. Let me tell you something I learned on this trip. Those people who take care of the incontinence in hospitals and nursing homes are God's angels here on Earth. That's all I'm gonna say on that subject, but that is the honest truth. As for other charges, I'm gonna see if we can get suspended sentences and put him on parole. I've never seen a man suffer like he did on the way back here. And that's just the beginning. He'll be in a wheelchair for the rest of his life. By God, I wouldn't want to do it."

"I have some news, too, Joe," Zane said proudly, "Lily said 'yes,' and we went to the holy man. We're married according to tribal custom, and we're going to the county next week to finish off our marriage."

"Well, congratulations, Zane. You couldn't do better. Lily, I'm happy for you."

"Thank you, Sheriff," she said. "I hope you don't have to arrest my mother. She is not happy."

"Is she causing trouble?"

"Yelling and screaming, so far. Veiled threats."

"Joe," Minnie said, "if she comes around here mouthing threats to burn me out, I'm gonna cap her ass."

"Has she threatened to use fire, Lily?" Yellowhenry asked.

"I hate to say it, but she did make that threat."

"Any witnesses?"

"Just my family."

"Okay, I'll call her into a conference with Cecil Crow and Albert Silverhorn. We'll discuss her threat to burn, restraining orders, and her position on the tribal council. If she doesn't calm down, she will find herself in more hot water than she's imagined."

"If something bad happens," Lily asked, "who'll take care of my brothers and sisters?"

"Well, you will, Mrs. Hammond," he answered. "You will."

With the stock put away, Yellowhenry dragged his galvanized bathtub into the kitchen, where Amy helped him bathe, scrubbing off five days of trail crud. With that task completed and the tub emptied and lugged outside, he lay beside his wife, gazing overhead drowsily. "You know what, Ames?" he said.

"No, what?" her muffled response was barely audible.

"I'm gonna build us an indoor bathroom. What do you think of that?"

Her soft snoring made him think about how to do that himself.

Liam Greene was laid on his back with his legs elevated and attached to a cable and pulley device. Dr. Laurence was checking his vital signs and asking him how he felt. "I'm glad to be off that travois," he assured her.

"Do you feel a burning sensation anywhere below your waist?" she asked.

"My toes feel funny," he said. "Like they're trying to curl."

"That's encouraging," she said. "Be patient because your recovery is going to be long-term. You will undergo surgery, therapy, and bouts of traction. You may never regain full function in your legs, but three-quarters to ninety percent is possible. How you didn't suffer a severed spinal cord is a miracle. The Sheriff's tying your legs on that drag is the only thing that saved it."

"That's good news, Liam," Yellowhenry said from where he was standing in the doorway.

"Hey, Joe, you saved my legs," Liam said happily.

"Hello, Sheriff Yellowhenry," Dr. Laurence said. "When you've finished talking with Mr. Greene, I'd like a moment with you."

"Did you hear what she said? My cord is pinched but not cut. You're tying me down, saved it."

"I'm glad, Liam, but it was just blind luck. I was sure that cow had cut your cord. If I'd had any clue, I would have been more careful. I guess," he said lamely.

"Ah, Joe, don't blame yourself. If you hadn't dragged my sorry ass out of there, I'd be wolf or coyote shit by now."

"Well, Liam, I'm gonna do my best to get your charges dismissed or reduced so you can be paroled. No promises. I'll let you know as soon as I know."

"Thanks, Joe. I know I don't deserve it. I promise you'll never regret anything you can do for me."

"Okay, Liam. I'll see you later."

When Yellowhenry walked into the hallway, he looked for Dr. Laurence, but when she wasn't in sight, he headed for the exit past the nurse's station. "Sheriff Yellowhenry," one of the nurses called, "Dr. Laurence would like to see you in her office. If you'll come this way, please."

She led him behind the counter and into one of three offices that faced the station. Dr. Laurence was sitting behind her desk. "Thank you for stopping, Sheriff Yellowhenry."

"How may I help you?" he asked.

"Actually, I have it in mind to help you."

"How so?"

"That you didn't sever Liam Greene's spinal cord was a miracle. I'm sure you were convinced that the animal attack had already done that. The X-ray and bruising showed an impression from a hoofprint that would have, had it been half an inch to the right."

"Dr. Laurence, even if I had known, under the circumstances, I could very easily have done that despite my best efforts not to."

"I know. What I have in mind is a tutorial, for lack of a better word, for you and your department on back, neck, and spinal injuries. Techniques on how to immobilize, stabilize, and support injuries and specifics on what not to do. Would you entertain such a training program?"

"I will advise the tribal chairman that I believe your offer should be embraced. The final decision will be his."

"Why wouldn't you decide, Sheriff? This is certainly within your purview as the head of the police department."

"There are circumstances right now about which I am not at liberty to speak. So, if you are in a hurry, you'll have to seek the approval of Cecil Crow."

"In that case, I'll wait. For reasons I also do not care to speak," Dr. Laurence said.

Yellowhenry requested a conference with Cecil Crow, Albert Silverhorn, and Emmy Chandler in his office. Without his knowing it, word of mouth had spread rapidly about his bringing Liam Greene in from the Moose's Ass strapped to a travois with his spinal cord intact. Greene was singing the Sheriff's praises and relating how he was nearly killed by an enraged moose. Greene regaled the nursing staff with his heroic whistling, bringing Yellowhenry to the rescue.

By the time of the conference at four o'clock in the afternoon, Albert Silverhorn was the only one who hadn't heard a version of the rescue. Cecil Crow had heard plenty about the heroic rescue. Emmy Chandler had also heard about the great humanitarian exploit. Her bile was in full roar by the time she came stomping into the Sheriff's office. The three men were already there, eyeballing one another uncomfortably. "It's about time, Emmy," Crow groused.

"What is this all about, Sheriff," she demanded.

"Sit down, Emmy," Yellowhenry said, "this going to take a while."

She looked at Crow, and he gestured for her to be seated. When she finally perched herself on the edge of a chair, Yellowhenry began. "I called this meeting to discuss the case of Liam Greene. It is my desire, under the circumstances that now exist, to see him paroled so that he can pursue the medical protocol to save him from paralysis."

"He is a horsethief, for God's sake," Emmy exclaimed. "Your horse to boot."

"I am not pressing charges."

"How about Ben Thomas? Greene stole his horse, too," she said in disbelief.

"The mare has been returned, and Ben is letting it go at that," Yellowhenry answered.

"He broke into the general store. I suppose you want a slap on the wrist for that, too," she fairly shouted.

"I've spoken to Langston. They are sympathetic to parole."

"Is there anything else you want to overlook?"

"Yes, Emmy, there is. Your role as an accessory to attempted murder and your threats to burn Minnie Graves home to the ground."

She was about to say something derisive but caught herself with her mouth open. She sat back in her chair and shot a furtive glance at Crow and Silverhorn. They looked at her, and Silverhorn blurted, "Attempted murder? Arson?"

"Yes, she made a rifle available to Greene when his intent was to shoot me when I pursued him into the backcountry, and when her nineteen-year-old daughter married a man she didn't approve of, she threatened to burn them out. They are renting from Minnie."

"Emmy, what did you do?" Crow rose a bit in his chair and stared at her malevolently.

"I didn't provide the gun?" she said. "My son did. I wasn't really gonna burn Minnie out. I was just mad."

"And you looked the other way, according to your sixteen-year-old son, Brian. But maybe you'd rather throw him under the bus, Emmy. Is that what you want?" Yellowhenry asked.

"Of course not. I didn't know about it until after he did it."

"And that's when you filed a police report?"

She didn't say anything but sat looking nervously at the men. "Well, Emmy?" Crow asked.

"I didn't file a report," she murmured.

"Oh, my," Crow said, looking to Silverhorn, "what's the upshot of that?"

"Since Sheriff Yellowhenry was apparently not shot at, legally, no statute was breached unless Emmy wants to press charges against her son."

She perked up, "No. I do not. The return of the rifle is all I ask."

"It's lost up there in Moose Creek. Ask Liam Greene what he had planned for it. When that story gets out, what do you suppose the odds of your staying on the tribal council will be, Mrs. Chandler?" Yellowhenry asked. "You know, a gun owned by a vindictive tribal council member in the hands of a potential killer who was saved by the Sheriff she wanted to see dead. Not a pretty picture, is it?"

"Cecil," she said, "do something."

"All right, Emmy. Jesus. Enough already. What is it you want again, Joe?" Crow asked.

With Silverhorn's help, the charges against Liam Greene were plea-bargained down. After he pled guilty to breaking and entering into Langston's General Store, he was sentenced to a suspended sentence of one year in prison. He was put on probation for two years. A specific restraining order was issued against Emmy, prohibiting her from getting closer than two hundred feet to Minnie Graves's property. The strained relations between Yellowhenry, Crow, and Emmy Chandler simmered down as the Sheriff's approval rating soared across the reservation. Emmy's prestige suffered proportionally.

Chapter Thirty-Two

True to his word, Yellowhenry looked into adding indoor plumbing to his house. With no experience other than priming a hand pump, he found himself more and more overwhelmed with the concept. Hot water from a tank in the house became a passion, along with a washer and dryer. An electric foot pump at the bottom of his well-plumbed pipes leading to a tub, bathroom sink, kitchen sink, and commode, all inside the house, was another element above his knowledge bowl. Then, the need for a septic tank and drain field had him standing back, tapping his boot, wondering just what the hell he was thinking about.

Amy got a kick out of needling him gently about when he was going to get started. She was not unhappy with her home as it was. With oil heat, carrying water was the only real burden she detested. The rest of it just came with the territory of being a wife. Still, she dreamed a little.

Yellowhenry took it upon himself to monitor Liam Greene's progress. Greene would have to be moved into his mother's home. She would help him as much as she could, but a wheelchair ramp had to be installed so that he could access the house and also use the outhouse. The outhouse would also need to be remodeled. Instead, Yellowhenry organized work parties backed by materials donors to build a new one, leaving the old outhouse in place. The new one was prepared with a packed, crushed brick pathway leading from the foot of the ramp to the ground-level entry of the extra-wide door of the new outhouse. Grab bars were installed. Finally, the doors inside the house were widened to accommodate a wheelchair.

Greene had remained in the hospital for ten days so heavy anti-inflammatories could take effect. Learning to use a wheelchair was also essential; it took training and practice. When he was delivered to his mother's home, he was amazed at the setup. He had been intentionally kept in the dark about the home improvements."Mom, how did you accomplish this?" he asked.

"I didn't. Sheriff Yellowhenry got everything donated and organized volunteer labor parties to do the work. He's the one to thank."

Greene broke into tears, "That crazy sonofabitch," he said. "And to think I wanted to shoot him."

Just then, Yellowhenry and a half dozen people who had worked on the project stepped from the front door and spread out in front of Greene as he sat in his wheelchair. "Welcome home, Liam," Yellowhenry grinned. "No shittin' your pants here. We've got it all set up for you."

"Joe, you bastard, you," Greene said, his voice breaking through a fresh flood of tears. "I don't know how to thank you."

"Just get better, Liam. That's all. Just get better," Yellowhenry said through his own moist eyes. "Also, thank these guys. They're the ones who did all the work," he continued. The men moved to shake hands with Greene and to wish him well. He knew all of them, and his genuine thanks drew tears from them as well.

The brick path had been extended to form an intersection from the curb to the path leading to the ramp. Greene wheeled himself to test the path. Then, he noticed the outhouse. "What the hell," he exclaimed. He wheeled to the new facility and looked inside. All the grab bars he would need to use the commode were installed in the proper places. "This means so much that I can't put it into words," he said. "Believe me when I tell you this is my greatest worry. Joe knows. He knows firsthand. I can't thank you enough."

A week later, Yellowhenry received notice from the highway patrol that he had been requested to contact the human resources office in Helena. Word got around, and the people began questioning one another about why their sheriff was unhappy. Then they began asking him. He declined to comment, but it didn't take long for the understory of the horse war to come out. The tribal council began scurrying for cover and pointing fingers. An undercurrent began circulating about the adequacy of Chairman Cecil Crow. Emmy Chandler's judgment was brought into question, especially when the restraining order for the protection of Minnie Grave's property was discovered. An emergency council meeting was called.

"I told you it was a mistake not to give Yellowhenry some kind of a raise. Hell, half of what he asked for probably would have headed off this shit storm," raged Jordy Kelly, a fifty-year-old who owned his own car repair shop and filling station.

"So, what do you recommend we do now?" shouted Sally Jack. "What they pay a highway patrolman is half again as much as we pay him."

"You wanted him reprimanded for pointing out how little we pay our tribal policemen. Well, guess what, Sally? The truth hurts, doesn't it?" Kelly retorted.

"Settle down, settle down," Cecil Crow yelled as he pounded his gavel. "Now, let's take a look at our finances and see what the hell we can offer Joe Yellowhenry. Even if he doesn't stay, a good-faith offer should save our collective asses. Show our good faith, even if it is a little late."

An hour of haggling ensued, and those who had been against Yellowhenry argued that a courtesy offer would be enough to save face. "We could probably get a sheriff for less than what we're payin' Yellowhenry," Sally Jack asserted.

"I say let the smart-assed bastard go," Emmy Chandler added.

"For someone he gave one helluva big pass to, Emmy," Crow retorted, "you're showing a damned short memory."

"Oh, what was that?" Kelly asked.

"Okay, Cecil, I'll go for an offer to keep him on," she said, quickly turning away from Kelly.

"Let me guess, then," Kelly said, pursuing with his voice. "you'd feel a lot better with him gone. Ease your guilty conscience. Is that it?"

"Mr. Kelly," Crow shouted, "that's enough."

"How about you, Cecil?" Kelly yelled. "Is there something you know about this you're hidin', too?"

"This is not the time nor the venue, Mr. Kelly."

"Oh, yeah? Why the hell not?"

"We're not going into police cases that are confidential," Crow returned shouting down others who began questioning what the hell the rhubarb was about.

"Wait a minute, there, Cec," Rory Blue, a well-respected elder, spoke up. "You, the sheriff, and a tribal council member have had your names brought up in a case in which the sheriff could have, apparently, brought charges against the council member but didn't. We're in a closed-door session regarding that very sheriff. I think we should all hear that story."

"All right. Emmy, do you want to tell or should I?"

"You do it," she said.

"Emmy and the sheriff, shall I say, are not bosom buddies. Everyone is aware of that. When Liam Greene returned and stole a horse and headed into the Moose's Ass, he was carryin' a rifle. Emmy's rifle. Her son had taken it and given it to Greene. If Greene hadn't been attacked by a moose, it's likely he and Yellowhenry would have engaged in gunplay. Didn't happen, but Emmy didn't report the gun stolen, either. Technically, she was an accessory to a situation of endangerment to a police officer. Yellowhenry said to hell with it. You all know the rest of it. He has helped Greene as he tries to recover from a broken back."

"That sounds like the kind of sheriff I would want if something like that happened to my family," Blue observed. There was a general murmur of assent.

"Well, then," Crow said, "are we ready to vote on a raise for the sheriff?"

"So moved," Billy Roundbelly said. A second quickly came from the floor.

"Those in favor raise your hands," Crow said.

Sixteen of eighteen hands were counted. Sally Jack and Emmy Chandler sat stoically.

"Those opposed," Crow said. Sally Jack raised her hand with her face turned downward, but Emmy didn't move.

"The motion carries sixteen ayes, one nay," Crow said.

"And one abstention," Emmy spoke up.

"All right. The secretary will note one abstention."

"Put my name next to it," Emmy said.

"We don't do that, Emmy," Crow said.

"Well, start," she said loudly.

"Mrs. Chandler, you are out of order and overruled," Crow said firmly, rapping his gavel. He was getting tired of haggling, tired of challenges, very tired of Emmy Chandler, and just tired and fed up generally.

"You can go to hell, Cecil," she yelled, springing to her feet and shaking her finger at him angrily.

Crow looked at her for a moment before quietly saying, "The sergeant at arms will remove Mrs. Chandler from this meeting."

"Are you serious?" Albert Tenpenny asked. He was the officer called upon, but he was a man in his late sixties who was suffering from arthritis. Stretched out, he would have been five feet ten inches tall and a hundred and seventy pounds. His usual stooped height, however, was four inches shorter than his maximum. He wore his silver hair in braids that drooped forward to the middle of his chest. It was topped by a black felt western hat. He wore a beaded vest, blue jeans, and scuffed and worn western boots. In a physical struggle, he would have been no match for Emmy Chandler.

"Hold on there, Cec," Jordy Kelly said. "Havin' her removed by the sergeant at arms calls for a vote for her dismissal from the council, too. You know that, don't you?"

"Of course, I know that," Crow snapped. "But when she tells the chairman, whether it's me or someone else, to go to hell, she shouldn't be on the council in the first place. Her behavior lately doesn't measure up to council standards, either. She has an active restraining order against her. What else do you want?"

"What if she leaves voluntarily?"

Crow looked upward and heaved a great sigh, "She could remain on the council with a reprimand which would call for her immediate dismissal should her behavior breach protocol or decorum of behavior again."

"How about it, Emmy?" Kelly asked. "By sergeant at arms or on your own?"

"I'll leave on my own, and I'll decide on my own if I still want to be on a council with all you fine-haired sonsabitches," she said from the angry crouch of a crone as she slowly shook an accusatory finger at the men and women staring at her in disbelief. Then she stalked to the door which Tenpenny had opened for her. She grabbed the door and jerked it free so she could slam it against the wall. The doorknob punched a round hole in the drywall before it bounced back.

"Are we agreed that Mr. Tenpenny, by his assistance in opening the door, did indeed escort Mrs. Emmy Chandler from this chamber?" Crow said, resuming the meeting.

"So moved," said Billy Roundbelly. An instantaneous second followed.

"To remove a council member requires a unanimous vote of all those present, provided a quorum is present. The quorum having been reached, an anonymous vote of those present is hereby ordered. The sergeant at arms will hand each member a white and black glass ball. The members will file one at a time past the secretary and deposit the glass balls into the box. Dropping a black ball into the right side will signify the aye vote. At the same time, the second ball will be dropped to the left. A black ball to the right is a vote for expulsion. There will be no discussion during this process."

The voting took about ten minutes as each member passed by Tenpenny, who handed each a white and a black ball. Then, the voters moved past the box, which had a raised neck, ensuring that no one could see the color of the balls as they were dropped into the receptacle. When all the members were seated, Crow asked the secretary to simply look into the right side. "Is there a unanimous vote?" Crow asked.

"There is not," she said. No count of the dissenter or dissenters was given, and no one but the secretary ever knew the number of white balls that kept Emmy Chandler on the council. No one knew who dropped the white ball or balls, either.

"The motion fails for lack of a unanimous vote," Crow announced. "However, a letter of reprimand will be forwarded to Mrs. Chandler regarding her conduct. Any repeat of a like nature will be grounds for her dismissal by the chairman."

"I move that the chairman, Jordy Kelly, and Rory Blue be appointed to negotiate with Sheriff Yellowhenry, a raise, not to exceed three times the normal annual raise awarded to our tribal sheriffs," Si Huff said. A second followed.

Crow repeated the motion, and it was carried unanimously. To Crow's relief, the meeting was adjourned.

Chapter Thirty-Three

The meeting with Yellowhenry and the committee was a tense one. Chairman Crow's disapproval of Yellowhenry's suggestion that Enos Clay be promoted to serve as the next sheriff for the tribe was palpable. "This sounds like you've written us off before we have a chance to counteroffer," Crow said, his voice stiff with displeasure.

"No, that's not it at all, Cecil," he said. "Maybe you've forgotten that you came to me and said, "No raise and you are reprimanded.""

"Since then, the council has had a chance to reassess your work record," Crow retorted.

"Well, that's so noble of you all," Yellowhenry said. "All I did was cover my own ass. It was clear that you and the council were about one vote short of tying a can to my tail. Between you and Emmy Chandler, it became crystal clear that I am unwanted on the police force here. So, what's your problem, Cec? I thought I was taking the action you and the council wanted."

Rory Blue rose to his feet, "Cecil," he said, "It's pretty clear that you and your cohort have pissed in the spring water, and now you want Sheriff Yellowhenry to drink it. I find this whole exercise repugnant."

"I don't see that's what it is at all," Crow said. "We're here in good faith, making him an honest offer."

"I can't believe this," Kelly said. "You're rattling the oat bucket after the horse is out of the barn, Cecil, and you want Rory and me to stand beside you and try to pretend that the tribal council and you have behaved all along in good faith. Well, I'm not going to do that. Sheriff Yellowhenry, I wish you the best in this career move to Montana Highway Patrol. Just be assured that the door is always available on the reservation."

As the three councilmen walked out of the sheriff's office, Cecil Crow said indignantly, "Thanks a lot for all your support, boys."

"Good god, Cecil," Rory said, "go screw yourself."

Yellowhenry's interview with the state patrol in Helena followed a set of guidelines applicable to all prospective officers. He was told that his application was approved for a second interview. He was in a pool of three candidates who had, so to speak, made the cut for three job offerings. The second interview would establish his territory. He would most likely be assigned to the Havre office. However, there was no guarantee when dealing with a state bureaucracy. The bureau sometimes did the opposite of what, on the surface, seemed obvious.

The bureau did not obfuscate, and Joe Yellowhenry became Trooper Joe, assigned to the Havre office of the highway patrol beginning two weeks later. His first month on the job was a ride-along break-in and training period. The officer he was assigned to was Art McClintock, a veteran of twelve years on the job, who had transferred to Havre from Butte three months prior. The pair had not seen each other before, as no overlap cases between the reservation and patrol had occurred in that time. McClintock was a curious, bluff, abrupt man. Forty-some years of age and single, he looked a dozen years older than he was. His hair was an iron-gray buzzcut. He was a formidable presence at a very broad-shouldered, six feet four inches in height, and two hundred thirty pounds. Arms that hung to his knees and oversized hands lent his physique a rather simian look, especially when he was in his customary slumped posture. His face was craggy with a pronounced brow and dark eyebrows over one brown eye and one blue eye. He appeared nearly lipless as he possessed one of those slash mouths that was narrow below a Hitleresque brush of a dark brown mustache shot with gray. A pointed chin and the beginning droop of a double chin coupled with huge ears he could flap made him an arresting figure whose mere presence made people pause and cast sidelong glances.

It took a few glances to take him all in. He was a fitness addict who also loved keeping sharp on the shooting range. Despite his appearance, his moods ranged from kindness and humor, to occasional anger and rage. With a nearly genius IQ, he was a voracious reader on a wide variety of subjects, and he was the possessor of an insatiable curiosity which could, at times, make him tactless.

"You the breed to balance our equity, eh?" he grinned as he extended a hand that swallowed Yellowhenry's.

"I'm a half, so if that meets the criteria, I guess I am," Yellowhenry answered, his face flashing a startled expression.

McClintock laughed, "Take a good look, Joe." Then he flapped his ears. Yellowhenry burst into laughter. He couldn't help himself.

"Art," he said, "you could make money in a carnival doing that."

"You know," McClintock grinned, "when I was in high school, people thought so. In the A.S.B. fundraisers, I was the one to dunk in the tank, stick my mug out in the Halloween horror tunnel, or just sit in a booth and flap my ears for a nickel. I had a great time in those days. What the hell's with rocks in your pocket?"

"Oh, those," Yellowhenry said, "on the reservation, I bag my supper with 'em when I'm out for very long, and I run short of supplies. I guess I'll have to give that up."

"No shit?" McClintock said. "The first thing we're doin' today is goin' to the range, gettin' ready for our qualification test on sidearms. I want to see you throw a couple of those rocks."

The firing range was outdoors and removed three miles west of town on the way to Shelby. It was set up on state property that had been a gravel pit. A long, low building had been erected to accommodate indoor shooting on one side and sheltered long-distance shooting on the other. The indoor range was configured with mechanical target devices that ran targets out to fifty feet. Five open-faced stalls sectioned off the range, which was thirty feet wide. McClintock set up a paper target and ran it out to thirty feet. "Can you hit that with a rock, Joe?"

Yellowhenry shrugged out of his uniform jacket. "Where do you want me to hit it?" he asked.

"Right between the goddamned eyes," McClintock said.

The rock ripped through the target and shattered against the back wall with no discernible drop in velocity.

"Damn," Yellowhenry frowned, "that was my third most favorite rock."

"Holy shit, Joe!" McClintock said, shocked. "You coulda been a major league pitcher."

"Wrong color for that in my high school days," Yellowhenry laughed.

"My god, that rock went right through the center of the eyes on that target. Hell, I'd say if you can't shoot for shit, you could throw rocks. How'd you get so accurate?"

"Had to. To get a grouse, it's best to hit 'em in the head. They'll sit for you up to thirty feet or so. Body strikes tear 'em up pretty good. Rabbit's the same. Got to hit the head."

"Did you ever take down a man with a rock?"

"Talon Greene up in the Moose's Ass."

"Kill him?"

"No, I pulled my punch, so to speak. I just wanted him out cold. Not dead."

"Well, if I could throw like that, I'd carry rocks myself."

"It just takes practice. You start at fifteen feet and move out. A lot of it is in the rock. The best is water-tumbled pebbles. Specific size, shape, and weight."

"I've got enough to do to keep qualified on the old Roscoe. But I'd say you should keep sharpened up with your rocks," McClintock said.

The men practiced shooting for a half hour. It was concentrated at thirty feet. With ear protection in place, neither was interested in conversation. After fifty rounds with his Glock nine millimeter, Yellowhenry felt somewhat adequate. McClintock cut the ten ring out of every target he shot. "I'd get a Sig if I was you," he told Yellowhenry.

"I'll get along with department issues. Have to put in a septic tank, running hot and cold water, and an electric foot pump in my well."

"You live on the rez, and you're staying there, eh?"

"That's the plan."

"Family man?"

"Wife and three kids. Two from her former husband. Marvin Fletcher. Killed in a traffic stop. You probably heard. It was four years ago, and the killer was never caught. We have a baby daughter of our own now."

"Handy for you, eh?"

Yellowhenry looked at the man and stepped back. "Art, my family is my business. If I want you rooting around in it, I'll give you an engraved invitation. Is that okay with you?"

McClintock grinned, "I like that, Trooper Joe. You got some spine. A guy to ride the river with. No offense intended."

"We'll see about that, Art."

"Hey, okay, okay," Art laughed. "I get it. Too much, too soon, but I got a good feelin' about you, Joe. Let's go check out your cruiser. Hey, come to think of it, how'd you get here this morning?"

"Sheriff Enos Clay gave me a lift."

"Still friendly with the rez police, eh?"

"No reason not to be," Yellowhenry answered.

"So, no bad blood. You left for more money, eh?"

"Something like that."

"Oh, you're the guy," Art beamed. "The papers called it 'The Last Pony War' down in Butte. Had your horse in jail under protective custody. We laughed ourselves sick."

"Yeah, I'm the guy," Yellowhenry frowned.

"Hey, I won't pry. But, man, that was epic. Someday, you have to tell me what the hell went down in that conflict, eh?"

"Maybe, someday. Don't hold your breath."

"Moving along, then," McClintock chuckled. "Jump in the buggy, and we'll run back to the equipment yard." The ride back was taken in silence. Yellowhenry stared out the side window at the flat, featureless terrain. McClintock whistled softly and tonelessly, apparently dry of questions. When they pulled into the yard, he said, "You'll get that car up on the rack in the shop. It's three years old, a quarter of a million miles, and an oil pan leak the mechanics are takin' care of. The car will be cycled out at the end of the year, and you'll move up to a two-year-old unit. And so on, eh?"

"Yeah, I get it," Yellowhenry said. "I'll get hand-me-downs for years. Maybe always. Doesn't matter to me as long as they run."

"It's the way of the world for rookies, Trooper Joe. Seniority rules, eh?"

"I'm not here to complain about the cruisers I drive, Art. Since I'll be ridin' with you for a month, that will give me time to make sure my piece of shit is at least tuned up."

"Ho, I like that, Joe. You're gonna be all right. I'm tellin' you, I got a good feelin'. Let's see how long before they drop the rack."

The two officers walked into the office, and McClintock spoke to a man dressed like a mechanic in greasy coveralls. "Hey, Bert," he asked, "how long till you drop the one on the rack?"

"Hey, Art. Not today. Waiting on a fuel pump and a power steering pump. Coming out of a warehouse in Salt Lake City. Got the oil leak stopped, then the sonofabitch started dumping brake fluid. Damned near had a fire. If I'd been smart, I would let it burn. Got that fixed, and it started dumping power steering fluid."

Art looked at Yellowhenry, "Sorry, Joe. You might be better off on your horse, eh?"

"I'll make do, Art. I'll need a ride to and from home until I'm checked out a set of wheels."

"Bert, we got anything. Joe can run back and forth from the rez until his beauty gets fixed?"

"He can use the parts runner as long as it's left here for us during the day."

"Perfect, he'll be ridin' with me for a month."

"We'll want to put a tarp in there for a seat cover. Get him a pair of gloves. It's a greasy old dog, but it's a runner."

"Good enough," Yellowhenry said. "I'll take it."

"Then, let's hit the high and dusty," Art beamed. "We'll run out to Shelby, make a couple of traffic stops, and have lunch. Addy's Bar and Grill. The greatest toasted tuna fish sandwich you ever locked a lip on, Joe."

Shelby was a hundred miles to the west on the Highline, the road that ran along roughly parallel to the Canadian border thirty to sixty miles to the south. They made two traffic stops, one for crossing over the yellow line, and one for an expired license plate on a trailer. McClintock had Yellowhenry shadow him so he could hear what was said. His style was friendly and folksy, almost to the point of being apologetic. Still, he wrote both citations.

"Do you ever give warnings?" Yellowhenry asked.

"Sure, after my quota."

"Quota? No one said anything about that. So, what's the quota?"

"Well, Trooper Joe, no one ever will say anything either."

"What's your personal number?"

"It varies depending on the type I've written. It's just understood that half of what you make needs to be generated through citations. It runs between twenty and forty for me. I'd guess fifteen to twenty-five for you. With radar, cutting the nut is much easier than it used to be. You won't have any trouble making a quota. I wouldn't worry about it."

"Radar? There's no speed limit," Yellowhenry said.

"Oh, yes, there is, my man. It's fifty-five at night. No grace, either. You'll have your shot at night shifts when you need 'em. The stops have to pay you in cash or in kind at the time of the stops, or they spend the night in jail. You can score some booty you wouldn't believe. They offer guns, cameras, sports equipment, jewelry, and anything of value to cover twenty-five bucks. You pay the fine in cash and convert the booty into so much more. It's an unspoken perk."

"Oh, I won't do that," Yellowhenry said.

"That's what they all say," McClintock said. Yellowhenry's private thinking was a turmoil of duty and guilt. He knew that he would be more of a teacher than a legal grifter, preying on the people he encountered. How that would play in Peoria was anybody's guess.

Chapter Thirty-Four

After Yellowhenry pulled up to his home that night in the parts runner, he took a new look at his neighborhood. The street was in disrepair, and the properties along it were no better. Even though his own place, with its dirt yard and wooden walkway to the front door, was upscale, it seemed unkempt. Other properties on the street had weed-filled yards with footpaths. Amy was walking with a five-gallon bucket toward the yard pump to get the evening's water. His thoughts went to the homes off the reservation with their neat lawns and white picket fences. It occurred to him that a place like that on his street would cause discrimination against his family. He decided to talk to Amy and Minnie before launching his home improvement plans.

"Why don't you add a second story while you're at it?" Minnie said when he laid out what he had in mind. "Build a garage to put your police car in. Add one of those white picket fences with rose bushes."

"I take it you aren't high on whitening up the place," Yellowhenry chuckled.

"There's stuff you can do, but I wouldn't do it to the outside."

"I would like running water in the house," Amy said. "I'd like to take a bath in a tub, pull the plug, and let the water drain out."

"What about that, Minnie?" Yellowhenry asked.

"Why are you asking me these questions?" she demanded.

"Because I honor the wisdom of elders," he answered.

"Elders, my ass. It was elders who fought the Horse War against you," Minnie said.

"Well, there was that," he agreed. "So, how far should I go with improvements and still live here."

"Hot and cold running water. A cesspool until you install a commode. Let the people get used to your extravagances before you burn your outhouse. Maybe share the improvements once in a while. You know, have some of the boys over for coffee so they can see what turning on a faucet in a home is like. Let them see what they're keeping from their women. Ease into your upgraded lifestyle. As a highway patrolman, it will be expected and, over time, accepted."

"Amy, what do you think?"

"Anything. Cold running water and a bathtub that drains."

"We're going with Minnie. We'll still use the outhouse, but we'll start with a bathtub, hot water tank, and a drain into a cesspool."

"Where are you puttin' the bathtub?" Minnie asked.

"A bathroom," Yellowhenry answered.

"Where?" Amy wondered, looking around. "We got a living room, a nursery, a kitchen, and two bedrooms."

"The nursery was my mudroom. It's in the back of the house where pipes can be brought in, and a cesspool can be dug. We can put a false wall in there. There will be room for a tub and a sink. Eventually, a commode. We'll have it plumbed so that we can add a septic tank at some point in the future," he said. "The front part of that room can still be the nursery. Smaller, but I don't think Bella will care."

"You need a plumber, honey," Amy said. "With your new job, 1 don't want to watch you shoveling away for six months with a winter in between."

"We'll have to pay a bunch for one of those, Ames," he pointed out.

"I still have some money, and with your new job, we can borrow the rest."

"Eeee," he said with a grimace. "Banks and redskins rarely mix."

"Well, you aren't one of those; you are a highway patrolman. If they don't give you a loan, you can hound them on the highway," she grinned.

"I'll see a couple of plumbers and get estimates. A banker can probably give us a heads up on a reputable plumber."

"I can't wait," Minnie said. "I get the second bath in Amy's new tub."

The two estimates shocked Yellowhenry. One was for twenty-five hundred, and the other was twenty-seven ninety-five. Between him and Amy, they pooled a thousand dollars. On a lunch break, when he was in town, he called on the

Havre First State Bank. In his uniform, Yellowhenry cut an impressive figure. The loan officer looked at the estimates. "This is going into your home on the reservation?"

"It is," Yellowhenry answered. "We were hoping you could help us select the plumber."

"We can do that, but I can't approve a home improvement loan on the reservation because we can't place a surety lien on the property," the officer said. "You'll have to apply for a personal loan with our bank's vice-president. He's Mr. VanDyke. If you'll come with me, I'll introduce you."

VanDyke was a small man with a toilet bowl fringe around his bald head. He looked over the estimates. "You're that Yellowhenry who was the tribal sheriff?"

"Yes. I'm a trooper with the highway patrol now."

"Damned good job. Better than your sheriff gig, but I must tell you the Horse War was some of the best reading I've had in the last ten years. I'll be proud to give you a personal loan. But, Mr. Yellowhenry, these bids are way out of line. This is your basic two thousand dollar job. Go see Hugh Roberts at All Clear Plumbing Service. Don't tell him about these bids. Just tell him I recommended him. Then come back, and we'll get you signed up."

A week later, Yellowhenry was back with a seventeen hundred and twenty-five dollar bid sheet from All Clear Plumbing Service. "There you go, a reasonable bid," VanDyke said. "Hugh will do it right, too. You'll be happy with how completely he does this stuff. Pay him twelve hundred up front and the rest upon completion. It's standard practice in the industry."

It took another month to complete the work. Yellowhenry put up the divider wall himself. He and Amy took the first bath together after putting the kids to bed. Later, Amy swore that was when she began expecting again. Minnie came over the following morning. Her bath was taken with bubbles. She delighted in the experience so much that Amy assured her she could have a tub bath whenever she felt like it.

Yellowhenry's cruiser was finally put together. The front seat on the driver's side was crushed out of shape, so he drove to the local wrecking yard and made a deal on a replacement seat. His submission for reimbursement was turned down. He didn't object, but he didn't forget, either. With a month of running patrol on his own under his belt, he felt like he was getting the hang of the job. Then, the captain called him in for a one-on-one conference. The captain was a spare sixty-two-year-old veteran of the force. With a full head of iron-grey hair, bristling eyebrows, a beaked nose, and a downward-turning mouth, John Harbold looked severe and sour. Most of the time, he was just that.

"Captain Harbold," Yellowhenry said, "I was told you wanted to see me."

"Yes, Trooper Joe," Harbold said. "we haven't had a chance to sit down and chew the fat. I always like to do that with my new men after they've been out on their own for a few weeks. How are you feeling about the place?"

"I'm getting more comfortable as time goes on. Art was a good instructor. He still helps with my questions."

"Good. That's good he's helpin'. Seems like a good man. Hasn't been here all that long, either. You were a tribal sheriff, is that right?"

"Yes Sir."

"Just for my own curious goddamned self, what spurred you to tie your horse up on Main Street?"

"Well," Yellowhenry said, looking down. "I probably shouldn't have done that."

"If you did it as the chief law enforcement officer, why would you want to back water on it now?"

"A lot of embarrassment to some people who didn't really deserve it."

"Oh, come on, Joe," Harbold snorted, "you jailed that horse, too. Did you not?"

"I did do that after threats were made to shoot him."

"Hah! I knew there was a good reason. Protective custody, by god. You know, I've been with the patrol forty years and never had anything that good happen to me or around me. Why would you want to leave a job like that?"

"Pay and the threat to can me," Yellowhenry smiled.

"Two damned good reasons. So, let me assure you that sort of thing won't happen with you as a state trooper. Of course, you won't have to jail a horse either."

"I won't miss that."

"Yeah, I see your point," Harbold laughed. "Got something to show you, though, that is peculiar to this office," Harbold said, pulling out stacks of copies of citations. All of them contained twenty to thirty sheets. The last, only five. "You know what these are, don't you?"

"Copies of citations written by officers."

"Yes. Now, there are a dozen officers working the three shifts out of this office seven days a week. I don't espouse a quota. But, look at these stacks," he said, pulling out stacks that contained three to seven sheets, except for the last, which was twenty items thick. "You know what these are, too, don't you?"

"Warnings," Yellowhenry said.

"Right now, I don't expect you to write as many tickets as the rest, but I've noticed you've warned a few of the subjects of these stops three times. Is there some reason why?"

"I guess I have the attitude of teaching as much as punishing."

"I thought so, and I believe in encouraging corrective behavior. But some folks will start to feel like they don't have to take you seriously. They'll think the only thing you ever do is write warnings. Then, when you need them to take decisive action for their own good, they won't do that either."

"Yeah, I think so," Yellowhenry answered.

"You don't have to be a prick about it, but you do need to be in charge of your territory. It's a rather fine line. You just can't be everyone's best friend. Nice chat, Trooper Joe. Thanks for stoppin'."

Chapter Thirty-Five

With the meeting terminated abruptly, Yellowhenry walked out to his cruiser and drove east out the Highline toward Saco, ninety miles away. He drove at a comfortable sixty miles per hour. The weather was warm and pleasant on a late October Tuesday morning. Traffic was light, and driving was moderately fast. There were a couple of places where he could pull over on a point high enough and perpendicular to the road that his cruiser could be seen by traffic coming from both directions for a mile. He turned on his radar unit just to watch the traffic reaction. He found it amusing that cars dropped suddenly from seventy-five and eighty to sixty-five or less by the time they passed where he was.

He was about to pull out when a car coming from the east coasted past and came to a stop on the shoulder of the highway a little beyond where Yellowhenry was parked. He got out of the car and waited to see what was wanted. A good-looking woman dressed in typical ranch wear came striding to where Yellowhenry was standing at the front fender of his vehicle. "Can I help you?" he asked.

"I hope so," she said. "My husband's missing."

"Missing or just late getting home?"

"I'd like to think late, but yesterday, he was out looking for a stock that got out of a pasture. He didn't come home last night and is still not back."

"Okay, what's your husband's name?"

"Roy. Roy Malone. He's thirty-three, six feet tall, a hundred and eighty-five pounds. Brown hair and eyes. He is a veteran of the war in Iraq. I mention that because he lost his left hand. He wears a hook on that arm. He was wearing a black hat and a dark brown duster over a sheepskin vest. I'm telling you all this because I know that's the kind of description you policemen like to have."

Yellowhenry had his pocket tablet out and was writing as fast as he could in cop's shorthand. "Okay, I think I've got it. What's your name?"

"Mrs. Malone."

"I mean your first name, mam."

"Carolyn. Carolyn Susan Malone."

"All right, Mrs. Malone. Where was he going to check on the stock?"

"He took a horse in the pickup and drove to up back of our place.. The stock could be five, maybe six miles out."

"That doesn't seem so far a distance that you couldn't check on him yourself or a hired man could do it."

"The road's too rough for the car, and I can't leave the kids. We don't have a hired man."

"The kids?"

"We have one-year-old triplets. They're in the backseat of the car."

"Carolyn, have you called this into the sheriff's office?"

"No phone. I know you sit here, so I took a chance you'd be here today."

"Where's your ranch?"

"Five miles north and two miles east of Dodson. It's the Bar H Seven. Branded on the gate post."

"Let me call this in, and we'll get the sheriff's office activated. Then you and I will drive to your ranch. See if your husband has come back. Oh, by the way, did the horse happen to come back on its own."

"Not by the time I left to come out for help."

"Give me a minute to call in, then I'll follow you to your ranch."

Twenty minutes later, Yellowhenry was bumping along the rutted road that led to the Malone ranch house. The complex of buildings was set so that the house and barn were separated by a spacious yard. He pulled off to the side of the two-story house behind Carolyn's car. He helped her carry her children into the house and then walked out to the barn. The gate from the barn into the corral was open, and the gate from the corral into a fenced pasture that extended over a hill and was out of sight was also open. He found the horse standing in the breezeway of the barn with its head down and the saddle turned under its belly. He looked the horse over for injury, straightened the saddle, and walked the horse around for a bit. He didn't find anything amiss, so he tied it up to the corral and walked back to the house.

He knocked on the door, and when Carolyn answered, he said, "The horse is back. I'm gonna ride him back the way he came. I didn't see another horse or mule."

"We just have the one."

"Okay. Saddlebags?"

"In the tack room."

"All right. When the sheriff's office guys get here, tell 'em where to go."

"Is he gonna be all right?" she asked, suddenly tearful.

"I'm sure. He probably got thrown by his horse. I expect to find him walkin' back. Should know in two or three hours. I'll take my first aid kit just in case."

"How will you know where to look?" she asked.

"I am half Cree. Still live on the reservation where I've lived all my life. I know how to track animals comin' and goin'. I'll find your husband, Mrs. Malone, by backtracking his horse."

He left her and moved his cruiser down to the corral. From the trunk he pulled out his first aid kit. He also grabbed his old saddle gun and a carton of ammunition. He also exchanged his troopers hat and jacket for a camo cap and sweatshirt. He walked into the barn and located the tackroom. With the kit and ammo tucked into the saddle bags, and the saddle gun in its scabbard strapped on, he mounted the horse and rode back the way it had come.

The horse had come, once it got its head, in a beeline for the barn. The country was a jumble of rock ridges and dried shin-high grass that broke off with every hoof strike. Yellowhenry found where the stock had broken through the back line fence of the pasture. The horse had returned that way. Once he found the line of travel the horse had covered approaching the downed fence, the trail led out directly for a high ridge that loomed across the northern horizon a few miles ahead. When he topped out on high points, he could see a line of green at the base of the ridge. A half-hour later, he spotted the ranch truck parked on a road that rose out of a low draw off to the west a mile or so. Yellowhenry trotted that way.

The truck was empty, and there was no sign of anything or anyone around it except for where the rancher had unloaded the horse and ridden toward the big ridge. Yellowhenry followed the tracks for a half hour toward where he could see a concentration of magpies. When the horse began to shy and bob its head, he said soothingly, "Whoa boy, what do you smell?" The horse became more agitated the further they went, so Yellowhenry rode off at an angle toward a higher point he hoped would give him a view. The line of vegetation was an extensive growth of willows that marked the course of a stream along the bottom of the long ridge. He could see a few head of cattle well up on its flanks. All of them were nervous and looking down at the bottom. He reached into a saddle bag and pulled out his binoculars. The horse was looking at something that was moving around in the willows.

"Oh, shit," Yellowhenry breathed. "Grizzly." He watched for a few minutes until he had figured out that the bear was feeding on a dead Hereford bull. It was about four hundred yards off, and the wind was blowing lightly from where the bear was feeding toward Yellowhenry. He dismounted and led the horse back the way they had come so it was out of sight of the bear. He pulled his rifle from its scabbard and checked its loads. After anchoring the horse's bridle reins in the rocks, he circled back around into a low swale out of sight of the bear and into the willows. He walked in a careful, quiet crouch just inside the line of willows and upwind toward where the bear was feeding.

Using his binoculars every few seconds, he scanned the ground between him and the bear. When he was two hundred yards or so from where the big animal was feeding, he saw in the willows what he was looking for. The prone body of a man lay with his left arm thrown over the back of his head. The end of the arm was a hook. Yellowhenry studied the figure for a couple of minutes without dropping his binoculars. Then the hooked arm moved to help lever the man toward the water that was pooled ten feet in front of him in the willows. With what appeared to be superhuman effort, the rancher heaved himself up to his hands and knees and slowly began crawling ahead.

"Oh, Christ, no!" Yellowhenry wanted to shout. Instead, he moved out of the willows for a better line of sight, sat down on his butt, and braced his elbows on his knees. The distance from the crawling man to the bear was only seventy-five yards. The big animal could cover that in three or four seconds. It took a moment before the bear noticed the man moving. Then it roared and charged. Yellowhenry began firing as soon as the bear turned. He continued shooting as fast as he could work the lever action on his .30-30. His first two shots seemed to have no effect, but his third hit the bear's right shoulder, causing him to stumble. His fourth caught the bear in the right rib as it reached the man who had plunged off the bank into the water pool. The shot caused the eruption of a great bawl, and the grizzly spun as if to swat at a mighty hornet that had just stung its side. Then it sprinted back toward where it had been feeding and disappeared into the willows.

Yellowhenry was instantly on his feet and racing to the stream's edge, where the rancher was floating belly down in the shallow pool. He dropped his rifle on the bank and jumped to the man's side, pulling his head up by the hair. Malone, who had been sucking in great gulps of water, groaned, "Lemme drown."

"Not a chance," Yellowhenry said, pulling the man to his back, using the water's buoyancy to jerk him back to the water's edge and out onto the bank. He took a quick look at the man's injuries. The bear had attempted to kill him with bites to the back of the head, but the metal hook had kept its jaws from closing enough for the bites to be fatal. They had, however, partially scalped him, and Yellowhenry had nearly completed the task when he pulled Malone's face out of the water. He pushed the hair and scalp back into place as well as he could. The bear had clawed and bitten arms, legs, butt, and face. How badly Yellowhenry couldn't tell from all the blood and mud that coated the man. His only thought was to get Malone the hell out of there before the bear returned.

"You've got to help me, Roy," he demanded. "Let's get you to your feet."

"Who are you?" Malone mumbled. "Just let me go. I can't stand up. Bear gets me every time. Save yourself and let me die," he groaned. "My god, my ribs. He broke every fuckin' rib I got."

"Oh, bullshit, Roy. I'm Joe Yellowhenry, and I've seen sicker cows than you get well. Now, come on, your wife and kids are waitin' for ya."

Malone cursed and moaned as Yellowhenry dragged him to his feet. Fortunately, his legs suffered no broken bones, and after picking up his rifle with his left hand, Yellowhenry reached around with his right hand gripped Malone's belt, and started him walking. Apparently inspired to live, he was able to help himself admirably. Adrenaline surged through him as Yellowhenry kept insisting that they had to get the hell out of there before that damned bear came back. "He ain't gonna go far before he comes back to defend that bull, Roy. We don't want to be here when he does. My .30-30 won't do much more than piss him off."

After what seemed forever, the men reached the horse. By turning the animal downhill and positioning Malone on the uphill side, Yellowhenry managed to heave him into the saddle where he sat weaving and threatening to fall off. "My ass, my ass. It's all torn up," he wailed.

"Goddamnit, Roy," Yellowhenry shouted, "get a grip. Stand in the stirrups. If you fall off, we're both fucked." The tongue-lashing seemed to have the desired effect as Malone stiffened in the seat and gripped the saddle horn with his right hand. Yellowhenry led the horse to the ranch truck while keeping a close eye on its rider.

He eased Malone off the horse's back and lugged him to the passenger's side, where he opened the door and shoved him inside. With the truck started and warming up, he pulled the gear from the horse and turned it loose with a slap on its butt that sent it on its way toward the ranch headquarters. Then he plundered his first aid kit and wrapped Malone's head wounds with a roll of gauze. He gave him a handful of aspirin, which Malone chewed and swallowed dry. After tossing the saddle and bridle into the back of the truck and setting the tailgate back into place, Yellowhenry began the long, slow drive back to the ranch house.

As they drove, between bouts of painful moaning, Malone filled Yellowhenry in on what had happened. "I lost my best bull to that goddamned bear. It must have been about noon when I was ridin' alongside the willows to a crossing when my horse suddenly shied and turned tail. Dumped me. Bear came boilin' out of where he had the bull down and had me before I could run twenty feet. Blew me down to my belly and went for my head. I crossed my arms over the back of my head and held on. Shook me like a rat. Just sat down on his haunches and lifted me clear off the ground. I played possum. Funny thing. I didn't feel anything. After a while, he left, and I got up to run. He was back on me in an instant. Dragged me that time, probably thirty or forty yards. It struck me that he was gonna kill me and stash me for later. I must have blacked out, so he figured he'd killed me. He dropped me and clawed some branches and dirt over the top of me. I came to just before dark. Got up to leave, and that sonofabitch was still there.

"Down I go again with him all over me. That time, he didn't shake me. He just went to bitin' my arms, back, and legs. Pumped up and down on me with his front legs. I could hear my ribs crack and break. Finally grabbed me by my ass and dragged me some more. I blacked out again. Didn't come to it until way after daylight. Heard him workin' over my bull. Growlin' and runnin' around chasin' the birds when they got too close. He'd covered me with grass and dirt again. I got a little smarter and didn't stand up. I was diein' of thirst, so I started crawlin' toward the crick. I'd crawl and stop, crawl and stop. I guess that's when you came up. I'd just got to my hands and knees when I heard him comin'. I figured to hell with it. If he's gonna kill me, he'll do it with me takin' my last drink of water. Then you started shootin'. Funny thing about it, the only thing that mattered was gettin' that last damned drink of water. More critical than dyin.' Why do you suppose that was? Bein' thirsty meant more than diein'."

"I don't know its importance, but bein' so thirsty has to do with blood loss, Roy," Yellowhenry answered. "You've lost quite a bit."

"Christ, I'm covered in it," he said, trying to wipe it off.

"Hey, stop that," Yellowhenry commanded. "You'll just start some of those cuts to bleedin' again. You got to hang onto all you've got."

"I don't want Carolyn to see me like this. It'd turn her stomach."

"She's better than that, Roy. Give her some credit."

Malone started to weep, "I know it, Joe. How does a guy like me end up with a woman like her? I don't deserve a woman like her."

"Roy, none of us who get lucky enough to get a good woman ever deserve 'em. Just count yourself fortunate and take the best care of her that you can."

"Like stayin' away from bears," Malone actually chuckled through his tears.

"Yeah, like that. Just remember, there's stuff worse than bear bites, too. Stuff that hurts a woman's heart," Yellowhenry said.

"I know. That's why I said I don't deserve her."

"Well, all right then," Yellowhenry said, cutting off too personal a conversation, "I'll take you at your word. The details are your business, not mine. We don't have time for it, anyway. We're just about to your house. There's someone out in the yard waitin' for us."

Yellowhenry pulled to a stop near the ranch house and stepped out of the truck. He caught Carolyn before she could get to where her husband sat slumped against the passenger side door. "He'll be all right, Mrs. Malone. He was attacked by a bear. I got him out in time. What hospital do you want him taken to?"

"Hospital? Can't I just take care of him here?"

"He needs blood and stitchin' up. A lot of broken bones. Where do you want him to go?"

"Can he make it to Havre?"

"Yes."

"Havre General, then. Are you takin' him?"

"Yes. Put some hay and water out for your horse. He'll be back by tonight," Yellowhenry said.

"Hey, Trooper," a Phillips County deputy sheriff called as he walked hurriedly toward the truck, "could I talk to you for a minute. I need to file a report on this."

"Help me get him into the back seat of my car. Ask your questions while we do that."

"I have a form. You'll need to sign it."

"I'd rather Malone not die, deputy, while we were going over your goddamned form," Yellowhenry growled. "Now give me a hand. Mail your form to the highway patrol in Havre. I'll fill it out and send it back."

"My sheriff isn't gonna like this."

"Tell your sheriff he can kiss my ass. That should help keep him from kickin' yours."

Malone began moaning and cursing as the men pulled him down from the cab of the truck. "Carolyn, Carolyn," he shouted when he got to where he could stand. "Where's Carolyn?"

"Roy," Yellowhenry yelled, "she's in the house getting your kids ready to go to the hospital. Come on, let's get you into the car."

"I have to see her. I have to tell her I love her. That I always did," Malone suddenly began sobbing.

"There'll be plenty of time for that, Roy. Right now we need to get you to a doctor."

"Joe, I'm afraid I'm not gonna make it," he moaned.

"All right, get in the car. I'll go get her so you can talk to her for a minute. Just let's get you into the car."

"Promise me, Joe," he said, desperation straining his voice.

"You got it, Roy," Yellowhenry said as he helped him stretch out on the backseat of the patrol car. "I'll be right back." Then he ran for the ranch house. He bounded into the living room and began shouting for Carolyn.

She came to the head of the stairs, "What? What's happened?" she said as she hurried down.

"Roy has to see you for a minute before we leave."

Carolyn squeezed into the back seat and sat listening as her husband raved. She stroked his face, and Yellowhenry could see her smiling as she spoke reassuringly. She finally helped him lay his head down, and she kissed his forehead. She sat back and wiped tears from her cheeks before slowly backing out. She stood up. "He's gone," she said simply. She walked past Yellowhenry and the deputy sheriff and into the house.

"Does she mean he's dead?" the deputy asked, astonished.

"I think so. Get on the horn and call your county coroner. Might as well run it through your office. I'm sure your boss will want to come out and strut around."

"Okay. Who are you, anyway?"

"Joe Yellowhenry. Montana Highway Patrol."

"Well, I'm Will Peters, Phillips County Deputy Sheriff, Joe. It's good to meet you."

"Same here," Yellowhenry said. "I'm going to check and see if Malone really is dead. Go make your call."

The inspection took only a few moments. There was no hope. Blood was pouring from Malone's mouth, and he was staring fixedly with wide-open eyes. Yellowhenry checked for breathing and for a pulse. He got nothing, so he closed Malone's eyes, closed the back door, and wearily climbed into the front. He called in and related what had happened. He was asked to stand by.

A few minutes later, his radio squawked, and Captain Harbold said, "You're sure the man is dead, Joe?"

"Yes Sir."

"All right, you'll have to stay there until the coroner gets there and confirms the death. Is there somewhere there for you to stay overnight if you have to?"

"I'll be all right. Would you mind letting my wife know?"

"You got it, Joe. We'll see you tomorrow. Check in before you leave."

"Will do."

The coroner didn't make an appearance until eight-thirty. In the meantime, the sheriff had come out to the ranch along with members of the media. Yellowhenry made himself scarce by retreating to the barn so the sheriff could swagger and bloviate. Mrs. Malone remained in seclusion. When the media had the story and left, Yellowhenry came out of the barn from taking care of the Malone horse, which had come back. He answered the sheriff's and coroner's questions so they could complete their reports. The coroner certified the death as injuries received from a bear attack. The sheriff wanted to know where the bear was last seen, and Yellowhenry pinpointed it for him on a map.

It was close to ten by the time the sheriff and coroner pulled out. Yellowhenry decided to check on the widow. A light was still on in the house, so he knocked on the door. She answered and asked, "Mr. Yellowhenry, is there something you need?"

"No, ma'am," he answered, "we are finished out here, and I just wanted to check on you before I leave."

"Do you have time for a cup of coffee?"

"That's not necessary," he said. "I'm okay."

"It's not really for you, as much as it is for me," she said. "Please come in. I'd like to talk for a while."

"Well, all right," he said.

They sat at the kitchen table. She talked, and he listened. "I've only been back in the house for a month," she began. "Roy had been married twice before. Neither lasted more than a year. He just had a wandering eye, and he was too damned good-looking for his own good. Women swarmed him at dances, stared at him in restaurants, and offered themselves to him. We were only married six months when he was seduced by a woman in Glendive. He'd gone down there to buy a bull and had to stay for a weekend. I was eight months pregnant, so you can tell by the math that I seduced him, too, before we got married. The thing about it was that it was so easy to get along with him. We never fought, and he was thoughtful and helpful.

"I guess it was too good to be true. Well, he admitted to a one-night fling with that woman in Glendive and asked for forgiveness. I forgave him, of course. With the babies on the way, I was desperate to have a husband. When I had the triplets, I was amazed and so happy. He was just the best father. Proud. We had two little boys and a girl. Boyd and Lloyd after his father and my grandfather, and Nicole after my late sister.

"Then we were in town shopping in Glasgow when the kids were eight months old. We have a triple stroller, and I was pushing the kids down the street when this pregnant young woman came jay-walking toward us. Roy said kind of quickly that he saw a gun in a store window we'd just passed, and he was gonna check it out. He ducked into the store just as the woman stepped up onto the sidewalk. 'I see he gave you triplets, Mrs. Malone. He only gave me twins,' she announced. Then she followed him into the store, where I heard them shouting at each other. When he came out, you could see her handprint on his face where she had slapped him. He acted guilty as hell. I didn't say anything till we got back to the car. I didn't ask him to admit a damned thing. My folks live in Miles City, and I told him straight out. 'Take me there.'

"Our separation lasted until just before the kids' birthdays last month. Thank God we were back together, and he was there for that. I'll miss him, of course, but strangely, I do not feel a lot of grief. It's the loneliness that's going to be difficult. Despite his infidelity, he was just so easy to get along with. He was a man who should have had five wives at the same time. He and all of them would have been so happy."

"Well, Carolyn," Yellowhenry said, "how you grieve if you do is no one's business but yours. If you don't mind my asking, what are you going to do now that he's gone?"

"Well, since you asked," she smiled. "The one thing Roy did for me, for which I will be forever grateful, was to take out a life insurance policy for a hundred thousand dollars. I'll sell the ranch, too. He inherited it, free and clear, from his father. I'm going to be here for another few months, I'd guess, until I get all my paperwork handled and the money banked. Then I'm moving to town. I don't know where, but I'm going to live where there are people."

"You strike me as a people person, Carolyn," he said. "Moving to town would suit you. Well, I'd better be going." He yawned widely as he spoke.

"Joe," she said quickly, "you should stay here tonight. We have a guest room with a good bed. You have to be exhausted. I'd feel horrible if you tried driving and fell asleep at the wheel. Please, I'd be so grateful if you were in the house tonight."

"Thank you, but it would be best if I bunked in the barn."

"No. I will not have a Montana State Patrolman as a guest at my ranch sleeping in the barn. That, I won't tolerate, Joe."

"Well, since you put it that way, where is your guest room?"

"Follow me," she said as she rose from the table and took the stairs to the second story.

The guest room was down a wide hall with three bedrooms on either side. The last room on the left was the one she showed him. He thanked her, and since he didn't have an overnight kit, he simply undressed and stretched out on the turned-down bed. He went to sleep almost immediately. Three hours later, he was disturbed by Carolyn as she crawled into bed behind him. Completely startled, he sat up and blurted, "What are you doing here?"

"I have to be with someone tonight. I can't sleep, and my conscience is driving me crazy. I'm not here for sex, Joe. Please lie down and let me hold you."

"Okay," he said, "but you understand this is all in the line of duty."

"I do," she agreed. "And I'll never tell anyone, either."

He lay back down with her cuddled behind him and her left arm thrown around him. She was asleep in moments. Yellowhenry lay as still as a man in a coma. After an hour of listening to her deep rhythmic breathing, he dozed. He never really slept. They were not intimate.

Chapter Thirty-Six

Yellowhenry's quiet return was anything but. The local newspaper and radio station wanted sit-down interviews. A TV station out of Great Falls had a team on site for a recorded report they hoped to air that night. Captain Harbold had called the Phillips County Sheriff, Al Sparks, to see if next of kin had been notified. Sparks had sent Deputy Sheriff Will Peters back to the ranch to ask Carolyn Malone about releasing her husband's identity. She approved the release, and Peters radioed the news back to Sparks, who relayed it to Harbold. He sicced the ghouls on Yellowhenry.

The newspaper took the first shot. "Mr. Yellowhenry, why was Roy Malone attacked by the bear?"

"He rode too close to a kill the bear had made. His horse shied, dumping him to the ground. The bear caught him as he tried to run."

"This happened three days ago from what we've been told, and yet, he was alive for you to rescue the following day. Why was that possible if the bear killed him when he was first attacked?"

"He wasn't killed outright."

"So, that means he was attacked again?"

"Twice."

"How do you know that?"

"He told me."

"Why wouldn't the bear just have killed him?"

"Malone wore a hook on his left arm. Kept the bear from delivering a fatal bite to his head and neck. Malone passed out. Bear thought he was dead. Scratched debris over him both times."

"Did the bear maul him three times, then?"

"Yes."

"If the bear thought he was dead, why did he cover Malone? Why wouldn't he just have fed on him?"

"The bear was gorged on a bull he had killed. He was stashin' Malone for later."

"Did he describe the attacks at all?"

"Lot of biting. Stomping. Dragging. Bowling him over as he was running. Broke most of his ribs."

"How did you figure out how to stop the attacks?"

"I shot the bear. Hit him hard enough to turn him and run him off. I wish I'd had a heavier rifle than a .30-30. Wouldn't have saved Malone, but the bear wouldn't still be out there wounded."

"When you shot the bear, was he attacking you?"

"No. He was after Malone again."

"That would be four times, wouldn't it?"

"Yes."

"What was Malone doing while you were shooting at the bear? Weren't you in danger of hitting Malone?"

"He was crawlin', tryin' to reach the creek for a drink of water. Said he didn't care if the bear killed him as long as he got a drink first."

"How did you get Malone out of there?"

"I got him to stand up and helped him walk to the horse. Managed to get him aboard and led the horse to the pickup he'd driven up there to look for stray stock."

"What happened at the pickup?"

"I started the rig, loaded Malone, and stripped the horse of gear before turning him loose. Then I drove back to the ranch house."

"When you reached the house, what happened?"

"With the help of Phillips County Deputy Sheriff Will Peters, we transferred him from the pickup to the back seat of my patrol car."

"Did he say anything at that point?"

"Yes. He feared he wouldn't make it and insisted on speaking to his wife, Carolyn."

"And did he?"

"Yes. I ran and got her from the house. He died as they spoke."

"Do you know what they spoke about?"

"You'll have to ask her."

"Why didn't you wait for an ambulance?"

"He died before I could radio for help. So, the Phillips County Coroner was called instead."

"Did you attempt CPR at all?"

"No. His ribs on both sides of his body were broken. CPR would have shredded his lungs and internal organs."

"How did you know the condition of his ribs?"

"I walked him a half mile to his horse. I could feel and hear his ribs grating end on broken end. I loaded him into his pickup and into my car. And he told me all about it all the way."

"Wouldn't the pain have made it impossible for him to walk?"

"Adrenaline masks pain. The fear of the bear's return overwhelmed everything else."

"Did it overwhelm you?"

"Absolutely. We did everything but panic."

"Who declared him deceased?"

"His wife. I checked. No breathing, no pulse, eyes fixated and unmoving."

"Anyone else?"

"Yes. The coroner."

"Did the coroner question the way you handled Mr. Malone?"

"No, he did not."

"In retrospect, what would you do differently?"

"Had I known I would be facing a bear, I would have carried a heavier rifle and killed the bear. Then, I could have left Malone where he was when I pulled him out of the creek.

Maybe he could have been stabilized and brought out on a stretcher. Unfortunately, I didn't have that option."

"But you had a rifle. Couldn't you have waited for the bear to return and killed him then?"

"You don't know much about eight hundred-pound grizzly bears, do you?" Yellowhenry asked.

"Well, if you shoot them with a rifle, they die. Don't they?"

"Oh, of course. I forgot. What's your name?"

"Shelley Shannon."

"Well, Shelley, be sure to put in your article that any .22 or .30-30 rifle is adequate to kill a charging full-grown grizzly bear. One that had killed a fifteen hundred-pound Hereford bull. That will establish your credibility, and everyone will blame me for getting Malone out of there in a manner that most assuredly was responsible for his death. Yes Sir, I just should have waited for hours or maybe a day until that bear came back and said, 'Here I am. You can shoot me now. Then go for help.' Be sure to write that up in your article," Yellowhenry said as he walked out of the interview office.

"Mr. Yellowhenry," the TV reporter called as he walked toward the exit. "Could you give us a few minutes, please?"

"Ask Miss Shannon for a statement. She has accused me of being responsible for Malone's death. I'm afraid to talk to the press now. Hell, I'll be charged for murder after another interview," Yellowhenry said, and then he walked on out of the police station.

In his wake, Shelley Shannon, having collected her tape recorder and briefcase, walked out into the bullpen where the radio and TV reporters were. "Hey, lady," the radio reporter said, "way to turn the hero into a murder suspect."

"I only questioned his method of moving the victim. He was armed with a rifle. At least a .22. He could have waited, killed the bear, and more sensibly evacuated the victim."

"Holy shit," the TV man said. "You have just become the story. What's your name, and who do you write for?"

"I'm Shelley Shannon of the Mid-Montana Sentinel if you have to know," the young belligerent brunette said.

"You aren't from Montana, are you?"

"No, I'm not. I'm from Delaware, and if you Montanans can't answer sensible questions, don't blame me for asking them."

"Oh, we're going to answer your sensible questions, all right. Especially the one about holding off grizzly bears with a pea shooter."

"He said it was at least a .22 caliber, whatever that is."

"Wow," the radioman exclaimed, "this gets better every time you open your mouth."

"I have proof on my tape recorder," she said indignantly.

"And I have a tape of this interview, too," he said. "I'll interview the patrol captain for his statement, fill in some details, and voila, you can be the butt of every breakfast joke in Montana for the next month or two. Thank you for making my day so complete."

"You haven't even talked to the trooper yet."

"Thanks to you, he isn't available. So, we'll run with the next option. That's you. And you aren't gonna like how we report the story."

The squabble in the press did become a sidebar to the main story. Enough to send Miss Shannon back to Delaware and climes with which she was more familiar. At the behest of Captain Harbold, Yellowhenry cooperated with the media. The result, despite Shelley Shannon's silly attempt to smear him, was to elevate his stature to that of a minor local celebrity.

Three days later, he was asked to lead an attempt to locate the bear and see to its disposal. The concern for a wounded grizzly with a taste for livestock and little to no fear of man spurred the Phillips County sheriff to mount the attempt. Three days of searching were in vain, however. The only positive was the return of Carolyn Malone's stock and the repair of the downed fence.

Hunting for a wounded grizzly was less frightening to Yellowhenry than his admission to Amy that he had slept beside Carolyn Malone. His concern was to convince Amy that it had been perfectly platonic and that Carolyn was no threat to their relationship. He was concerned that he didn't tar Carolyn in the process. Amy gave him the opening when they were in bed, and she asked, "Where did you spend the night?"

"Guest room in the ranch house."

"Really? Just you and the widow?"

"Well, she has one-year-old triplets."

"I don't envy her. Did you get any rest at all?"

"Oh, yeah. Some."

"Those kids keep you awake?"

"Well, no. It wasn't that."

"What was it then?"

"She, uh, came into my room in the middle of the night and slept with me."

"Joe, you didn't, did you?"

"Not a chance. She was distraught. Needed company. We didn't talk; she slept, and I dozed until morning. The kids woke her up about daylight; she got up and took care of them. She didn't come back. I got up, dressed, thanked her for her hospitality, refused breakfast, and left the place. She's a nice lady, Amy. I think you'd like her."

"What's she gonna do without her husband. Use mine?"

Yellowhenry chuckled, "Cash in her chips and move to town. She will inherit the ranch from her husband, who inherited it, free and clear. And, she has a hundred thousand dollar life insurance policy on her husband."

"How did you find all that out?"

"Before going to bed the night before, she wanted to talk, so we drank coffee. I listened. It was a catharsis for her. They had had an off-and-on marriage. He was, from what she said, quite a lady's man. Couldn't help himself. Too good lookin' for his own good was the way she put it."

"You heard that as she crawled into bed with you, and there was no sex?"

"Hey, I was going to sleep in the barn. Believe me, I would have slept a lot better. But, you know what? She had no interest in sex at all. She fell asleep almost as soon as she laid down."

"Behind you?"

"Yes. She just wanted contact with another human being. Loneliness was already getting to her. She says she wants to be around people. Calls herself a people person."

"Well, I'm a people person, too," she said. "Yours. So you don't forget, rollover. I'm comin' on top."

Chapter Thirty-Seven

On the tenth of November, a blizzard blew down out of Canada. Temperatures dropped to twenty-three below, and the winds blew a steady fifty miles per hour, higher in gusts. The storm lasted for three days. Yellowhenry and everybody else in law enforcement were blown undercover. Roads were blocked off to everything, including essential and emergency travel. People were simply on their own. Yellowhenry parked his patrol car in the breezeway of his stable. All the stock was stalled, and a small stream of water was left running in the sink and bathtub of the house. With the constant heat provided by the oil stove and everyone sleeping in the living room in their winter clothes, the Yellowhenry family was comfortable enough. Joe carried water to the mules and horses. He strung rope to the outhouse and escorted everyone to and from the facility.

On the second day of the blow, Joe made his way to Minnie's to see how she and the Hammonds were doing. After a short discussion, they moved down to Yellowhenry's for the storm's duration. Despite the crowded conditions, a festive air dominated the home for the remaining twenty-four hours of the storm. The fourth day dawned clear and cold. Snow had drifted against buildings and filled in hollows.

Before Yellowhenry left for work with the patrol, he spent an hour with Deputy Hammond checking on neighbors. Many of them wanted the pair to stop for coffee, but they explained that they were just making as many courtesy calls as possible before Yellowhenry had to move on for his work with the highway patrol. Still, his appearance in his patrol car lent an air of appreciation to his efforts. The tribal members felt less alienated from the law enforcement that was usual to off-reservation service.

When Yellowhenry checked into the patrol headquarters, he was dispatched to tail the eastbound snowplows. Both a blade-and-sand truck and a rotary unit had been sent out early. They were thirty miles out when Yellowhenry caught up. The rotary unit driver was working on a heavy drift when he suddenly turned off the rotary equipment and backed out. He climbed down from the cab of his plow and waved at Yellowhenry to come to him. When the two had finished with their greeting, the driver, Lane Dawson, said, "The reason this drift is here is because a rig of some kind is buried in it."

"Can you tell what it is?"

"Looks like a pickup with a stock rack to me. I saw the tailgate before I hit it."

Yellowhenry walked with the driver, who had grabbed a short-handled snow shovel from his rig and moved it to the bogged vehicle. "I think I recognize this truck, Lane," Yellowhenry said. "Let me see that shovel for a second." He chopped at the snowpack at the rear of the pickup truck. "Oh, my god," he yelled a few seconds later. "This is that Malone widow's rig. She has three one-year-old babies. Lane, can you plow up alongside so we can see if she's in there?"

"Sure can. Give me a minute." He backed his plow up and maneuvered his equipment to blow snow off to the left side of the road. With the rotary cranked to full power, he eased alongside the Truck as close as he dared. When he reached the rig's front end, he shut everything down and backed up out of the way. Yellowhenry moved in with the shovel and began hacking away at the snow plastered against the driver's side door. When he had enough removed that he could wipe at the window with his gloved hand, he was relieved not to see anyone inside. He continued to remove snow until he could open the door. When he finally was able to jerk the door open, he found a note. It read: "Truck died. I caught a ride with Willis Beasley. Difficult conditions. We are trying for Harlem. Carolyn Malone."

Yellowhenry stuffed the note inside his coat and climbed down. "Lane, do you know Willis Beasley?"

"Sure do. Big rancher south of Malta about ten miles."

"What kind of rig is he likely drivin'?"

"New. Four wheel drive diesel one ton GMC."

"That's a relief. He picked up Caroline and her triplets, no doubt. They were going to lay over in Harlem."

"Well, we'll see. Should be there in an hour or two. We need to mark this pickup with flags, though. Otherwise, some stupid sonofabitch will drive right into it."

"I don't doubt it a bit," Yellowhenry laughed. "Do you have the flags.?"

"Tobe does in his truck." Dawson waved at the driver of the bladed Truck. He waved back and sat still. "That stupid bastard is gonna get it this time."

Yellowhenry watched as Dawson stalked to the driver's side door of the idling plow. "What do ya want?" he heard as the door was snatched open and the driver jerked down from the seat. Then, both drivers were sprawled onto the road beside the snow plow, flailing ineffectively at each other. With their winter boots, snow pants, insulated gloves, and heavy parkas, they resembled overgrown school kids wallowing around over some overblown insult.

Yellowhenry watched for a bit before muttering, "For the love of Pete." He walked around the blade of the plow and found the pair in the middle of a spitting contest. Both sported full beards that reached the middle of their chests. Both of them had a one-handed grip on the other's beard while pushing away the opponent's face with their free hand, and they spit at each other whenever they got an opening. "Hey," Yellowhenry bellowed. "Knock it off before I arrest both of you."

"He started it," the one called Tobe shouted as they continued to tussle.

"Stop!" Yellowhenry yelled. "Right now."

The pair ceased their struggle and reared back on their haunches, puffing, and glaring at each other.

"What the hell is the matter with you two?"

"He's the laziest sonofabitch on the entire plowing crew," Dawson declared.

"I do what I was hired to do. Drive that truck. If the fuckin' road department wants a shoveler and a flagger, they should hire one."

"Everybody knows there's shovelin' and flaggin' in snow removal," Dawson insisted.

"Then it oughta be in the goddamned job description."

"You want an asswiper added to it while you're at it, Tobe?" Dawson yelled.

"Hey, stick it up your ass, Lane. The union has been negotiating for that position for the past three years."

"That union has to be recognized first, ya dumb shit."

"No help to you," Tobe retorted.

"All right, that's enough," Yellowhenry interrupted. "The next one of you starts, goes in the back of my car for assault and battery."

"What about our truck if you do that?" Tobe asked.

"I'll call in, and the road department will have to send someone out to take over."

"Say something, Tobe," Dawson prodded. "If they jail ya, maybe you'll get fired."

"Hey, he started it," Tobe demanded, "arrest him and throw his ass in the back of your car."

"Just get back in your truck, Tobe. Give me the flags, and I'll do it," Yellowhenry ordered.

"All right, Trooper Joe," Tobe said, hauling himself upright, "but it ain't in your job description either."

"Just toss the stuff down, Tobe."

"I told you he's a lazy sonofabitch," Lane groused as he and Yellowhenry walked to plant the flags on the buried pickup.

"Punching him out isn't the answer, Lane. You should know that."

"You ain't gonna turn me in, are ya?"

"No. He might, though," Yellowhenry said.

"Yeah, I'm sure the lazy bastard will. Probably charge me with assault and battery while claiming self-defense."

"Well, Lane, that's the description of it."

"So, why aren't you arresting me, then?"

"Because your spittin' contest doesn't take precedence over the necessity for public safety in getting this road cleared."

"What's likely to happen when we get back to town? Are you gonna throw me in the hoosegow?"

"No. If you're charged, I'll probably be subpoenaed to testify," Yellowhenry responded.

"So, what are you gonna say?"

"The truth, Lane. You wouldn't want me to perjure myself, would you?"

"No, I guess not. What am I likely to be hit with?"

"A lot of laughin', for one thing. But, I think you were winnin' if that makes you feel any better."

Dawson grinned, "Yeah, I got in a couple of real good gobs, didn't I?"

"I can testify to that, Lane."

With the Malone ranch truck flagged, the plowing began afresh. With the blade truck leading, the trio of vehicles made it to Harlem an hour later. The Merry Maiden Motel had a GMC one-ton parked on the lee side. A private snowplow operator had cleared the parking lot in front of the motel, so Yellowhenry radioed to the snowplows he was working with that he was going to stop and check on Carolyn Malone. "I'll catch up with you in a little while."

He got the room number from the front desk, walked to unit number six, and knocked on the door. When she opened the door, Carolyn was both surprised and pleased to see Yellowhenry. "Why, Trooper Joe," she exclaimed. "I wouldn't have expected to see you here, of all people. Please come in. I have a pot of coffee made. Have a cup with me."

"How have you been, Carolyn? We found your vehicle. It was completely snowed in. I was afraid you were still in it. I have your note. You were lucky Willis Beasley came along."

"You have no idea. He had to tromp the snow down at the side of my pickup to get the door open. I really thought we were going to freeze to death. Willis is my hero."

They sat and chatted for a bit. Yellowhenry held one of the triplets while Carolyn bottle-fed another.

"Something's been bothering me," she commented after a while. "Did you tell your wife I borrowed you the night I slept with you?"

"I did."

"How did she respond?"

"With sex," Yellowhenry chuckled.

Carolyn laughed, "Your wife is smart. That's the way we keep you guys in our beds. Did she mind my using you for a Teddy Bear?"

"As long as it's a one-time event, she'll trust us, but never again, I'm afraid."

"Darn," she grinned, "I was sort of hoping for a night of reversed positions."

He laughed, "I'm afraid the Teddy Bear would be a little more than cuddly if we did that. Have you decided where you want to live when you leave the ranch?"

"My folks want me to go to Miles City so they can be close to my kids. It's either there or Havre. I have friends there, and to tell you the truth, I'd like to get to know your wife."

"Then, you'd get to know Minnie Graves. She lives next door and is a pseudo-grandmother to my kids. You'll love her. She's a white-haired little old lady, but she calls my horse 'our horse,' and she rides him around without a bridle. She guards him like a hawk and will shoot anyone trying to steal him. In fact, she already has."

Carolyn laughed, "You're kidding, of course."

"Not for a minute. She didn't kill that guy. She only wounded him. I killed him later."

"Really?" Carolyn asked.

"When someone is shooting at you, especially when you are an officer of the law, you shoot back."

"What happened?"

"It was just a thing, Carolyn. Not something I talk about, if you don't mind."

"I'm sorry, Joe. You're just so easy to talk to, I didn't think."

"Maybe another time. Well, I need to catch up to those snow plows. I am so relieved that you and the little ones are all right. Do you need help getting your rig back to your ranch?"

"I think I have it handled. I've hired a snow plow operator here in town to go dig my pickup out and plow my road for me."

"Do you have anyone handling your stock?"

"Yes. After Roy died, I hired a ranch hand. He's there in the place. I was in Havre visiting my attorney when the storm hit. Roy's brother is challenging the transfer of the ranch to me."

"Really? Were you inheriting the ranch in a will?"

"Yes. He's trying to say the will was made under duress because I was pregnant when Roy and I were married."

"Sounds like he's hoping to shame you into giving him a piece of the estate."

"That's what my attorney thinks, too. Ain't gonna happen. Hell, I sleep with strange men."

Yellowhenry was on his feet at that moment. "Well, I wouldn't announce that in court if I were you," he laughed. "I have to go chase those plow guys before they stop and fight each other."

"Why would they do that?" she asked.

"Idiots. They disagree about union representation. I've already broken up a spit fight between those two."

"A spit fight. What on Earth is a spit fight?"

"It requires a full beard so you can hang onto the other guy's beard with one hand while you try to deflect his spit with your other hand as you are spitting at him. The fight takes place while you roll around on the ground."

She began laughing, "You'd best be going, Joe, before they run out of spit and actually hurt each other."

Yellowhenry caught up to the plows when they were twenty miles beyond Harlem. He followed without further incident to the turnaround at Saco. On the return, they encountered the snow plow operator at Carolyn's rig. He had parked his snow plow in front of the disabled vehicle, shoveled the pickup free of snow, and had the hood up on the truck. He and another man were working under the hood.

The snow plows pushed through the snow they had loosened on the outward leg of their assignment and continued plowing back toward Havre. Yellowhenry stopped, flipped on his lights, and walked over to where the man was working. "How bad is it?" he asked as he approached the pickup.

"Hey, Trooper Joe," the man sang out. "It's probably a little moisture in her fuel tank. I've put in an additive that dries out the fuel. The battery is dead, too. I'm about ready to jump-start it. If that doesn't work, I have a replacement in my truck. I'm hopin' I don't have to pull the carburetor."

Yellowhenry watched as the men started their plow rig and attached the jumper cables. "We'll give it a few minutes to charge before we try startin' Mrs. Malone's rig," the operator said.

"I'm Joe Yellowhenry, by the way."

"Hell, Trooper Joe, you're famous. Everybody in this neck of the woods knows who you are. I'm Larry Benson. This is Kyle Cramer. If we can get this thing started, Kyle will drive it down to Mrs. Malone at the motel. I'm gonna plow her road out while he does that. Hopefully, she'll be home by tonight."

"A lot of moving pieces. How about you guys take the pickup to her place, and I'll go get her and her kids."

"Sure," Benson said, "That'll save us some miles and time. She's paying me a set amount, so that works for her and me."

"How long till you try the truck?" Yellowhenry asked.

"Couple of minutes."

It was more like ten minutes later when the men stopped bullshitting and remembered to fire up the truck. It was probably ten minutes well spent. The truck's battery needed the charge time. It took several attempts, but the rig finally turned over and, with heavy pumping of the foot feed, stayed running. When the men were sure it would stay running, they headed out. Yellowhenry stopped at the motel in Harlem. The snow plow and ranch truck continued on to the Dodson turnoff to the ranch.

When Yellowhenry knocked on the door, he found Carolyn dressed for travel. "Joe," she said in surprise as she looked past him at the parking lot, "what are you doing here? Where's my truck?"

"A little change of plans," he said. "I'm driving you to the ranch. Your snow plow guy and his helper are driving rig for you."

"Well, that's not necessary, but it is awfully nice. Thank you. I have the kids ready to go."

With Yellowhenry's help, she loaded the kids into the back seat of his cruiser. On the way to the turnoff to the ranch, she asked about his tires. "You'll probably have to chain up to get to the house. I'm sorry, Joe."

"Glad you mentioned that. I'll toss 'em on before we leave the highway."

When Yellowhenry pulled up to the front door of Carolyn's house, the snow plow guys were talking to the hired man. Smoke was rising from the ranch house chimney. "Looks like my house is going to be warm and friendly, Joe," Carolyn said. "Why don't you come in for a minute? Help me get my kids undressed and ready for their supper."

"Okay, I can help you with the kids," he said.

"Good, let me talk to Hank Jonas for a second. He's my hired man."

Yellowhenry started carrying the kids into the house. He was toting in the last one when Carolyn led the three-person train into her kitchen. They all sat down at the kitchen table. "Joe, I'm putting a pot of coffee on. Why don't you stay for a while? This is Hank Jonas. Hank, meet Joe Yellowhenry."

"Well, I'd say this is an honor," Jonas said as he shook hands. "You're the fella jailed a horse under a protective custody order. Had that town bein' known, in fact, as a one-horse shit hole? The whole damned country was laughin'."

"There were a lot of extenuating circumstances," Yellowhenry said with a deprecatory smile.

"I've been around a long time, Trooper Joe," Jonas continued. "There are damned few stories like that. Makes them a treasure for decades." The man sat back easily in a straight-backed wooden chair. Yellowhenry guessed he was sixty years old. He had a full head of iron-gray hair, which he wore loosely and swept back. He sported long white sideburns and a white Fu Manchu mustache. He was five feet ten inches tall and weighed about one-seventy. His teeth were uneven and stained from smoking and chewing tobacco. From the Bull Durham string tab hanging from his shirt pocket, it looked like he rolled his own.

"How did the stock make it through the blizzard?" Carolyn asked.

"They made it. You don't have but forty heads. I was able to herd 'em into the barn. With all the stall doors open, there was enough room. I worked my ass off gettin' water to 'em. I kept a fire goin' here in the house. Kept a little stream of water runnin'. Carried water to a galvanized tub I used as a water trough. Moved the tub around. Moved the stock. Eventually, I got 'em all watered at least once. Hay was no problem. I tossed it down from the loft."

"It's none of my business, Carolyn," Yellowhenry asked, "but how did you and Roy make it with forty head of stock?"

"Sold the herd down. Roy was going to build it up with better. That bull the bear got was supposed to be the start. Doesn't matter now, though. The ranch is going up for sale next spring."

"I wish I had the money," Jonas said. "This ranch is a fine spread. It's not too big for a one-man operation. As long as he didn't get greedy, a man could make a good living here for a good long time."

"You look like a man who could be happy here," Yellowhenry offered.

"Oh, yeah. I could hang my hat right here till the Grim Reaper comes to a callin'."

The group visited and drank coffee for a half hour before Yellowhenry stood up. "Carolyn, thank you for the coffee. I've got to get on down the road. Larry, Kyle, Hank, it was a pleasure meeting you."

The men stood and shook hands with the minor celebrity, all expressing their appreciation for the honor of sharing a cup of coffee with him. He felt strange and a touch embarrassed by their admiration. "I'll walk you out, Joe," Carolyn said. When she closed the door behind her, she whispered, "Joe." He turned, and she embraced him.

He awkwardly returned the embrace in a one-armed half hug. "Are you all right?" he asked.

"I have to become a good friend of your wife, Joe. If I don't, I'm going to try to seduce you every chance I get."

"Whoa, Carolyn," he said, alarmed. "Where did that come from?"

"Hell, if I knew, I wouldn't do it, Joe. It just did. Good night," she said and walked back to her house.

Yellowhenry stopped at the highway and pulled his chains. It had been dark for nearly an hour, and he had a two-hour low speed drive back to town. He called in for a status report and was cleared to head for the barn. Thinking about the Bar H Seven ranch, he had his head spinning. He liked ranching and had often thought that if he got lucky somehow, he'd buy one. Carolyn's ranch and what Hank Jonas said about it tantalized his thinking. 'What if she'd let Hank and me run it for her?' was his first thought. The more he considered that, the less appealing it became. He finally reconciled himself to his lease on the reservation. Thinking about that gave birth to another idea. 'What if Amy applied to the tribe for a lease of her own adjacent to his?' Then, he could manage a small operation right there at home and still work for the highway patrol. He weighed that idea for a while and finally decided he didn't have the capital to fence in 360 acres. Nothing he came up with made sense. The one thing that did stick with him was that he would not be caught alone with Carolyn Malone.

Chapter Thirty-Eight

The weather moderated following the blizzard. Carolyn Malone received the proceeds of her life insurance policy and decided to look for a nanny. As a result, she drove with the triplets to Havre and checked into a motel. She paid for a three-day stay. She then placed an ad in the local newspaper for a full-time nanny with pay commensurate with experience. Then, she drove out to hunt up Amy Yellowhenry.

"Hello," Amy said to the stranger on her doorstep.

"Are you Amy Yellowhenry?"

"Yes."

"I'm Carolyn Malone. I borrowed your husband for a Teddy Bear, and I feel like I owe you an explanation."

Amy giggled, "I know. He told me. Won't you come in?"

"I have my children in the car. Let me get them."

"I'll help you," Amy said.

With the triplets settled in with baby bottles plugged in, Carolyn explained her trauma. "It was horrible looking at my husband. His face had been terribly distorted from being bitten and nearly torn off by the bear. Blood and mud-caked his face into a grotesque mask I couldn't recognize. I tried to hold him, but the pain of his broken ribs was too much. I just knelt beside him as he asked for forgiveness for cheating on me and not being a better husband. Of course, I forgave him. He tried to smile, but his pain was overwhelming him. It was just a grimace, but I knew. Then he drew a great last breath and let it out in a long sigh. I kissed him on his forehead and said goodbye as he died.

"I didn't feel deep grief like a wife should. Probably because he was unfaithful so often. Maybe it was guilt that drove me into your husband's bed. He was the only adult on the ranch besides me. I was suddenly feeling so lonely. My husband, despite his dalliances, was a good and helpful father. With him gone, the thought of raising triplets by myself just stunned me. I grabbed at the only stable thing I could. Your husband. I want to thank you. I assure you that I climbed into bed behind him. He was mortified. He was a perfect gentleman. He lay there all night, stiff as a plank."

"My poor husband," Amy said. "He gets shot on one assignment, rescues a man who dies on another and sleeps with the guy's wife. Has to tell his own wife nothin' happened. I believed him, but he wasn't totally sure I bought it. Your coming here helps a lot. I believe you."

"Thank the lord," Carolyn said. "I have more confessing to do, Amy. I want to become your good friend if you'll let me."

"Well, of course. We both have a houseful of children. Having another good friend with kids will be great. But what does that have to do with confessing?"

"I want to quit wanting your husband."

Amy began laughing. At first, Carolyn smiled. Then she caught the sillies. "Why do you find this so funny, Amy?" she finally said.

"I don't know," she said amidst more peals of laughter.

The noisy women disturbed the triplets. So Carolyn tended to her babies, and after a half hour of getting to know Amy a little better, she left to return to the motel. There, she put her babies down so they could toddle and crawl around. Then she went into the bathroom to change into her night clothes. She looked at herself in the mirror. She saw a woman who was attractive but clearly over the bloom of youthful beauty. At twenty-eight, she had to draw her elbows back to stand her breasts in their best position. "Well, they're heavy," she said out loud. Then she turned to look at her derriere. She frowned at the spread she hadn't noticed. Her face, when she looked closely, was showing sun damage and fine line wrinkles. She didn't like her hair either. It seemed to be a dark blonde lanky mess that hung down to shoulder length. It was naturally fairly curly, which caused it to tangle. At the moment, it needed a tint and trim. She pulled her hair down and wrenched her mouth down at the corners. "You don't have to worry about sleeping with Joe Yellowhenry," she said. "As soon as he sees you naked, he'll run for the hills."

It took two days of interviewing and observing nanny prospects before Carolyn finally hired an older lady from Chinook. Betty Dashell was a widow who was renting a room in a boarding house. She was available immediately as she had given notice of her intent to vacate her room. She was a fifty-five-year-old widow of a fireman and the grandmother of three teenagers, all the children of her only son. All of them lived in Bend, Oregon. Betty had been working as a waitress for minimum wage plus a percentage of the tips collected during her shift. She had barely managed to pay for her rent and the minimum of necessities. To Betty, the job offer seemed too good to be true. Her plans had been to buy a bus ticket to Bend and try to restart her life there.

Carolyn offered to pay her room and board plus a hundred-fifty per month. It seemed like a fortune to Betty. Her duties were to assist with the triplets and to cook for the household, including the hired man. With the terms all set, the women and children drove back to the ranch.

Yellowhenry was filing a trip report when Harbold called him into his office. "Joe," he said, "I need you on a special assignment. You are a capable tracker, aren't you?"

"Yes, I am."

"You can be away from home for a few days?"

"Yes, I can."

"How about the use of your horse?"

"If I need a horse, I have one."

"You'll be compensated for riding your own horse. How about a horse trailer?"

"Don't have one."

"Not a problem, the patrol will rent one for you. Here's what's happening. There's a poaching ring operating out of Choteau. That's in the Great Falls sector. They're forming a joint task force of county, fish and game, and highway patrol personnel to put a stop to it. The poachers concentrate on elk, bears, wolves, cougars, and deer. It's a pretty sophisticated bunch. Bow hunters. They operate on the eastern slopes of the Continental Divide. They have portable processing and refrigeration units. Security details go out with those units, and they are guarded with high-powered weapons. It's believed that there are two families involved. The Elmores and the Creeds. With inlaws, fathers, and brothers, the estimate is that a dozen or so people are involved. Undoubtedly, there will be women involved with the paperwork. The sheriffs of Teton, Lewis, and Clark Counties are spearheading the operation.

"The usual method of operation for the poachers is to pack horse into the mountains, shoot the game and field dress it, then load the carcasses, hides, antlers, gallbladders, and anything else they can sell on the black market onto pack horses and transport it all down to the processing and refrigeration units. This has been going on for a couple of years. Now, with animals down out of the high country onto their winter range where they are concentrated, the poachers work the foothills. They've become brazen and bold. We've been asked to add a man to the team. I decided to ask you if you would accept the assignment. It qualifies for hazardous duty pay. Would you be interested?"

"When do I report?"

"Good man. We need to have you on the road tomorrow. A truck and trailer will be ready to roll out of here by seven in the morning. All you'll need is to grab it and get your horse. You should be in Great Falls about mid-afternoon. You'll be briefed on the details of the operation, which is slated to kick off tomorrow night. I'd throw in a bale of hay and maybe some oats for your horse. Pack your saddle gun for sure."

Chapter Thirty-Nine

Yellowhenry pulled up in front of the Great Falls Highway Patrol Office and parked on the street. He walked into the reception area and was buzzed into the bullpen. "Joe Yellowhenry," a heavyset, neatly bearded sheriff said, extending a hand. "I'm Harry Graymeier, sheriff of Teton County. Where's your hoss?"

"Horse trailer out front."

"Okay, we have a stable on the way out to Choteau. Come on back and meet the rest of the crew."

The pair walked back to a conference room where four men were looking at a topographic map. "Gents," Graymeier said, "meet Joe Yellowhenry."

"Well, the famous man. I'm Leo Altarena, the poor bastard in charge of this outfit. This is Lance Porter, Lewis and Clark County Sheriff, and these guys are Troopers Shane Maxwell and Dominick Petricelli."

After shaking hands the men looked at him. "You were an Indian sheriff?" Porter asked.

"Up until I signed on with the patrol," Yellowhenry answered.

"You got into that shooting scrape with Wes Edom over Christina way, then," Porter said.

"Yes."

"Killed horses and wounded Wes?"

"Yes."

"Wasn't that sort of extreme?"

"Well," Yellowhenry said, "I was shot twice in that exchange. Does that qualify as extreme?"

"Wes was protecting property on his own land," Porter said.

"The property was stolen stock. My horse and a pair of mules belonging to the Cree people."

"Wes didn't steal that stock."

"I didn't sell my horse. The people didn't sell their mules. Edom agreed that the stock was stolen. All three were branded."

"But you were on Wes's ranch."

"With a written agreement to be there."

"I heard you were cutting fences."

"The fences were already down. Our cuts made no difference."

"Didn't that seem unlawful?"

"No. All the fences in that place were down in many places. Edom hid the animals and started shooting when he saw me and my team loading them. I shot back. All of that is a matter of record, Mr. Porter. I am not on trial, here. And I was not the one who faced criminal charges," Yellowhenry said, looking Porter directly in the eyes.

"Hey, I'm just bein' curious."

"No. You were givin' me the accusatory third degree. And, you can stick it up your ass, Sheriff."

"Hey," Altarena said sternly, "there's no call for that."

"Who are you referring to?" Yellowhenry asked.

"Both of you, but the language needs to be toned down."

"No, it doesn't," Yellowhenry retorted. "I just met this guy and he's accusing me, a fellow lawman, of being a criminal. Probably because he has a problem with Native Americans as lawmen."

"That ain't true," Porter protested. "On the reservation, they're absolutely necessary."

"Any questions, Captain Altarena?" Yellowhenry asked. "Or, would you rather I just drive on back to the reservation where I'm more legitimate."

"Now, now, Trooper Yellowhenry, let's not play the racist card here," Altarena said. "I'm sure Lance only meant that generally."

"Okay, hold on for a second," Yellowhenry said, pulling his pocket tablet. "Let me get this down on paper so when this whole shit show blows up because the Indian was involved, I can at least tell the review board how it all started. Is that fair?"

"Ah, now, let's take a step back and start from scratch," Altarena said looking from Porter to Yellowhenry who was busy writing on his tablet.

"Give me just a minute," Yellowhenry said. "I use Indian shorthand. I'll have this down to the word in a jiffy." Then he quoted word for word what everyone, including himself, had said. "Does anyone want to correct any of that?"

The group looked, stunned, at one another, waiting for someone to speak. Finally, Sheriff Graymeier said, "That's what was said. I'd like you to add that I had nothing to say."

"Well, let's get to the briefing," Altarena said, "before the shit show blows up before it has a chance to be a shit show. Is that all right, Joe?"

"You're the leader, aren't you? Or, is Lance in charge. I'd sorta like to know, and, so far, that hasn't been made clear."

"I've been delegated to lead this operation," Altarena said.

"Ah, good to know," Joe said. "Does Lance know that?"

"Yes, Lance knows that," Porter said, as he turned to the topo map. Then under his breath, he muttered, "Fuckin' war hoop." Only Altarena heard the mutter. He nudged the sheriff and grinned.

After reviewing how the poachers moved their product out of the field to their processing plants and on into the black market, Altarena assigned Joe with the task of locating the pair of poacher security guards, disarming them, and moving them to where they were not a threat to the officers doing the important work of arresting the main criminals. "I see," Yellowhenry said, innocently. "I'm supposed to slip up on 'em like an Indian. Use some of the skills that Indians are born with. Is that it? I'm not allowed to just shoot 'em from a hundred yards away, Captain Altarena?"

"No, for God's sake. Don't do that," Altarena said annoyed.

"That'd really throw a monkey wrench into the middle of the entire operation. Just ease up on 'em and take 'em out of the equation."

"That's why you were brought in on this deal," Porter said. "You'll be a natural. The rest of us would have to work at it. You were born to it."

"I'm just so proud, Leo," Yellowhenry said somberly. "You won't mind that if I get into firefights and wind up killin' some of those guys, I lift just one scalp, will you?"

Altarena looked at him quickly. "Ha, ha, ho, ho, Joe. I'd like you to take this a little more seriously is what I'd like."

"Oh, but I am, Leo. I am. One thing I'm gonna need is a silencer. Otherwise, if there's a shift in the wind direction and one of those guys smells Indian, I'm gonna need to take him out before he can start shootin' at me. I mean we don't want them shootin' at me and throwin' the monkey wrench into the operation either, do we, Leo? Eh?"

"Just use the natural cover like you're supposed to and they won't see you comin'."

"Okay, then. I'm gettin' the picture a little better. In which case, I'll carry a tomahawk just in case things go sideways."

"A tomahawk? Come on Yellowhenry. You need to start takin' this seriously."

"Oh, but I am," Yellowhenry said, pulling a rock from his pocket. Pick a target anywhere in this room, Leo. One you don't mind seeing destroyed."

"What the hell are you drivin' at, Joe?"

Yellowhenry shrugged out of his uniform jacket. "I won't be wearin' this in the field."

"I'm not pickin' out a target, for God's sake. What the hell do you think this is?"

"Okay," Yellowhenry said, looking at the far end of the squad room. "See that bowling trophy on the last desk. The one with the bowling ball extended behind the bowler. That's about fifty feet from here, so the demonstration is a little unfair, it being so close. Just watch the ball." His move seemed casual and the bowling ball disappeared before the trophy toppled off the desk. The rock ricocheted off the back wall, leaving a neat inverted eyeball impression in the paneling.

"Holy shit," Porter exclaimed. "I never saw that fuckin' rock at all."

Yellowhenry walked to where the rock had come to rest halfway back from the wall in the middle of the room. "This is my favorite rock. Don't want to lose it. I throw a tomahawk like I throw this rock. So, either you provide a silenced firearm, or I'm carryin' a tomahawk."

Chapter Forty

The operation launched a day later. Altarena knew where the meat processing and refrigerator trucks were stashed on a landing at the terminus of a dead-end logging road in the Lewis and Clark National Forest. The area leading to the location was rolling hills that pitched sharply and quickly upward near the rising flanks of the Rockies. The hills were sparsely blanketed by water-starved pine and fir trees. The canopy ranged from twenty-five to forty feet high. It was a winter range for deer and elk, which were intermingled and populous, even though the population would be tripled a month later.

Yellowhenry rode Hi Boy within a half mile of the pair of processing rigs. He could hear the refrigerator unit running. Riding the horse was less frightening to the game animals than being on foot, so there was no concerted disturbance amidst the elk and deer.After he dismounted and tied Hi Boy to tree branches, he looped higher on the slope above the processing site. He was dressed in combed cotton winter weight camouflage from head to foot. He carried a scope-mounted .220 Swift silenced rifle. He had stopped on the way to the operation launch point and sighted the rifle in at one hundred yards.

He moved slowly and deliberately. Every foot plant was made carefully, and he stayed in the screen of cover as much as possible. He used the scope to scan ahead and to the sides. He also checked behind. At last, he was rewarded. What surprised him was that the guard was a teenage girl. She was carelessly sitting with her back toward him as she straddled a log in the open seventy yards below him. Her rifle was propped against the log at her side. Boredom was obvious as she swung her legs back and forth. She was dressed for the weather, including a brown stocking cap.

Yellowhenry scoped out the cover between himself and the girl. He grinned to himself and began his creep. Twenty minutes later, he eased the girl's rifle away from where she sat, stood up, and stepped silently back uphill two strides. Then he said quietly, "I haven't heard any shots bein' fired."

"That's because the hunters shoot bows," she answered automatically before pivoting in alarm, "Who are you?"

"I'm an Indian. Shhhh. It's okay. But, just to make sure you don't holler, this rifle has a silencer attached. Don't make me shoot you. No one would even hear the shot. Do we have a deal?"

"Yes," she said, her voice trembling.

"Good. Now, what's your name?"

"Celia. Celia Creed."

"Celia, how old are you?"

"Fourteen."

"Where is the other guard?"

"In the trees on the other side of the trucks."

"Mmmhmm. Let me guess. Your brother, who is twelve?"

"How'd you know that?" she blurted.

"Shhh, not so loud. What's your brother's name?"

"Lee. How'd you know he's twelve?"

"Because the older kids either hunt or cut up meat. What are their names and ages?"

"Why do you want to know that?"

"So if I have to shoot someone, I don't shoot kids."

"Shoot someone," she whispered, "what would make you do that?"

"Because I'm a Montana State Highway Patrolman. I'm here on an assignment to break up a poaching ring. The one you are a part of."

"Breakin' us up? Why? We have been payin' all along."

Yellowhenry paused before his next question. "I haven't been gettin' my cut."

"That's not Papa's fault. You need to talk to Leo. He's the one who spreads out the cuts."

"That's good advice, Celia. I'll be sure to do that. Now, we've got a bit of a problem."

"We do?"

"Yeah, you see, the people who sent us out here want us to make a big show of stoppin' your folks' poachin'. I need you to pretend that you've been caught. Nothing will happen to you because you're a minor. You'll be told, 'Naughty, naughty, Celia. Quit helpin' your dad.' We'll go away with baggy britches because we have done our duty. Your dad will have to quit for a month or so until everything settles down. Then it'll be back to business, as usual. Can you help me with that?"

"Yeah, sure."

"Good. Now, who are the other kids?"

"There's Stan; he's my sixteen-year-old brother and Clarence Elmore, my fifteen-year-old cousin, and Fred Elmore. He's seventeen. Oh, and there's Sissy, but she just cuts up the meat. She's seventeen. She's my sister."

"Who is at the trucks right now?"

"Nobody. The game has to be brought in first. Then Daddy, Uncle Gordy, and Ted break it down into quarters and hang it in the refrigerator truck for twenty-four hours. Then it's cut and wrapped and boxed and delivered to our outlet in Great Falls."

"Does Ted have a last name?"

"Yeah. Smith, but Daddy doesn't believe that because he's an ex-convict."

"Okay, if we walk to the trucks, can you call Lee to come down?"

"I think so."

"All right, let's give that a try." Yellowhenry let her lead the way. He packed both rifles.

At the trucks, Celia hollered for Lee to come down.

"Why?" came floating down through the timber.

"Yeah," Celia asked. "Why?"

"To learn about the new plan."

"There's a new plan," she hollered again.

"What is it?"

"Tell him he has to see it," Yellowhenry instructed.

"Lee," Celia yelled impatiently. "You have to see it. Get down here."

"All right," Lee shouted. "Don't get so bossy. I'm comin'."

A few minutes later, the youngster came walking into the clearing. As he walked around the back rear corner of the processing truck, Yellowhenry greeted him, "Hello, Lee," he said, sticking out his hand as though to shake. The kid brought his rifle from across his chest down to his left hand as he stuck out his right. Instead of shaking the kid's hand, Yellowhenry smoothly seized the weapon and pulled it away from the youngster. "Sorry, Lee," he said. "I'm the new plan. I'm with the Montana State Highway Patrol. We're conducting a police action against poaching."

"But Pa pays you guys," Lee protested.

"It's all right, son," Yellowhenry said. "Your sister can explain what's going on. Now, the three of us need to leave. Come with me. We have to take a hike and then a horseback ride."

"What about my gun?"

"We'll unload it. Then you can have it back as long as you keep it unloaded. I won't take a boy's rifle away from him. Don't worry about that."

"Where are we goin'?" Celia asked.

"You'll see. It'll be fun," Yellowhenry smiled.

Sam Creed and his brother-in-law Gordy Elmore were working together just after daybreak. They both wore camouflage, including broad-brimmed hats under black see-through netting. They had also painted their faces with black and green striping. Elmore was convinced that animals could spot a hunter's eyeshine. "If you stare at a game animal or any wild animal, they'll pick you off. Trust me. I've field-tested it. I know," he declared. "That's why you wear the black net."

Creed didn't care one way or the other. He had little desire to spark another argument with his overbearing brother-in-law. The pair were paralleling each other a hundred yards apart along a wooded sidehill of an unnamed and insignificant fork of Deep Creek. Creed was at the bottom. They knew they were pushing ahead of them a small band of elk. He could hear the animals as he sneaked along, looking for a shot. Then he saw the dark legs of the elk through the trees as they followed the lead cow. So far, they hadn't run, but Sam knew that he would need to take a chance and hurry through an opening thirty yards ahead of him. He could see a break in the trees and brush ahead of the elk. The animals would have to cross there, and that would place them forty yards above him. He hoped to get arrows into at least two of the animals.

Elmore, meantime, was hiking over the crest of the sidehill. When he had cleared enough so that he wouldn't be seen, he began running. His concern wasn't so much to be quiet as it was to be unseen. He knew that elk made enough noise as they moved and that he wouldn't necessarily be enough to cause them to run. By getting ahead and off to the side so that his scent plume wouldn't be blown to the animals, he was pretty sure of intercepting the band and getting off a shot. Both men carried seventy-pound bows. Elmore's was a Hoyt, and Creed's was a Mathews. Despite the excellence of both bows, the pair argued constantly about which was better.

Creed was halfway across the opening when the lead cow barked. He knelt and drew his bow. The herd had turned to run over the top of the low ridge. He was able to take a shot at a spike bull just as it dropped down to dig into a sprint. The arrow caught the bull on the right side just behind its ribs as it quartered away. It was a kill shot, and Creed knew it. He clenched his right fist around his release and raised his arm in triumph.

Elmore heard the elk herd coming on the run with calves mewing. He bounded downhill behind a pair of pine trees as the animals came over the brow of the hill. He carried a mouth call and began calling as the herd ran by at twenty-five yards. He kept up the call and watched as the animals disappeared. A spike suddenly dived head-first into the ground and piled up at the foot of a pine. He watched carefully as he worked his call. He was rewarded when a cow circled back and stood nervously at forty yards. She was facing him at first. But as she finally turned to run, she gave him a broadside shot. He led her slightly, and she ran into the arrow. He could see the arrow as it bobbed up and down in her side as she raced through the trees.

Elmore was standing by the spike when Creed came over the hill. "I got two. This spike and a cow, downhill about a hundred yards," Elmore said.

"Not that it matters, Gordy, but I shot this spike."

"Like hell. How do you figure."

"How about a hundred-yard blood trail, you stupid bastard."

"Oh, I suppose so."

"Let's get to work. We need to get these two over to the trucks so we can get caught by Leo's men. The boys should be down at the bottom with the horses. We don't need to do more than field dress 'em," Creed said.

Yellowhenry and the two kids rode Hi Boy triple down to the pickup and trailer. He loaded the horse and drove back to the Great Falls highway patrol office. Then he escorted the pair inside. He bought both of them a soft drink and took them to a vacant desk. "Just wait here for a couple of minutes," he smiled. "I'll be right back." Then he spoke to the receptionist and explained that he needed a tape recorder.

"What's that for?" Celia asked.

"It's so you don't have to sit here for an hour writing out a whole bunch of stuff. You can just say it."

"Will I get in trouble?"

"The only way you can do that is to lie about what you know. Then you could go to the reformatory for girls. You know what that is, don't you?"

"No way do I wanna go there," she said.

"Good," Yellowhenry said.

"I don't either," Lee said.

"All right," Yellowhenry said. "Lee, I have to interview Celia first.

By herself. Here's another quarter. Go to the vending machines and get yourself a candy bar. I'll come get you when we're done."

"Thanks, Injin Joe," Lee said happily as he walked quickly toward the machines.

Yellowhenry went through the process of identifying himself, the case he was working on, and Celia. Then, he asked her questions to elicit what she knew about the poaching operation. "Very good, Celia," he said. "Go get yourself a candy bar and ask Lee to come see me."

When he was finished, he asked the receptionist for an evidence bag. He placed the tape into the bag, had the receptionist sign the seal, and witnessed her signature. "Do you want to leave this with me?" she asked.

"No. I'll take care of it," he said. "These two kids need to hang out here until Captain Altarena returns this afternoon."

"Aren't you going to be here?" she asked.

"No, I have to return to Havre to care for my horse. My part in the case is completed."

Then he walked the kids into the break room. He gave each one fifty cents. "Your dad will be here this afternoon, kids," he said. "You've both been terrific, and I'm happy to have met you. I have to get on the road. I want to get Hi Boy home today.”

“I like your horse,” Celia said.

“Yeah, me, too,” Lee added.

“Well, by golly,” Yellowhenry said, “I think he liked you, too. Bye now.”

Chapter Forty-One

Two days later, *the Great Falls Herald* ran a banner headline: HIGHWAY PATROL BUSTS POACHING RING. The accompanying article lavishly praised the local captain, Leo Altarena, and the members of the sting operation. Yellowhenry was not mentioned. Gordy Elmore and Sam Creed had been arrested and a pair of elk were confiscated. A week later they were arraigned and charged with two counts of illegally harvesting game animals. They were stripped of their hunting privileges for five years, given six months of suspended jail sentences, fined five hundred dollars each, and had the poached animals confiscated. The meat was donated to the local food bank.

When Yellowhenry arrived back home, it was nearly midnight. He put Hi Boy away in the midst of softly falling snow. By morning, there was a four-inch accumulation, and it was still falling. Amy asked him to describe how things had gone in Great Falls. "Well, I was the unwanted Injin. The token, if you will. But, I met a couple of great kids. Brother and sister. They were honest to the core, and they gave me recorded statements of what was goin' on down there. I put the tape in an evidence bag and then stole out of there like a thief in the night. I can't say what was goin' on because of confidentiality. I have to speak to Captain Harbold and file a report. Then I'll know whether to make things very uncomfortable for all the wagon-burner haters in the Great Falls environs."

"Well, honey," Amy said, "I'm sure if you'd just known you were gonna be the token, you could have ridden Hi Boy bareback."

"I agree, Ames," he said. "They're just so unthoughtful."

The meeting with Harbold took place at mid-morning after Yellowhenry had returned the rental truck and trailer. "Grab a cup of mud and come on in," Harbold said. "Give me the lowdown on how they broke that bunch of poachers down there."

"Well, John, hang onto your hat. Leo is in on it," Yellowhenry said.

"What? How did you come by that piece of intelligence?" Harbold asked.

"Well, I have a tape that lays it all out. They gave me the duty of taking out the guards of the processing units. Turned out to be the kids of the main man. Fourteen-year-old girl and her twelve-year-old brother. Both of 'em are honest as the day is long. Their statements are on tape in this evidence bag."

"Okay, let's hear what the kids had to say about their old man and his poaching ring," Harbold said.

Yellowhenry handed him the bag and sat back to listen as his captain pulled a portable tape recorder from his desk. Twenty minutes later Harbold turned off the recorder. "This is bad," he said. "Those kids laid it all out. Named names. I can see why you didn't share that with Leo. He would have burned it and denied it ever existed."

"So, what do we do with it?" Yellowhenry asked.

"I'm going to put a cover letter with it, send it to Helena, and wait for the sparks to fly," Harbold said. "How did they treat you, by the way?"

"Like the unwanted token Injin," Yellowhenry replied.

"That sounds like Leo, all right. He has a sour disposition when it comes to the Native Americans. I can tell you right now, this tape isn't gonna improve it none."

The tribal council was having an internal war about the tribal police force. Cecil Crow and Emmy Chandler were at odds with most of the other members of the council about appointing Enos Clay as police chief. Crow still had a rosy ass over the episode that made him the lead man in a one-horse shithole town. Every time he saw Clay or Zane Hammond, he wondered just how much they had to do with the Yellowhenry escapade. Emmy was pissed that Hammond was even whiter than Yellowhenry and seemed on a fast track to permanent status on the force.

Their solution had been to advertise for a replacement with experience as a tribal police officer. Applicants needed to be at least three-quarters, Cree. They found two. One was an old man who was simply worn out with the boredom of retirement. He was at least seventy and perhaps closer to eighty. When attorney Albert Silverhorn asked him what his greatest ambition was he said, "I'd like to get in one more gunfight before I die."

The second applicant was, at first, promising. He checked off most of the boxes. He was a hundred-percenter, thirty-five years old, in excellent physical condition, and a man with five years of experience. "I notice on your application a break in law enforcement employment. What? A couple of years. Why is that?" Rory Blue wanted to know.

"I lost interest in the physical part of it. Saw too many cases of people with communicable diseases. Being the chief of the department, I wouldn't be involved in takedowns of that sort. I'd dispatch a deputy."

"You mean you wouldn't even assist?" Blue asked.

"The deputies would be on call twenty-four hours a day. That way, as police chief, there would be no need for me to get involved."

"Without getting personal," Blue said, "doesn't that describe a physical coward?"

"While some view it in that light, I choose to believe that the dignity of the office is preserved when the police chief is not required to roll around in the dirt."

"Well," Crow said, "there is certainly nothing wrong with that point of view. Our last chief wallowed in dirt, shit, and piss. And look what it got us."

"I have a question," Jordy Kelly said. "How much does having deputies on call twenty-four hours a day cost?"

"It depends somewhat on what they're making now," the fellow answered.

When he was told what the deputies were being paid, he seemed stunned. "That's it?" he asked.

"What's wrong with that?" Emmy Chandler demanded.

"It makes me immediately ask what you pay your chief officer?"

When he was advised, he laughed, thanked them for their interest, and left.

"Well, that was damned rude," Emmy declared.

"I recall what Chief Yellowhenry told us when we canceled his raise and basically told him to go to hell. He said in tribes of our size we're dead last in what we dedicate to our police department. I think we should examine that part of this endeavor before we embarrass ourselves further by being so damned cheap," Billy Roundbelly offered.

"That bastard was overpaid, in my opinion." Emmy fired back.

"Well, that bastard is making double as a highway patrolman, and he works eight-hour shifts. I'd say that reflects back on us. And that bastard didn't sit on his dead ass and act like King Tut, either," Blue retorted.

"He still stays in touch with the people, too," Roundbelly added. "After that last blizzard, he drove all over town checking on us. He didn't need to do that. So, maybe we need a bastard like that one, Emmy, whether you and Cecil like it or not."

After another half hour of wrangling, the council did elevate Enos Clay to Yellowhenry's vacated position as police chief. At the same time, they instructed him to seek out a deputy to replace him. They also voted for an across-the-board increase in the police department's budget of twenty percent. It was left up to Clay how the additional funds would be used.

Clay's first action was to install Zane Hammond as a full-time deputy. Thanks to Yellowhenry each of the two tribal officers was assigned his own patrol car. Then Clay began a quiet talent search for a second deputy. A most surprising applicant mailed in a resume, including a picture. Enos and Zane were opening the morning mail. "This has the look of a job applicant, Sheriff," Zane said.

"Would you stop that?" Enos said. "Just call me Enos. Callin' me 'Sheriff' makes me half think you're resentful. So knock it off."

"Respect for the office, Enos. You just aren't used to it yet."

"What the hell," Clay suddenly exclaimed. "Do you know who this applicant is?"

"Not a clue."

"It's Barbara."

"Front desk, Barbara?"

"Yeah. She says in her cover letter that promoting her and hiring someone to take her place would be a much more efficient process. She also points out that a woman deputy provides value in handling and processing women arrestees. Did you know she's only thirty-three years old?"

"I've never thought of her as of any age," Zane replied.

"I haven't either, but we need to take a serious look at her now. I don't want to start my new job being thought of as sexist."

Let's see—five foot eight, one thirty-five, works out regularly. Single, lives on the reservation. Formerly, she was a high school lacrosse player and spent two years studying social work and police forensics at Montana Tech in Butte. Her folks live in Shelby, where her father is an elementary school teacher. She has five siblings. Both parents are white, and her maternal grandfather was full-blood Cree," Enos said, laying the application on his desk. "What do you think?

"I'd say give her an interview," Zane said. "You'd be sexist if you didn't. And she's just as much Cree as I am."

"Well, no time like the present," Enos said. He buzzed Barbara and asked her to come back to his office.

"I see you have my application," she said.

"Just came in the mail," Enos said. "As a matter of curiosity, why did you mail it?"

"To make sure that it gets noted on the daily mail log. And to remove any possible taint of favoritism. I want to be considered on merit," Barbara answered.

"So noted," Enos said. "You have two years of study in law enforcement at Montana Tech. No degree, though. I think that's a two-year program. Why didn't you get a degree?"

"I was also studying social work. I didn't have enough credits for a degree in either one. I just ran out of money."

"After you graduated from high school until you went to Tech, some ten years, you show no work record. Did you work during that time?"

"No. I was married, but it didn't work out. We divorced."

"No children?"

"Three miscarriages. I just never was able to complete a pregnancy. It was one of the factors in the divorce. My ex has remarried and has two children now."

"Are you bitter about that?"

"No. Disappointed in myself and pleased for him."

"Is it your ultimate goal to remarry and have children?"

"No. I plan to enjoy your kids," she smiled.

"Lucky them," Enos said, returning her smile. "Do you have plans to complete your degree?"

"In conjunction with a job, after I've had some experience, I would consider night school or correspondence classes. I have a couple semesters of work to complete, yet."

"Tell me why you want this job?"

"The experience I have working for Sheriff Yellowhenry has given me a good look at what the job entails. I feel capable and it's what I was preparing myself for at Montana Tech. So, instead of starting with a degree, I would be starting with on the job training."

"All right then. I'll keep your application right on top of the stack, Barbara. We'll make our final decision sometime next week."

Enos Clay's search for a deputy of Cree extraction yielded one more applicant. The old man came back in and requested an oral interview only. More from amusement than anything else, Enos granted his request. "Explain why you are interested in going back into law enforcement," he began.

"I have much experience that would benefit a sheriff."

"I see. Do you drive?"

"No. I would need a desk job and be an advisor."

"A long head is always appreciated. You are known as Ned Long, but what is your Cree name?"

"Cold Hawk. My father was Bold Hawk who named a canyon Moose's Ass. I was born in the coldest winter in memory. My father honored the Great Spirit by naming me Cold Hawk."

"Very honorable. When were you in law enforcement?"

"Too many moons ago to remember."

"Why did you quit?"

"I killed a man too many."

"Can you explain that?"

"Yes. I was in a gunfight. The sheriff back then was Black Nose—one trigger-happy sonofabitch. We chased rustlers up into Lost Horse. Together we had 'em in a crossfire. Killed all four. But I killed Black Nose, too. Maybe accidentally. Who knows?" Long said sadly. "The council didn't want me after that."

"Okay, Ned, I will write out your application for you. Do you know your age?"

"Maybe fifty."

"Maybe seventy, too?" Enos asked.

"Maybe."

Chapter Forty-Two

In the Montana State Highway Patrol Office, the Tape from Choteau came to be known as the Tape from Hell. The state patrol launched an in-depth investigation that worked from the ground up. The team started by verifying the statements from the two Creed kids. At first, in fear of their father, they attempted to deny what they had said. When they were assured that their father would not be charged further due to double jeopardy, but that if they lied about their prior statements, they could be sent to reformatories, the little canaries spilled their guts.

The next layer of the onion involved Sissy Creed, who was in charge of the finances. The bank records were subpoenaed. They showed payments of several thousand dollars to Leo Altarena. His bank accounts showed cash withdrawals that corresponded to payments from the poaching consortium. One of the patrolmen confessed to accepting graft to hide the poaching activities. He fingered three others. When Altarena finally relented after cutting a deal with the prosecuting attorney, admitting to paying cuts, and naming who was receiving them, Ted Smith disappeared. Altarena and four other officers were discharged and agreed to pay fines in lieu of incarceration. Temporary staff was assigned while interviews for permanent staff were conducted. Sheriff Lance Porter of Lewis and Clark County also lost his job.

A month later, the patrol was still looking for a patrolman and a captain for Great Falls. It was mid-December when Captain Harbold called Yellowhenry into his office. "Joe, the patrol is having a hell of a time filling those positions in the Great Falls office. Especially the captain's slot. They want me to go down there with a very healthy raise, but I have to find a replacement for here. Someone who has at least been a sheriff. The only guy in sight is you."

"Me?" Yellowhenry blurted. "Sheriff of a three-person Indian office? There are officers here who have a lot of seniority over me. What's wrong with Art?"

"Never had experience above the patrolman level. I know it's a stretch, Joe, but think about this. The circumstances surrounding this opportunity are something I've never heard of or seen before. They're likely never to occur again. If you turn this down, you're also likely never to get the chance to move up again. It's a once-in-a-career opportunity. Take a couple of days to think it over, Joe. You'd be doing me one hell of a big favor if you'd take the leap."

Yellowhenry invited his old staff and Minnie to come to his place for a cold-weather barbeque to take place the evening of the following day. Minnie agreed to spend the afternoon tending pork ribs on a charcoal grill and rotisserie set up in the breezeway of the stable. Amy prepared Boston Baked Beans and potato salad. Pitchers of lemonade and water were the beverages of choice. Dinner was served à la carte at six o'clock. When everyone was fed and all the youngsters settled down, Yellowhenry announced that it was time for everyone to pay for their dinner by giving him some advice.

"Enos, you pay first," he began. "What I want is your opinion of my taking over the job of running the state patrol office here in Havre. Go."

"Well, I'd say you'd piss off a whole bunch of troopers who have seniority over you."

"That's what I said, but I have a required qualification they don't. I was a sheriff. So, Zane, your turn. What do you think?"

"I think you'll have a job from hell. Those staters, like that Tibbetts we ran into coming back from Lewistown, have a pretty low opinion of Indians. Having to work for one is gonna make 'em resentful as hell."

"Minnie, your turn," Yellowhenry directed.

"Joe, you're as much white as you are Indian. Hell, you live like a white man. Make 'em believe you're white, and that you didn't take the job as a favor to the red man."

"Amy, your turn."

"If it gets me a septic tank, do it."

"Okay," Yellowhenry laughed. "Lily, what are you thinking?"

"After the trouble you had with Cecil Crow, my mother, the lawyer, and the council, I'd say you're as ready as anyone else for a job like that."

"Shirley, what do you think?" he asked.

"You know what everybody does in that office. Just take the reins from Captain Harbold and do what he does."

"Barbara, what say you?"

"Montana Tech has an excellent law enforcement and management program you can sign up for and take by correspondence. If I were you, I'd sign up right away and start cementing your credentials."

"All right. Thank you all," he concluded. "I have some thinking to do, but I appreciate what you've said."

Yellowhenry waited another day so he could talk to Amy in depth about making the move. She was supportive. "Joe, you've proven your capability," she said. "Don't doubt yourself. But I think Barbara had an excellent suggestion. Elevate your qualifications. Just starting a law enforcement program will make your patrolmen believe you are a professional and dedicated lawman. It will also give you belief in yourself. When you have an empty place, like self-doubt, doing something constructive and positive to fill it is what you should do. The doing is what's important. It becomes its own objective. But, honey, do what's in your heart. I'll be happy either way."

The following morning, Yellowhenry walked into Harbold's office with a cup of coffee in hand. "Well, Joe," Harbold said. "Let me guess. You've come to a decision. Is that right?"

"One question, Captain. Does the patrol have a program so that I could get some financial aid in going after a degree in law enforcement?"

"You mean by correspondence?"

"Yes. It's the only way I could do it."

"Do you have a school in mind?"

"Montana Tech in Butte."

"I believe they do. It's a hell of a good idea, Joe. So, how does that impact your thinking?"

"If the job is available and I qualify, I'll take it."

"If the work-study is offered, that is. Is that what you're telling me?"

"No. I'll take the job either way," Yellowhenry grinned. "I just want the state to pay for my schooling."

"I like that," Harbold laughed, "and I agree with you. The state will be the one benefitting from it, so why shouldn't they pay for it?"

"I'll let Helena know that we're making the switch up here, and I'll put the bee on 'em at the same time for your studies. You need to recruit someone to take your spot. Have anyone in mind?"

"As a matter of fact, I do. Not a for-sure thing, but I'll talk to him as soon as I'm sure I'm solid here."

"Excellent," Harbold said, rubbing his hands together. "Let's get the ball rolling."

Forty-eight hours later, the announcement was made at an all-staff assembly that Captain Harbold was transferring to Great Falls and that Joe Yellowhenry would be assuming the captain's position in Havre. The reaction was mixed. Congratulations for Harbold were uniform, but caution and disbelief were just as uniform for Yellowhenry. Harbold spoke for a couple of minutes, laying out the necessary requirements as defined by Human Resources in Helena.

That having, at minimum, sheriff's credentials was questioned by one of the patrolmen, who pointed out that Harbold himself had never been a sheriff.

"You're right," he said, "and I wouldn't qualify under the new guidelines. But times have changed. Now, Joe has a few words for you."

"Thank you, Captain," he said. "You are all professional lawmen and lawwomen. My job as captain doesn't alter the expectation from the Montana State Highway Patrol that you will continue to function as a professionals. My job is to assist you, just as Captain Harbold has, in building and maintaining that professionalism. That is what I intend to do. My door will always be open to you. Thank you."

When the assemblage had dispersed and its members had started their daily routine, Harbold and Yellowhenry retreated to the captain's private office, where Harbold began the work of preparing the new captain for the duties of supervising twelve patrol officers and four female staff members.

They had barely sat down when a patrolman rapped on the frame of the open door. Harbold looked up and greeted him. "Hello, Pete. What do you need?"

"Turnin' in my badge and equipment, Captain."

"All right. Come in and have a seat. Close the door, if you will, please. Captain Yellowhenry," Harbold said, "this is Pete Leeman, one of your patrol officers. Pete, meet Captain Joe Yellowhenry."

The men shook hands as Harbold pulled out a drawer of hanging folders. "This is Pete's file, Joe," he said, pulling a manila folder from the alphabetized material in the drawer. "I'll leave you two to conduct Pete's exit interview." With that, he rose and left the office.

Yellowhenry took a minute to look over the folder. "Pete, you've been on the force for six years. Are you still married?"

"What business is that of yours?" Leeman asked.

"Your folder doesn't appear to have been updated for a while. When you signed on, you were twenty-eight and had two children and a wife, Ida. The business that's mine is that if you walk out on patrol today and get killed in the line of duty, the State of Montana needs to know who your next of kin is, and who stands as the beneficiary of the life insurance this file indicates is in force on your life."

"How much life insurance?"

"The state carries ten thousand, and according to this, at sometime three years ago, you added twenty-five more. Ida Joann Leeman is named as the beneficiary," Yellowhenry said.

"Well, that's right. So what?"

"Are you and Ida still married and living together?"

"Yes, but so what? If I quit, what difference will it make?"

"The insurance stays in effect for some time after you leave the employment of the state."

"Well, there aren't any changes to my insurance status."

"Good. We got that handled. Now, Pete, how many kids do you have these days?"

"Four, but, again, so what?"

"It's winter, Pete. If you need a job, I'd advise you to hang onto this one. You've been, according to your file, a damned fine officer. Why would you want to piss in your own spring water by suddenly, and for no valid reason, becoming a quitter?"

"I don't like this change of captains. There are guys who have been with the patrol for fifteen years. One of them should be the new captain."

"Pete, I don't disagree with how you feel," Yellowhenry said, looking the officer directly in the eye. "But I don't make the rules, and neither do you. I won't accept your badge until you have another job to go to. If you're dead set on leaving the patrol, so be it. But you have a family to take care of first. Go do that. Find a job to go to, come back and resign, and I'll wish you all the best."

Leeman looked at Yellowhenry for a thoughtful moment. "I expected something completely different, Captain. I thought you'd tell me to go to hell. You know, be resentful and throw your weight around."

"I'm here to help my officers however I can. I don't want to lose any of them. If they decide to leave, that's their business, but running away from something without something to run to doesn't make sense," Yellowhenry said. "And I'd like to say something positive to their prospective employers—not that they just quit without notice. It can be damned difficult to get a new job when that happens.”

“All right, Joe,” Leeman said, standing and extending his right hand. “No hard feelings, I hope.”

“None at all, Pete. Just let me know what you decide.”

When Leeman walked out, he passed Harbold. “He’s gonna be all right, Captain,” Leeman said as he walked past. Harbold paused and looked at the back of the departing man. He didn’t see the posture he expected. Leeman was carrying his service belt, and he gave a little tip of the cap and a shrug to the woman at the reception desk. She smiled and glanced over her shoulder at Harbold. Twila Allen had been a mainstay in the office for fifteen years. Yellowhenry would be her third captain. Harbold raised his eyebrows, and she shrugged her shoulders.

Harbold walked back into his office to find Yellowhenry sitting in the command chair, looking at personnel files. “I can help you with that,” he said.

“Oh, that’s all right, John,” Yellowhenry said. “I’ve got it.”

“What’s up with Pete? How did the interview go?”

“I told him to go find another job first. With four kids, he needs to keep a paycheck comin’ in.”

“He didn’t look to me like he planned to quit at all,” Harbold said.

“I left that up to him. He can stay or go. No hard feelings. Say, I notice some of these files don’t seem to be updated.”

"These are just backups. The real ones are in Helena."

"Of course. Should have thought of that myself. For my own edification, though, I'm going to use these as a way of getting to know my staff," Yellowhenry said.

For the rest of the day, Harbold worked over the new captain's shoulder. At day's end, he had a sinking feeling that it seemed too easy for Yellowhenry. That, and an aching back from leaning over as his successor maintained his position squarely behind the captain's desk.

The man seemed to be elevating the captain's position in one day. Harbold began to wonder how much more he could have done while he had had the job. He vowed to see what else he could learn from Yellowhenry in the next three days before he headed for Great Falls.

Chapter Forty-Three

The state patrol, as things shook out, wasn't the only agency having to scrape for replacement personnel. Yellowhenry pulled a raid on the reservation police force and convinced Zane Hammond to transfer to the highway patrol. Enos felt betrayed until Yellowhenry revealed how much Zane would be making as a patrolman. Then, he couldn't blame Zane. Enos wondered if there were any more positions open. "No," Yellowhenry said, "but having some experience as a sheriff would qualify you as a captain at some point in the future. Double the patrolman's salary. You're better off getting some experience here on the rez, Enos. A year, or so. But, if another patrolman's position comes open, you better believe I'll come knocking on your door."

"That's what I'd hope you'd do, Joe. Now, who do I put on the front desk? With Barbara as my only patrol officer, I'll have to take the field to help her, but I need someone to keep the office open and man the phone and radio."

"Until you can find someone permanent, put Ned on as a temp," Yellowhenry said.

Enos looked at his friend to see if there was a joke behind the suggestion. "Why would you suggest him?"

"He knows reservation law. Speaks fluent Cree. Former officer. Don't expect much. It will probably work for Emmy Chandler's wages. If you give him a little training on the phones and radio, he could hold down your fort until you can locate a permanent replacement.”

“Can you imagine what Emmy will say if she walks in or even hears of Ned’s being on the desk?” Enos chortled.

“She’ll demand he be fired. Perfect excuse for a lawsuit for age discrimination,” Yellowhenry grinned. “Cecil will have a cow.”

“God, yes. I’m gonna dress him up in full uniform, badge and all. He’ll look like a prop in a carnival, and they’ll have to take him seriously.”

As a result, Ned, Cold Hawk, Long took up the receptionist’s position at the front desk of the tribal police force offices.

Three days after Harbold left for Great Falls, Yellowhenry had his seat-and-greet meeting with Art McClintock. After updating the file, McClintock asked, “You’re gonna ask me what the boyos and goils really think of ya, eh?”

“No, Art, I’m not. They’re perfectly capable of doing that themselves and I’m not interested in hearsay,” Yellowhenry replied. “This office qualifies for a sergeant. It doesn’t have one. I’d like to put you in for the position.”

McClintock sat frozen as though he hadn’t heard. Then he shook himself a little and said, “I’m just sort of the court jester around here with my looks and all. Really, shouldn’t ya be lookin’ for a more serious lookin’ kind of a fella, eh?”

“You can drop the brogue, Art. It won’t change my mind. You’re the man for the position if you’re willing to accept it. If you don't want it, just say so. I'm not gonna try to get you to change your mind."

"Don't you want to poll the others to see what they'd think of it?"

"No, Art, I don't. That would give them the idea that this office is run by a committee or, even worse, a council. It isn't. I decide on personnel issues. If you have to get their approval, then you aren't the man for the job, either. It's your decision. Yours and nobody else's."

"All right, Captain Yellowhenry put me up for the stripes."

"Good. And, Art, stop bein' the court jester. This isn't high school anymore."

The Christmas holidays came and went. Amy was not too much into the spirit of the white man's festivities. She and Yellowhenry hosted a dinner and gave the guests small practical gifts. The children were given candy canes. Juneteenth and Indigenous People's Day were much more meaningful times for the people. Yellowhenry did give Amy a written promise that as soon as the frost came out of the ground in the spring, she would get her septic tank. It was at the dinner that Zane and Lily announced that they were expecting. Neither Amy nor Shirley were, and they both announced that they were happy they weren't.

Then, Minnie went into one of the bedrooms unseen. When she returned she was featuring a bump. "I have an announcement," she said. "I've been hiding it long enough. Cold Hawk and I are expecting." Everyone laughed, except for Ned Long, himself.

"Like father, like son," he finally said when the laughter died.

That sent Minnie into peals of laughter, "How did you find out?" she asked as she pulled the pillow from under her jacket.

"It made his year. He was too proud to keep it secret. He would be unhappy with me if all I begat was a pillow."

She threw the pillow at him and said, "That's what you get for wasting all those years."

"Maybe, but we were both with others," he said.

"I know, but I wouldn't have told 'em if you wouldn't have."

"And there you have it, folks," Ned grinned, "the story of my life. Just a pile of sand behind the teepee."

Ned's work at the tribal police reception desk was impeccable. He was smooth, professional, and informed. Cecil Crow was the first to object. "Is Sheriff Clay here?" he had asked.

"No sir. He is on patrol. Radio dispatched, however. If your business is urgent, I can call him and request his immediate return. I just need your name and the nature of your business."

"I am the tribal chairman, Cecil Crow. I want to talk to the sheriff about personnel matters."

"Very good, sir," Ned said. He turned and keyed the mic to Clay's car. "Base to Sheriff Clay."

"Clay, here. Go ahead."

"Cecil Crow requests your immediate return to base to discuss personnel matters."

"Acknowledged. ETA to base, ten minutes. Clay clear."

"Base clear," Ned said. "Mr. Crow, let me buzz you in. We have a fresh pot of coffee if you'd care for a cup while you wait."

Crow was somewhat taken aback by the efficiency with which Ned whisked him into Clay's private office and set him up with coffee just the way he liked it. The man was also dressed in a clean pressed uniform. The only thing he had against Ned Long was his age. His problem was how to replace the old man without legal repercussions or the appearance of being guilty of old age discrimination.

"Cecil, what can I do for you?" Enos asked.

"Close the door, Sheriff Clay. What I have to discuss with you is personal and confidential," Crow said.

"Okay," Enos said. He closed the door, returned to his desk, and rummaged around in one of the desk drawers. He pulled out a tape recorder and set it up by recording the date and time, the nature of the conference, and who was involved.

"Hey," Cecil said. "I didn't want this talk on the record."

"As the chief of police, I need the conversation documented, Cecil. This is a lot cheaper than having a court recorder take it down. You understand?"

"I just wanted to toss some suggestions around, was all. More of a brainstorming session."

"When it involves police force personnel, even a brainstorming session needs to have documentation," Enos said. "I checked with Albert Silverhorn and he agrees. So what do you have in mind?"

"It just seems that a younger man on the desk might be better in the long run. You know, someone with longer-term employment prospects."

"We tried that and it didn't yield someone willing to work for the pay we offer. In fact, Ned Long is proving to be reliable and capable. He also is working for a little more than half pay for his position. Until a permanent prospect can be located, Ned is doing a fine job. But, you have the authority to fire him, if you want. He'll sue in federal district court for wrongful dismissal under age discrimination laws, though. Just give me the word, Cec, and I'll cut him loose. That's really why I'm taping this conversation. So, do you want him gone bad enough to fire him?"

"No, I'm merely suggesting that you could be more diligent in looking for permanent prospects," Crow answered quickly.

"I'm spending twenty-five dollars a week on radio ads, forty on newspaper ads, and I have a notice posted at the Langston's General Store. Liam Greene answered that. He's younger, a horse thief, and in a wheelchair. Does that disqualify him?"

"Oh, for chrissakes, you don't need me to tell you that."

"I'll take that as a 'yes'," Enos said.

"I have more trouble with this department than any department on the reservation. Can you explain that?"

"Maybe because law enforcement is the most problematic. Maybe because the pay scale is barely above the poverty level. What is it in your opinion?" Enos asked, turning the question back to Crow.

"We added twenty percent to your budget. What else do you want?"

"Thank you for that. But inflation is running at six percent, we were at least ten percent under par to begin with, so, the effective positive influence is four percent. Doesn't exactly stimulate a job rush, does it?"

"When you put it like that, I suppose not."

"How would you put it?" Enos asked.

"I'm not an economist, so I wouldn't. I have things to do, so you can turn that thing off."

"That's fine, Cecil, I'll get it after you leave. Thanks for your input."

"There are subjects I wanted to talk about that do not need recording, Sheriff," Crow snapped.

"I'd say that's why I should record them. I'm not interested in backroom conversations, Cecil."

"Even the council has closed-door sessions, Sheriff. That's all I'm talking about."

"I'm not the council and anything you have to say about my department is something I want a record of. It's not for public consumption, Cecil, unless it's contrary to law, tribal code, or custom. It's not that, is it?"

"We had some real problems with Yellowhenry if you care to remember."

"So, you're saying Joe broke code or law?"

"Not specifically. But he was on the line."

"No, he wasn't. If you contend that, you're stating he operated lawlessly. He did some things you didn't like, but Silverhorn advised you throughout that entire period. He found nothing Joe did outside the law. Maybe you should go ask Albert to quit if he can't give you the advice you want."

"Oh, for God's sake. Let me outta here," Crow stormed.

"Thanks for the visit, Cecil," Enos hollered at the chairman's retreating back. "Good talk."

As he went sailing past Ned, the old fellow commented, "Nice to see you, Mr. Crow. Feel free to come back anytime."

"Yeah, right," Crow growled as he stalked out and returned to his own office.

Chapter Forty-Four

The first crisis Yellowhenry had to face was a cadre of officers who tried to undermine Art McClintock's authority. Of the four, two had more seniority and two were younger officers with less than five years on the force. McClintock had been assigned to monitor and control patrol assignments to balance coverage. Three patrol cars were taken out of commission in a multi-car accident during a late January snowstorm. That meant that patrol cars had to be shared from shift to shift. The obvious procedure was to pull cars from the three most junior members of the force who had vehicles permanently assigned to them. The rub was that two of the officers lived between fifteen and twenty miles out of town. They had to use their personal rigs to commute to work. So, they decided on their own to start their shifts, not when they arrived at headquarters, but when they left their homes. They also cut shifts to accommodate their returns. The two colluded and shaved an hour off each end of their shifts. The other pair supported their contention. McClintock disagreed.

They brought the complaint to Yellowhenry. "So, you two, Trooper Hamilton and Trooper Cole are the two involved directly in this matter. Troopers Costas and Lindley, what do you have to do with it?"

"We're here to give our support to Mike and Cory," Lindley answered.

"So noted, gentlemen," Yellowhenry said. "You're excused."

"We'd rather remain and serve as witnesses," Costas stated.

"I see, so you feel like you are likely to bear witness to something untoward which is, quite frankly, none of your business?" Yellowhenry asked.

"We don't see it that way," Lindley responded.

"Well, I see it this way. You two are meddling in my ability to administer this office. So be it. You may listen and not comment."

"Sergeant McClintock, you have concluded that Troopers Hamilton and Cole are inappropriately docking their time on the job. Two hours a shift in the case of each. Trooper Hamilton to cover a total of thirty miles. Trooper Lindley to cover thirty-eight miles. Trooper Hamilton, how do you justify the two-hour reduction in your on the job time to drive thirty miles, twenty of which is paved?"

"Well, ah, I just rounded it off. Didn't think too much of it. Wasn't a big deal."

"The state of Montana pays patrol officers portal to portal. When you have a patrol unit at home, that is your portal. When the unit is here at headquarters, that is your portal. You fellas know that," Yellowhenry explained. "Trooper Hamilton, do you have anything to add?"

"Not really. I think this whole thing is just part of the chickenshit program that came with Abe's phony promotion to Sergeant."

"Okay. Well, here's how we're going to settle this. Sergeant McClintock, how many hours have these officers reduced time on the job?" Yellowhenry asked.

"Hamilton, twelve hours, and Lindley ten hours."

"All right gentlemen, those hours will not be deducted from your pay provided that no future deductions occur. If they do, you will go on report and all hours will be deducted," Yellowhenry decided. "All of you are dismissed. Trooper Hamilton, I need to speak to you personally."

"We'll be staying to witness what you say to our fellow officer," Lindley asserted.

"Very well. All of this has been recorded and my remarks to Trooper Hamilton will also be recorded," Yellowhenry advised.

"I know what you're gonna say, so just get it over with," Hamilton said. "It won't be the first time I've had my ass chewed."

Yellowhenry smiled, "Well, Trooper Hamilton, your next reprimand won't take place in this office. You are now assigned to the Miles City office. You are being given a week's paid leave of absence to arrange your affairs and to report for duty. That is all. Turn your cruiser keys into Sergeant McClintock and leave immediately. You are dismissed."

"This is bullshit," Hamilton shouted as he left.

"Hey," Lindley said, "what gives you the right to just move an officer like that?"

"The superintendent of the Montana State Highway Patrol approved the transfer, Trooper Lindley. If you want to take the matter up with him, be my guest. If you continue to challenge my decisions, you will find yourself listed on the transfer register. Do you have something else you would like to add to these proceedings?"

"No. I just thought moving him away from his home was damned harsh, if I may be so bold."

"Trooper Lindley," Yellowhenry returned, "you've heard for weeks how Trooper Hamilton derogates me and Sergeant McClintock. He did it not five minutes ago. Helena left the matter in my hands but with a strong recommendation for dismissal. The transfer was the option I chose. When a man under my command delegates himself the duty of being a cancer to his superior officers, you may trust that his tenure here is going to be damned short. If I can transfer him to another assignment, I will do so. If I can't, he will be terminated. Is that clear Trooper Costas?"

"Oh, yes sir, Captain," Costas answered hastily. "And, don't get me wrong. I'm not agitatin' by bein' here."

"Trooper Lindley, do you have more input?"

"Ah, no. Not at the moment."

"Then let me put you on notice," Yellowhenry said severely. "If you have doubts or criticism about how I'm administering this office, you're advised to bring them to me personally. We'll discuss them on their merits. If they will improve how we operate, we'll put them into action, and I'll give you credit for them. If they are of the sort Hamilton has been spreading, come see me, and we'll talk it out. Do not make the mistake of fomenting dissension behind my back. Is that clear, Trooper Lindley?"

"Yes, Captain Yellowhenry. That's very clear. May I ask, however, that my name be entered on the transfer register?"

"Certainly. Are you available for immediate assignment?"

"That would depend upon where the transfer was."

"The State of Montana assures you a job. It doesn't allow you to select the place of your assignment. I'll move you to Libby immediately."

"No, no. Not there, Captain. Anywhere but there."

"That's all that's available right now, Trooper Lindley. So, you have three options: stay here and be a productive contributor, go to Libby, or quit. Pick one. I'll give you ten seconds to decide."

"How can you fill two positions just like that?"

"Graduates from the academy in Helena. Three seconds."

"I'll stay here, for now."

"No, Trooper Lindley. The slant of your conversation makes it clear that you are not dedicated to this office. You still have two choices. You can remain an officer—just not here—or you can quit. Ten seconds."

"Sir, I apologize. My family is here. My kids are in school. I have to work. I can't quit. Please, disregard my comments. They were not well thought out. I want to stay on the force here."

"Trooper Costas, you are dismissed," Yellowhenry said. Then he buzzed Sergeant McClintock's office. "Art, would you come to my office, please?"

A moment later, McClintock stepped into the captain's office. "Have a seat, Art," Yellowhenry said. "I need to discuss with you and Trooper Lindley his tenure here in this office. He has been challenging my decisions. How has he been in dealing with you?"

"To be honest, Captain," McClintock said, looking directly at Lindley, "things are beginning to look up, aren't they, Larry?"

"Definitely, Art," Lindley said, color draining from his face.

"All right, then. Trooper Lindley, I'm placing you on probation for thirty days. If either Sergeant McClintock or I have cause for a disciplinary hearing within that time frame because of your comments or your actions, you will be terminated. You are dismissed."

Lindley rose quickly and left Yellowhenry's office."Art, I've transferred Hamilton to Miles City. Pull his keys and lock the unit in the shop. Make sure he leaves immediately. If he gives you any grief, fire him. Be sure you protect yourself if you do. You'll have to pull his sidearm, service belt, and badge. Let me know if you need assistance."

"Right 'o, Captain," McClintock said as he rose and exited the office.

Chapter Forty-Five

Things in the patrol office took on the ambiance of people walking on eggshells. Most of the officers feared the transfer of Hamilton and the probationary status of Lindley to be the start of a major shakeup. They hurried past Yellowhenry's open door and wasted no time around the vending machines and coffee pots. Shifts were started right on time and radio communication became suddenly sharper and quite professional.

Twila Allen dropped into Yellowhenry's office a couple of days later. She closed his door and walked to stand in front of his desk. "Have a seat, Twila," he said. "What's on your mind?"

"Well," she said, sitting down uncomfortably, "you're my third captain, you know?"

"Yes," he said, waiting for her to continue.

"We've never had an incident like the one involving Mike and Larry before."

He looked at her and continued waiting. She crossed and recrossed her legs. Finally, he said, "Do you want to file a complaint, Twila?"

"No. I'd be afraid of being transferred."

He turned around and pulled a form from his credenza. "This is the form, in triplicate, if you'd like to detail the problem and send it along to Human Resources in Helena, Twila," he said. "You have every right to do so, and if I interfered, I would be called in on report. I would never transfer you or an officer for filing a legitimate complaint about how I manage this office. I could quite well learn from those complaints. So, you can file the complaint, or we can keep what you have to say in-house. I'll record our conversation, if you want, and give you a copy to protect the integrity of your comments. How do you want to do this?"

"I don't want to cause trouble. I just thought you'd like to know how people feel."

"I see. I take it they confide in you, then. Is that right?"

"They always have."

"Well, I can't think of anyone better," he said.

"How about you?" she asked.

"I'm not here for that. I'll be friendly and compassionate, but as their supervisor, there's a level of detachment I need to maintain so that our personal relationships don't become entangled in management or legal decisions. In short, I'm not going to be anyone's best friend in this office, Twila. That's just a management technique."

"Okay, I can see that. But the men think you're kind of a tyrant."

"Thanks for that, Twila," he chuckled. "I'll try smiling more often."

She grinned, "That would be a start."

The next day, Yellowhenry took a ride along with his daytime patrolman, Paul Norris, who was assigned to the eastern sector. When they reached Dodson, he instructed

Norris to turn north and then into the lane to the Bar H Seven ranch. "What's down here?" Norris asked.

"Lady rancher. Lost her husband in a bear attack. I helped her out."

"Hey, I remember that. Yeah, Yellowhenry. That was the officer who brought her husband out. The story sort of said if you'd left him there, he might have made it. Not accusing you, Captain, you understand," he said quickly.

"You ever try to stop a Grizzly with a .30-30, Paul?"

"Never been in that kind of situation."

"Would you?"

"Hell, no. Unless it was all I had."

"Good answer. I agree with you. That's why I brought Malone out. I wasn't willing to wait for the bear to come back to try out that reporter's contention. She thought I should have waited even if I was only armed with a .22. But, some fools thought a .30-30 would do the trick. I'd like to be a bird up a tree when one of those heroes puts that theory to the test," Yellowhenry said.

"Is there some follow-up reason for us to be here?" Norris asked.

"Just a friendly visit, Paul."

When the two knocked on the front door, Carolyn Malone answered the knock. "Joe," she said as she stepped forward and embraced him. "Come in," she insisted as she took his arm leading him through the living room and into the kitchen.

Along the way, he introduced Norris. She sat them down for cups of coffee. "Where are the triplets?" Yellowhenry asked.

"Taking naps. My nanny's with them."

"Damn," Yellowhenry smiled. "I had my heart set on bouncing them on my knee."

"They would have loved that, Joe."

"Well, maybe next time, Carolyn," he said. "How are things working out with Hank."

"He and my nanny are getting married. Here on the ranch. You'll get an invitation to come with your family. He's doing so good, Joe. He really knows horses and cattle, weather, fencing, wiring, plumbing, and carpentry. He's a good mechanic, too. Hell, I would have married him."

"Now, now, Carolyn," Yellowhenry laughed, "I'm not sure he'd survive that."

"Oh, Joe, I'd only sleep with him like I slept with you. Make sure he lasted to keep on ranchin'."

"Paul, I'll explain that to you later," Yellowhenry grinned.

"I can't wait," Norris laughed. "That ought to be good."

"Amy is still okay with that, isn't she, Joe?" Carolyn giggled. "We could do a rehearsal to prove how good we were."

"That's very kind, but I'm a one-and-done kinda guy, I'm afraid. Well, I just wanted to stop by and see how you're doing. I'm pleased to hear it's all good. We'll be here for the wedding, for sure." He stood up and hugged her. "Just remember, if I can be of any help, let me know."

"I will, Joe. I'm going to be in town in a couple of days. Would you let Amy know I'll drop by for a visit."

"I'll do that. Give my best to Hank and Betty. Tell 'em congratulations for me."

On the way back to the highway, Norris asked, "Captain, that was a very friendly visit. Do you mind if I ask why you aren't like that around headquarters?"

"No, I don't mind. How would you like me to become a buddy and show favoritism to you?"

"As long as it was the same for everybody else, I wouldn't mind," Norris answered.

"Okay, so we're all pals. Then I have to put one of us up on report which leads to a termination. How do you suppose that would work out?"

"Well, there would be some who wouldn't understand, I suppose."

"That's right. I would have to justify my actions to everyone individually. Some would blame me regardless of the circumstances. In other words, it would be ruled by a committee. My position as Captain would be subjugated to the feelings of my buddies. Isn't that right?" Yellowhenry asked.

"When you put it like that, yeah, I see your point."

"I hope so, Paul. I'll be your professional friend but understand that I am the captain. No one else. Me."

"All right, Captain," Norris said. "I understand where you're coming from."

Chapter Forty-Six

Yellowhenry, following the success of his ridealong with Paul Norris, decided to repeat the activity with the rest of his officers, including those on swing and graveyard shifts. Some were more successful than others, but the overall effect was to establish that he was the boss. A good one. The result was that the talk around the office cooler was respectful of the boss and absent the snide comments that so often get leveled at managers.

Art McClintock followed the example of the ride-along, but only on the day shift. With a lot less to prove, he still benefited from his effort. He and Yellowhenry were regarded as a team; it was a privilege to work with them. The working relationship was proven late that winter when a high-speed chase out of Missoula required a roadblock on the highway to Shelby. The culprits were three bank robbers who had taken a pair of hostages. The women were a thirty-five-year-old woman and her eighteen-year-old daughter. Both became repeated victims of rape. The three criminals were an escaped convict, Vaughan Reynolds, his brother Henry, and a pal of Henry's, Allen Clasper. Henry and Allen were both nineteen-year-olds with extensive juvenile histories of crime. Vaughan had been sentenced to a term of ten years for second-degree manslaughter. The crime had been plea-bargained down from murder. He had been imprisoned for five years at the time of his escape. At six feet four inches and two hundred twenty-five pounds, the thirty-year-old was a ripped physical specimen. He shaved his head, but he wore a full dark brown beard. His black eyes were sunk deeply into his flat face, which featured a button nose. After five years without a woman, he was sexually voracious.

The two women were, unfortunately, waiting for a bank officer to help them with a loan for the daughter's tuition to attend Arizona State University. The three bank robbers, brandishing firearms, had hit the teller's cages and were shooting into the ceiling as they backed out toward the street where they had parked a stolen Chevrolet Impala. Vaughan Reynolds noticed the women cowering down as they embraced each other in huddled fear. He hustled them out of the bank at gunpoint and into the back seat of the roomy Impala.

Lorna Christensen and her daughter Phyllis were attractive, blonde, and devoted to daily workout regimens. They were dressed in workout clothes. Both had been high school athletes. Lorna was a divorcee. With Henry driving and Allen Clasper watching from the passenger front seat, Vaughan took a screaming, crying Phyllis first. The rape was a rage of bloody passion as he vented himself on the virgin. A half-hour later, he was on the mother. Clasper hooted and cheered as he masturbated in the front seat.

The men traded positions over the next several hours. The women whose pleading, crying, and screaming seemed to be as much a stimulant as a deterrant, became numb as the continuous ravaging exhausted them both physically and mentally. They finally became silent sufferers who endured the assaults with closed eyes. From one man to the next, they scarcely knew who of the three was raping them.

The route of travel was by way of back roads. By the time the highway patrol had set up roadblocks on the interstate both north and south of Missoula, the trio was onto back roads leading northeast toward Conrad and Shelby. They had been lucky, missing two different county roadblocks. Yellowhenry's roadblock was set up twenty-five miles east of Shelby, where the highway intersected a gravel road that led to the north and south. The stop's location was just beyond the crest of a hill, concealed by head-high brush. Hidden in the brush, a spotter equipped with binoculars and a handheld two-way radio was calling in vehicles heading east. However, the white Impala the patrol was searching for was nowhere in sight.

Henry was the one who noticed that the car was low on fuel. "What are we gonna do with these two while we gas up?" Clasper asked.

"In the trunk," Vaughan answered.

"What's to keep 'em from kicking the trunk lid and hollerin'," Clasper asked.

"You."

"Me?"

"Yeah, you. You're the only one of us small enough to lay in there with 'em."

"Not to be a pussy, but those two could be damned difficult to keep quiet," Clasper said.

"You'll have a gun. Keep it on the daughter. Right under her chin. The mother won't move for fear you'll shoot the daughter," Vaughan said.

"Fine, but I get to be doin' one of 'em while I'm back there."

"Couldn't think of anything fairer than that, Allen," Vaughan said.

"We got another problem," Henry said. "The young one bled all over the back seat. How are we gonna hide that?"

"Little brother, you look awful tired to me. You'll be in the back seat taking a nap. Right over that blood spot."

"I can do that."

With everyone in place, Vaughan said, "Let's roll. Five miles to Choteau. We'll gas up there."

The women were forced into the trunk. Lorna was pressed in first followed by Allen. Phyllis was placed where he could spoon her from behind while pressing a handgun in his left hand under her chin. He forced himself into her as soon as the trunk lid closed.

Vaughan pulled into a Texaco full-serve station ten minutes later. Henry was stretched out in the back seat. "Fill 'er up," Vaughan instructed the attendant as he walked around the front of the car to use the restroom. He noticed the attendant take a double take as he glanced at the front of Vaughan's pants when they passed each other. He looked down at himself and saw a dark red stain that was spread across both sides of the crotch of his gray canvas pants. "Had to heave a road-killed deer off the road," he explained. "Damned thing must have dumped blood on me."

"Bad place for a blood spot," the attendant laughed.

"You got that right," Vaughan called back over his shoulder. In the restroom, he used wet paper towels to work on the smear. It wasn't perfect but he figured when it dried, he could get by. He also decided it was time to ditch the hostages. After paying for the fuel, he pulled away from the Texaco and headed for Conrad. Ten miles out he pulled over into a passing lane wideout and stopped. After emptying the trunk of its three occupants, he announced, "Change of plans, boys. Get your last piece. The ladies need to go. They've served their purpose."

"I'm good," Allen grinned. "That last piece in the trunk was kinky and special. She gripped. It was probably the power of suggestion."

"Yeah, I'll bet," Vaughan chuckled. "A whisper in the ear and a gun to the chin. Hell, I'd clinch like a python if that was me in there."

"They're so loose now that I'm fine," Henry said.

"That's a wrap then. Let's boogey," Vaughan commanded.

They had been on the road for a while when Henry asked his brother, "Where are we gonna dump the broads?"

"Let's look for someplace with some cover or a canyon or a big open field. It'll be dark pretty soon. We'll do it then."

What the men hadn't noticed was the fierce whispering of Lorna into Phyllis' ear, "When we get out there, you run one way and I'll run the other. Zig zag. When we get away, we'll circle back toward each other. It'll be all right, honey. It'll be all right."

"Hey, you two back there, what the hell are you whisperin' about?" Vaughan called loudly. "Henry, what are they sayin'?"

"The old one's sayin' 'It'll be all right' over and over."

"Well, just shut up," Vaughan shouted, "you're gettin' on my nerves."

The only sound that continued from that corner of the car was the soft sobbing of Phyllis as she hugged her mother.

"That looks pretty good up there," Henry said from the back seat. He was referring to an area of prairie that was swept mostly clean of snow. It dropped off toward what looked like the brushy drainage of a watercourse of some kind. In the gathering gloom, it was difficult to tell how deep the draw might be.

Vaughan pulled over, "Beggars can't be choosers. Allen, take 'em down to that brush line and put 'em down."

"Me," Allen exclaimed. "You're the one with the plan. You do it."

"All right, if that's what you want. I'll go with you. Two down or three down. It's all the same to me," Vaughan said in a flat, cold tone of voice. "I'd rather cut the take two ways, anyway."

"All right, all right, Vaughan," Allen said, a touch of fear in his voice. "I'll do it. Come on you bitches. You're comin' with me," he ordered as he quickly stepped out of the car and walked around to the driver's side passenger door. He jerked the door open and grabbed Lorna's left wrist. "Get out of there." He pulled her roughly and shoved her clear of

Phyllis who was following her mother. He shoved her, too. "Over there. Across the road. We're going to that brush line."

The women walked roughly with Allen shoving and prodding them with the pistol he gripped in his right hand. What he didn't notice was the eye contact they made as they seemed to stumble excessively over the terrain which made walking only moderately difficult. He assumed they were just exhausted and too frightened to control their steps. It made him confident that he was in complete control of the situation as he directed them toward a break in the brush bristling at the edge of the bank.

When they reached the brush line, suddenly, Lorna shouted, "Now!" just as Allen pushed her in the middle of her back. She spun and lashed out viciously, aiming for his face with her right elbow. There was a satisfying crunch that caught him flush, flattening his nose and dropping him to his knees. She immediately ran into the brush, following Phyllis who had fled as soon as her mother yelled.

"Come back here," Allen bellowed as he straightened up and fired a wild shot over the fleeing forms of the two women. Groggily he lurched to his feet and lumbered to the edge where the women had disappeared. In the deeper darkness of the brush, he couldn't see them, but he could hear them as they floundered and moved away down the slope.

"What the hell did you do?" Vaughan's voice boomed from the car.

"They jumped me. They're runnin' down into the bottom," Allen yelled back. "I need some help."

"Henry, stay here," Vaughan ordered. Then he grabbed his handgun and set off across the flat toward where Allen was standing near the brush line taking potshots over the edge of the break in the prairie.

"I can hear 'em, but I can't see 'em," Allen said as Vaughan arrived.

"What the hell happened to your nose?" Vaughan asked, looking at Allen's face.

"The old one caught me with an elbow, damn her. If I don't kill her before I catch her, I'm gonna do her good."

"Jesus," Vaughan exclaimed, "you look like you've been butchered. You've got blood clear to your belt buckle."

"I'll worry about that later. We've got to get after 'em before they get too much further, or we might lose 'em," Allen said.

"Yeah, right, "Vaughan said. "They'll head downstream. You go down here, and I'll run down and see if I can get in front of 'em."

"Okay," Allen said as he turned to step off the edge. He didn't hear the blast of the shot that hit him behind his right ear and blew out his left eye. His body flew forward and off into the brush out of sight.

Vaughan could hear it for a short while as it rolled and tumbled before finally coming to rest in the thicket of thornbush halfway to the bottom. Then he fired a pair of random shots down into the brush before turning back toward the car.

"What happened to Allen? I couldn't see what was going on over there in the dark," Henry asked anxiously when Vaughan came out of the gloom at the edge of the road.

"He lost the women. You heard him hollerin' for help. One of 'em nailed him with her elbow. Knocked him down. Damned near out. He was still groggy when I got over there. Then he went over the bank after the women, stumbled, and shot himself. There was nothin' I could do, Henry. He took it right through the boiler room. Just an accident, unlucky as hell. I popped off some shots but I doubt I hit anything. Let's go. We need to get out of here."

"Shouldn't we go after the women?"

"Hell, no. Down in that brush after dark would be impossible," Vaughan declared. "Our best bet is to get out of here and ditch this car as quick as we can get a different set of wheels. We've been lucky, so far. But you better believe there are gonna be roadblocks from here on out."

Chapter Forty-Seven

Yellowhenry's crew kept their roadblock in place until midnight. The spotter in the brush on the hill was nearly frozen stiff when McClintock called it off. All drivers going through the roadblock had been questioned to see if they had seen a white Chevrolet Impala. None had. The officers had retreated to the outskirts of Havre where they turned the traffic stop over to the day shift. Yellowhenry had stayed in the office and approved the move, including overtime for the officers who put in extra time. There was no way the fugitives could avoid Havre because of the condition of side roads which were closed due to deep snow.

Lorna and Phyllis scrambled frantically, ignoring the snags to their hair and clothing and the bloody scratches to exposed skin as they heaved themselves forcibly through the thick mat of thornbush and wild roses in their downhill flight. The gunfire above the rim of the creek bank sent charges of adrenaline coursing through their arms and legs. Bullets spanging past sounded like angry bees they ignored. It was the gun cracks that followed that lent power to their efforts. After half an hour of bushwhacking in the brush that seemed determined to prop them up as targets, they hit the frozen stream bottom. The gunfire from above had stopped. "What do we do now, Momma," Phyllis whispered.

"That way," Lorna answered, pointing downstream. "Be quiet and hurry." She followed her daughter who was walking briskly into gloom that was approaching total darkness. Ten minutes later, she bumped into Phyllis who abruptly stopped.

"What's that noise?" Phyllis asked.

Lorna listened until she heard what her daughter had heard. "It's sheep or goats. It's getting cold. We're gonna need shelter if we can get away from those bastards. Maybe there's a sheep shed down that way."

"I think they're gone. I heard a car pull away." Phyllis said.

"When?"

"Just before we hit the bottom. I was held up in the brush and you were moving. I'm sure I heard them leave."

"Oh, God, honey. Pray it's so," Lorna said tearfully.

"I believe it, Momma. They're gone."

"Okay, let's go, then. Pray there's a barn ahead of us."

Complete darkness had settled into the creek bottom as the two women stumbled onward. It was slow going that included stumbles and falls. Lorna began cursing under her breath as the relief of escape was frustrated by the annoyance of having to feel their way through the dark. Phyllis began to snicker when her mother would cut loose with, "Rotten sonofabitch. Bastard."

She finally broke out in stifled laughter when Lorna kicked a rock, stumbled, and fell to her knees, "Cocksucker," she said vehemently. "What are you laughin' at?"

"You, Momma," Phyllis said, catching her breath, "and us. It's like we jumped out of the frying pan right into the fire, and all we can do about it is cuss our luck."

"Yeah, well. You wait. We're gonna jump right back into that goddamned frying pan."

Suddenly sober, Phyllis asked, "What are you talkin' about, Momma?"

"Those sonsabitches owe us. Big time. I'll tell you what I'm thinkin' about later." She stumbled again, "Damn it to hell. Where is that fuckin' barn?" she said angrily.

They got to where they could hear a steady intermittent bleating that was a beacon for them. They found the barn when Lorna bumped into it. "We found it, honey," she said triumphantly. "Let's find the door."

A few minutes later, a sheep stampede piled up against the back wall of the structure as the two women swung the barn door open. "What the hell's with them?" Phyllis asked.

"They'll be all right as soon as they realize we aren't after them. Let's close the door and let 'em settle down," Lorna answered.

"All I want to do is lay down and sleep," Phyllis said.

"Oh, God, yes," Lorna exclaimed. "Let's get over to the side where we can stretch out." A few minutes later the two were sound asleep in each other's arms in rough straw as curious sheep sniffed them before lying down themselves.

The Reynolds brothers pulled into Shelby under the cover of darkness. Vaughan was driving and he pulled into a motel on the southern outskirts of town. The place was old and rundown with garages in between the units. "I've got to change my look, Henry. We're gonna check in here first. You check us in. I've got to stay out of sight. Then I'll need to shave. Ask the desk jockey where an all-night drug store would be located.   Tomorrow, we gotta get new wheels and a change of clothes."

It took an hour for the men to get to a drug store and get set up in the motel room. They stashed the car in the garage that went with unit number nineteen. Vaughan shaved his beard. He let his hair go, intending to let it grow out. The men counted their take and were pleasantly surprised. Henry exclaimed, "You've got to be shittin' me. Seventeen grand?"

"And six hundred fifteen dollars," Vaughan grinned. "Plenty to get our next set of wheels. Legal ones."

The pair hung out in the motel room the next morning long enough for businesses to be open before walking away from the motel. By looking through the phone book, they knew where a used clothing and second-hand store was located. After a half hour, a pair of cowboys walked down the street to a used car lot. Dickering for an hour netted them a 1968 Ford Fairlane for five hundred dollars, including a title signed off but undated. The plates were good for another three months. The cowboys would file for the new title at that time. The car was gassed up and ready to roll for its second hundred thousand miles. Its somewhat faded robin's egg blue color was nothing if close to white. When it rolled to a stop at mid-afternoon at a roadblock just outside Havre, Henry was driving. He was asked for his driver's license, and he produced one that identified him as John DeAndre. The photo was two years old but looked sort of like Henry. The officer thanked him and when he returned the license, suggested he get a better photo when he renewed the license.

"Have you fellas seen a White Chevy Impala coming this way?"

"No, sir, we haven't," Henry replied.

"Okay, you have a nice day," the officer said and sent them on their way.

Henry wanted to break out in loud laughter, but Vaughan, who was watching behind them through the sun visor mirror on the passenger side, said sternly, "Keep your cool, little brother. We'll celebrate later. This is no time to be noticed by anybody." As a result, the Fairlane rolled serenely through Havre without stopping. At Malta, as darkness fell, the car rolled into a full-service gas station. While the attendant added fuel to the car, the cowboys walked inside and filled styrofoam cups with coffee. They grabbed a box of powdered doughnuts and waited for the attendant to come in and check them out. He charged them for the doughnuts and gas, stating that coffee came with a fill-up. They thanked him and headed out for Glasgow where they overnighted at another obscure motel. Three days later they crossed the eastern border of North Dakota and disappeared into Minnesota.

Lorna was awakened by the sound of a barking dog. She sat up disturbing Phyllis, "What's going on?" she asked.

"Someone's coming to check on the sheep," Lorna replied. "Their dog is barking at the door. We need to get up and off this floor. The last thing we need is to get dog bit." It was daylight so they could see in the gloom of the barn a ladder extending into an overhead loft stuffed with hay.

Phyllis spotted it first, "There," she shouted, running across the breezeway and splitting panicked sheep that ran in a circle to pile up at the backside of the barn.

Lorna was halfway up when a voice shouted, "Hey, who are you?" The dog leaped and snapped just missing her foot but causing her to scramble to the top of the ladder and into the loft.

"Call your damned dog off," she yelled.

"Tell me who you are and I will," the herder returned.

"We were kidnapped by those bank robbers in Missoula," Lorna said.

"Hey, Lobo, heel," the man shouted at the dog. The black and white border collie stopped barking and slunk in that crouched, belly-down posture of the breed back to its master where it sat up in an alert position behind him. "You were kidnapped? Did I hear that right?"

"Yes."

"I never heard about no kidnappin'. How the hell did you get down here?"

"The kidnappers dumped us off up at the highway. They tried to shoot us, but we got away."

"Was that what all that shootin' was last night?"

"Yes."

"Are you all right?"

"Yes."

"Momma," Phyllis whispered. "We're not all right."

Lorna looked at her daughter with tears springing to her eyes. "I know, honey," she murmured, "but this isn't the guy to talk to about it."

"You can come down now," the sheep herder called from the base of the ladder. "Lobo won't bother you."

"Momma, you go first. I'm still bleeding," Phyllis said nervously.

Lorna, realizing what her daughter referred to, pressed Phyllis' hand. "I'm sorry, sweetheart," she said. "I'll go." The pair climbed down in tandem with Lorna shielding her daughter.

When they were standing on the floor with Phyllis standing behind her mother, Lorna introduced themselves. "I'm Lorna Christensen and this is my daughter, Phyllis," she said extending her right hand.

The shepherd who was holding a traditional shepherd's staff, awkwardly reached forward and loosely gripped Lorna's fingers, "I'm Tad Jenkins," he said. He and Phyllis nodded at each other. Tad was an eighteen-year-old high school senior. At six feet one inches tall and one hundred sixty pounds, he was mostly a rail. He was a sufferer of acne which had scarred his thin face, and he had a long straight-beaked nose. His teeth were uneven and he had a pronounced Adam's apple. His shoulders were narrow and slumped. His hair was a brown mop. He was bundled up in a heavy coat and he wore orange cloth work gloves and a badly pilled brown stocking cap. Silence was his default demeanor. "You're all scratched up," he said, after an uncertain moment as the three stood staring at one another.

"Yes. We had to escape through the brush. Are your folks home, Tad?" Lorna asked as she decided to move things along.

"It's just me and Mom. Dad died five years ago. She's down at the house. Just go on down. Ain't but a quarter mile."

"Can you lead us?" Lorna asked.

"Naw. Gotta take care of the sheep. I'll be here for a couple of hours. Just tell Mom I sent you."

"Okay. We just follow a path, is that it?" Lorna asked.

"Sure. It follows the crick. You'll see the smoke from the house."

"Thank you, Tad," Lorna said as she turned so that Phyllis could step past her, then she followed, shielding her from Tad's prying eyes.

As the pair walked through the barn door, Phyllis said quietly over her shoulder to her mother, "I hope this woman has some Kotex."

"I'll ask for you, honey," Lorna said. The path was in the middle of a snow-covered dirt road on a gradual downhill slope beside a small stream that was intermittently hidden beneath ice and snow. The women could see their breath with every exhalation. After a couple of hundred yards, the path turned to the left around a shoulder of the broad drainage basin of the creek which dumped into a larger stream a half mile further on. A slender column of smoke rose from the sole chimney of an unpainted, one-story clapboard house.

"There's the house," Phyllis said. 'I don't even see power lines coming to the place, though."

"Well, one step at a time, honey," Lorna said. "That's all we can do right now."

Chapter Forty-Eight

The woman who answered Lorna's knock on the door did so with a shotgun at the ready. "What do you want?" she asked.

"Tad sent us down."

"Where'd you see Tad?"

"Up at the sheep barn. We stayed there last night. We were kidnapped by some bad men in Missoula, and they dumped us out at the highway up above here. We need your help," Lorna answered.

"Lands sake, come on in. We heard a buncha shootin' up that way. Were you involved?"

"Yes. They were going to kill us, but we escaped by jumping down in the brush. They shot at us, but we got away."

"No wonder you look like you been tryin' to handle wild cats with your bare hands," the woman said leaning her shotgun against the wall behind the door. "That thicket is nothin' I'd try to tackle. I'm Wanda, by the way. Wanda Jenkins. Lost my man five years back. Only had one baby to survive. Tad. You girls just sit down at the table there and let me have a look at you."

"We have a big favor to ask right away," Lorna interrupted.

"Well, I'll help if I can," Wanda said.

"My daughter needs a sanitary napkin."

"Well, heavens sake, dearie. That time of the month doesn't wait for nobody does it? Let me get you what you need. Outhouse is out behind the house."

Wanda left to fetch the product. "Momma, I'm not having my period."

"Shhh, honey. Wanda doesn't need to know."

"Here you go," Wanda said returning happily. "There's a couple extras for ya."

"Thank you," Phyllis said as the rose from the table.

"Oops, sweetie," Wanda said, "you've been leakin'. Don't worry. Tad won't be back for over an hour. As soon as you get back, we'll set the tub up so you can clean up. Jeez, here I've been carryin' on, and I don't even know your names."

"I'm Lorna Christensen and my daughter is Phyllis."

"Well, I'm just happy to help, Lorna. There's a tub hangin' on the wall around to the side. If you'll grab that, I'll pump some water and get the fire stirred up. You gals look about my size. I don't have any duds like those you two are wearin', but I got a dress Phyllis can wear. You look like you could use a change of clothes, too."

"I'd be grateful," Lorna called as she stepped out to get the tub. A half hour later Phyllis eased into a galvanized tub inside Wanda's bedroom. A towel was laid out on the bed with soap and shampoo resting on it. When she came out twenty minutes later, her hair was wet and she was wearing a blue and white flowered beltless shift.

"Honey," Wanda laughed, "I hope you washed your hair first."

Phyllis smiled, "I did."

"Okay," Wanda said. "Come on, Mom, let's dump that tub and get you into it."

By the time Tad returned, the three women were sitting at the kitchen table. Lorna and Phyllis were eating pancakes and eggs. All three were drinking coffee. "Oh, there you are, Tad," Wanda said gaily. "Everything fine with the sheep?"

"Yes, Momma. No new ones last night."

"Our ewes are havin' their lambs," Wanda explained. "Tad, will you drive these ladies over to Spurlocks? They need to use a phone. They'll wait there. The sheriff or the highway patrol will come get 'em. Lorna, just send those clothes back to me General Delivery, Conrad. I'll burn yours like you said."

The Spurlock cattle ranch was seven miles from the Jenkins. By mid-afternoon, Lorna and Phyllis had been picked up by a sheriff's deputy and were waiting at the Buckhorn Café in Shelby. They would be transported back to Missoula by the highway patrol. The women refused to say anything about what had happened to them other than that they had been abducted and had escaped. When they were resettled at their home in Missoula, the Federal Bureau of Investigation called on the women, escorted them to the FBI office, and debriefed them.

The lead investigator was Dolan Aimes, an old hand at investigating a bank robbery. He separated Lorna and Phyllis. His partner Amanda Canfield interviewed Phyllis while he deposed Lorna. He recorded the interview and maintained a placid face as she detailed the rape she and her daughter endured. "You say there were three men. We located the Impala at a motel in Shelby. The fella at the motel saw two men. A bearded guy. Tall and well built and a younger one. The young one checked them in. Do you have any idea where the third fella might be?"

"The last I saw of him was where I elbowed him before I jumped into the brush above the Jenkins place," she answered.

"We'll send a team up there. See if we find anything. It would help if either you or your daughter could accompany us. Would that be possible?"

"I have to go back to work. My daughter could probably get time off from school. She's a straight-A student and after this experience, some time off would definitely be a good idea."

"Would she know where that spot is?" he asked.

"I think Tad Jenkins would know better than we would. He and his mom heard the shooting. It was close to dark when they pulled over and Allen marched us over to the brush. Phyllis and I weren't looking for landmarks."

"Okay. You work for the city of Missoula. Parks department. We may need to interview you again as the investigation develops. We would appreciate your not speaking to the press."

"Believe me," Lorna said, "when I say I appreciate your request. The last thing I want to do is relive that nightmare in public."

When Lorna and Phyllis were dropped off at the apartment Lorna had rented, they compared notes. Phyllis, too, had been advised not to speak to members of the press. "Momma," Phyllis asked, "You said we were going to jump back into the frying pan. That's bothered me ever since you said it. Can you tell me what you meant?"

"Not for a while, honey. Maybe never. We'll have to wait and see if the FBI catches those two sonsabitches."

"Two? There were three."

"Not anymore," Lorna said. "The detective I spoke to said they'd traced them to a motel outside Shelby. Only two checked in. I'd bet money on the two brothers. I'd also bet the FBI is gonna find Allen's body up there where we jumped down into the brush."

"I just hope they do," Phyllis said fiercely. "That little bastard deserved to die."

"They all do, honey," Lorna said. "They all do."

Chapter Forty-Nine

Lorna had delayed revealing her true intentions to her daughter until she knew whether or not either of them were late in their monthly cycles. As it happened, they both were. Phyllis admitted it to her mother after ten days. "Mom," she said tearfully, "I'm afraid I'm pregnant."

"Damn," Lorna said. "We both are."

"What are we gonna do, Momma?" Phyllis cried.

"You are going to Dr. Zimmerman for an abortion."

"What if I don't want to? Not even our church condones abortion."

"Well, honey, you are old enough to decide for yourself. There is still time for you to change your mind."

"I already have decided, Momma," Phyllis said. "My baby had nothing to do with how it was conceived. I just can't kill my baby for that reason."

"Have you thought about giving it up for adoption?"

"Yes. I don't know about that part yet, either. What are you gonna do, Momma?"

"I'm going after the father. I know it was Vaughan. I'm going to marry that bastard and make his life a living hell."

"I think he fathered my baby, too, Momma. He was first."

"Could be. Testing is the only way to really find out. Do you want that?"

"Not really. I want nothing to do with any of them," Phyllis said. "How are you going to find Vaughan? The FBI lost his trail. They don't even know where Henry and Vaughan are."

"I overheard where they were headed. It's in Wisconsin."

"When are you going after him?"

"After school is out. I'm going to take my vacation. It'll take a few days to find him. I'll have a bump by then he can't deny. The choice I'll give him is matrimony or penitentiary."

"Are you going to live with him?"

"No. I'm going to make him pay for what he did. Every month. When he doesn't, it'll be FBI time. I just hope they don't catch him before I do."

"Momma, you're bein' crazy. The guy is an escaped convict. Probably a murderer. A kidnapper and rapist. He's also in flight to avoid arrest. The FBI is after his ass. And you think you can marry him? He doesn't even have identification that is his own."

"Well, there are some details that will have to be worked out."

"Momma, the only detail to be worked out is to tell the FBI where you suspect they are."

"Honey, I want my own pound of flesh first. Even if all I get to do is kill the sonofabitch."

Tad Jenkins found Allen Clasper. He left him where he was after relieving him of his wallet. The greatest find, however, was the handgun Clasper had planned to use on Lorna and Phyllis. It was a Glock nine. It became his greatest treasure. One he told no one about. Even when the FBI retrieved the body, he said nothing. After removing seventeen dollars and two driver's licenses from Clasper's wallet, Tad burned it.

Yellowhenry was listening to one of his officers, Loren Muse. "I got to thinking about a couple of cowboys we checked through. I think the driver gave me a fake ID. John DeAndre. Didn't look too much like the driver. The passenger was a big guy. Looked pretty damned buff. They were driving a '68 Ford Fairlane. Robin's egg blue. License plate M6940S. Expiration in April."

"Okay, run the license plate. Let's see if we can figure out if they are the pair that dumped the Chevy Impala. Now that we have something that might help their tight-assed investigation, maybe the FBI can include us," Yellowhenry said. Then he placed a call to Dolan Aimes in Missoula.

"Captain Yellowhenry," Aimes said. "What can I do for you?"

"You probably need to be looking for a 68 Ford Fairlane. Robin's egg blue. A couple of cowboys drove it through our checkpoint. Has a license plate with an April expiration. Number M6940S. Headed east. One overnight stop before they hit the North Dakota border. Hell, Dolan, those guys are probably in Chicago by now."

"Well, we haven't found hide nor hair of the brothers. One of them shot Allen Clasper in the head. Funny thing, they apparently took time to climb down into a thornbush thicket in the dark to retrieve the gun he was carrying and to relieve him of any identification he might have been carrying."

"Was there anyone else who might have gotten to him before you did?"

"Couldn't tell. It snowed before we got in there," Aimes said. "Perfect cover for someone to go in during daylight hours. Those assholes wouldn't have gone searching in brush like that in the dark. They wanted to get away from there as fast as they could," Yellowhenry said.

"That's what I think, too. I have a guy in mind but no proof. I'll alert our office in Chicago about the car. They already know about the Reynolds brothers because of the bank robbery. They'll put out a net for that Fairlane. It's a long shot, but it's better than anything we have working right now. Thanks for your help. I owe you one."

Chapter Fifty

The Fairlane proved to be a very nice car. Reliable and economical, the Reynolds brothers thought of it as a keeper. So, they stayed in Milwaukee for two days and had it painted black. "Our next step is to get rid of these Montana plates," Vaughan declared. So he stole a set of Wisconsin plates. From his time in prison, he had a lead to a source in Milwaukee for acquiring fake identification. Four hundred dollars later Vaughan became Richard Westfall. Henry became Phillip Hendrickson. They had Wisconsin driver's licenses, Social Security cards, and Wisconsin birth certificates.

From Milwaukee, the boys drove to Sheboygan where they planned to completely disappear. Gone was the cowboy look. Both men went to work as stevedores on the Lake Michigan waterfront. Vaughan took their Montana title to a Wisconsin licensing agent and filed for a title in the name of Richard Westfall. He gave Henry three hundred dollars for his interest in the car. The pair shared an apartment and began studying the local dialect to purge their voices of any Western twang. They set up a pair of mistake jars. A slip of the tongue, including using their old names, cost twenty-five cents to the other brother's jar. Two weeks later the new title and license plates for the Fairlane came in the mail. The brothers tossed the stolen plates and grinned at each other. "Now, all we do is wait," Vaughan said. "I don't trust the FBI any further than I could throw Missoula. We'll keep getaway bags packed at all times."

Lorna and Phyllis became their own support group as both determined to carry their babies to full term. Phyllis was by no means the only pregnant girl at her school. She drew strength and courage from a support group of girls who met weekly with school counselors. The puzzle to most of the others was how she was so determined to carry a rapist's baby to term. Her answer was always that she could not bring herself to kill a baby that had nothing to do with how it was conceived. "My baby is half me," she insisted stubbornly. "I will decide after it is born whether I'll put it up for adoption. I just know that right now, I'm seeing it through till it's born." While none of the other girls agreed with her, they admired her determination. Most of them were able to arrange for abortions in Washington State.

Her counselor pointed out that her dreams of going to Arizona State University would be very difficult to achieve as an unmarried co-ed with an infant. "Just the dynamic of caring for your baby, attending classes, and studying will be a demanding and exhaustive undertaking, Phyllis," the counselor advised. "Perhaps you should consider the University of Montana right here in Missoula. With your mother living here, all of that would be considerably more manageable." Phyllis agreed to investigate.

Lorna experienced two different influences. Three men proposed to her, stating that she would need a good man around the house. "Thank you," she said to each, "but this is something I have to do myself." She didn't explain further.

The other influence was universal condemnation from fellow working women. It was summed up by a co-worker who said, "You need to set an example for the victims of rape and incest. Get rid of that bastard you're packin' around. You're giving rapists a good name if you don't."

"I'm sorry," Lorna said. "I'm making a decision only for me. Killing my baby would be giving its murder a good name. I'll give the baby up for adoption before I do that."

As winter wound down toward spring, Amy was lying in bed waiting for Yellowhenry to come join her. When he finally put down a novel he was trying to get into and went to bed, he found her with a folded piece of paper in her hand. "Ho, ho, ho!" she exclaimed with a deep voice.

"What?" he asked.

"Shhlushsh," she grinned.

"Oh, yeah, that," he frowned. "Honey, maybe this fall."

"Why?"

"So we can save enough to pay cash."

"Oh, I think I see what this is all about," Amy said, stunned and suddenly angry. "I see it all. Amy goes to the shitter with all the lovely smells, and Joe goes to the lavatory and shhlushsh. No wonder cash is more important than shhlushsh for Amy. Joe doesn't have to go sit with the lovely smells. Okay. We need cash. Amy has a source Joe doesn't have to get some."

"What's that?"

"Pussy," she said as she tore up his promise and handed it to him. "I won't need this. You can have it back." Then she rolled under the covers and turned her back to him.

"Hey, Ames. You're right. I'm sorry. We'll put the tank in right away."

"I don't want your tank. I'll earn my own."

"Honey, come on. It'll still be our tank. You aren't gonna go whoring yourself around."

"Oh, I'm not gonna go anywhere. I'm gonna charge you. Cash in advance. A hundred bucks a throw."

"That's funny," he laughed.

"Is it?" she turned to him, tears streaming down her face.

He tried placating her. "I'll call some contractors tomorrow."

"If you do that, I'll never use your goddamned commode. I'll shit in your outhouse for the rest of my life."

"Amy," he said sitting down and reaching for her, "come on. Let's talk."

"Don't you touch me. You get to do that when you've paid first," she said venomously.

He looked at her in disbelief. "Ames, why are you doing this?"

"Because I just saw my value," she said, gritting her teeth.

"Oh, come on, honey," he said alarmed. "I'm putting in your tank. I'm sorry. I just wasn't thinking. I don't want us to be like this."

But they were. Yellowhenry did have the tank installed. Amy relented in charging him for her favors. In a gesture of community spirit, Yellowhenry put in an oversized drain field and added a septic tank and bathroom for Minnie which was connected to his drain field. The bathrooms were set up quite nicely in both houses and the Yellowhenry's cesspool was covered and abandoned. It was months before Yellowhenry figured out that Amy would not use the commode in their house. She would walk over to Minnie's or use the old outhouse. He never asked her why.

Chapter Fifty-One

School let out for the summer for Missoula area high schools in late May. The Christensen women were well into their second trimesters. Their bumps were pronounced and they found that they had to talk to each other about completing their terms to keep their courage up. They didn't talk about the rapes. Lorna had not sought counseling but she listened to Phyllis talk about her sessions from school. "Are we supposed to learn anything about humanity from abortionists?" Lorna asked.

"They struggled with me. They all thought I was being stupid. When I told them that I was only deciding for myself, they seemed to feel guilty. All of them wanted complete unanimity. What really got to them was that they were all for aborting the babies of known fathers. That I was raped by three different rapists and still wanted my baby, they just didn't understand. I just know, Momma, that I want to see my baby."

"Honey, we're going to see our babies together," Lorna said. "Just think, it's possible that within a week in September, I'll be a new mother and a grandmother. You will be a sister and a mother. Our babies are in for a lot of lovin'."

With school out, Phyllis began sleeping in until she rarely rose before nine-thirty or ten AM. During the week leading up to the Saturday of the second full week of June, she had not noticed her mother stocking up the refrigerator and pantry. When she awakened that Saturday morning and wandered out of her bedroom she noticed an unusual stillness in the apartment. She walked to the living room windows and looked out toward the street. Her mother's car was parked in its usual spot, so she assumed her mom was sleeping in for once. After showering and getting dressed in slop-around Saturday attire, she walked into the kitchenette poured a glass of orange juice, and prepared a bowl of cereal. "Yech," she said to her baby. "If you weren't in there, I wouldn't be eating at all this morning."

After eating and quietly putting the dirty dishes into the dishwasher, Phyllis turned on the TV and with the sound muted, she channel surfed until she found a program featuring an archeological dig in Egypt. She tuned in with the sound lowered and watched for half an hour. It was after eleven when she finally decided to check on her mother. What she found was her mother's car keys, some money, and a note. The note read: I'm taking a week of vacation. The refrigerator and pantry are stocked for you. Use the money for anything else you need. Don't wreck the car! Love you, honey.

"Mom!" Phyllis screamed. "You didn't."

By the time Phyllis discovered her mother's absence, the bus Lorna was on had stopped to take on passengers in Bozeman. By Tuesday she was renting a car in Milwaukee, Wisconsin. From there, she commuted to Sheboygan about sixty miles to the north on the shore of Lake Michigan. She spent the next two days, using binoculars as she employed a cruise and stop method of prowling the Sheboygan waterfront. Under a blanket on the front seat of her rental car rested a .22 magnum semiautomatic peep sighted rifle that was her favorite rockchuck and prairie dog gun. It was loaded with a ten-round clip. It had been her father's and had never been registered. She had broken it down and packed it in her suitcase. With it reassembled, she could take down a rodent quarry at over 150 yards. She had no reservations about hitting targets under a hundred yards.

In addition to looking for the Reynolds brothers, she was also looking for Ford Fairlanes. She had picked up that tidbit from a follow-up interview in Missoula with FBI agent Aimes. Any color drew her scrutiny. A shiny new black one drew her attention, so she sat on it until shift change at six o'clock on that Thursday evening.

Vaughn Reynolds walked wearily to his Fairlane, tossed his lunch bucket and hard hat in the back seat, stretched out his back, and looked around before stepping into the car. He fiddled for a moment with his radio and then backed out of his parking space. He made the decision to stop for a hamburger and fries to go. He planned on eating at home with a cold brew. He didn't notice the car that tailed him. A woman wearing a head scarf and dark sunglasses followed him to the hamburger joint and waited across the strip mall where the fast food business was located. When he pulled back out onto the main street leading toward the west side of town she followed, stuck like a tick. He pulled into an apartment complex and backed into the space assigned to G-6. The tailing car drove slowly past and continued on toward the visitor's parking lot. The driver parked and watched as Reynolds grabbed his lunch bucket and the bag with his takeout order. He looked around carefully before setting off to a flight of stairs that led to the second story of an eightplex set of apartments.

Lorna watched until Reynolds disappeared before preparing to follow him. She was leaning down when a Volkswagen Bug pulled up in front of her on the opposite side of the parking island. She glanced at the driver and froze. Then she pretended to be getting something from her glove box. With surreptitious glances, she tracked Henry Reynolds as he climbed from the bug and began walking toward the eightplex his brother had entered. She let him disappear before she finally sat up and opened her car door. When she stepped out, she pulled on a lightweight full-length raincoat and a pair of ladies' cloth dress gloves. Then she leaned inside the opened door and drew her rifle up under her right arm. She held it beneath the coat and under her armpit by clasping the forearm through the fabric of her coat and crossing her left hand to the pistol grip so that her coat remained closed. She muttered, "All right, sports fans. It's game time."

Walking purposefully, neither hurrying nor walking slowly, she followed the brothers. Apartment number G-6 was on the northwest corner of the block of apartments. It had a spyhole set in the door. Lorna knocked on the door and stepped to the side out of sight. She pulled her rifle to the ready and listened intently for movement. She heard someone walk to the door and stop. Then a voice called, "Who is it?"

"There's no one there. I think it's those damned kids nigger knockin' again."

"Well, take a look and run 'em off if they're out there."

Lorna tensed as she heard a chain lock being slid open. The door swung in and Henry stuck his head out. She planted the muzzle of her rifle under his chin and pulled the trigger. He staggered backward with shocked staring eyes as he fell to his back where his feet began drumming on the floor. The report was a sharp crack as though someone had dropped something fairly heavy on a wooden floor. She stepped swiftly into the apartment and closed the door behind her. Vaughan was seated straight ahead at a dinette table with his hamburger, fries, and a beer set out in front of him He was too shocked to move. "Hello, lover," she said leveling the rifle at him. "Do not move. I'll kill you just as quick as I shot your brother."

He raised his hands and said, "Hey lady, whoever you are. I'm not movin'. If it's money you want, you can have what I got."

"Well, isn't that thoughtful," she said. "And look, you have my dinner all laid out for me. Oh, I'm sorry. I meant to say for us. Me and our baby."

"Our baby? What the hell are you talkin' about? I don't have a kid comin'."

"Well, Vaughan, honey, you could be right. You were just one of the three who raped me and my daughter back in Montana," she said. "Have a look." She swept her coat off her bulging belly. "We'd have to have some tests done to be sure."

"Oh shit," he exclaimed. "It's you."

"Yes, it is," she said sweetly. "And now it's my turn."

"I'm sorry, lady," he whispered. "I didn't mean to knock you up. It was just pussy. I'd been in jail for five years.

I wasn't in control of myself. Let me make it up. I've got money. A lot of money. Just don't shoot me."

"Get it," she said as she moved around to get an angle on him.

He rose from the table with his hands still in the air and stepped away from his chair. As soon as he straightened up she shot him in the right knee. He fell and squealed, "What did you do that for?"

"I haven't shot anyone for five years and I just lost control of myself," she said. "You understand, don't you?"

"Please, lady," he began sobbing. "Don't kill me."

"Now where have I heard that before?" Lorna said. "Now I remember. My daughter was crying and saying, 'Don't rape me.' It's about the same thing, sweetheart, isn't it?"

"Oh, Jesus, I'm so sorry. I shouldn't have. I know it, now. Please, don't shoot me," he continued.

"Ah, darn. I have to think about that. I'll give you time to get the money. Start crawlin' before I shoot some other body parts."

He pulled himself up and began hobbling around a short divider wall and down a short hallway to a bedroom. She followed a step behind him with her rifle on her shoulder. The door was open and he stumbled inside the room and fell on an unmade bed. He rolled over with a handgun clutched in his right hand. She was ready for the move and shot him between the eyes before he could get a shot off. "Well, I guess we won't be doing any prairie dog hunting together this year, sweetheart," she said.

Then she laid her rifle down and did a quick search of a chest of drawers, under the bed, and in the closet. Overhead on the shelf above the hanging clothes, she found a cardboard box. She pulled it down to the bed. Inside was a cloth bag containing money. Then she retrieved the spent shells from where they had ejected and tucked them into a pants pocket. She tucked the money bag and her rifle under her coat and left the apartment, locking the door behind her. On the way out, she noticed a free-weight bench set up in the living room where everyone else would have placed a television set.

A man was standing on the landing of the stairs as she walked by. "What was that bangin', lady?" he asked.

"One of those guys dropped a couple of weights on the floor."

"Are they all right?"

"Oh, yes. They're just fine," she smiled as she swept past.

The man watched her as she walked down the steps. He wiped his mouth with his right hand. "Aw, to hell with it," he muttered and returned to his own apartment.

Lorna tossed her coat, gun, and cloth bag into the back seat of her rental car. She pulled off the gloves laid them on the passenger seat and headed for Milwaukee where she pulled into the Lakeside Motel and carried all the stuff she had used in Sheboygan into her room. She tossed everything on the bed before going into the bathroom. Naked, she looked at herself straight on and in profile. "Hopefully, they won't catch us before you pop out of there," she said as she patted her swollen abdomen. "I have to thank you, sweetie. Momma is finally getting some tits."

After showering and dressing in clean pants, a blouse, and running shoes, she began eliminating trace evidence. Wearing the cloth gloves, she broke down her rifle. With a bath towel, she wiped it, the clip, and the used ammunition free of fingerprints. After loading her suitcase with her extra clothing and toiletries, she packed everything out to her car. She did not take the little bottles of shampoo and hand cream nor the small complimentary bars of soap. It was dark when she pulled away from the motel and drove to a city park on the shore of Lake Michigan. There, she pulled out the two parts of her disabled rifle. Again, she was wearing her raincoat and gloves. She used the coat to conceal the firearm parts. In a wooded area off a walking path along the lake, she threw the barrel and attached breech into the water. Further on she slung the clip well out into the water. Then she found an overloaded dumpster and buried the stock inside it under some trash. Back at the car, she removed the gloves and headed for the Milwaukee Mitchell International Airport some fifty miles away. She threw a glove out the window at the ten-mile mark. The other at the thirty-mile mark.

After turning her suitcase over to a Redcap at the terminal, Lorna drove her rental car to the Hertz Rental facility. She had used an airline ticket as identification in the name of Allison Parker to rent the car. She returned the car without incident. From there she walked to the departure lounge for flights heading to the west. She stretched out on a divan and went to sleep. She had an open ticket for a flight to Seattle. The flight wouldn't leave until five thirty the following morning.

Lorna began using her own identity in Seattle. She spent Friday unwinding in Pioneer Square where she took the underground tour of Old Seattle. The thrilling experience of having lunch atop the Space Needle, and paying for it with Vaughan Reynolds money was the highlight of the visit, even though she caught a Mariner's baseball game on Saturday night. For that entertainment, she used her credit card. An early morning flight to Spokane on the opposite side of the state with a connecting flight to Missoula had her calling Phyllis to come to the Missoula airport to pick her up. It was eleven o'clock when she faced her infuriated daughter who had waited until they were in the car and driving home to unload her umbrage. "Mother," she shouted, "what the hell did you do?"

Lorna waited until Phyllis, who was driving, took a breath. "Listen carefully. I'm going to say this once. I went to Seattle on vacation period. Everything else is not something you need to know. I won't tell you, so let it go."

"Mother, I've been a wreck. Your rifle was gone. I was sure you went somewhere to commit suicide. You owe me an explanation."

Lorna became angry, "Quit calling me Mother. It's alien. I'll be damned if I'll tell you more than I have. Accept it. Get it into your head that I went to Seattle because I did. That is what you can attest to. So do it. Leave everything else up to me."

"I deserve more than that," Phyllis continued shouting.

"No, Phyllis. Deserving has nothing to do with it. So, quit yelling at me. I'm done. And, so are you."

Despite Phyllis' attempted interrogation, Lorna didn't say another word all the way to their home. For the next month, the two were stiff with each other. Phyllis kept up a stubborn insistence that her mother needed to come clean. "Your conscience will haunt you forever, Mom," she said.

"I know, honey. I just don't want it to spread to you. So, let it go," Lorna said. "It's a burden that I'll bear. Alone. My baby will make it possible."

In the eighth month of her pregnancy, Lorna was asked to come to the local office of the FBI. Agent Aimes had called her in. "Lorna," he smiled. "What is it about pregnant ladies that makes them so beautiful?"

"If you think this is beautiful, why don't you try it?" she said.

"Ha," he snorted. "You got me there. Thanks for coming in. I have some news and some questions about the Reynolds boys. Have a seat."

She sat in a padded folding chair that faced his desk. "First, the news. They're dead. Took quite a while to figure out who they were. They had false IDs. The FBI office in Milwaukee caught the case. Ran their fingerprints through the Integrated Automated Fingerprint Identification System. IAFIS, for short, thank God. Our boy Vaughan came through with flying colors. Perfect fingerprint match. Then it was a simple matter of facial identification for Henry. Did you shoot those boys, Lorna?"

"Now, Dolan, you know that I'm not going to grieve for either one of those bastards. They raped me and my daughter in front of each other repeatedly for days. Then they dumped us and tried to kill us with gunfire. We're both pregnant. Neither of us believes in abortion. Our children will be born bastards. We will have to care for and defend those children all the days of their lives. They may resent us, their mothers, because we'll be the only targets they'll have to vent their spleens on. I have one hell of a big job ahead of me. So does my daughter. No. I didn't shoot them."

"Well, we know you were out of town at the same time those boys were shot. You took two weekends and a week off. Plenty of time to make your way to Wisconsin and back, Lorna. From a witness, it is known that a woman was present at the apartment at the time of the shooting. I can't think of a woman with a better motive than you have. So, we have motive and opportunity and a woman at the scene."

"That woman has my support."

"Well, there is also evidence that in addition to a double homicide, a robbery took place. Now, the money from the bank robbery has yet to be found," Aimes said. "Do you have that money, Lorna?"

"No."

"We'd like to fingerprint you. There were prints in that apartment that were unidentified. Would you be willing to be fingerprinted?"

"Sure."

"All right. Good, now we're getting someplace. Lorna, where did you go during that time you were off?"

"Seattle."

"Can you prove that?"

"Sure. I have receipts from places I visited, and my airplane ticket stub."

"If we check, will we find evidence that you also traveled to Wisconsin?"

"Be my guest."

"Well, we have," he said. "What do you think of that?"

"I don't. Am I under arrest, Dolan?"

"No, the evidence isn't in to prove that. We are still working on it, though, Lorna. Just a matter of time. Come with me and we'll get you fingerprinted."

Lorna went home from the FBI office and burned the rest of the money from the cloth bag. There was eleven thousand, two hundred dollars in all.

Chapter Fifty-Two

On a Saturday morning in late August, Yellowhenry came home early from a shift he'd planned to end at noon. "James," he asked his nine-year-old stepson, "Where's your mother?"

"She went over to Minnie's to take a shit."

"Hey, watch your language in the house."

"Okay, to take a dump. Dad, why won't she use our crapper?"

"She's teaching me a lesson," Yellowhenry answered.

"What's that?"

"Never to break a promise. I promised her a septic tank in the spring of last year. Then I tried to push it to the fall. That made her mad."

"You did have it put in during the spring, though. So, what's her point?"

"It's a constant reminder about promises. She had to make that one to herself to make me keep mine. That one and any others I might make."

"Well, you'd think she would get over the septic tank thing," James said.

"That was a promise she made to herself. She felt like I betrayed her with a false promise."

"I think that making promises is too much of a big deal, don't you?"

"I'd like to agree, Son, but I can't. A promise is your word. If your word isn't any good, then neither are you."

"That's pretty harsh, Dad. You're, like, sayin' you're no good your own self."

"Made me realize how important my word is. I have to work at it. So does everyone else. Mom just called me on it. Maybe someday she'll get over it. I've come to know that it's up to her. She's the only one who can forgive her promise to herself. It all depends on how many broken promises she's willing to carry around in her life. We all end up with some," Yellowhenry said.

"It just seems weird," James said. "Why is promising not to use our shitter such a big thing?"

"Call it a commode, Son," Yellowhenry grinned. "Don't irritate your mother with your street language. She might promise only to feed you on the porch."

"The way she keeps promises, I don't wanna risk that," James said.

Amy came in through the back door just then. Both her men turned to look at her with neither saying anything. "You've been talkin' about me," she declared. "It better have been good."

"Mom, you're weird," James said.

"Yeah? Well sometimes you have to be," she said as she walked to the table and sat down. "Honey, what are you doing here? Shouldn't you be at work?"

"I'm going out on a special assignment. I need a three-day grub pack."

"It must involve Hi Boy. You've got a truck and trailer parked out front," she observed.

"That grizzly's back in Carolyn's place. They finally have a phone line into the ranch house. Hank called me. The bear took down a calf a half mile above the barn ten days ago. Then his border collie started raising hell a couple of mornings ago. The bear was standing on its hind legs as the dog ran around it in circles. Fifty yards out in front of the chicken coop. Before Hank could get his rifle down, the bear broke and ran. He has a limp in his right front shoulder. It's the same bear that got Roy."

"Isn't it the job of fish and game to go after the bear?"

"It is. They're leading, but I'm the guy with experience and a horse. I know the country that bear's in, too. They figure that Indian knowledge is essential," he grinned.

"Oh, brother," she rolled her eyes. "Grizzlies kill us just as fast as they kill Anglos. That whole idea is just so stupid."

"Well, those old notions die hard. Anyway, sweetie, while I load Hi Boy, could I get you to lay out a grub pack?"

"Sure. Bread and jerky isn't hard," she chuckled.

"Come on James," Yellowhenry said. "You can help me load the stock."

"Are you takin' the mules?"

"Just one. Bray. Jay's too close to foaling."

"Dad, at school we were taught jennies are sterile."

"Most are. It's very rare for them to have foals. Wild horse stallions, though, don't care. When Jay got out last winter, she mated with a wild horse before we got her back. So, she's gonna have a little one."

"The mules belong to the tribe, huh?"

"Yes."

"Could I have Jay's baby?" James asked.

"You mean as your own special animal?"

"Yeah. I think it would be neat. I'd teach it to be a riding mule."

"Well, I don't know," Yellowhenry said thinking aloud. "I know the council complains every time they have to pay me for room and board for Bray and Jay. Maybe if I don't charge them for a third mule, they'd give it to us. In that case, sure. You could have Jay's foal."

"When will we know?" the boy asked eagerly.

"We'll get right on it as soon as I get back," Yellowhenry smiled as he ruffled his son's hair.

"Can I tell Mom?"

"Yeah, but swear her to secrecy. A pregnant mule is very rare. If people get to thinking about it, others might want your foal. In that case, we might not get it at all."

"I will. I won't tell anyone else."

"That's wise, Son. Let's just keep our powder dry."

"Huh?" James said.

"That means to be careful. In other words, if we started blabbing about our foal, it would be like pouring water on our gunpowder. It wouldn't be any good when we pitch our idea to the tribal council," Yellowhenry explained. "Get it?"

"Not really. But I'll keep my mouth shut."

"That'll be good enough."

For the next half hour, Yellowhenry and James worked on packing the pack saddle and loading the stock. When they went into the house, James shouted, "Mom, guess what. Dad's giving me Jay's foal."

"How can you do that, honey? We don't own it."

"It depends on the tribe's giving it to us. There's a good chance they will. The way the council groans about paying my board and feed bill, they might just give it to us or sell it to us real cheap," Yellowhenry answered.

"Don't tell anyone, Mom," James said. "It'll wet our powder."

"What?" she asked.

"We want to keep our powder dry," Yellowhenry explained. "A mule's having a foal is very rare. It might prove to be valuable to others."

"Okay," she frowned ominously looking at her husband. "We'll talk. Look at what I've set out for you. I assume you will pack provisions for others. I just set out stuff for you, though."

"Let's add food and utensils for one more. That will cover the guy who shows up with nothing expecting everything."

"Should you toss in an extra sleeping bag, then?" she asked.

"Good idea. I'll do that."

With everything loaded, he kissed his wife goodbye and ruffled James' hair, again. "Let's keep our powder dry," he smiled. He left to a small frown of concern clouding Amy's face.

When Yellowhenry pulled into the ranch yard at the Bar H Seven ranch, he was amazed at the collection of vehicles, stock, and personnel milling around the barn and stable. He parked off to the side where he had room to unload Bray and Hi Boy. He went unnoticed until he rode to the barn and corral on Hi Boy with Bray trailing on a tether tied to the horse's tail. Hank Jonas saw him and walked over to where Yellowhenry sat his horse, looking over the menagerie. Jonas looked up at him, "This is a shit show from hell, Joe," he grinned. "There's a TV crew here for God's sake."

"Well, if we don't accomplish anything else, we'll drive that bear clear to Canada," Yellowhenry laughed. "Who's in charge?"

"They're saying you are."

"Me?" Yellowhenry blurted in disbelief. "I'm not gonna be in charge of this hoorah. Where's the fish and game guy?"

Jonas looked around, "There he is. Comin' this way."

A small, wiry figure dressed in jeans and a Montana Fish and Game shirt was striding purposefully across the ranch yard. He wore a ball cap adorned with the seal and insignia of the department. He also wore work boots. Facially, he was thin-cheeked and clean-shaven. He sported a receding chin and hairline. His mouth which was generally turned down gave him a sour look. His overall demeanor was negative, and his being a five foot seven inch, hundred forty-five pound small man contributed to it.

"You Yellowhenry?" he asked as soon as he got close enough to start talking.

"I am."

"You're late," the man said. "The rest of us have been here for a couple of hours."

Yellowhenry looked at the figure who was standing fifteen feet away with his hands on his hips and an accusatory look on his face. Then he looked at Jonas and spoke to him. "Who is this asshole?"

Jonas began a grin he tried to keep suppressed. "Joe Yellowhenry, meet Francis Elliott."

"I go by Frank," Elliott growled as he looked up at Yellowhenry without offering to shake hands. "How do you want to do this?"

Yellowhenry glanced around at the accumulation before settling his gaze upon Elliott.

"I don't. But if I have to do it, I'll take Hank with me. The rest of you can stay here."

"Maybe you weren't advised thoroughly on this project mister Yellowhenry, but we're going to dart this animal and move him to a zoo in Cincinnati, Ohio."

Yellowhenry nodded. "I go by Captain Yellowhenry. If you can organize this bunch, and get a sore-legged griz to lay down so you can plug him full of darts, more power to you. If you want him killed, come see me. Hank and I will be having coffee in the ranch house." With that he swung Hi Boy around, forcing Elliott to give ground. He rode over to his outfit and tied the horse to the rear of the horse trailer. Then he joined Jonas and the pair walked to the ranch house where they disappeared inside without speaking further to Elliott.

Carolyn Malone greeted Yellowhenry with a hug. "Hello, Joe," she said. "I thought you'd have everything lined out and headed for the mountain by now."

"Yeah, sure," he said. "I was told we're supposed to dart that bear so it can be moved to a zoo in Ohio."

"I knew you'd be flummoxed when you heard that," she laughed delightedly. "That's why you came in here to drink coffee, isn't it?"

"Yes. I am completely flummoxed. I was asked this morning if I could assist. Then I was told by that Elliott fella that I was late to arrive and that I am in charge of that carnival out there."

At that moment Betty came down, trailed by the triplets. They waited until she reached the landing before they sat down and launched themselves into butt bumping their way down to where she waited. Then they repeated the process to the main floor where they ran into the kitchen. They climbed into the laps of the three seated at the table. For a while, all the attention was centered on the toddlers.

Then the phone rang. Betty answered and announced that it was for Yellowhenry.

He handed off the triplet he had in his lap to her and took the receiver. "This is Joe Yellowhenry," he said.

"Mr. Yellowhenry, this is director Kirk Poston of Montana Fish and Wildlife. I'm told we have a problem with you on this bear project. Is that right?"

"No. Not at all. I will help if the objective is to kill the bear. I'm set up for a three-day trip with a horse and pack mule. I'll take the ranch foreman with me and we'll see what we can do. If this is really a darting project like I've been told, I'm out," Yellowhenry replied.

"There is a big commitment behind this," Poston said. "A zoo in Cincinnati will take the animal. A man killing a bear would be a great calling card at the zoo. We really need to pull this off."

"Mr. Poston," Yellowhenry began patiently, "I, personally, am not going to involve myself in what I consider to be a foolhardy adventure. That bear is dangerous as hell. It also is wounded from my previous encounter with it. It's coming down to the ranch for easy food. Going after it with a TV crew is just going to chase it into a country where it can hide out and bother other ranches, probably after it kills the TV crew. If you want it that bad, set up a barrel trap and give it a week. You can use road kills to keep the bear coming in."

"That's a fallback strategy. You have a marketable reputation the TV people would like to take advantage of.

What they'd like is to get some footage of you stalking the bear and darting it."

"You're kidding," Yellowhenry said.

"Not at all. This is a chance for you to capitalize on your reputation."

"Not going to happen. As the captain of the patrol office, I am not interested in becoming a color in your TV production. I'll help the rancher get rid of a nuisance bear that is killing stock and prowling the ranch headquarters at night. But I will not get involved in your dog and pony show."

"All right, then I'll put Frank Elliott in charge and relieve you of any chance you have to participate."

"Okay. I'll advise Mrs. Malone of your intention. That way, if anything goes wrong, she'll know who to sue," Yellowhenry said as he hung up the phone.

"What are they going to do, Joe?" Carolyn asked.

"They want to take the bear alive in cowboy fashion. Hank, I'm out, but you might propose that for a fee, your services are available. They aren't gonna be able to dart that bear unless it's in a barrel trap. I told that fool as much. That doesn't have the Hollywood honey attached, however. This bear is hungry or he wouldn't be down here," Yellowhenry explained. "He's a good candidate to trap. But he is one dangerous bear to go hunting. They're determined to get TV footage of some kind, though. Hank, you have the looks. Go for it."

"If the children weren't here, Joe, you know what I'd say."

"Honey," Betty said. "If they'll pay you to go riding around with your saddle gun and cowboy hat, do it. We could use the money."

"Oh, do," Carolyn interjected excitably. "I'd love to see you and the ranch on TV."

"Well, if they'll pay, I'll do it," Hank said brightly. "Joe, will you tell them for me?"

"You bet," Yellowhenry said. "I'll set it up for you."

The friends visited for a while. Yellowhenry occasionally walked to the kitchen window to keep track of the organizational effort. Elliott could be seen strutting his stuff. Finally, Yellowhenry announced, "Okay Hank. Give me five minutes. Then shuffle off toward the barn kinda slow. If our timing is right, the TV people will come after you."

As he walked from the house toward where the TV crew was located, Yellowhenry was cut off by Elliott who called to him, "You're no longer needed here, Captain Yellowhenry. You can load your horse and mule and vamoose."

Yellowhenry ignored the man and walked past him to the publicity seekers. "Who's in charge here?" he asked.

Elliott, who had turned to follow him, grabbed his arm and attempted to spin him around. Instead, Yellowhenry jerked the little man around in front of him where he stumbled and fell on his ass. "You saw it," Elliott hollered. "He slugged me."

The three members of the crew laughed. "Forget that. We have a general coverage camera that will show that you fell on your own ass after grabbing Mr. Yellowhenry's arm," one of them said.

Elliott scrambled to his feet, "Did you hear what I said, Yellowhenry?" he demanded.

"I'm Harv Tilly," one of the men said. "I'm in charge of the camera crew. What can I do for you Captain Yellowhenry?"

"Tell that jackass to get out of here before I arrest him for assault on a lawman."

Elliott began walking backward before turning to stalk off toward the corrals.

"That guy wants us to put him on film. What a pain in the ass," Tilly said.

"You guys will not film anyone darting a bear out here," Yellowhenry said, "but I get that you need some footage of the country. I'm not going to offer my services for that, but for a fee, that cowboy walking toward the barn will help you with what you need. Nice meeting you Mr. Tilly."

Yellowhenry watched the TV man approach Hank who acted surprised. Yellowhenry laughed as he reloaded Bray and Hi Boy. He was still chuckling when he pulled out and left the ranch.

Chapter Fifty-Three

When Yellowhenry pulled into his corral to unload, it was midafternoon. Amy came walking from the house. "What happened?" she asked.

"Turns out they don't want the bear shot. Some zoo in Ohio wants a man killing bear as a drawing card."

"Oh, they must be planning to catch it in a barrel trap," she said.

"Nope. The fish and game guy wants to dart him in the wild. They have a TV crew to document it all."

"Joe, that's impossible. They'll never get a barrel trap to that bear in time before it wakes up, even if they do get a dart in it to start with."

"I know."

"They'll just chase that bear onto somebody else's ranch, Joe. That isn't right."

"Publicity is more important than practicality. I told the director of Fish and Game to use road kill to lure that bear into a barrel trap. That didn't fit the scenario. I did get them to use Hank for some background filming, though," he grinned. "Can't wait to see how much he got for that."

Later that night, Amy braced Yellowhenry about the jennie's foal. "Joe," she said. "I don't think you should be teaching James to try and cheat the tribe to get Jay's foal."

He looked at her and gritted his teeth before speaking. Sore points in their relationship and his just having had a bad day rushed into his head. The problem of the septic tank and now this, an accusation that he was a cheat, crowded out any thought of being considerate. "I won't. But don't ask me to do the research for the tribe about the possible value of a foal they had nothing to do with and about which they don't care," he said angrily. "I don't appreciate your busting my balls, either."

He jerked the covers back and swung his feet to the floor where he thrust them into his slippers. Then he grabbed his bathrobe and stalked out of the bedroom. "Oh, shit," she said through clenched teeth. "I've done it this time." She rolled out on her side and hurried after him. "Joe," she called. "Joe, I'm sorry. I didn't mean it that way." As she was speaking, he was closing the back door to the kitchen. She watched through the window until he disappeared into the stable.

At first, Yellowhenry thought just to sleep in the stable, but it suddenly came to him that he wanted nothing more than to be alone for a few days. So, he decided to go back out to Carolyn Malone's ranch and go bear hunting. He hadn't unloaded the pack saddle so he was basically already packed. He returned to the house and dressed. He didn't speak to his wife. Amy followed him and watched as he loaded the horse and mule. She spoke to him through the window of the truck. "Joe," she asked. "What are you doing?"

"Why do you care?" he asked.

"I do, Joe. I didn't express myself very well. I'm sorry. But your children deserve to know where their father is."

"I'm goin' after that bear before it hurts someone on the ranch. It's comin' down at night to raid the chicken coop. That's too close," he said.

"Okay, Joe. I understand. Please take Hank with you."

"Right now, Amy, I need some alone time."

"Then go up into the Moose's Ass, Joe. I'm scared if you go after that bear alone."

"I'll be careful. I've got to go. I'll see you in a few days."

"I love you, Joe," she said as he rolled up the window and pulled away. He didn't reply.

Yellowhenry pulled his crew cab pickup onto the road leading back to where he had found Roy Malone's truck when the man had been attacked by the bear. He found a level spot and parked. Then he stepped out and looked around. The land was bathed by a full moon which lit up the night. He walked around, trying to clear his head. Finally, he sat down on a rock and watched the moon. An hour later after weighing his options, he realized he didn't have any. So, he went to the truck and stretched out on the back seat. His final thought as sleep overcame him hours later was that he should have told Amy he loved her.

Frank Elliott eventually got the darting party headed for the bear's country. Hank Jonas was riding his horse onto high points where he would look over the terrain with binoculars in a very deliberate fashion. Then he would shift his rifle in its scabbard before using full arm motions to direct the crowd that followed him. The TV crew got it all on film. They didn't know it, but the man-pack jumped the bear from its day bed. It loped along toward the big ridge where it disappeared into the willows. Hank got a glimpse of it but decided it was pointless to encourage the fools into following the big bruin. Nothing good would come from letting the Francis' and fans' sideshow head into the thicket of willows after an eight-hundred-pound grizzly bear.

After sleeping fitfully, Yellowhenry had no problem with starting early. Just after daylight he was riding Hi Boy and trailing Bray into the line of willows that ran along the bottom of the big ridge. He stopped to lean over so he could examine a bear track in the mud next to the creek. "That's our boy," he said to his horse. Then he rode through the willows and out onto the open ridge beyond and above the willow line. He tethered the horse and mule down into a fold in the side hill and pulled his rifle from the saddle scabbard and his binoculars from his left side saddlebag. A short hike later found him sitting with his knees drawn up and his arms braced as he combed the willows two hundred yards below. His rifle lay on the ground beside him as he worked methodically in a grid pattern.

An hour later he gave up and massaged his eyes. Just as he was putting a hand down to help him get to his feet, he caught movement off to his right. Something was running in the willows. Shortly, it darted out on the opposite side of the willows from where Yellowhenry sat tracking its movements through his binoculars. A forked horn mule deer buck began stotting up the far slope. Yellowhenry pulled his gaze back to the willows and watched to see what might have chased the buck out onto the hillside. The big cat moved without shaking the willows. He just stepped out and stared at where the buck was moving steadily away. His tail waved slowly from side to side. Then he turned back and disappeared inside the line of trees.

For the rest of the day, Yellowhenry rode along the highlands above the willow-blanketed stream. He figured he combed five miles, or so. With nothing to prove for his efforts, he fell back on his plan two. He was carrying his hunting license and tag for the early buck season which began the following morning. The balance of his day after watering his stock at the creek was spent at his vehicle where he fed the animals before settling down for another night of moon watching after a cold dinner washed down by water from a canteen.

It wasn't much of a buck, and normally Yellowhenry wouldn't have shot him, but there was bigger prey in play. He tagged the spike, slit its belly open, and dragged the deer's corpse behind Hi Boy beside the line of willows and past the death scene of Roy Malone's prize bull. Only the bleached skull and backbone of the bull remained. A quarter mile from there, Yellowhenry pulled up and finished gutting the buck. Then he hung the carcass in a willow tree by its hind legs, using wire to tie it in place. He also wired the buck's head snugly to the tree trunk as well.

He rode to a high point a couple of hundred yards downstream where he could hide his horse. Then he walked back fifty yards and settled butt down into a screen of sagebrush with his rifle propped between his knees and settled down to wait. The breeze was blowing steadily into his face. Occasionally, he would pull up his binoculars and scan along the dragline of his bait. A couple of hours later a coyote came out of the willows. It stood on the gut pile and gorged as fast as it could on the liver, heart, and other organs as it looked fearfully around. Suddenly the coyote took off, darting through the willows and onto the open hillside above the stream. There it stopped and looked back over its shoulder before it continued on to disappear over the edge of the drainage.

A few minutes later Yellowhenry was fixated on the big cat that had frightened the coyote. He was working on pulling the buck out of the tree when Yellowhenry heard Hi Boy's squeal. He leaped to his feet and ran toward where he had tied the horse in the rocks. When he reached a vantage point from which he could see what was happening he could hear the enraged growling of the bear and the terrified screaming of the horse that was beneath it. As Yellowhenry threw his rifle to his shoulder, Hi Boy managed to kick the bear in the mouth causing it to rear back and lift its head. The blast of the rifle caused the bear to turn away. The bullet had taken him high in the neck. He sprinted away toward the willows downstream. Yellowhenry rushed to Hi Boy.

The horse was down, breathing heavily, and bleeding from several deep claw marks on its haunches. He jerked his jacket off and wrapped it around the horse's head. "Easy, easy," he said soothingly. After the horse began to recover from fright, Yellowhenry worked its head up and pulled on the reins. With the horse standing on trembling legs, Yellowhenry looked at his wounds. The bear had tackled him from behind, knocking him to his knees. In the process, he raked the horse's haunches as he fought the struggling horse which had rolled and begun kicking with his hind legs. That had kept the bear from eviscerating him. Yellowhenry had appeared at that moment and shot the bear turning it and running it off.

The saddle had turned under Hi Boy's belly, so Yellowhenry reset it and removed his jacket. With a calm reassuring voice, he began leading the horse back to the truck and trailer.

It took nearly an hour to get his horse to the vehicle. Hi Boy was limping on his left front leg. Yellowhenry had examined the leg and found the knee had been gouged in the rocks. He was hopeful that the injury was only a bone bruise. The claw marks on the horse's haunches had mostly stopped bleeding. Several would need cleaning and stitching. Without checking in with his office or going home, he drove to Davidson's Veterinary Clinic. Dr. Harold Davidson came out as soon as Yellowhenry explained what had happened. It took both men working and coaxing the horse to ease him out of the trailer. When they had him to where Davidson could get a good look at him, he announced, "He'll live. The knee is just bruised. Four of those lacerations on his rump will need suturing. The others will need to be flushed. I'll give him injections of antibiotics. He's damned lucky, Joe. Another thirty seconds, maybe less, and that bear would have killed him. Let's keep him here for a few days. I'll keep an eye on those wounds." Then he laughed, "You know what's going to happen when the hair grows back in those claw marks, don't you?"

"Oh, what's that?" Yellowhenry replied.

"The hair will be white."

Chapter Fifty-Four

Lorna's and Phyllis Christensen's babies were born ten days apart in September. Lorna's came first. Both were girls and despite how hard they looked and thought, the women could not figure out which of the rapists was the father of either one. Lorna named her baby Elise Ann and Phyllis named hers Elaine Lorna. The babies were normal and healthy. Lorna took maternity leave of thirty days and the tidy little family of females began a new chapter in all their lives.

Toward the end of her maternity leave, Lorna received a call from FBI agent Aimes requesting that she come to the field office for an interview. She took Elise with her along with a diaper bag. "Well," Aimes smiled when he saw the baby. "She's beautiful. Gets it from her mother."

"Thank you," Lorna said, taking a seat in front of his desk.

"I've received some additional details on the murders of the Reynolds brothers. I remember from years ago when your father and I were huntin' prairie dogs together that he had a .22 magnum rifle. Turns out that the gun used on the brothers was a .22 magnum. The ballistics aren't on file with the National Integrated Ballistics Information Network. Another one of those registries with a tongue-twister of a name. Call it NIBIN and be done with it, I say. Do you happen to have your dad's gun, Lorna?"

"No."

"You had it at one time. Hunted prairie dogs with it. You were a damned good shot. Where is it now?"

"I sold it."

"Who to?"

"Didn't get a name," she said.

"Is it someone from around here?"

"No."

"Oh, then where from?"

"Fella from out of state."

"Can you describe him?" Aimes asked, peering intently at Lorna.

She looked at Elise who was squirming in her arms and fussing. So she bared a breast and tucked a nipple into the baby's mouth. It began nursing vigorously making little sucking noises. "What was your question, Dolan?" she asked.

He was suddenly discomfited and began looking away. "Uh, I was wonderin' what the fella bought your gun looked like."

"Well, he was an Indian from Washington. He was Indian colored with black hair and black eyes. Maybe five feet ten, a hundred and sixty pounds. Gave me a hundred and fifty dollars in cash. That was three years ago, last April."

"I see. What was he drivin'?"

"A pickup."

"Make?"

"I didn't notice."

"Color?"

"Gray."

"How did this Indian from Washington find out about your rifle?"

"He said he was visiting relatives. One of them saw the notice I posted on the bulletin board at the Community Center."

"What was the relative's name?"

"I didn't catch it."

"What if I told you that you're lying through your teeth?"

"I'd tell you to go ahead and think that."

"You killed those boys just as sure as I'm sittin' here, Lorna. I'd like you to take a lie detector test."

"Is that something you can make me do?"

"No, Lorna, it isn't, but it would clear your name. What do you say?"

"Sorry."

"Why not?"

"Because, Dolan, I'd miss all these lovely inquisitions of yours. Is there anything else because when Elise feeds, she fills her diaper?" she asked.

"No. You can go, but just know that I know you killed those two. It's just a matter of time till I prove it."

"Goodbye, Dolan. The next time you call me, have some charges ready to file or talk to my attorney. Your freebies are over. I'm through with your harassment."

"Lorna, I hope you're not upset," he said quickly. "I'm just doing my job."

"No, you're not," she shouted. "You have no evidence against me. You call me down here and accuse me of murder. You've never once read me my Miranda rights. You're harassing me."

"What's going on here?" a man's voice asked loudly from Aime's office door.

"He is accusing me of murder. He has never advised me of my rights," she began crying loudly. Elise joined her. "He keeps harassing me and calling me a murderer and he has no evidence. I'm a nervous wreck."

"Dolan," the man asked, "have you Mirandized her?"

"I'm not to that point," he said rising from his chair.

"Have you accused her of murder?"

"Not officially."

"We need to talk," the man said. "Mam, you're free to go."

"Who was that man?" Lorna demanded.

"You don't need to know," Aimes said.

"Yes, I do. He is a witness to the fact that you have accused me of murder and have not read me my Miranda rights. My attorney will want his name."

"Aw, hell," Aimes gave up. "He's the director here. William Devisiter."

"How do you spell that?" she demanded.

"Look it up. It's on the directory out front," he said as he hurried out of his office and down the hall behind the back of his retreating boss.

Two conversations followed Aimes last interview with Lorna. The one at the FBI office involved Devisiter and Aimes. When the two men were seated in the boss' office, Devisiter pointed at a five-drawer filing cabinet against a sidewall. "You know what that is, don't you Dolan?" he said pleasantly.

"Of course. The cold case file cabinet."

"Yes, it is. There are cases awaiting the delivery of justice. People who were victimized by criminals who are still on the loose. People who continue to have hope that someday we'll get a break and those villainous sonsabitches will get theirs."

"Well, of course," Dolan said, "that's why we continue to work them on a rotating basis or as new procedures arise regarding the collection of evidence."

"That's right, Dolan. Evidence that will solve cases and deliver justice. You, however, continue to drub that woman who has the world weighing her down as you continue to try to serve justice to a bunch of bastards for whom justice was delivered perfectly. Does that really make sense to you?"

"No, but isn't justice supposed to be blind?" Dolan asked.

"In a perfect world, yes. We aren't in one of those, though, are we?"

"Are you directing me to cold case Lorna Christensen's file, sir?"

"I'm glad we had this little chat, Dolan. I'm sure it will help us move ahead with our work."

When Lorna returned home she cared for her baby and then asked her daughter to join her at the kitchen table. "I spoke to that FBI agent again. Something came up. I have to advise you of something I lied about. I told him I sold my prairie dog gun to an Indian from Washington three years ago in April. I got a hundred and fifty dollars for it. If he asks you about it, honey, you have to tell him that."

Phyllis looked at her mother. "Don't look so concerned, Mom," she said. "I know where you went. Of course, I remember that Indian. He bought your gun. Other than that I wasn't concerned. I was just a young virgin dreaming about men."

Chapter Fifty-Five

It was with dread that Yellowhenry pulled up in front of his place and unloaded the big mule. Minnie saw that Hi Boy wasn't there, and she came hustling over. "What did you do to our horse?" she demanded.

"Bear attack, Minnie, but he's okay. Got him down at Davidson's. He got chewed up and clawed up some. Doc's gonna sew up some claw marks on his ass."

She looked dumbfounded. "Damn you and the sand in your shoes, Yellowhenry. Amy told me that you left on one of your getaways. Now you're back after damned near killing our horse? What the hell is wrong with you? As a captain of the highway patrol, I'd expect better than that."

"I won't argue with you on that," he said.

"What the hell were you tryin' to accomplish, anyway?"

"I was after that bear on Carolyn's place. Got some leads into him."

"Kill him?'

"No, ran him off. He was attacking Hi Boy at the time."

"You were by yourself, weren't you?"

"Yes, Minnie, I was."

"It shouldn't be an old white-haired Indian woman to have to tell you this, but just how stupid can you get, Joe?"

"Well, I knew better than to try and tranquilize the sonofabitch, Minnie," he said in a voice that told her not to press her luck.

"Okay, Joe. There is that. Let me help you get unloaded. I'd like that manure over at my place."

Yellowhenry didn't take the time to talk to Amy. She watched him from the kitchen window as he unloaded and spoke to Minnie. She saw that their exchange was growing somewhat heated and decided to let him come to her. When he didn't, she cried.

After returning the truck and trailer, Yellowhenry drove to his office headquarters. He greeted his office staff, before entering his private office. He tossed his hat on a chair and called Sergeant McClintock to come in for a conference.

"Anything goin' on, Art?" he asked.

"Your bear hunt," he answered. "I know the game commission didn't do squat. How'd you do?"

"Got some lead into him. He damned near killed my horse. He's over at Davidson's getting sewn up."

"How bad?"

"Had his ass carved up pretty good. Lamed in the left foreleg, but the doc says it's just a bone bruise. He'll get over that. Says the hair in those claw marks will come back white," Yellowhenry chuckled.

McClintock grinned, "He'll look damned interesting in parades. What's next with that bear?"

"I'm hoping the game commission comes to their senses and puts a barrel trap out for him. There's a zoo in

Ohio that wants him. But if they leave it up to that fool they had in charge the other day, that won't happen. Hank Jonas will have to kill that griz. Damned bear has been comin' down to the ranch house at night. I'm hoping I'm done with the whole damned thing."

"Want to bet?"

"No, why?"

"You've made headlines. Got on TV, too. The game commission has a red ass over their idiotic darting plan. The TV boys got some film of you sitting on your horse with the mule trailing behind. Good stuff of Jonas, too. You two were the stars of the show. They even got the futility of trying to tranquilize the bear for capture down right. Your pulling out of the caper made the news. You came off as the only one with any sense."

"Holy Christ," Yellowhenry exclaimed. "What's gonna be next?"

"With that bear still on the loose, your saga is ongoing. Yes sir, stand by for more coverage, Captain."

"I don't want that. Why can't they just let it rest?"

"The public doesn't want it to. It's just too good a story. Indian lawman in a deadly struggle with a man-killer. How do you stop that?"

"I kill the bear. Will that do it?"

"Sure it will after a wrap-up. Interviews and feature stories. Face it, Captain. You're developing a hell of a reputation. Celebrity-like shit."

"Well, I don't want it."

"That's the perfect approach to it. The reluctant man of action," McClintock grinned. "Hell, if you keep going, you'll be needing an agent." He flapped his ears.

Yellowhenry laughed, "You've got it Art. You can be my agent. What else is happening that I need to be briefed on?"

"The new cars came in. Yours is over in the shop being set up and painted."

"Painted? They should have come in painted. What's left to do?"

"Some small personal touches on your car, Captain. I think you'll like 'em."

"Whose idea was that, for God's sake?" Yellowhenry asked.

"Everybody's. The whole staff had a contest. Put in ten bucks apiece. One of those newbie cadets came up with the prize-winning graphic."

"That sort of thing has to be approved, Art."

"Oh, it was. The boys down in Helena were all for it."

"Is it done so we can look at it?"

"Should be. We can call the shop and check, but you can't see it now," Art said.

"Why not?"

"Everybody wants to be here for the presentation."

"When are we gonna do that?"

“End of day shift, tomorrow. Act appreciative, Captain. Everybody wants you to be pleased.”

“All right. I’ll do my best,” Yellowhenry said.

Chapter Fifty-Six

After finishing his shift, Yellowhenry braced himself for the dreaded confrontation with his wife. He knew he had to apologize, but he couldn't get over being a touch bitter. Amy was warm and loving. She listened attentively as he told her about shooting the deer and setting a trap only to have the bear come in behind him and attack Hi Boy.

"Are you going back after that bear, Joe?" she asked.

"I hope not. I'm trying to get the game commission to set up a barrel trap. Otherwise, the bear will have to be put down before he kills someone else."

"You're going back in there, Joe. I know you will."

"Only as a last result, honey," he said noticing the fear in her eyes. "But, I won't go alone."

"Why does it have to be you, Joe?"

"I guess I have the skill set for it more than others is all I can think of. I know the country and where the bear hangs out. That gives me an edge, I guess."

"Probably. I just wish that bear would die. I am so afraid he'll get you like he got Roy."

"Well, like I said, I'll take help if I have to go again."

"Joe," she said, broaching the subject she knew needed to be sorted out, "I was wrong to say what I did about Jay's foal."

"I don't want to talk about that," he said. "I'm sorry for taking off. Let's just let it go."

"I don't want it to come between us," she said with tears forming in her eyes.

"Then don't bring it up, Amy. You said I was teaching your son to be a cheat. You've apologized. You can't unsay it, so just let it go. I'll be more careful with what I say and do with the kids. Okay?"

"I guess so," she said. "I'm just feeling like it has come between us."

"Give it some time, Ames," he said.

"Are you all right?" she said as tears began running down her cheeks.

"I'm getting there," he said. Then he smiled, "What's for dinner, sweetheart?"

She leaned against him as he kissed her. "Me," she answered.

At work the next day, Yellowhenry played dumb about the car. Twila Allen led him out to the parking lot at shift change time. Even the men from the graveyard shift were there. The unit was parked broadside and covered with a lightweight car cover. Sergeant McClintock made the presentation. "It isn't very often that someone of the rank of raw recruit rises above the ranks, rules over them, and they like it. Captain Yellowhenry is that exception. He has our backs and because of that our respect. To honor his commitment to law enforcement and his officers, we have a special presentation to commemorate this very unusual circumstance. Gentlemen, please reveal the special police cruiser."

No one had seen the patrol car in its finished version. A gasp of appreciation and approval swept the faces of the officers. The circle of the Great Seal of the State of Montana was stenciled on the doors and the hood of the solid black cruiser. On the lower half of the circle in the bright yellow script was printed 'Captain Yellowhenry'. Set off at the near end of the name before the capital 'C' was the profile of an Indian chief in a headdress of red, white, and blue. The far end was finished with a shock of wheat in silver and gold representing the wheat farmers in the area and the words 'oral y plata' which appears across the lower quarter of the great seal of the State of Montana.

Yellowhenry was blown away. "Speech, speech," was called by several officers.

"Holy crap, guys," Yellowhenry said. "I'm not sure I can live up to this. If the name on that cruiser was one of yours, I'd have it displayed out front on a pedestal. All I can say is 'thank you. ' You can't know how much I appreciate the car, but the acclaim and respect you have afforded me is so much more. That's what matters the most. Before I drive this cruiser, I want each one of you to take it out on patrol. Thank you."

The applause was spontaneous and genuine. McClintock took over. "All right back inside everyone." With everyone gathered he had Twila hand out slips of paper. The patrol officers wrote their names on the slips and they were drawn in the order that the special patrol cruiser would be assigned.

Officer Pete Leeman was drawn first. He stepped into Yellowhenry's office. "Remember when you refused to accept my resignation, Captain."

"I gave you options. I'm glad you stayed," Yellowhenry smiled.

"So am I, Captain. That was the best decision I ever made. I have you to thank."

"No, Pete. That was a decision you made by considering your family first. Enjoy that cruiser. Let me know how it rides."

"Will do, Captain."

Jay dropped her foal three weeks later. James and Yellowhenry were there in the stable with her. As soon as the tiny jenny was able to stand and suckle, James named her. "Miracle," he said. "Dad. I'm going to call her Miracle. Do you think I can keep her?"

"That might be another miracle, Son," Yellowhenry answered, "but I will make an honest effort to make that miracle happen."

Two days later, Yellowhenry was sitting in Cecil Crow's office. "So, you want to make a deal, Joe, on what?"

"On a foal the tribe's jenny had. I'd like to keep it for my son."

"Mules are sterile. What the hell are you sayin', Joe?"

"It's very rare, Cecil, but it can happen. The tribe's mule got out last winter. She was with some wild horses for a while. The stallion covered her. She dropped the foal, another jenny, three nights ago."

"So, the tribe has three mules, now."

"Yes. I'd like to work out a deal on the foal."

"What do you have in mind?"

"No board on the foal."

"So, we just give it to you?"

"Sure. In six months I'll be billing the tribe for half again as much as I do now."

"We've got to do better than that, Joe. I'll consider that as value, but I'll have to explain to the council that it's a pending deal. It could be shot down given our history."

"So, what do you need?"

"How much is this critter worth on the open market?"

"A hundred and a half."

"Give me a hundred, and I'll give you a bill of sale."

"Done," Yellowhenry said extending his hand. The men shook and the deal was made.

That afternoon, Yellowhenry came home early to meet his son when he came home from school. He and Amy were all grins when James came home. "What's up?" he asked, throwing his books on the sofa.

"Got something for you," Yellowhenry said, handing him the bill of sale.

"Dad," James yelled, "It's a miracle."

A few days later when Yellowhenry arrived home from work, Amy came hurrying out to meet him. He immediately saw her concern. "Don't tell me something happened to Miracle," he said.

"No, honey. The bear came back. He killed Hank."

"Goddamnit," he shouted. "How did it happen?"

"Carolyn said Hank's dog was barking, so he went out to see what it was all about. The bear was right outside the kitchen door. Hank had his gun, but the bear got him before he could get off a shot. The dog chased the bear out into the pasture and Carolyn somehow got hold of Hank's rifle and shot a couple of times. The bear took off."

"How could the bear get past the dog to the kitchen door?"

"They bring the dog in at night."

"Dirty rotten sonofabitch," he raged. "How is Betty?"

"They're waiting for the coroner. Betty is sitting with Hank, washing his wounds."

"I'll have to get a work waiver in the morning for a special assignment. This time I'm taking that bastard out."

"Honey, what about a barrel trap?" she asked.

"That would let him live. Not gonna happen, Ames. Not gonna happen. I've figured out where he lays up in those willows. I'll get him."

"Can't you get some help?"

"Maybe. Hi Boy is out. I'll need to rustle up a horse. I'll take Zane if I can get him cleared. His horse is here. Let's get inside. I want to call Carolyn. I want her, Betty, and the kids off the ranch. We'll bring them here. Between us and Minnie we can put them up till this is over."

It took some convincing to get Carolyn to agree to come into town. The coroner was still there when she took Yellowhenry's call. He had to agree to let her take care of her stock before she left. "The sheriff is here, Joe. He's actin' like he wants to go after the bear."

"Just tell him no. He doesn't know where that bear hides out. I do. Tell him if he wants to help, have him assign a deputy to care for the stock. If he insists, tell him he can come with me."

"Hold on, Joe. He's right here." There was a pause while she spoke to the man. "He wants to speak to you, Joe."

"All right, put him on."

"Yellowhenry, this is Al Sparks, sheriff of this county. We don't need you on this. We'll handle it."

"All right. I'll come out and take care of Mrs. Malone's stock while you go kill the bear."

"Well, maybe you could give me some information on where to look."

"Go hunt the willows, Al. That's where he'll find you."

"You mean he'll come after me?"

"He's killed two men. He is habituated to humans. If he feels pushed or cornered, he will turn on you. Good luck, Al. I'll see you tomorrow. Let me talk to Carolyn."

"Joe, he's sayin' he wants to talk to you some more before he goes after the bear."

"Okay. Can I borrow your horse if I need it? Mine is out of action for a while."

"Of course."

"All right. This isn't what I had in mind, but if Sparks wants to give it a shot, let's let him do it. I'll be out mid-morning tomorrow."

It took a couple of hours for Yellowhenry and Hammond to gain permission and get organized the next morning. By the time they reached the Bar H Seven ranch, Sheriff Al Sparks had his bravado up. He had a horse with saddlebags strapped on behind the cantle of his saddle ready to go. Sparks, himself, was dressed for bear. He was wearing chaps, cowboy boots, a big western straw hat, and a leather fringed vest. At five feet ten inches tall and a hundred eighty pounds, the red-headed sheriff was physically capable of comporting himself adequately on a bear hunt in which the animal was lured to a baited stand. As a stalker of the bear in question, he was more a snack than a hunter.

"Look at that clown," Hammond said. "If he insists on going in alone, we're gonna have to pull him out, Joe, sure as shit."

"Well, it's his county, Zane. If he insists, we'll wish him well. Hell, he might get lucky. I don't care who kills that griz. I just want him dead. Before we unload, let's talk to him."

"Captain Yellowhenry," Sparks asked as he thrust his leather gauntlet-clad hand out to shake. "What is this, round four with this sonofabitch?"

"Whatever it is, it's the last one," Yellowhenry said. "This is Zane Hammond. He's one of my troopers."

After shaking Hammond's hand, Sparks said, "I just need a probable on where to find this bear. With my .300 magnum, it shouldn't be too much of a problem takin' him down."

"It's a pleasure having someone else take a shot at this, Al," Yellowhenry said. "I wish you all the luck in the world. I sure as hell haven't had any. Let me diagram where I think he holes up in those willows."

Using his finger in the dirt, Yellowhenry drew in the big ridge and the band of willows that straddled the stream at its base. "The willows are anywhere from a hundred to three hundred yards, or so, wide, fifteen to thirty feet high, and thick as hair on a dog's back," he added. "Sightlines are from zero to twenty feet. There are game trails in there where sightlines will reach around thirty, maybe forty feet. The danger is that if the wind shifts and carries your scent to him, the bear will know where you are."

"What do you think he'll do?" Sparks asked.

"Oh, I'd guess he'll try to kill you," Yellowhenry answered. "He's been wounded. Most recently, about ten days ago, I hit him in the neck as near as I could tell. He was attacking my horse at the time. He also took a hell of a shot to the chops from a kick from the horse. All of that could affect how he can feed. I'm just guessing that he was looking for easy food when he killed Hank Jonas. At the least, he'll be laid up and pissed off. In those willows, I'd advise you not to be wearing chaps."

"I don't know about doin' this alone," Sparks said as he squatted gazing at Yellowhenry's diagram.

"Right in here upstream from where the bear killed that Hereford bull, you'll find an old beaver dam."

"He killed a bull?" Sparks asked.

"Oh, yes. That was before I shot him in the shoulder, though. He's turned to smaller prey now," Yellowhenry continued. "The beaver dam still has a small pond behind it. Thirty or forty yards long, twenty wide, and maybe four to six feet deep. No beaver left. A couple of lodges. I haven't found it, but I believe that Griz has a den somewhere above that beaver pond. Probably under a cut bank of the creek. Every time I've seen him he was in that general vicinity. Well, we have to take care of Carolyn's stock so she and the kids can get out of here. Good luck, Al."

As Yellowhenry and Hammond took off toward the barn and corrals, Sparks called, "Hey, just a minute. I'm thinkin' I could use your help."

Yellowhenry turned and looked at the comic figure looking hopefully at him. "No offense, Al, but going in there with an inexperienced man is the quickest way I can think of to get mauled or killed."

"Hey, I am a pretty damned good shot."

"When did you last sight in that three hundred?"

"Well, I borrowed it, but the fella said it's just a little high and right at two hundred yards."

"I see," Yellowhenry said, "so, where is it at seventy-five?"

"I'd guess pretty close to dead on."

"Uh, huh. How many grains are you shooting?"

"I don't know. It's a three hundred magnum. What difference does that make?"

"What was it sighted in for?"

"Jesus Christ, what's with the third degree?"

"Difference between life and death," Yellowhenry said. "That's all." He turned and continued walking, ignoring the additional pleas of the sheriff.

"What do you think he'll do, Joe?" Hammond asked.

"I think he'll ride out there. It's three hours. He'll sit up on a point above the creek and take potshots into the willows, hoping the bear will run out so he can shoot at him in the open. Hell, he might get lucky. Otherwise, he'll come back sometime after dark, scared shitless, and declare that he put the bear on the run. Out of the country. Nothing more to worry about."

"What does that mean for us?"

"Best case, he'll spook the bear out for a couple of days. Then, he'll be back. Leerier than ever and even more dangerous. I think he has a broken jaw. Hi Boy caught him right on the lower jaw. Didn't dislocate it, but I'd bet it rearranged some teeth. Gave him a hell of a toothache. Those chickens could be pretty damned tempting."

"We don't have that much time, do we?"

"Nope. We'll have to leave and come back. Carolyn will have to stay. Let's take care of her stock. We'll need to ride out and check her cattle. Make sure the fences are up. Kill some time until Sparks gets back."

The two lawmen did their riding and caring for animals at the barn. Yellowhenry had advised Carolyn that plans had changed and she needed to stay home for an indefinite period. He spent some time with Betty Jonas consoling her as best he could. He anticipated Sparks return close to sundown. Carolyn had insisted that the men have dinner with her family. Yellowhenry had called Amy to let her know he planned to be home late. So, they waited, but Sparks didn't come back. "What do you think happened, Joe?" Carolyn asked.

"I don't want to speculate. We'll have to wait for daylight. I just don't know and stumbling around out there in the dark is pointless. Zane and I will start investigating at first light." He called Amy again and told her of the new plans.

Hammond called Lily and told her what was going on, then he and Yellowhenry went out and stabled their stock for the night. Carolyn put them up in the house on the ground floor so they could get an early start. Yellowhenry had decided to step out and make water before bedding down when he glanced toward the barn and saw a shadow that moved. He walked out to where he could get a better look. Then he stepped back into the bunkhouse. "Hey, Zane," he called, "Spark's horse is back. Let's go take a look."

The horse, a bald-faced black of indistinct lineage had come down the lane and was standing outside the barn. "Let's get him inside and have a look in the light." The men pulled the saddle and examined it for blood. There was none.

Neither was there blood or injury to the horse. The reins, however, were broken from the bridle. They stabled him and went to bed.

Chapter Fifty-Seven

Yellowhenry and Hammond loaded their horses in the dark and drove out the road toward the willows as far as they could. There they waited for daylight before unloading and riding their horses on a parallel line to the willows. The weather was clear and breezy, but it promised to be a warm day. Three-quarters of a mile later they crossed Spark's horse's tracks where they were leading towards the area Yellowhenry had shown him in the dirt diagram. They tracked him to where they found the broken reins. They were jammed into a crack in a rock crevice. From there they tracked Spark's to a point twenty-five yards away and above the horse. The point overlooked the willows above the remains of the Hereford bull. There they found three spent .300 magnum shell casings.

"Well, he was shooting his gun," Hammond said. "Do you think he was on the bear?"

"Until we find him, we won't know. He definitely walked toward the willows. Maybe he got lucky." The pair split apart ten yards with Spark's tracks between them, loaded rounds into their rifles, placed them on safety, and began slowly working their way toward the willows. A half hour later they were inside the willows on high alert still patiently working Spark's tracks which were overlaying bear tracks on a game trail next to the creek. Spots of blood were appearing about every third step. The men were nearly shoulder to shoulder. The breeze, what there was of it, was wafting into their faces, but Yellowhenry could feel an occasional puff behind his neck. He indicated with hand signals to Hammond that the wind was swirling. Hammond nodded.

It took fifteen minutes to reach the Beaver Dam. Spark's tracks led along the left side of the pond. "Joe," Hammond hissed. "His rifle is stuck barrel down in the mud." He pointed to where the scope-mounted firearm was just visible five feet off the edge of the game trail at the side of the beaver pond. Yellowhenry dropped to a knee and began scoping into the willows in a sweep that covered a hundred eighty degrees of the area around the pond. Hammond stood poised and braced to shoot at any second.

"You see anything?" Yellowhenry whispered.

"Just that rifle. He's got to be right here someplace."

"Unless the bear packed him off," Yellowhenry returned. "Look at that second beaver lodge. It's torn all to hell."

"Yeah," Hammond agreed. "Fresh, too. Wonder why?"

The lodge was one of two. Both were pretty much centered in the pond. The one upstream of the other and in shallower water had been ripped open. Yellowhenry scoped it with his rifle. "There's blood on the debris, Zane," he warned. "Stay alert."

"If I was any more alert, I'd be shittin' my pants," Hammond said.

"Look at the tracks. Sparks was runnin' back this way. I think he threw his rifle and jumped into the pond. What's that in the water up there?"

Hammond scoped a half-submerged object suspended in the water forty feet ahead of them. "That's his hat. He had to dive into the pond."

"Do you suppose he swam into that lodge and the bear dug him out?" Yellowhenry asked.

"Why wouldn't he swim back out? That blood could be from the bear," Hammond answered.

"Yeah, why wouldn't he? I'm gonna try something. Hold my rifle," Yellowhenry said. Then he reached into his pocket and pulled out a pair of rocks. He planted his feet and fired at the first beaver lodge. The rock clattered around in the dry branches before ricocheting into the water. He waited for a minute and threw the other one. Two minutes later, there was a swirl of water from under the lodge and presently Spark's head popped up. He treaded water and spun quickly in a circle.

"Oh, my god, I'm saved," he croaked as he swam smoothly across the pond despite the drag of his cowboy boots. "Praise God, you're here."

"Give me a hand," Yellowhenry commanded. "We're not out of the woods yet."

Sparks gripped the extended hand and Yellowhenry pulled him out of the sucking mud of the pond's edge.

"You won't believe what happened," Sparks began.

"Save it," Yellowhenry said curtly. "Your rifle is stuck up there in the mud. Come on. Let's grab it and get out of here."

With Sparks sloshing alongside him, Yellowhenry hurried to where the gun stood on its barrel five feet off the bank. "Give me a hand and get in there, Al," Yellowhenry ordered.

"Christ, I'm all wet," he protested.

"Do you want to leave the rifle?"

"No."

"Then, move, goddamnit. It ain't mine."

"All right then, damn it," Sparks said angrily, as he stepped in and sank up to his knees. Yellowhenry anchored him at arm's length and Sparks was able to reach and grasp the rifle's pistol grip. Shortly, the man was pulled to shore and the pair were hustling back to where Hammond stood guard.

"Let's get out of here," Yellowhenry said as he took his rifle back. He and Hammond retreated carefully watching their backtrail. They let Sparks walk ahead. When they reached the bull's bones they cut uphill out of the willows to a bench overlooking the creek. "All right, Al, this is where you shot at the bear, I take it?"

Sparks looked around. "Yeah, I spotted him goin' up the crick. My first shot made him jump and bawl. I shot a couple more times, but I doubt I hit him. He was runnin' by then. Goddamned horse jerked the reins loose and took off."

"No, that horse broke the reins, Al," Hammond said.

"Those .300 magnum are damned loud. Spooked your horse. He wasn't where he could see the bear, so I doubt the bear had anything to do with it," Yellowhenry added. "Next time, stake him out a hundred yards, or so."

"Tell me about it," Sparks said. "This was the first time I ever shot one. I'll never do it again without muffs. I wanted the horse close so I could make a quick getaway."

"So, how hard do you figure you hit the bear," Yellowhenry asked.

"I thought it was a pretty good shot, but I jerked a little. May have been low."

"That figures. A pretty good guess would be a flesh wound, low, and between his front legs. Didn't damage bone, or he couldn't have ripped that beaver lodge apart. He left some blood there," Yellowhenry said.

"I thought he had me there," Sparks said.

"Why did you drop your rifle and jump into the pond?" Hammond asked.

"Have you ever had a grizzly stand up and roar at you from fifteen feet?"

"Well, no."

"I didn't drop the rifle. I pitched it. But I did a lot of other stuff, too. Pissed myself right off," Sparks explained. "I headed for the pond because I'm a damned good swimmer. Dived in and went deep with that sonofabitch right on my ass. He lost me for a little bit because I stayed down as long as I could. He stirred up the mud when he ran in. The water's deep enough that he couldn't stand on all fours and touch the bottom. He stood up and was lookin' around for me the first time I came up for air. When he spotted me, he jumped. Knocked me forward but he didn't get a grip. I swam like a fuckin' otter, let me tell you.

"Got behind him and bumped into that beaver lodge. There was an access hole underneath it and I went for it. I thought I was okay, but he saw me go under and followed. I could hear him growlin' and snarlin', and I could feel the lodge breakin' apart. So, I backed down real easy like and stayed deep. I just held my breath for close to three minutes because it took a while to find that second beaver pile. It was bigger and I got up there where the beavers hang out. Talk about stink. I puked. I'm tellin' you, boys, I've never been much for prayin', but I sent up a big one inside that beaver den. I figure you guys are the answer to that prayer," Sparks finished with tears running down his face. "I'll never in my life be able to thank you enough."

Yellowhenry let him finish. "Well, you're welcome, Al. But we still haven't killed that sonofabitch. There's a big job ahead of us."

"I'm done," Sparks declared. "I'll resign my office and quit law enforcement altogether before I go after that griz. Hell, any griz. That sonofabitch towered ten feet tall and bellered like a freight train right over the top of me. I'd be dead right now if that pond hadn't been right there. No sir. Once is enough. You guys go on ahead. I'll see if I can get the barrel of this rifle cleared and cover you as much as I can from here. If it gets along toward dark and you guys aren't back, I'm outta here. I'll send people back to bring in your scraps, but that's it for me."

Hammond looked at Yellowhenry, "What do you want to do?" he asked.

"I want that cannon of Al's. Then, I'm going after that bastard. He'll kill someone else at the ranch house if he's left out here."

"You've got it, Joe," Sparks said. "I've got some extra shells in my pocket. They're yours."

"That's a plan then. I'm in," Hammond said.

"Okay, cover me," Yellowhenry said. "I'm going to get a willow stick to clear the barrel of Al's rifle."

Sparks began stripping off his soaked and muddy clothes and spreading them out on the sagebrush. Hammond stood guard as Yellowhenry collected some sucker limbs from a big willow tree rooted above the shallow hollow where the bull bones were scattered. A half hour later Yellowhenry took off on a hike. After a quarter-hour and over a hill, the boom of the big rifle rolled off the ridge. When he returned, he said, "Okay, Zane. The barrel's clear. We're back in business. Let's go kill us a bear."

Chapter Fifty-Eight

The first thing Yellowhenry did before reentering the willows was to strip the scope from Spark's .300 magnum. "Why?" Sparks asked.

"Inside thirty feet, I'll be shooting from the hip with this thing. The scope would be useless that close. It's easier to work the bolt with the scope out of the way, too," Yellowhenry said. "I'm hoping to get in a couple of shots before I get steamrolled."

When Hammond and Yellowhenry reached the beaver pond, Yellowhenry set some verbal cues. "Straight ahead is twelve o'clock, so we're working nine to three. 'Pivot' means we turn back to back. You turn at six o'clock. If he lays doggo, we could walk right past him. We don't want to be ambushed from behind. Expect to pivot several times. Just call numbers. 'Ho' means stop. It's an unvoiced word. We'll talk with low voices."

The men moved fairly quickly to the upper end of the beaver pond. Then they started a step and search procedure similar to before. When they had to move a single file, Yellowhenry led. The stream meandered through the willows and the game trail followed, but it took sharp angles around trees and downed logs. Sight lines were always short. The men looked on both sides of the blocking vegetation. They kneeled and checked every color change thoroughly before moving. It took an hour to cover two hundred yards. They bumped deer, rabbits, coyotes, quail, and other birds. The men let all of them leave or move out of the way of their own accord and speed before they moved ahead.

After two and a half hours the stream began crowding the left towards a steep sand bank. The men were on the sandy trail when Yellowhenry said, "Ho." Then he leaned close to Hammond and whispered softly. "I think the bear has a den somewhere in here along this sand bank. Be ready."

Just then a soft thermal caressed the back of the men's necks, disturbed the surface of a long pool that lay under the face of the sand bank and beside them, and ruffled the leaves of the willows along the opposite side creek bank. "Get ready," Yellowhenry said. Hammond moved up beside him and both men brought their rifles to their shoulders.

The bear had been holed up for hours licking the wound to his left underarm. Nothing had disturbed him until the air current swept to him the sharp odor of men close by. He lifted his head and listened for a moment before rolling to his feet. When he stuck his head out of his scooped-out declivity in the sandbank, the men were standing side by side thirty feet away. He charged with a deep-throated roar.

Despite running head-on into a stunning force that hammered him to a stop, he recovered and launched himself in a sand-churning leap that blew the man on the streamside of the trail into the creek. The uphill man was brushed aside and staggered from the glancing blow of the bear's right shoulder. The grizzly, however, was focused on the man in the water. He had him by the face and had squatted to shake him when a blow like thunder struck him in the right side wiping him over to the left and onto his back. He lost his grip on the man he had in his mouth. As the man scrambled away, the bear that had always been cat-quick, did his best to follow, but thunder cracked beside him again, and the unseen force knocked him sideways. Still, he struggled after his tormentor, but the water was just too heavy. He lunged but it only stretched him out and he pushed the man away. It became suddenly peaceful. He laid his head, heavy with sleep into the water and closed his eyes.

Yellowhenry dropped the .300 magnum and dived into the water after Hammond who was floating face down. He pulled him out of the water and turned him over. His face had been crushed. Deep lacerations and puncture wounds in the shape of the bear's bite were bleeding heavily and his left eye was laid out on his cheek.

Yellowhenry, without thinking, reflexively shoved the eyeball back into the socket. "Zane, can you hear me?" he yelled. "Zane. Zane listen to me. We got him."

Hammond moaned, "Joe, he had me in his mouth. Is my face gone? I can't see anything."

Yellowhenry looked at Hammond's right eye. Although flooded with blood, it looked okay, so he waved his hand in front of the eye. "Zane, can you see my hand?"

"Just a moving shadow, Joe. Shouldn't we be getting out of here? He could come back," Zane said fearfully, struggling to his feet.

"No, Zane, we got him! We got him!" Yellowhenry shouted. "Let's get you out of the creek and onto the trail." With that accomplished Yellowhenry had him stand still while he retrieved their rifles. Then he removed his own shirt and cut off the left sleeve. He tied it around Hammond's face binding his eyes. He put his shirt back on and removed his belt. He looped it through a pants loop on the back of his jeans and buckled it. "All right, Zane, this is how we're going to do this," he said. "I'll lead and tell you what your steps are going to be. Hang onto the belt. I've got the rifles. We'll take it nice and easy. Just listen to what I tell you."

Getting back to Al Sparks took nearly two hours. The men worked out a system of taking five steps. Zane cracked his shins a few times and stumbled at first, but Yellowhenry thought about how the blind used their white canes to probe for what they couldn't see. He found a willow branch and made an ersatz cane of it. Hammond was able to use it with Yellowhenry's instruction of what to tap for. By the time they reached the bull bones hollow, the pair were moving with surprising dispatch.

Sparks was agitated. "I heard the shooting," he called out. "Did you get him?"

"He's dead," Yellowhenry replied.

"Thank Christ," Sparks said. "What happened to Zane?"

"That sonofabitch got to him. He'll be All right, but we've got to get him to a hospital. Let's go."

"I'm sorry as hell," Sparks said. "But if it had been me, he'd have killed me. That's a fact."

"Yeah, well, let's get to the horses. I'll ride double with Zane," Yellowhenry said as he guided Hammond with voice commands down to where they had tied the horses.

Chapter Fifty-Nine

An hour later, Sparks was headed back to his office in Malta, and Hammond and Yellowhenry were on their way to Havre. Yellowhenry paused long enough to use the phone Carolyn Malone had installed following her husband's death to call his office. Twila Allen took the call. He had her call the hospital to get set for emergency surgery for the bear attack on Hammond. Then he had her call Amy to let her know that he was coming home.

The staff at the Havre General Hospital cleaned up the punctures and stitched the lacerations to Hammond's face. They rebound his eyes with clean gauze bandages, but they booked him out on an emergency medical flight to a hospital in Spokane, Washington, for reconstructive surgery by plastic surgeons and ophthalmologists. Lily flew with him. The specialists saved his right eye, but he wore thick glasses for the rest of his life. The left side of his face sported a glass eye. His face was permanently scarred, but whenever he told the story, he never blamed the bear. "He was just bein' a bear," was his stock statement.

Yellowhenry reported the bear kill to the Montana State Fish and Game Department. Francis Elliott wanted the carcass brought out for examination. Yellowhenry gave him instructions on where it was and advised the man to hop right to it. After an insulting comment about lazy Native Americans, Yellowhenry told him to go to hell and hung up.

His next confrontation came with Minnie and his wife. Hi Boy was back and Minnie was babying him almost to the point of sleeping in his stable. She had his knee wrapped with her special poultice. He was walking with only the slightest limp. Before turning to his house, Yellowhenry spoke to Minnie first. "How did Hi Boy get back here?" he wanted to know.

"That big fella with the flappy ears got hold of a truck and trailer and brought him home," Minnie said.

"McClintock?"

"Yeah. Very nice man. I fed him and he ate like a horse. I don't think he has a woman."

"He's my sergeant. No woman that I know of."

"Well, my, my," she grinned. "Maybe I'll feed him more often."

"I know he wouldn't regret it, Minnie. Say, Hi Boy is doing all right ain't he? That poultice of yours works on him, too, doesn't it?"

"Yes. Horses and men are a lot alike when it comes to doctorin' 'em up."

Yellowhenry laughed, "I'll take your word for it, Minnie. I wouldn't doubt it for a minute."

"How bad is Zane, Joe?"

"About as bad as it gets, Minnie. The bear had him by the face and was getting set to shake him when I got a couple of shots in, but the damage was done. I doubt if he'll ever see out of his left eye again. It was crushed out of the socket. It was bad, Minnie, really bad. He and Lily are being flown for emergency surgery to Spokane."

"If there is ever another rogue bear, you know you'll be expected to take it out, Joe," she said.

"I expect so. My being an expert and all."

"Don't do it, Joe. Experience doesn't mean scuat bear to bear."

"Probably not, but it's a start. It's also comes with the territory."

"Try telling that to Amy. See how far you get with that. Here she comes now."

"Joe," Amy said as she rushed into his arms, "how bad is Zane? Twila said he was hurt."

"I don't know for sure, but he couldn't see after he was attacked. He's being flown to Spokane to some specialists. We'll just have to wait and see."

"That could have been you, Joe," she cried. "Why do you keep doing this?"

"Because I get the job done, Ames. That's why."

"I'm so afraid that the next time your number will be up like it was with Hank," she said, her eyes brimming with tears.

"Honey, my number will likely come up with you in bed," he grinned.

She kissed him. "Well, guess what?"

"Oh, no," he groaned. "Not again."

"Yes, again. But, after this one, we're going to be talking about the V word."

"How about the H word?" he suggested.

"To hell with that. After your next bear hunt, I could very well wind up with another man. He'll want to have his own kids. I'll need to be ready to be a first-timer so I can reel him in like I did with you."

He looked at her, still in his arms. "Do you know what I love most about you?" he asked.

"No, what?"

"You're so subtle, honey," he said as he kissed her warmly.

About The Author

Stevens McClellan is the pen name of Tom Kendall, a sixth generation Oregonian. He is a retired English and science teacher whose life experiences include growing up on farms and ranches, working as a United States Forest Service fire lookout and fire fighter. He also worked as a railway clerk, a slaughter house worker, and branch manager of an international finance company. He is a published poet. His home is the Spokane Valley, WA, where he lives with his wife, Judy.

www.ingramcontent.com/pod-product-compliance
Lightning Source LLC
Chambersburg PA
CBHW071752310726
48976CB00001BA/104